It's Raining Men!

**So open these pages and let
these delicious, sensual men
come to you...**

Dear Reader,

Happy New Year!

Welcome to this month's selection of two-in-one Desires—two full length novels for one great-value price.

This month sees the start of a new mini-series THE MILLIONAIRE'S CLUB with *Millionaire MD* by Jennifer Greene and *World's Most Eligible Texan* by Sara Orwig, both books are together in one volume entitled **Millionaire's Club**. If you think you can handle a double dose of some of the richest, most sensual men around then this is the series for you!

You definitely won't be out in the rain and cold with our second volume—**It's Raining Men!** including *Reese's Wild Wager* by Barbara McCauley and *The Temptation of Rory Monahan* by Elizabeth Bevarly. These stories are just hot, hot, hot!

Completing the month is *Baby at His Door* by Katherine Garbera and *Cheyenne Dad* by Sheri WhiteFeather in a volume entitled **Dads in Demand**. These bachelors are about to find out that fatherhood—and marriage!—is exactly what they've been searching for.

We hope you enjoy them all!

The Editors

It's Raining Men!

BARBARA McCAULEY
ELIZABETH BEVARLY

*Silhouette, Silhouette Desire and Colophon
are registered trademarks of Harlequin Books S.A.,
used under licence.*

*First published in Great Britain 2002
Silhouette Books, Eton House, 18-24 Paradise Road,
Richmond, Surrey TW9 1SR*

IT'S RAINING MEN! © Harlequin Books S.A. 2002

The publisher acknowledges the copyright holders of the
individual works as follows:

Reese's Wild Wager © Barbara Joel 2001
The Temptation of Rory Monahan © Elizabeth Bevarly 2001

ISBN 0 373 04736 3

51-0102

*Printed and bound in Spain
by Litografia Rosés S.A., Barcelona*

REESE'S WILD WAGER

by
Barbara McCauley

BARBARA McCAULEY

was born and raised in California and has spent a good portion of her life exploring the mountains, beaches and deserts so abundant there. The youngest of five children, she grew up in a small house, and her only chance for a moment alone was to sneak into the garden with a book and quietly hide away.

With two children of her own now and a busy household, she still finds herself slipping away to enjoy a good novel. A daydreamer and incurable romantic, she says writing has fulfilled her most incredible dream of all—breathing life into the people in her mind and making them real. She has one loud and demanding Amazon parrot named Fred and a German shepherd named Max. When she can manage the time, she loves to sink her hands into freshly turned soil and make things grow.

To Cris Grace, the Queen of Cuisine—
this one's for you!

One

Cigar smoke lay like a heavy hand in the small back office of Squire's Tavern and Inn. Four men, brothers, sat around the table, cards in hand, their dark gazes intent on the current deal. Gabe Sinclair, the eldest of the four, frowned at his luck while Callan, brother number two in order of birth, considered the possibility of drawing another king for a pair. Beside him, Lucian, brother number three, smiled inwardly at a pair of jacks and deuce wild, while Reese, the proprietor of the inn and the youngest Sinclair at thirty-two, all but did mental backflips over the three queens in his hand.

They were a handsome lot, the Sinclair men. Each of them, with their thick, dark hair and rugged good looks, had broken more than their share of hearts in Bloomfield County.

Some said that Reese held the record, though. He had eyes that made women forget to breathe. Deep green, like a forest, and curtained with heavy, dark lashes. And his smile. Lord, that smile of his could charm the stripes off a zebra.

It also didn't hurt that he was six foot three, solid muscle and had won the honorary award of "Best Butt in a Pair of Blue Jeans" three years running by the females in Bloomfield. Reese proudly displayed his silver-framed certificate on the wall right beside his plaque from the Bloomfield County Chamber of Commerce for "Top Restaurant of the Year."

How sweet life is, Reese thought as he clamped his cigar between his teeth. Three queens, a ten-dollar stogie and two fingers of Patron Gold tequila. He grabbed a handful of chips from his winnings stack and tossed them onto the table. He was on a date with Lady Luck and about to score.

"Five dollars says that pot is mine." Reese grinned at his brothers. "Again."

Lucian glanced up from his hand of cards and bit down on his own cigar. "You close that mouth of yours long enough and you won't have to put your foot in it. I'll see your five and double it."

"Too steep for me." Gabe threw his cards down and pushed away from the table. "Gotta go, kids. Kevin and I have a fishing date at the crack of dawn."

"I'm out, too. Abby's waiting up for me." Callan stood, and wiggled his brow. "Far be it from me to keep a lady waiting."

Reese stared at his brothers and shook his head. The Saturday night games were getting shorter and fewer since Callan had married Abby six months earlier and then Gabe got engaged to Melanie a few weeks ago. When they'd all been unattached, these games had lasted until three or four in the morning. Abby and Melanie were great, Reese thought, and he knew he couldn't ask for better sisters-in-law. He was happy for his brothers, but now the Sinclair reputation of devout bachelorhood lay in the hands of himself and Lucian.

And speaking for himself, Reese thought, it was a reputation he was proud to uphold.

"Looks like it's just you and me, Bro." Reese tipped his chair back on two legs while Gabe and Callan pulled on their jackets. "I see you…" he tossed a few more chips into the pile "…and I—"

The door to the office flew open.

"Reese Sinclair, this has got to stop immediately!"

Reese swiveled to look at the woman standing in the doorway.

Sydney Taylor.

Uh-oh.

Sydney's pale blond hair tumbled around her flushed face and fell in wild waves over the shoulders of the red-plaid cotton bathrobe she wore. She brought the crisp early November night air in with her, and the earthy scent of autumn leaves. In her arms she held Boomer, Reese's Border collie-terrier-Lab. Boomer was covered with mud. So was Sydney. All the way down to her fluffy brown slippers.

Mud on Sydney Taylor? Definitely a Kodak moment, Reese thought. He wanted to laugh, desperately, but the look of ice-cold fury on Sydney's face stopped him. She'd murder him if he so much as smiled. Everyone knew that Sydney Taylor could cut a man off at the knees with just a glance. She might be pretty, but she was so damn bossy everyone called her Sydney the Hun. Not to her face, of course. After all, she was the granddaughter of the Honorable Judge Randolph Howland, and that did deserve a certain amount of respect.

Reese glanced at his brothers. Based on their slack jaws, they were obviously just as shocked as he was to see the impeccable Sydney Taylor in her bathrobe, covered with mud, holding a dog in her arms. Somehow, even in her disheveled state, she had an air of royalty.

"Well, if it bothers you that much, Syd—" Reese brought his chair back down on four legs "—the game's just about over."

Narrowing eyes the color of blue ice at Reese, Sydney lifted one finely arched eyebrow and pressed her lips tightly together. "You know perfectly well what I'm talking about. Your dog was in my flower bed again."

Sydney had recently moved into the upstairs apartment of the historic brick building directly across the street from Squire's Tavern. She'd also rented the store downstairs and had been renovating to open a restaurant. She'd installed a deep-blue awning over beveled glass French doors and created a garden-like entrance. Hence the flowers which Boomer had become so attracted to.

"Are you sure it was my dog?" Reese asked innocently. "I could have sworn I saw Madge Evans's poodle out earlier."

"Madge is a responsible pet owner," Sydney said irritably. "You, on the other hand, are not. This is the fourth time in three weeks I've caught Boomer in my flowers, He's all but ruined my pansies, dug up my bulbs twice and chewed up my chrysanthemums."

Boomer barked, his guilt sealed when bright yellow petals fell from his jaw. Sydney stalked across the room and dumped the dog on top of the table. Boomer danced excitedly; chips and cards flew. Then Boomer gave a fierce shake of his long black-and-white coat and mud flew, as well. With an oath, Lucian jumped up, wiping at the splattered mud on the front of his white shirt.

Miss Lady Luck had suddenly been replaced by Miss Fortune, alias Sydney Taylor. Reese glanced forlornly at the queens in his hand, sighed, then threw his cards down and swiped at the dirt on his face. Boomer jumped off the table, sat at Reese's feet and looked up at his master expectantly. The dog's nose was covered with damp mud.

Reese knew he should be repentant, he really did. But there was just something about Sydney. Something about that haughty, patronizing air of hers that made him want to puff up his chest and bring that cute little chin of hers down a notch or two. Reese glanced at his brothers for a little moral support, but based on the gleam of amusement in their eyes, he was obviously on his own.

Reese stood and looked down at Sydney, considered telling her that she had a slash of dirt across her temple, then thought better of it. "I'll buy you some more flowers and bulbs."

Folding her arms tightly, she met his gaze. "What good will it do if your dog keeps digging them up? Need I remind you that my grand opening for Le Petit Bistro is in four weeks?"

Hardly. There was very little in Bloomfield County that everybody didn't know about everybody else, some of which was even true. Since Sydney had returned three months ago from culinary school in France, the whole town had been talking. Not about the restaurant she was planning to open as much as the reason why she'd left town over a year ago: Sydney had been left high and dry at the altar by Bobby Williams, Head Coach at Bloomfield High School. Bobby had been offered a position at NYU, only he'd neglected to mention the job to Sydney, along with the fact that he'd decided not to get married. At least, not to her. Bobby and Lorna Green, a cocktail waitress from Reese's tavern, had eloped on their way to New York.

No one had seen Bobby or Lorna since, but there had been talk that Lorna had been looking rather plump around the middle at the time she and Bobby had taken off together.

Reese had certainly never missed Bobby; he'd never liked the egotistical jerk, anyway. But Lorna, though a little dim-witted, had been a good employee, a rare commodity these days. Especially at the moment. With one waitress out on maternity leave, another on vacation, and a new girl who was sweet but couldn't remember what time to show up for work, the tavern had been in chaos for the past two weeks.

And now Hurricane Sydney had blown in.

Nothing I can't handle, Reese told himself and gave her his best smile. "I'm really sorry, Syd. It won't happen again."

"Spare me the charm." Sydney rolled her eyes. "I realize that works on most of the women in this town, but it's wasted on me."

From any other woman, Reese would have wholeheartedly risen to the challenge. But this was Sydney, for Heaven's sake. Sydney was starched stiff as a nun's habit. Going up against Sydney would be sort of like the *Titanic* taking on the iceberg. And those were icy waters he'd rather not swim in.

Except, at the moment, with her hair all rumpled, dressed in her robe and slippers, Sydney didn't look quite so starched or quite so stiff. She looked kind of…soft. Soft and cute.

Startled by his thoughts, he looked at her again, saw the rigid lift of her shoulders and tight press of her lips. Geez, what had he been thinking? Sydney Taylor might be an attractive woman, but soft and cute? And those frumpy robe and slippers she had on were not exactly Victoria's Secret.

"Reese Sinclair, are you listening to me?" Sydney narrowed her eyes. "I'm not leaving here until we settle this once and for all."

"You could have him destroyed," Callan offered from the sidelines.

Boomer jumped up and barked shrilly.

With a gasp, Sydney whirled. "I would never harm an animal."

"Not the dog." Callan looked offended that Sydney would think such a thing. "I meant Reese."

The look Sydney gave Callan could have wiped out spring crops. Reese glared at his brothers. He knew they were having a good laugh at his expense. He didn't even blame them. If the situation were reversed, he'd want a front row seat. With popcorn. But if he was going to go one-on-one with Sydney Taylor, he sure as hell didn't want an audience. "Weren't you all just leaving?"

"Not me." Lucian glanced at the cards still in his hand.

"No hurry." Gabe started to take his coat back off and Callan followed suit. "We could squeeze in a couple more rounds."

"Game's over." *And so's the show.* Reese snatched the cards out of Lucian's hands, helped Gabe put his coat back on, then shoved all three of his brothers out the door and closed it behind them.

"Okay." Reese turned and faced Sydney. "Now, where were we?"

"You were about to tell me how you intend to keep your dog inside your own yard and out of my flowers."

"Oh. Right. Well, here's the thing." Reese glanced at the dog, then moved beside Sydney, lowering his voice as he bent his head close to hers. The scent of lavender mixed with something else he couldn't identify drifted from her skin. He hesitated, not only to appreciate the smell, but because he was surprised. He'd never thought about Sydney smelling so...nice.

Brow furrowed, she frowned at him. "What thing?"

"What? Oh, well, you see, Boomer's sensitive about being locked up. Ever since I found him out on the highway and brought him home with me, he gets depressed if I try to keep him in."

Boomer, who heard his name and seemed to understand he was the topic of conversation, lifted his head and thumped his tail on the floor.

"Depressed?" The tilt of Sydney's head signified her skepticism. "Maybe he requires more attention than you can give him."

"Shoot, Boomer gets more attention than a baby with a bonnet. He just can't stand to be fenced in. He needs to...stretch his legs a little."

"Gabe just bought the Witherspoon house," Sydney said matter-of-factly. "That's five acres of farmland, surrounded by several more acres. Plenty of room for a dog to 'stretch his legs.' I'm sure Boomer would be extremely happy there. He can dig to his heart's content."

"I couldn't do that to Boomer. He was already abandoned once when he was a pup. If I just gave him away like that, he wouldn't understand. He'd think I deserted him."

She stiffened, then took a step back from him and lifted cool blue eyes to his. "Like Bobby deserted me? Left me standing in my wedding dress to face a crowded church on my own, is that what you're trying to say?"

Dammit, dammit. That wasn't what he'd meant at all. "No, Syd, really, I—"

"Forget it, Sinclair. You think you can soften me up with that killer smile of yours and make me feel sorry for your dog, and I'll just go away. Well, I'm not going away." She folded her arms. "Life is just one big lark to you, isn't it, including this bar you run."

"Hey, now, this is a tavern, not a bar. There's a big—"

"Maybe you think I'm being petty, or that a few chewed up flowers are irrelevant, but your lack of respect for my property is irresponsible and insensitive."

"Hey, I'm as sensitive as the next guy," Reese protested.

"If that next guy happens to be Bobby Williams," Sydney said, and pointed her chin at him.

That did it. Reese clenched his jaw. He wasn't anything like Bobby Williams. He'd had enough of Sydney's insults for one night. He glanced at Boomer. *This is the thanks I get for saving your sorry butt.* He looked at the table where cards and chips were scattered.

Irresponsible, was he? Life was one big lark, huh?

Well, fine, then.

"Tell you what, Syd," he said slowly, turning back to her. "What say we let a friendly card game settle this for us?"

Her head came up, and her brow came down. "What?"

"A card game. Go Fish, Crazy Eights. Maybe a couple hands of Old Maid?"

His jab struck home. She straightened; her eyes shot blue daggers at him. "What on earth are you talking about?"

"A game of chance to settle this once and for all. If you win, I'll keep Boomer fenced in, and if I win…" *What did he need? Something to not only shut Sydney up, but put her in her place. Think, Sinclair, what do you need?*

He grinned suddenly. She'd never go for it. He knew she wouldn't. He just wanted to see the expression on her face, wanted to see her back down from a challenge.

"…if I win," he continued, "you have to come work at the tavern for a week. I'm short two servers right now. Wages included, of course, plus tips."

Sydney's jaw went slack; she was silent for all of fifteen seconds. "You expect us to settle this with a *card* game? That's preposterous!"

He grinned at her. "That's my middle name."

"You're serious. You're really serious."

"Yep." She'd back out now, Reese thought with smug satisfaction. No way she'd go through with anything as foolhardy as this. And since he had her attention, he'd up the ante till she squeaked. "Under my direct supervision, of course. You have to do what I say."

"What!"

"Don't go looking so hopeful, Sydney," Reese said, thoroughly enjoying the flush on her face. "I'm only referring to business here, though we could certainly discuss job perks and options, if you like."

"Let me get this straight." She blew a wisp of hair from her cheek. "If I win, you promise to take care of Boomer and keep him out of my flowers. If I lose, I have to work for you, here, for a week."

"Just three hours a day. Someone as tidy and organized as you could surely work three hours into your schedule."

Sydney's laugh was dry and short. "Even coming from Reese Sinclair, this is the most absurd proposal I've ever heard."

He knew she wouldn't go for it, but it had been fun, anyway. Still, he couldn't resist giving her pride one more tug. "If you're afraid to lose…"

"Afraid?" Her eyes narrowed sharply, and she stepped closer to him. "I'm not afraid."

"Okay." He shrugged and rolled his eyes. "Whatever you say, Syd."

"All right, Sinclair." That chin of hers went up again. "What do you say we make it more interesting? If I lose, Boomer's not only free as a bird, I'll come work for you for *two* weeks. If *I* win, though, Boomer not only gets kept in…" she leaned in close "…*you* have to come work for *me* for two weeks after my restaurant opens."

He gave a bark of laughter. "You're kidding, right?"

"Afraid *you'll* lose?" she asked sweetly.

"You mean it." He stared at her incredulously. "You'll actually go through with it?"

"I'll not only go through with it, I'll honor my bet, win or lose. Will *you,* Sinclair?"

A muscle jumped in Reese's jaw. "You're on."

"Fine."

"Fine."

They marched to the table and sat down opposite one

another. Reese scooped up the scattered cards and started to shuffle them. It had been a long time since he'd played Go Fish or Crazy Eights. He hoped like hell he could remember.

"So what's it gonna be, Syd?"

She sat straight in her chair, her hands laced primly on the table. "How 'bout five card stud, one-eyed jacks wild?"

Reese nearly dropped the deck of cards in his hand. "You want to play poker?"

"What did you think we'd play? Gin rummy?" She lifted one brow. "My father taught me to count with a deck of cards when I was two. When the other kids were playing Chutes and Ladders, I learned how to double down with an eleven in blackjack." She smiled, held her cool eyes steady with his. "Now deal the cards, Sinclair. I'm about to kick your behind."

One hour and ten hands later, to Sydney's delight— and Reese's annoyance—her stack of chips was twice the size of his. It was a glorious sight, Sydney thought. Each tall, neat column of red, white and blue signifying her victory.

And Reese's defeat.

Of course, she hadn't officially won yet, but it was just a matter of time—a short matter of time, based on the past three hands. At the rate he was losing, she should be able to put him out of his misery in the next hand or two.

She still couldn't believe she'd let him goad her into this. At twenty-six, she liked to pride herself on being a mature woman, in control at all times, one who had a solid handle on her emotions. A woman who used logic and practicality to make decisions, not childish grammar-school antics of one-upmanship.

But he'd looked at her with such arrogance, such smug amusement, she'd simply accepted the challenge, as much to her surprise as his.

Glancing over the cards she held, she watched him study the hand she'd dealt him. Those incredible eyes of his were narrowed with concentration, and one shock of thick, dark hair tumbled over his furrowed forehead. Absently, he brushed his thumb back and forth over the strong line of his chiseled jaw; the quiet rasp of thumbnail against the shadow of his beard was the only sound in the office.

She'd never had the opportunity to stare so openly at a man before. It was not only rude, it was extremely forward. In this situation, though, she considered it a necessity. After all, this *was* poker. The most important rule of the game, her father had taught her when she was a child, was to closely assess an opponent. Every movement, every blink, every twitch, was to be noted, then analyzed. If her father had taught her nothing else before he'd left when she was twelve, she had learned to be observant. If she ever saw him again, she just might have to thank him for that one thing. But seeing her father again was one bet she'd never take. He'd called a few times, sent a couple of birthday cards, but he'd never come back once to see her after he'd walked out fourteen years ago.

Knowing what an extremely difficult woman her mother had been to live with, Sydney could understand the lack of visits. What she couldn't understand, what she couldn't forgive, was him leaving her alone with her mother, who had no one else to take out her bitterness on except her daughter.

But that was water under the bridge, Sydney thought with a sigh. She was twenty-six now and in a few short weeks she'd have the business she'd dreamed of for so many years. The past would be behind her, including the humiliation of Bobby and Lorna.

Sydney Taylor was going to be a new woman. She was going to be the woman everyone thought she was: confident, self-assured, poised. A woman who didn't give a damn what anyone thought or said about her.

All the things she wasn't, but desperately wanted to be.

Realizing that she'd lost focus of the game while her mind wandered, Sydney snapped her attention back to Reese. She'd learned that when he touched his finger to the cleft in his chin he had at least a pair, when he scratched his neck just under his left ear, he probably had three of a kind or better. When he brushed his jaw with his thumb, as he was doing now, odds were he was bluffing.

And so she watched him. Closely. Strictly for the game, of course.

She'd never noticed the scar just under that firm mouth of his, or the slight bump at the bridge of what she would consider an otherwise perfect nose. He wore his hair combed back, and the ends just brushed the collar of his blue flannel shirt. The sleeves were rolled to his elbows, his forearms muscled and sprinkled lightly with the same dark hair that peeked from the vee of his shirt.

No question about it, he was an amazing specimen of masculinity. He wasn't her type, of course. After Bobby, she'd sworn off smooth-talking, shallow playboys who had more muscle than brain. While she could certainly appreciate Reese Sinclair's blatant maleness, she had no intention of being a victim of it, as were most of the women in town.

But then, Sydney knew she wasn't Reese's type, either. He went for the bubbleheads, the women who giggled at every joke and endlessly batted their eyelashes. She'd seen Heather Wilkins hanging on his arm last month at the pumpkin festival in town, then Laurie Bomgarden had been snuggling with him a week ago at the Women's Auxiliary's annual fall charity drive. Sydney doubted that Heather and Laurie's IQs combined was equal to the current outside temperature. And considering it was only the beginning of November, she was being generous.

But who Reese Sinclair spent his free time with was of no concern to her. Her only concern was beating the pants off that arrogant butt of his that the women of Bloomfield were so crazy about.

She glanced at the "Best Butt in a Pair of Blue Jeans" award he'd hung on the wall in his office. The conceit of the man, she thought with a sniff. Maybe they'd give *her* an award when she kicked that butt in poker.

"You vote for me, Syd?"

"What?" Realizing that she'd been caught staring at the award, Sydney snapped her gaze back to the table. Reese was watching her, and the amusement she saw in his eyes made her stiffen.

With a grin, he nodded toward the wall. "Did you vote for me?"

"Certainly not."

It was a bald-faced lie. She'd considered it her civic duty to vote when the ballot box went around for the annual "best butt" election. The contest had been close this year, between Lucian and Reese and the sheriff,

Matt Stoker. It had been a difficult choice, but in the end—she almost smiled at her own pun—she'd voted for Reese.

And she'd die before she told him that.

"Who'd you vote for, then?"

She straightened the cards in her hand, lining them up perfectly. "What makes you think I voted for anyone?"

"Sydney Taylor miss an opportunity to express her opinion on something?" He settled back in his chair and regarded her with a curious gaze. "So why didn't you vote for me? Don't you think I deserved it?"

She was becoming increasingly flustered by this rather personal topic of conversation. "I wouldn't know if you deserved it or not. I've never noticed."

"You've never noticed?" He looked slightly wounded. "You come over to the tavern every Wednesday night for the book review club. How could you not notice?"

"Reese Sinclair!" She slammed her cards down on the table. "In spite of your high opinion of yourself, I do not go to the book review meeting to stare at your butt!"

He looked at her for a long moment, then blinked. "Excuse me?"

"I said, I do not—"

"I heard what you said, I just don't under— Oh." He glanced at the wall, then back at her. "I was talking about the *restaurant* award. You are a member of the Chamber of Commerce, aren't you? And you did vote for the top restaurant in Bloomfield County, didn't you?"

The restaurant award. She felt her cheeks burn. He was talking about the *restaurant* award.

He clucked his tongue and shook his head. "Sydney Taylor, shame on you. Where *is* your mind tonight?"

Her entire face was on fire now, the heat spreading down her neck. "I…well…I—"

"I've never seen you stutter and blush, Syd." Reese gave her a lopsided grin. "You *were* thinking about my—"

"I was not!" She scooped up her cards again and stared at them. "The sun will be up in a few hours and you can crow all you want, Sinclair. Right now, this game is gathering moss. Could we get on with it, or do you need some ice for that swelling in your head?"

"You know, darlin'—" Reese picked up the cigar he'd put out an hour ago and bit on it "—that mouth of yours is going to get you into trouble one of these days. You need to learn to lighten up and have some fun."

"I am having fun." She smiled sweetly at him. "I have twice as many chips as you do. Bet's to you, *darlin'*."

Reese grabbed a large handful of chips and tossed them on the table, then grinned at her. "Five dollars."

It was a steep bet, the largest he'd made since they started playing. He was bluffing, she thought. She'd seen him brush his thumb over his jaw a few moments ago. Sydney matched the bet, then slid another column across the table. "And I raise you."

And then he scratched his neck under his left ear.

Oh, dear.

Now she wasn't sure.

She stared at her own cards. She had three jacks, ace high. A good hand, but not great.

His thumb brushed his jaw again. She chewed on her bottom lip.

"Let's have some real fun," Reese said casually and glanced up from his cards. "Let's bet it all."

Bet it all? Her throat went dry. "You're kidding."

"Nope." He shifted the cigar from one side of his mouth to the other and leveled his gaze at her. "Winner take all."

She knew enough not to look away, not to so much as glance at her cards. Confidence was everything in this game. Never sweat, never falter. Absolute self-assurance.

"Do you know how to make quiche, Sinclair? With a splash of goat cheese and a kiss of basil? It's a little more complicated than flipping burgers and pouring beer, but you'll get the hang of it." Without so much as a blink, she pushed her stack to the middle of the table. "Or maybe I'll have you put on a tux and wait on tables. There are plenty of people who'd pay to see that."

"Not as many who would pay to see you wearing a wench outfit toting a load of drinks." Reese shoved his chips across the table. "Hell, I'd give a month's salary for that, myself."

They stared at each other, neither one flinching.

"You show me yours, I'll show you mine." Reese raised one corner of his mouth.

Sydney laid her cards on the table without even looking at them. Reese glanced down. Without any expression at all, he laid his hand down, too.

Breath held, she slowly lowered her gaze.

Three tens.

And a one-eyed jack.

Four of a kind.

Her breath shuddered out of her. She felt a pounding in her head, as if her skull were a tin drum and someone was beating on it. Boomer, who'd started this whole business in the first place, lay under the table, softly snoring.

But she could hardly blame the dog for her own stupidity.

"We don't open until tomorrow," Reese said cheerfully. "But show up at eight to get ready for Sunday breakfast. The *Philadelphia Gazette* ran an article about the tavern winning the Chamber of Commerce award, so I'm expecting a crowd."

Numbly, she rose from the table, every limb stiff and cold. She'd lost. Dear Lord. Two weeks. She had to work for Reese Sinclair for two entire weeks. Under his "personal supervision" as he'd put it.

She couldn't think right now. Couldn't let Reese see how completely humiliated she was.

She'd never let anyone see her like that again.

"All right, then." Drawing in a deep breath, she tightened the belt of her robe. "Eight o'clock it is."

"Sydney." Reese shook his head and chuckled. "You don't think I was serious about this, do you? I was just having some fun."

She lifted her chin and narrowed a cold look at him, praying he wouldn't see how badly her hands were shaking. "That's just one difference between you and me, Reese. Everything's a big lark to you, a game. You don't take anything seriously, where as I intend to honor my bet and the deal we made. I said I'd be here at eight, and I will."

A muscle jumped in Reese's jaw, and she watched as his eyes darkened. "Have it your way, Syd," he said with a shrug. "Just remember if it gets too rough for you, that I gave you an out."

"I can handle whatever you dish out," she said in a

voice so serene it surprised even her. "What remains to be seen is if you can handle me."

His brow shot up at that, and she simply smiled, turned on her muddy, slippered feet and walked calmly out the door.

She intended to give Reese Sinclair two weeks in his life that he'd never forget.

Two

Sunday was the only morning that Reese allowed himself to sleep in. He cherished that day, was grateful that he had a manager like Corky to come in early, start the coffee brewing, the grills heating, and the cinnamon rolls baking. Squire's Tavern and Inn was well-known not only for their hamburgers and pizza, but also for their breakfasts—plump sausages, country potatoes, biscuits that melted in your mouth and eggs so fresh they were still warm from the nest. He loved the smells and the sounds of his business: the food grilling, people laughing, having a good time while they ate and talked.

It reminded him of meals in his house when he was a kid. With five kids at the table—four of them boys—you had to yell to be heard over dinner in the Sinclair house. His father had always joined in with his children's antics, while his mother frowned and made a convincing effort to keep order. But as strict and rigid as she'd tried to be, they'd have her laughing and acting silly right along with the rest of them before the meal was over.

He missed those meals almost as much as he missed his parents. Twelve years had passed since the car accident that had taken them both. Sometimes it seemed like only yesterday, other times it seemed like an eternity.

Yawning, he rolled into the softness of the mattress and his pillow, cracked one eye open to glance at the bedside clock. Eight o'clock. He frowned and slammed his eye closed again, shutting out the early-morning light that poured through the open slats of his wooden blinds. He was up every other morning by six, but he never woke up before nine-thirty on Sunday. He still had an hour and a half to go, and he intended to savor every minute of it. The cottage he lived in was directly behind the tavern, a redbrick carriage house he'd converted into living quarters after he'd bought the abandoned tavern and completely renovated it four years ago. He was close enough to his business to handle whatever problems might arise, but it offered enough privacy for him to have alone time when he needed it. Or to entertain company.

Specifically, female company.

He was a man who fully appreciated women. The female gender, with their exotic smells and delicious curves, fascinated him almost as much as they intrigued him. They were complicated and mysterious; sweet and coy one minute, difficult and confusing the next. An absolute enigma that completely enchanted him.

Fortunately for him, women enjoyed his company as much as he enjoyed theirs. He understood the game well enough to know that, as an unattached male, he was open season for all the single women. But he was honest and up front with every woman he dated: he wasn't looking for marriage. Still, they had a way of pausing at jewelry-store windows, dragging him to movies that included at least one wedding, and somehow ending up in the department store housewares section, specifically china and silver.

But he was content with his life exactly as it was. He loved his business and his freedom. No one telling him what to do or when to do it. He never had to answer to anyone. No complications, no problems—

He buried his head in his pillow and groaned.

Except for Sydney Taylor.

Damn.

Sydney was one *big* problem.

He'd really never expected her to take him seriously when he'd made that bet with her, and he'd certainly never expected her to know how to play poker, let alone be so good at the game. But if there was one thing predictable about Sydney, it was the fact that she was unpredictable. He knew he never should have challenged her like that, but once he had, and she'd refused to back down, he couldn't just walk away. A guy had his pride, after all, and Sydney had tweaked his.

Knowing the woman, she was probably in the kitchen with Corky right now, telling him what to do and how to do it. Corky would have a fit about that, Reese knew. The man had been in the New York restaurant business for twenty-five years before he'd given up the fast pace of the big city and moved to Bloomfield. He'd applied for the position of chief cook and bottle washer one week before Squire's Tavern and Inn had opened its doors. For the past four years, Corky had been more like a partner to Reese than an employee, and even more, he'd been a good friend.

But Corky was particular about his kitchen. He had his own way of doing things. He wouldn't like Sydney messing with his pots and pans. Reese could see her now, with that stubborn little chin of hers pointed at Corky while she informed him of the proper method of cracking an egg or peeling a potato. That long, slender neck stretched high as she swished him out of her way. That sassy mouth giving orders.

Reese had known Sydney most of his life, but had never noticed before last night what a perfect mouth she had. Her lips were wide and full, rosy pink. She didn't know she did it, but every time she'd have a mediocre hand, she'd catch that lush bottom lip of hers between her perfectly straight, perfectly white teeth and nibble. More than once, that little action had distracted him. Then he'd remind himself he was thinking lustful thoughts about *Sydney,* of all people, and force his mind back to the game.

But he'd never seen her with that blond hair all mussed up like that, or streaks of mud on that smooth, porcelain skin. And he'd certainly never seen her in a bathrobe. As plain as the garment had been, there'd been something appealing about that red-plaid robe. Something strangely…sexy. Something that made him curious about what she wore *under* that robe.

And further still, what was under that.

Good Lord. He flipped onto his back and snorted. His brothers would have a good laugh if they could hear his thoughts about Sydney. Reese decided he needed to start dating more. He hadn't had much time for female companionship the past several weeks, and even Sydney was starting to look good to him. And that was ridiculous. Sydney Taylor was not even close to the type of woman he was interested in. Sydney was too uptight, too bossy, too—

"Are you going to sleep all day, Sinclair, or do you think we can get started?"

"What the—" On an oath, his eyes popped open. Arms folded, Sydney stood in his open bedroom door, a smile on those lips he'd been so foolishly fantasizing about and a gleam in her baby-blue eyes.

He was going to strangle her.

Eyes narrowed, he sat slowly. *This* was the Sydney he knew. Dressed in tailored black slacks, a pale blue, high-necked turtleneck that made her eyes shine, her hair pulled up tight in a smooth, golden knot on top of her head.

While, he, on the other hand, was buck naked under his sheets.

"Have you ever heard of knocking?"

"I did knock." Diamond studs sparkled on her earlobes as she tipped her head. "Twice, as a matter of fact. Corky told me to come on in if you didn't answer."

He decided he'd strangle Corky right after he finished with Sydney.

"This is my *bedroom*. You want to be specific about what it is you'd like to get *started?*"

"My duties, of course. What else would I possibly be talking about?"

He slipped down between the sheets and his white down comforter, plumped his pillow with his fist as he turned his back to her. "I sleep in on Sundays. Corky will show you what to do."

"Not a chance, Sinclair. Our bet was that I was to work under *your* supervision."

"Well, Syd, since I'm in my bed, what work under me would you suggest?"

"Why, Reese Sinclair." Sydney's voice dripped Southern debutante. "Sweet words like that do make a girl's heart flutter."

"If the girl had a heart," he muttered.

He heard her soft laughter and couldn't resist glancing over his shoulder to watch as she strolled around his bedroom, first inspecting a baseball trophy from the year his college team had won the state championship—he'd been pitcher—then squinting as she bent over his dresser and closely examined an oak-framed photograph of his sister Cara and her husband Ian that had been taken at their wedding last year, then another picture of his brother Callan and his wife Abby taken at their wedding six months ago.

She straightened, not even pretending to hide her curiosity as she continued to inspect his bedroom.

The woman was unbelievable.

"Tours don't begin until ten." Reese glared at her. "You can purchase tickets at the front desk."

Sydney smiled. "I'm sorry. It's just so overwhelming to be in the legendary Sinclair den of carnal delights. I expected to be stepping over the writhing bodies of scantily clad women."

"The maid cleaned up already this morning," he said dryly. "But there might still be a couple in the closet if you'd care to look."

She was actually heading for his closet when she stopped suddenly at the floor-to-ceiling bookcase he'd built beside an existing brick fireplace.

"Books!" she exclaimed. "You actually have *books* in here. Grisham, King, Follett—oh!" Her eyes lit up.

"Dickens and Shakespeare, too. Were they all left here by the previous owner?"

The sarcasm under that sweet smile of hers had Reese bristling. It wasn't bad enough she'd invaded his bedroom, now she was insulting his intellect. He'd read every one of those books, even had a signed copy of Fitzgerald's *The Great Gatsby* and Steinbeck's *Cannery Row.* His most recent purchase, though, and his most prized, was a first edition, leather-bound Alexandre Dumas *The Three Musketeers.* It had cost him a bundle, but it was worth every penny.

Still, he did have an image to maintain.

"Yeah, well, my comic books didn't take up much room and I needed something on the shelves." He sat, bent one knee while he stretched his arms wide. The comforter slipped down to his stomach. Sydney looked in his direction, and to his smug satisfaction, her eyes widened and she gasped.

Ha. That ought to send her running.

"Reese," she whispered, her voice filled with reverence. "How magnificent!"

Good Lord. Reese felt his face warm. He pulled the comforter back up as she hurried across the room toward him. Geez. He'd heard a lot of compliments, but never had a woman been quite so…exuberant.

"It's Louis XV, isn't it?" She stopped at the foot of his bed, touched one corner of his four-poster bed and ran her fingers over the dark grain. "Black walnut, right?"

"Ah, yeah." She was enthralled with his *bed,* for God's sake. He wasn't sure if he was relieved or annoyed. He watched as she stroked her fingertips over the round top of the smooth wood and made a small *O* with those pretty lips of hers.

His throat went dry.

"These rose carvings are amazing." Her fingers glided over the intricate petals and leaves. "Has it been refinished or is this the original stain?"

He dragged his gaze from those slender hands of hers and swallowed hard. What had she asked him? If the bed had been refinished? He had no idea. He'd just bought it last month at the Witherspoon estate auction after Cara had insisted it would be perfect for the inn. On a whim, he'd kept the bed for himself instead. Sydney was the first woman who had been in his bedroom since he'd set it up, but if it had this effect on all females, he would have to give his sister his undying gratitude.

Somehow, though, he couldn't imagine any of the women he'd invited here—and there weren't nearly as many as the gossipmongers proclaimed—noticing the grain of wood on his bed. He *did* know, however, that not one woman had ever commented on his book collection before.

He frowned as he remembered that Sydney's comment had been less than complimentary. And he certainly hadn't invited her here, either.

She bent on her knees and leaned closer still to inspect the carving, her hands moving over the post. Stroking. Up, down. Reese felt an arrow of liquid heat shoot straight to his groin.

Good God, as ridiculous as it was, the woman was turning him on!

"Gee, Syd—" Reese feigned a lightness to his voice, even though his entire body was wound up tighter than a steel spring "—now that you're such good friends, maybe you'd like me to leave so you can be alone here with Louis."

Shaking his head, Reese chuckled as he slipped out of bed. If there was one thing he could be certain of, the next two weeks were certainly going to be interesting.

War had been declared, and there was no question in Reese's mind who the victor would be.

Outside Reese's small carriage house, Sydney leaned back against the closed front door. Beside a black wrought-iron porch column, one large pot of rose-pink bouvardia sweetly scented the cool morning air, and a family of sparrows chattered excitedly in a nearby maple. Weathered clay pots of flowering cabbage dotted the moss-lined brick walkway that led back to the tavern, and a rusted metal tub nestled beside a concrete bench spilled the fading blooms of purple crocus.

Any other time, Sydney would have stopped to admire the beauty of the English-style garden with its double-tiered fountain and rose arbor. She'd had no idea such a lovely spot existed behind the tavern. But then, she'd never been in Reese Sinclair's bedroom before, either.

Her senses still reeled from the experience.

Closing her eyes, she drew in a slow, calming breath. Even now, outside in the fresh morning air, she could still see him as vividly as when she'd stood in his bedroom. The blush she'd managed to hold back inside now bloomed on her cheeks. Her skin felt warm and tingly. Heavens, but the man was something incredible to look at. Long and lean, with broad shoulders and a wide chest sprinkled with coarse, dark hair. His arms were muscled, his stomach tapered, without an ounce of fat.

When the blanket had slipped down, her heart had

skipped rope. He'd been naked under those covers, she was certain of that, and standing in his bedroom, surrounded by that masculine scent of him, staring into his sleepy, sexy eyes, she'd found it difficult to breathe.

And then she'd wondered what it would be like between those warm, rumpled sheets with him. What those sculpted muscles would feel like under her hands, how his tall, hard body would fit against her own.

She'd distracted those wayward thoughts by fawning over his bed. It was a beautiful piece of furniture, but the only reason she'd known specifics was because she'd actually been at the auction and she'd admired it then, as well. She'd picked up a French Victorian buffet herself that she intended to use in the entry of her restaurant.

But that buffet had definitely not been on her mind when she'd been kneeling beside Reese's bed. In spite of her yammering on about carvings and stains, she'd had more lascivious thoughts in mind. And she'd walk naked through a blizzard before she'd let Reese know that.

Honestly. If the man's empty head got any bigger, he'd have to wear lead shoes on a warm day to keep from floating away. The *last* thing Reese Sinclair needed was another female admirer. And the *last* thing she needed was to have her head turned by a superficial, immature rake whose single most recurring thought was about sex.

Tip her tiara, indeed.

Not likely.

Squaring her shoulders, she marched back to the tavern, determined not only to honor her end of this ridiculous bargain, but to put all prurient thoughts about Reese Sinclair out of her mind.

She hadn't spent nine months in culinary school and restaurant training for nothing. Squire's Tavern was distinctly eighteenth-century English: Tudor design with dark woods, rough-hewn oak beams, peg and groove floors, and a massive stone fireplace. There was a warmth to the tavern that welcomed its customers, and the food was very good. She was particular to the hamburgers and French fries herself.

Still, that didn't mean there weren't areas that could stand a little improvement. A tweak here, a nip there. Why not pass along a few of the ideas that had popped into her head as she'd walked through the main restaurant area this morning?

And anyway, Sydney thought as she let herself in the back door of the tavern, no matter what she did, Reese probably wouldn't notice at all.

Three

"**W**ho the *hell* put tablecloths on these tables?"

Fists on his hips, Reese stood in the center of the tavern and glanced around the room. Crisp, white linen tablecloths covered the black oak plank tables. In the center of every table, small crystal vases each held one single pink rose. Though he kept the tablecloths and vases in his back storage room, he'd only used them a few times for private parties.

"Sydney!"

He'd left her alone too long, dammit. He'd showered in record time, threw on a white shirt, his Sunday blue jeans and black bullhide boots, then hightailed it over here. And still that wasn't fast enough to keep the blasted woman from causing trouble.

Tablecloths and flowers, for God's sake.

"*Sydney!*" He turned and stalked toward the kitchen door. "Where the devil—"

He was going in as she was coming out. The door slammed into his nose with a loud *thwack*. An arrow of hot pain shot straight through his skull, then exploded into thousands of tiny, blinding white stars. His oath was loud and raw.

"Reese Sinclair, what kind of talk is that?" Shaking her head, she moved past him, a small blackboard and easel in her hand, oblivious to the fact she'd just rearranged his septum. "Are you always this cranky in the morning?"

"Cranky?" Holding his nose, he followed her to the front door. "You haven't even *begun* to see cranky." His growl was nasally. "But I guarantee you, Syd, it's coming in on a fast-moving train."

She clucked as she slid open the heavy wrought-iron latch on the front door. "Maybe you should have slept in. Lord knows you shouldn't be around people if this is how you behave in the morning."

"If you recall, I *was* sleeping until *you* barged into my bedroom. And what do you mean, *I* shouldn't be around people?" He winced as he gently touched the tender bridge of his nose, then pulled his hand away and checked for blood. Thank goodness there wasn't any. "You're a walking menace to society and *I'm* the one who shouldn't be around people?"

"What in the world are you so excited about?" She set the blackboard on the easel by the hostess podium, then turned to face him. "Why are you holding your nose like that?"

"Tablecloths," he snapped.

"Excuse me?"

"This is a tavern, not a teahouse. We don't use tablecloths."

She frowned at him. "That's why you're holding

your nose? Because you don't like the tablecloths? Heaven's, Reese, even for you, isn't that a bit childish?''

He counted to ten, drew in a slow breath. "No," he ground out between clenched teeth. "You slammed the kitchen door into my nose."

"Oh, dear." She stepped closer and looked up at him. "Let me see."

Protecting his nose with his hand, he backed away. "You've done enough, thank you very much. I'll take my chances with a hematoma."

"Stop being such a baby." She came after him. "I just want to look at it, for Heaven's sake. I won't even touch."

"Yeah, that's what they all say." He held up a hand to warn her off, but she just rolled her eyes at his nonsense and kept coming.

She backed him against the wooden bench for waiting guests, then laid her hands on his shoulders and pushed him down on the seat.

"Now, be still." With her lips pressed firmly together, she placed her hands gently on each side of his jaw and lifted his face. "Hmm. It does look a little red."

"Of course it's red," he complained, but the soft touch of her fingers on his cheeks made the pulsing pain subside. "You clobbered me with the door."

"I'd hardly use the word clobbered." She turned his head to the side, stared at him thoughtfully. "It does look a little crooked, though."

"It was already crooked. Lucian broke it when we were teenagers." Damn, but her fingers felt nice on his face. Her palms were smooth and warm, and she smelled good, too. Like last night. Lavender and something else. He breathed in deeply, concentrated on the familiar scent....

Vanilla. That was it. Sydney smelled like lavender and vanilla. It suited her, he decided.

"Your own brother broke your nose?" She gently touched the sides of his nose with her fingertips, raised her brows when he flinched. "That sounds a little barbaric."

She wore a gold, narrow-band wristwatch and the *tick-tick-tick* echoed in his ears and matched the *thump-thump-thump* in his temple. He couldn't remember a woman's fingers ever being so soft. "He didn't mean to do it. At least, not to me. He was swinging at Callan, who managed to duck the blow. I, unfortunately, was standing directly behind Callan."

Shaking her head with exasperation, she turned his head the other way and stepped between his knees as she leaned in for a closer inspection. "So all those stories I heard about the wild, reckless Sinclairs were true, huh?"

"Bad to the bone, sweetheart. Don't you forget it."

Her lips turned up at that, and he could see the laughter in her eyes. His gaze settled on that sassy mouth of hers and without his approval, his pulse jumped. Damn, but those lips were enticing, turned up slightly at the corners and the upper lip shaped like a cupid's bow. The kind of lips that would be a perfect fit for a man's mouth. And in spite of her sass, he knew she'd taste sweet. Somehow, just knowing that didn't seem to be enough. He had the craziest desire to experience that sweetness.

Something shifted in the air around them. As if an electrical storm were coming; a heaviness that made it hard to breathe. And with him sitting and her standing so close, directly in front of him, between his legs, no less, he became increasingly aware of Sydney as a woman. A woman with curves, very nice curves. He was certain she wasn't aware of it, but her breasts were no more than a handsbreadth from his face. From his mouth.

His heart started slamming around inside his chest like a punching bag. He couldn't be thinking this... *feeling* this way about Sydney. Sydney and sex simply didn't compute. The blow to his nose must have rattled his brain. Except for the fact that he'd already had a fleeting, mildly sexual thought about her earlier in his bedroom. Okay, so maybe the thought was a little more than mild, but it had been fleeting.

And now it was back. With nuclear force.

She moved in closer as she gently touched the bridge of his nose, and his blood began to boil. God help him, he wanted to kiss her. He wanted to slip his fingers under her sweater, feel the warmth of her skin and fill his palms with her soft flesh.

He fisted his hands at his sides and pressed his lips tightly together.

"We should probably put some ice on it," she suggested. There was hesitation in her voice. Uncertainty.

"Probably." But he didn't move, and neither did she. "Does it still hurt?" she asked softly, a little breathlessly.

"Yes." Only it wasn't his nose he was talking about. There was another part of his anatomy that was now throbbing.

"I'm sorry." Her cheeks were flushed, her lips slightly parted, and her hands had moved back to tenderly cup his face. "It does look a little swollen."

He started to choke at her choice of words and she

quickly pulled her hands away and slapped him on the back. ''Reese! Are you all right?''

Certain he couldn't speak, he simply nodded, then stood so fast that their bodies collided. Sydney started to fall back, but he grabbed her by the shoulders to steady her.

His hands tightened on her arms as he stared down at her.

Blue eyes wide and soft, she stared up at him.

Damn that mouth of hers.

Damn the torpedoes....

He started to lower his head—

The tavern door swung open wide; Gabe and Melanie came in first, with five-year-old Kevin, Melanie's son, Callan and Abby came next, then Cara and Ian. The noise level in the tavern increased tenfold as his family spilled like a burst dam into the room.

''Hail, hail, the gang's all here!'' Gabe scooped a laughing Kevin up in his arms, and Reese saw the lift of Gabe's brows as his gaze landed on the sight of Reese holding Sydney's arms. Reese quickly dropped his hands. Terrific, just terrific. He could only imagine how this must look to everyone. Exactly like what it was, he realized with a silent groan. Good Lord, he'd almost kissed Sydney!

Thank God his family had rescued him from making a mistake like that. Reese knew he'd take some ribbing for it, but that was a small price to pay to be saved from insanity.

''My mom won't let me say hell,'' Kevin announced to everyone in the way only a five-year-old can. ''She gets mad if I even say heck.''

''Hail—'' Melanie carefully enunciated the word as she pulled a black felt hat from her head, spilling her thick auburn hair around her shoulders "—means hello," she explained. "It also means hail as in pellets of ice, but we can talk about that later. Sydney, how nice to see you."

"Hello, Sydney." Abby smiled sweetly, ran an unconscious hand through the layered golden curls of a new hairdo she wasn't quite used to yet but her husband seemed to love.

"You here for Sunday brunch?" Cara asked, shrugging out of her navy peacoat. Though she had barely begun to show in her pregnancy, her hand instinctively moved to her stomach. Ian, her husband, slipped an arm around her from behind and covered her hand while he pressed his lips to the top of his wife's blond head.

"Sort of." Sydney folded her arms and looked up at Reese with a smug why-don't-you-tell-them expression on her face.

The room was once again quiet, all eyes on him.

Dammit, dammit. He'd never intended for that silly card game to go this far, let alone be standing here trying to explain to his family.

And based on that smirk on Sydney's face, she sure as hell had no intention of making it any easier on him, either.

"Well, it's kind of funny, actually..." He cleared his throat. "See, Sydney and I were playing poker last night—"

That certainly lifted a few eyebrows, but still, no one said anything. "Well, we sort of had a bet, and, uh, I, well, I won." He paused, blurted it out in one quick breath. "So Sydney's going to work here for me for a couple of weeks."

How absolutely ridiculous it sounded to say it out loud. Eight sets of eyes bored into him.

Then all hell broke loose.

"You did *what?*" Cara narrowed her eyes disapprovingly.

"A couple of *weeks?*" Ian's jaw went slack.

"This is a joke, right?" Gabe frowned.

"*Sydney* work *here?*" Callan started to laugh, but Abby elbowed him and shook her head in disbelief.

A pounding started in Reese's head. "I told her I'd waive the deal and cancel all debts. In fact, I even insisted. She refused my offer."

"A deal is a deal," Sydney concurred. "I lost, Reese won. I'm here for two weeks, three hours a day."

"With full pay and tips," Reese added quickly, hoping to redeem himself even a little. It was obvious his brothers thought it was hilarious, while the women all looked at him as if he'd kicked a puppy.

"Isn't your restaurant opening up in a few weeks?" Melanie asked. "How do you have time to be here?"

"I'm pretty much ready to go now, except for the counter that Lucian is installing for me this week," Sydney said. "The next couple of weeks after this one will be just handling details."

"Oooh, look," Abby murmured as she glanced around the room. "Tablecloths and flowers. How pretty everything looks."

"Nice touch, Reese." Cara nodded with approval. "Bringing a little elegance and sophistication to the tavern, are you?"

The tablecloths. Reese had gotten so caught up in his near kiss with Sydney, he'd forgotten about that. The pounding in his head increased. "It was Sydney's idea," he said tightly.

"Reese doesn't like them." Her neck stretched high, Sydney glanced at him. "We were about to discuss it, but we got distracted after I hit him in the nose. On accident, of course.''

Brows went back up again and everyone looked at Reese. He squirmed uncomfortably. ''I'm fine,'' he grumbled.

''Two minutes ago he was howling like a banshee.'' Sydney shook her head. ''You'd have thought I'd tried to murder the man.''

The only murder around here, Reese thought irritably, was going to be a long-necked blonde with a gorgeous mouth that wouldn't quit. The sudden image of how he might silence that mouth with his own only made him more irritable.

''Hey, everybody.'' Lucian burst through the door at that moment. ''Please tell me I didn't already miss hearing what happened with our dear baby brother and Sydney Taylor last night. She came storming into the tavern last night mad as a—'' He caught sight of Sydney then and stopped abruptly. ''Uh, mornin' Syd.''

''Morning, Lucian,'' Sydney said smoothly, then turned a bright smile on the group. ''I have a large table by the window up front. Why don't we get you all seated and I'll bring everyone drinks and tell you about today's specials.''

Teeth clenched, Reese watched as Sydney, with all the grace and charm of the queen of England, led his family to their table. Good grief, but the woman was infuriating. She wasn't here an hour and she'd taken over. Tablecloths and flowers and—

Today's specials?

He didn't have any today's specials. His gaze shot to the blackboard she'd carried in and set up by the hostess podium.

Crepes Almandine? Quiche Lorraine?

This was an English *tavern*, for God's sake, not some frou-frou French restaurant.

Muttering under his breath, he snatched up the blackboard and easel and headed back to the kitchen. Within the hour, the restaurant would be full, so at the moment, there was no time to "discuss" anything with Sydney.

Something told him that these three hours with Sydney were going to be the longest of his life.

Three hours somehow stretched to four, but with the tavern as busy as it was, Sydney hadn't even noticed she was an hour over her agreed schedule. Apparently Reese hadn't noticed, either, Sydney thought as she slipped into the small employee lounge behind the restrooms, because he hadn't booted her out yet.

With a tired sigh, she sat on the vinyl sofa in the lounge. After losing the poker game last night, she'd tossed and turned all night, then dragged herself out of bed early to get ready for the day. With only two waitresses, plus Reese and herself to see to the customers, she hadn't stopped until now.

The truth be known—and she'd certainly never admit it to Reese—she'd enjoyed every minute of it.

Even as a little girl, Sydney had loved helping out at her mother's endless string of dinner parties and her grandfather's business functions. Whether it was in the kitchen or helping serve in the dining room, she had loved the excitement, the elegant food, the pretty table settings, the flowers, all the wonderful smells and sounds of music and people having a good time.

Sydney had once foolishly told her mother about her dream of opening a small French restaurant in Bloomfield. "Absurd," "waste of time" and "exercise in futility,'' had only been a few of her mother's choice words for the idea.

Sydney had never brought the subject up again, but one year to the day after her mother had died, four weeks after Bobby had left her standing at the altar, Sydney enrolled in culinary school in Paris, bought a ticket for France and never looked back.

She knew people still talked about her behind her back: *Well, is it a surprise?*, they would whisper. *Nobody ever really thought that a handsome jock like Bobby would marry Sydney the Hun. He'd simply felt sorry for her after her mother had died, and after all, her grandfather is the town judge and her family does have loads of money.*

Sydney wasn't stupid. She'd known all that. But she'd really thought that Bobby, even if he hadn't loved her, had cared a little about her, enough that maybe, just maybe she could have a life at least close to what other women had. Husband, children—how desperately she wanted babies!—a little house with a yard.

So maybe she wouldn't have that. But she'd have her restaurant. That was one dream no one could take away from her. Just these few hours this morning in the tavern, showing customers to their tables, taking orders and serving food, had made her feel alive again. She'd felt…needed. And she'd enjoyed every minute. Almost as much as she had enjoyed aggravating Reese.

Closing her eyes, she laid her head back on the sofa and smiled slowly. She knew she was driving him crazy. He'd hated the tablecloths and flowers and had thrown a fit about her additions to the menu. Her smile widened.

Reese Sinclair would rue the day he made that bet with her.

She did feel bad about hitting him in the nose with the door, though. Thank goodness she hadn't broken anything or drawn blood. She didn't believe in physical violence of any kind, and even though it had been an accident, she would have felt terrible if she had seriously hurt him.

But what had happened afterward between them still had her head spinning.

She'd told herself that she'd only touched him because she was concerned he might need medical attention. But when she'd placed her hands on his face she'd had trouble remembering that her inspection was strictly of a clinical nature. His freshly shaved cheeks had felt smooth under her fingertips and the faint scent of his spicy aftershave mesmerized her senses, tempted her to draw his essence more deeply into her lungs. To move closer still.

Had he noticed her hands shaking? Or how difficult it had been for her to breathe? And worst of all—that she'd wanted him to kiss her?

No, she doubted that he had noticed. She'd learned well enough over the years to hide what she was feeling. How else would she have survived an angry, bitter mother who'd never accepted that her husband had left and was never coming back? To the day she'd died, not one thing had ever made her mother happy. Not the family's money or status in the community, not the traveling or fine home they'd lived in. Not even her daughter had ever brought her joy, Sydney thought sadly, though she knew she'd done her best. Her best simply hadn't been good enough.

She wondered if it ever would be.

"What are you still doing here?"

Her eyes flew open at the sound of Reese's voice. He

stood in the lounge doorway, watching her. *Not now,* she thought with a sigh. The last thing she felt like doing at this moment was playing verbal Ping-Pong with Reese Sinclair.

"Even the prisons give five minute breaks, Sinclair." She laid her head back. "I still have one minute left."

"I mean—" he moved into the room and closed the door behind him "—why are you still here at all? Your sentence was up an hour ago."

"I told Julie I'd cover her for a break in ten minutes. She hasn't stopped once in three hours."

"Neither have you. You're going beyond the call of duty here, Syd."

"Well, don't get any ideas that I'm doing it for you," she said, but there was no bite to her words. "I'm just trying to win Julie over so I can steal her away from you. It's not easy to find employees who work that hard."

"It's not easy to find employees, period," he said in agreement. "You have anyone lined up yet?"

She shook her head. "I'm putting an ad in this week."

"Well, if you want long-term, take it from me and stay away from aspiring actors and artists. One day they're here and the next, poof, they magically disappear."

"Sort of like fiancés," she said lightly, then wished she hadn't. She saw the change in Reese's eyes, the pity. More than she hated what people said about her, she hated the pity.

She felt the sofa dip as he sat beside her. Her senses went on immediate alert. She had no idea what was going on with her unexplained feelings toward Reese, but if she'd learned anything this morning, it was to keep as much space between her and him as possible. Especially when she was tired. Tired made her vulnerable, and that was the last thing she wanted to be around Reese. She knew better than to let her guard down with men like Reese Sinclair.

"Sydney." He said her name with such trepidation that she felt her insides wince. "I need to talk to you."

Good grief, if they'd been lovers, she'd have sworn he was getting ready to break it off. But they weren't lovers, of course, and that was a ridiculous thought, anyway.

With a sigh, she sat and leveled her gaze with his. He actually looked worried, she thought in amazement. As if he hated whatever lecture he was about to give her. It had been nice, for two minutes, to have a discussion with Reese without verbal barbs, to talk business as if they were equals. Peers. Only he didn't consider them equals or peers at all, she thought. She knew he considered her restaurant a lark, that she didn't know one little thing about owning a business or the hard work attached to it.

Well, she *did* know what she was doing, and what she didn't know she'd learn. And she'd be damned if she'd sit and cower while he reprimanded her like a child.

"If you're still upset about the flowers and tablecloths, then fine, I won't do that again. I simply thought it might add a certain…*je ne sais quoi*—" she gestured with her hand "—sophistication?"

"That's not what I wanted to—" He stopped, narrowed his eyes. "Sophistication?"

She tucked a stray strand of hair back into the knot on the top of her head. "I wasn't suggesting it for every day. I just thought that a couple of subtle changes would add a little refinement to your Sunday brunch.''

The green of his eyes darkened and a muscle twitched in his jaw. ''You stick that nose of yours up any higher, Syd, you're going to need a guide dog to lead you around.''

''Well, you certainly don't need to be rude.'' She forced her head to remain perfectly level. ''For all it matters to me, you can throw peanut shells on the floor and serve beer in paper cups.''

''Is that so?''

''Yes, that's so.'' She stood, shot a cool gaze at him. ''Well, it's been real, but if you'll excuse me, I'm going to cover for Julie's break before I leave. And I consider this hour overtime, Sinclair. Time-and-a-half.''

Guide dog, she fumed as she left the lounge without giving him a chance to respond. She wasn't a snob. And she most certainly did *not* stick her nose up in the—

She tripped over a brass potted plant in the hallway outside the lounge and stumbled forward, barely catching herself. She heard the sound of Reese's chuckle as he watched her from the doorway.

As childish as it was, Sydney wished she had a big fat banana cream pie in her hands. She'd love to rub it in that stupid grin Reese had on his face. Tugging her sweater down, she turned smoothly on her heels and walked away.

Four

Unless it was a holiday weekend or the height of tourist season, Mondays at the tavern were normally slow so Reese closed and used the time to catch up on errands and the never-ending paperwork that was part of owning his own business. There were always books to be balanced, supplies to be ordered, staff schedules to be juggled and phone calls to be returned. While it was not his favorite part of self-employment, he simply accepted it as a necessary evil, cranked up his favorite Jonny Lang CD and settled down at his desk with a gallon of coffee.

He'd been at it for two hours, and he'd accomplished zip.

All because his mind kept wandering to a completely irascible, highly frustrating, extremely uptight female.

Coffee mug in hand, he leaned back in his desk chair and swiveled around to stare out his office window at the garden he'd had restored after renovating the tavern and inn. In the spring and summer the plants were thick and lush, the flowers a brilliant splash of color, but now, in the fall, the foliage had been cut back and only a few hardy chrysanthemums and asters still bloomed. While Jonny's gravelly voice wailed about lies and sex, Reese watched a bumblebee explore one budding branch of Winter Heath and, for the hundredth time, his mind drifted to Sydney.

After only one day the situation had already gotten out of hand. When he'd gone to the employee's lounge yesterday, he'd had every intention of putting an end to this farce. She'd looked so tired sitting on the couch with her head back and her eyes closed. So guileless. Soft and serene.

Quiet.

He smiled at that thought. He'd certainly never admit it to anyone, but he was not only getting used to that sass of hers, he actually enjoyed it. She said what was on her mind, and even though he didn't always like it, he had to at least respect her honesty. She didn't use her femininity to get her way or manipulate. No games of seduction or flirtation. No pouting or sulking. Even when she'd had to wipe down tables or sweep up a spilled bottle of catsup, she simply applied herself to the task without hesitation.

Somehow he'd never pictured Sydney Taylor doing anything as menial as taking drink orders or clearing dishes. She'd been born with a silver spoon in that enticing mouth of hers, and he doubted she'd ever lifted a finger for anything more strenuous than a manicure.

But she certainly had yesterday morning. She'd run her cute little behind off and never once complained. If he hadn't known better, he would have sworn she'd actually *enjoyed* working. Other than those damn table-cloths and the admonishment she'd given George Hubbel for ordering the double pork sausage skillet breakfast with extra cheese—George had just been released from the hospital following a triple bypass—the morning had gone by great.

Then she'd just had to go and get all snooty on him again. Implying the tavern lacked "sophistication." It was a tavern, for crying out loud. Not Antoines. If he let her have her way, she probably would have put out finger bowls and chilled salad forks. To Reese, chilled salad forks were the epitome of nothingness.

So he'd been compelled to continue their little parody. Just for another day or two, he told himself. That ought to be long enough to make Sydney Taylor throw in the towel.

He was a man with a plan.

Smiling, he took a sip of coffee, watching as the bumblebee stumbled out of the Winter Heath like a drunken sailor, then flew off. Sydney just needed a little instruction on how to relax and not be so serious all the time, Reese told himself. Not to be so high-and-mighty.

To think he'd almost kissed her. He snorted at the thought, then frowned.

He *still* wanted to kiss her.

Dammit, what was it about the woman that had him thinking about her when he needed to be working? He'd never thought about Sydney like that before. Never noticed how smooth her skin was, or how soft the blue of her eyes was, how incredibly tantalizing her mouth was. And when she'd stepped between his legs and moved so close, her breasts only inches away from him, he could have simply leaned forward and—

"Yo, Reese, you in here?"

He jumped at the sound of Lucian's voice, swore when coffee spilled over the sides of the cup in his hand and stained the front of the blue denim shirt he had on. He was still swearing as Lucian plopped himself down in a chair on the opposite side of the desk.

When Reese swiveled his chair around, Lucian took in the wet spot on his brother's shirt and lifted his brow. "Been drinking long?"

Reese narrowed his eyes. "Been sneaking up on people long?"

"I didn't sneak. You were in a galaxy far, far away, or at least your mind was." Lucian stretched his long legs out in front of him and settled back comfortably. "So what's her name?"

"Whose name?" Reese swiped at the front of his shirt, rummaged through the paperwork on his desk looking for a napkin, found one underneath his quarterly federal tax form.

"Whoever you were lusting over when I came in. I know the look, Bro. So who is it? Susan Williams? I heard she and Larry split up."

"They split up once a week. I'm trying to work here, Lucian. Get lost."

Undaunted, Lucian dug in like a dog after a bone. "It's Nancy Turlow, isn't it? She came into the tavern last Saturday with Heather and couldn't take her eyes off you."

Reese clenched his jaw, then picked up a pencil and turned his attention back to the ledger on his desk. "If the construction business is so slow you've got nothing better to do than sit around and speculate on my love life," he said dryly, "I've got some cracked tile in one of the guest rooms. Work me up an estimate and get back to me tomorrow."

"Gosh, thanks," Lucian said flatly. "As soon as we finish the strip mall we're building over in Ridgeway, then the four-story office building in Angel City, I'll get right on that. But for the record, I am here on business. I'm looking for Sydney."

"Sydney?" His head came up. "What do you want with Sydney?"

"Gabe asked me to stop by her place and take measurements on the countertop she ordered from him. She wasn't there, so I thought she might be here."

"Do you see her here?"

"Nope. But since you won her in that poker game, I just thought—"

"I didn't win *her,* dammit." Reese pushed away from his desk and stalked to the window. He stared out into the garden, frowned at the sight of Boomer sunning himself on the soft leaves of a lamb's ear plant. He shook his head, then sighed. "How the hell was I to know that she really knew how to play poker?"

Lucian stared thoughtfully at his brother for a long time, then slowly raised his brows. "You cheated."

"What?" Reese turned sharply.

"You cheated." Lucian leaned back in his chair. "I know you, Bro. You can call a good bluff, but you can't lie to me. It's right there in your eyes. You cheated."

Reese shoved his hands into the front pockets of his jeans. "She was winning. And she was so damn smug about it. She just needed to be taken down a peg or two."

"And you, of course, were the man to do it?"

He shrugged. "I never expected her to go through with it. It was...a joke."

"Doesn't look like you're laughing," Lucian noted.

"I tried to call it off, especially yesterday, after she'd

worked so hard here at the tavern. I was even going to confess. Then she stuck that pretty little nose of hers up in the air again and for some reason, I just couldn't let it go.''

Lucian chuckled softly. ''Well, I'll be damned. That's lust in your eyes, Bro. Who would have ever believed you'd be hot for *Sydney?*''

Reese made a rude sound. ''Even coming from you, Lucian, that's about the stupidest thing I've ever heard. I am not remotely interested in Sydney that way.''

Reese's head went up at a sound from the hallway outside his office, then he relaxed when Marilyn, one of his night-shift waitresses poked her head in the door and smiled. ''Hey, boss, can I pick up my check now?'' Her gaze slid to Lucian and her smile turned provocative. ''Hi, Lucian.''

''Hey, Mar.'' Lucian easily slipped into charm mode. ''What's up?''

Reese found the woman's paycheck on his desk while she and Lucian bantered back and forth, then quickly hustled her out.

''Look, I know I got carried away.'' Reese dragged a hand through his hair. ''And believe me, I'm paying for it big time. But as far as there being anything between Sydney and me, that's just completely—''

''Knock, knock. Little sister's here.''

Reese groaned as Cara came waltzing into his office, her pink skirt swirling around her legs and her arms loaded with shopping bags. He might as well have a revolving door on his office the way people were coming in and out.

''What about Sydney?'' Cara asked.

''Reese has a thing for her.'' Lucian rose, took the bags from his sister's arms.

Cara hesitated, looked at Reese. "You have a thing for Sydney?"

Why the hell couldn't he have been an only child? he thought irritably. "I do *not* have a thing for Sydney," he snapped. "Doesn't anyone in my family work anymore?"

"Not on Mondays." Cara brushed her blond hair back with her fingers and sat in the chair Lucian had occupied. She'd once been a private investigator, but now she ran a women's shelter in Philadelphia founded by her husband's grandmother. "I brought decorations for the surprise party we're throwing here for Gabe and Melanie on Saturday."

"What surprise party?" Since it was off the subject of Sydney, Reese eagerly pursued his sister's announcement.

"We never celebrated their engagement, so Abby and I thought we'd give them a surprise dinner party here." Cara slipped her flats off her feet and frowned at her swollen feet. "Good Heavens, at this rate, my feet will be the size of shoe boxes by the time this baby's born."

"They're getting married in a month," Lucian said, setting her bags down beside the desk. "What do they need a party for now?"

"Men." Cara sighed and shook her head. "Of course we have to give them a party."

Confused, Reese and Lucian looked at each other and shrugged.

"Just family." Cara stretched her feet and wiggled her toes. "Something nice, but not fancy. I'll work up a menu with Corky."

"Work up a menu?" Reese frowned. "What's wrong with the menu I've already got?"

"There's nothing *wrong* with your menu," Cara said

with all the patience of a kindergarten teacher. "Abby and I just think we should do something special. Now what's this about you and Sydney?"

Reese groaned silently. He should have known she'd come back around to the one subject he didn't want to talk about. "There is *nothing* about me and Sydney. She's just…helping out here while I'm shorthanded. We explained all that yesterday. I tried to let her out of the agreement, but she's stubborn as a mule."

"Honorable is a better word," Cara said and stared at him thoughtfully. "And if you had lost this *bet* you'd made, then what?"

Dammit, Reese fumed. Big families were like small towns, only worse. They wanted to know every little teeny tiny detail of their sibling's life, whether it was their business or not. But it was one thing for Lucian to know that he'd cheated in the poker game with Sydney, and quite another if his sister found out. She'd have him drawn and quartered.

Well, she didn't need to find out. No one needed to find out, for that matter. Lucian might razz him endlessly in private, but he wouldn't tell Cara or anyone else, Reese was certain of that.

He just needed to act casual. Nonchalant. He picked up his pencil and entered gibberish in one of the columns. "I would have had to lock Boomer up so he'd stop digging up her flowers."

"What kind of a deal is that?" Cara stared at him in amazement. "You *should* keep him fenced in anyway, deal or no deal." Cara shook her head. "Sydney's smarter than to bet something as simple as that. What are you holding back, Reese?"

He kept his eyes glued to the page in front of him as

if it were a fascinating novel. "I'd have to work at her place for two weeks," he mumbled quickly.

Now it was Lucian and Cara's turn to stare at each other in wide-eyed amazement. When they both began to laugh, Reese slammed his pencil down. "What's so damn funny?"

"You—" Lucian's shoulders were shaking "—you work for Sydney Taylor in her French restaurant? I'd eat a whole plate of those slimy little cooked snails to see that."

"How 'bout you eat my fist instead?" Reese rose stiffly and glared at his brother.

"No violence in the presence of a pregnant lady," Cara warned, struggling to contain her mirth. "Now, Reese, you've got to admit it, if you'd lost, it would have been pretty funny."

Yeah, gut-splitting, he thought and sat back down in a huff. "Why don't you both take a hike? I've got better things to do than sit around thinking about Sydney all day."

Cara went still, and even Lucian stopped laughing long enough to stare at him. "*Thinking* about Sydney?" Cara asked, raising her brow.

Dammit, *dammit*. "Talking. I said *talking*."

"No, you didn't. You said thinking," Lucian said. "Well, well. So you and Sydney *do* have a thing for each other."

"*I do not have a thing for Sydney,*" he boomed.

"Of course he doesn't."

All heads turned at the sound of Sydney's voice coming from the doorway. She stood there, wearing a simple white silk, scoop-necked blouse and a calf-length, dark blue silk skirt. There was a long moment of strained silence as Sydney's ice-blue eyes met Reese's, then she moved as gracefully across the room as if she were performing *Swan Lake*.

"Hey, Syd." Lucian cleared his throat. "Ah, I was looking for you."

She turned those incredible eyes on Lucian. "Oh?"

"Yeah, ah, Gabe asked me to take some measurements for the countertop you ordered."

She reached into her skirt pocket and pulled out a set of keys. "You can leave them inside when you're finished. I have a duplicate set."

Grasping at the opportunity to escape, Lucian snatched up the keys. "Well, I'll just get to those measurements, then."

"Could you give me a hand with these packages, Lucian?" Cara quickly slipped her shoes back on and stood. "Just leave the two blue bags. They're for the party. Nice to see you again, Sydney," Cara said as she and Lucian moved toward the door. "Please give my best to your grandfather, will you?"

"Certainly." Sydney kept her gaze directly on Reese.

Cowards. Reese frowned after his brother and sister when they disappeared from the room. When he wanted them to leave they wouldn't. Now he wanted them to stay and they couldn't get out of here fast enough.

"Hey, Syd." He turned his attention to the woman who stood watching him, her arms folded primly across her chest. Unknowingly, the gesture lifted and pressed her breasts firmly upward. *Don't think about her breasts,* he told himself, but the more he told himself not to think about them, and certainly not to look, the more he wanted to.

"Where in the world would Lucian get such a preposterous idea that either one of us would have a *thing* for the other?" Sydney asked.

"Didn't you know that Lucian was dropped on his head when he was a baby?" Reese said easily and slipped back into his desk chair.

"Is that so?" She arched one delicate brow.

"God's truth." He raised his hand to emphasize the veracity of his statement. At the same time, he forced his gaze to stay steady with hers, but it felt like a fish on the end of a line, tugging and pulling, trying to draw his attention down to the neckline of her blouse. "My parents thought about an institution when it became apparent there was permanent damage, but since he wasn't dangerous, they kept him at home."

"Every Sinclair man is dangerous," Sydney said, shaking her head. "You should all come with a warning label that says you're hazardous to the female sex."

"I love it when you talk dirty," Reese said huskily. And even though he was teasing, the sudden image of pillow talk with Sydney did make his pulse race.

Keep your eyes on her face, he repeated over and over, though he desperately wanted to slide a long, slow look over those lovely breasts, then down her silk-covered slender hips. What was she wearing underneath? he wondered, then gave himself a mental shake and decided he was the one with brain damage.

"Reese Sinclair." Sydney shook her head and sighed. "Can't you be serious for even one minute? It's ludicrous to think that you would have feelings for me or that I would have feelings for you that were of a physical nature. I just don't want your family getting the wrong idea about us."

Her words had *snob* written all over them, Reese thought with annoyance. And just why was it so ludicrous for her to have any feelings for him that were of a "physical nature"? What the hell was wrong with him? *She* was the one walking around as if she had too much starch in her collar.

Just once, he'd like to shake that ivory tower she lived in. He stood slowly, moved toward her with intent. "What's wrong with physical, Syd? I happen to like physical. In fact, I'm feeling extremely physical at this very moment."

"I hear lifting weights is quite an effective release of energy."

"There are other ways to release energy that are a lot more enjoyable," he murmured, moving closer. His gaze dropped to her mouth, and though he had no intention of this going anywhere, the jolt of desire that shot to his groin obviously had a mind of its own.

"Tennis is an excellent form of exercise," she suggested.

Wary, Sydney watched Reese approach, but refused to back away. Refused to think about those large hands of his, that long, muscular body and broad shoulders. She forced herself to think about a brandy sauce she'd been experimenting with, if it had enough butter, maybe a little less brown sugar. Vanilla, she decided, she'd add a little extra vanilla.

"Never could really get into the game myself." Reese moved past her and closed the office door.

Sydney's insides immediately formed a conga line from her head to her toes. "Is that so?" she said, forcing a bored tone to her voice, when she was anything but.

He smiled, then came up behind her, touched the back of her neck with his fingertip. "I prefer contact sports myself. Something that works the circulatory system and strengthens muscle tone. Something that really gets the heart pumping."

Her heart *was* pumping furiously. It was one thing to exchange verbal banter with him, but this was something entirely different. Something much more... sensual. She knew that Reese was teasing her, and as much as it aggravated her, it also excited her.

He wanted her to put a stop to his nonsense, expected her to. This was a game to Reese, she realized. He was certain she would yell "uncle" first. He was counting on it. He wasn't interested in her that way. And she, of course, wasn't interested in him that way, either.

Well, he started it, she thought with annoyance. Let *him* be the one to finish it. In spite of herself, she shivered when he slid the tip of his finger over the bare skin on her neck.

"Did anyone ever tell you that you have a pretty neck? And hair, too." Her breath caught when he moved behind her and brought his mouth closer to her ear. "Do you ever let your hair down, Syd?"

The warmth of his breath on her neck and ear sent ripples of pleasure over her skin. Every warning system screamed at her to run, to get away as fast as she could, but she knew that was what he wanted. He'd know then that he'd won, that he was irresistible to even cold-as-ice Sydney Taylor. And if that ego of his got any bigger, Reese Sinclair wouldn't even be able to walk through a doorway.

"Of course I let my hair down," she said calmly, ignoring the dull, heavy thud of her heart against her ribs. "When I wash it, before I go to bed, when I go to the beauty salon for a trim, or there's this wonderful oil pack that—"

"I'd like to see it," he said, skimming two fingertips up her neck.

Sydney realized she wasn't breathing and forced herself to draw in air. "Well, if you really want to. It's highly irregular, but I'm sure I could arrange it with my stylist. They pour about a cup of hot oil over wet hair, put a shower cap on your head, then stick you under the dryer for about—"

"Your hair down, Syd," he interrupted. "I'd like to see you let your hair down."

She'd had no idea how sensitive the skin on her neck was. Reese's touch was light as a feather, yet it packed the punch of a boxer. As ridiculous as it seemed, her knees were actually *weak,* her pulse was racing and she felt…hot. Very hot.

"Do you mean that figuratively, or literally?" she asked, then winced at the breathless sound she heard in her voice.

"Both." He moved closer still, brought his mouth within a whisper of her ear. She shuddered, was furious that she couldn't stop it and that Reese must have seen, too.

What made her even more furious was that she liked it. What he was doing to her, the way she felt. She liked it a lot. Wanted him to keep doing exactly what he was doing, wanted to keep feeling exactly as she was feeling.

She struggled to breathe, struggled to remain composed and collected when she really wanted to run. Into his arms or for the door, she wasn't sure which. But if he kept looking at her the way he was, if he kept touching her, she was going to find out real soon.

A knock at the door made her jump.

"Delivery." The door opened, and a young man with bleached white hair and double nose rings stuck his head in. "Hey, Reese, you wanna show me where you want all these bags?"

Reese gave Sydney one short, intense look, then brushed past her and followed the other man into the tavern. The breath she'd been holding shuddered out and she stumbled over to the desk to steady herself. That was close. Much too close. She'd nearly thrown herself in his arms and begged him to kiss her. Talk about pathetic, she thought with disgust. If she wanted to kiss anybody, it should be that delivery man for interrupting.

But just once, she thought, just once she wished a man would say things like that to her, that she had pretty hair or a nice neck, and he would mean them. *Really* mean them. It wouldn't be a game, like with Reese, or a lie, like Bobby. Just once she wished someone would say sweet things to her and it would be sincere.

She sighed, then drew in a long, slow breath and followed Reese out into the tavern. He was signing for the delivery and joking with the young man—Jessie—about the multitude of piercings on his body.

Sydney waited for the deliveryman to leave, then cautiously made her way toward Reese, who was staring intently at a four-foot-high pile of large produce bags.

Maybe she should try to get along with him, she thought. There was no reason for the two of them to argue or constantly snipe at each other. Maybe he was right. Maybe she should let her hair down, just a little.

What if maybe, just maybe, he *had* actually felt something when he'd been teasing her?

She moved beside him, ready to be pleasant and agreeable, even if it killed her. He turned when he saw her, looked at her with an expression that could only be described as sheer joy.

She smiled back and relaxed a little. "Reese—"

"Ah, there you are," he said, grinning. "This might take a while, so you better get started."

"Take a while?" she repeated dumbly.

He slapped a hand on top of the bags. "I thought it was a great idea you had, sort of give the tavern a rustic ambiance."

"What on earth are you talking about?" She stared at him in confusion, then looked at the bags under his hand.

Peanuts. Bags and bags of peanuts. Hundreds and *thousands* of peanuts.

"You can start shelling these for the floor and throw the nuts into a container. We'll serve them at the bar."

She stared at him, blinked. "This is a joke, right?"

"No joke," he said easily. Gone was the dangerous, sexual predator she'd nearly thrown herself at. Frivolous, life-is-a-game Reese Sinclair was back.

"You really expect me to shell all these nuts? By hand?"

"Don't know any other way to do it, and since it was your idea, I figured you'd want to be in charge."

What a fool she'd been to let her guard down with this man! An idiot. Well, it wouldn't happen again. Folding her arms, she lifted her chin and pointed it at him. "This isn't nearly enough peanuts to evenly distribute and create the proper illusion of 'rustic' as you called it. If you're going to do something, Reese, you should at least do it right."

He cocked one brow and gave her his most charming smile. "Well, Syd, I'm sure I can trust you to handle this project all on your own. You have carte blanche, sweetheart, and since you're only here three hours, I suggest you get started right away. This is a whole lotta nuts."

Whistling, he snatched up his truck keys from the bar counter, then left her in the tavern, alone.

Sydney hurried across the tavern and stared out the front window, watched Reese get into his truck and drive off.

The nerve of him! It would take her hours to shell all these nuts. Days. She knew that wasn't really what he wanted. He was making a point here, hoping she'd back down. Give up. Throw in the towel.

Well, Sydney Taylor didn't give up. Not by a long shot.

Across the street, she saw Lucian come out of the front door of her building and head back toward the tavern. He stopped in the parking lot to talk to Jessie the Peanut Boy, who was standing inside the back of his delivery truck, moving bags of peanuts.

She watched the two men for a moment, then glanced back over her shoulder at the mountain of nuts she'd been left to shell.

A smile spread slowly across her face.

Shoulders squared, chin up, she went out to the parking lot.

Five

Reese stayed away from the tavern for the next two hours and fifteen minutes. He'd had several errands to run: the bank, Harry's Hardware, Sav-More Stationery, the post office, and garden center. He disliked errands as much as he disliked paperwork, but today he'd actually had a smile on his face as he'd strolled through the aisles of the stores and waited in line at the bank. Several times, to the confusion of anyone standing close to him, he'd even started laughing out loud.

The stunned look on Sydney's face when he'd told her she had to shell all those peanuts—Lord, it was priceless. He'd cherish that moment forever.

That oughta take a little starch out of that high-and-mighty collar of hers, he thought as he pulled his truck into a space in the front parking lot of the tavern. And a little lesson in humility certainly never hurt anyone.

He would have loved to stick around and watch her

shell peanut after endless peanut, but after their little…encounter…in his office earlier, he had thought it best to keep his distance from her for a while. He seemed to be having continuous lapses of sanity when it came to the woman.

He'd never admit it to a living soul, but Sydney Taylor made him nervous.

Women never made him nervous. He loved the female gender and everything about them: their mysteries and idiosyncrasies, the way they smelled, the way they moved. The curve of their legs and the sway of their hips. He'd always been comfortable with the opposite sex. Completely in control. If he was attracted to a woman, and she was attracted to him, it had always been easy to take it to the next step. He certainly didn't sleep with every woman that he dated, but he always enjoyed their company.

Simple and uncomplicated, that had always been his motto.

Then along came Sydney.

Sydney was anything but simple and uncomplicated. She was bullheaded, snooty, condescending and wound up tight as a new Swiss watch. No female had ever gotten under his skin the way Sydney had. He'd never spent hours thinking about any one particular woman, gnashing his teeth in exasperation one minute, then the next, fantasizing about the soft curve of her neck and what it would taste like, what it would feel like under his hands and mouth.

And earlier, when he had touched that lovely neck, he'd wanted to do a hell of a lot more than fantasize. He'd felt her shudder under his touch, and he knew that she wasn't so disinterested, wasn't so cool, as she'd have him believe. He could have kissed her right then—

he'd certainly wanted to—and she would have let him. It wouldn't have been a big deal. He'd kissed lots of women, for crying out loud, and while it might have been mutually pleasant, it hadn't really meant anything beyond that. Just a kiss.

So why, then, hadn't he just done it?

Why had he held back, been relieved, even, when Jessie had interrupted them?

And the biggest question of all: Why hadn't he ended this charade? Told her the truth and taken his lumps?

Pride. That's what it was. Every time Sydney looked down at him, every time she sniffed and lifted that little chin of hers, he couldn't let it go. He wanted her to surrender. To give up. It was that simple. And stupid, he admitted to himself.

Well, Ms. Sydney Taylor should be sufficiently humbled by now, he thought, climbing out of his truck and heading for the tavern entrance. He could only imagine the snit she would be in after two hours of shelling peanuts.

He grinned at the thought.

He found her sitting at the bar, perched primly on a barstool, her back to him. On the floor beside her was a cardboard box she'd tossed the empty shells into. To her right, on the counter, was a large bowl half-filled with shelled peanuts.

He shouldn't rub it in, he thought gleefully. There was certainly no need to rile her anymore than he already had.

Yeah, right. Not in a million years would he let an opportunity to ruffle Sydney Taylor's feathers pass him by.

Whistling cheerfully, he strode into the tavern right

up to her. "Hey, Syd, that's a whole bunch of nuts you got there. Looks like you've been a busy girl."

"'Idleness is only the refuge of weak minds,'" she said, blithely quoting Chesterfield.

He leaned close. "'Beauty stands in the admiration only of weak minds led captive,'" he quoted right back at her.

Astonishment widened her eyes. "You know Milton?"

"English Lit 102. Professor Lori Hunter. A hot babe I wanted to impress with my term paper."

Sydney arched one brow. "And did you?"

He grinned at her. "I got an A."

"I'm sure."

She turned her attention back to her task and he watched her quickly snap and shell the peanuts inside. She had long, slender, delicate hands and he remembered the touch of her fingers on his face the other day. Smooth and soft. Warm. *Don't go there, Reese,* he reminded himself.

"You've got a natural talent there, Syd," he said, forcing his mind back to his intention to ruffle her feathers, not stroke them.

"It's easy once you get into the rhythm." She didn't even glance at him, just dropped the empty shell into the box at her feet and reached for another peanut. "It's actually quite relaxing. Sort of like needlepoint or knitting."

Relaxing? Like needlepoint? Sure it was, he thought, holding back his grin. She was convincing, all right, but he knew she was bluffing. Trying to get his goat. *Not gonna work, Syd.*

"Shall I order more?" he suggested. "You didn't think there would be enough earlier."

"Won't be necessary." She looked up and smiled sweetly at him.

Ha. He didn't think so. But her smile captivated him, drew his attention to her mouth. She wasn't wearing lipstick, but still her lips were rosy. He quickly snapped his gaze back to hers. Which didn't help much. Her blue eyes were sparkling with pleasure.

Not this time, Sydney, he thought with smug satisfaction. No way was she going to distract him. He had no doubt that, inside, Sydney was seething mad. He intended to relish every moment of his conquest. Another ten pounds of peanuts and she'd cave. He was certain of it.

He couldn't wait.

"Well, Syd, it's been nice chatting with you. If you need anything—" *like a white flag or a towel* "—I'll be in my office."

She waved a hand, then turned back to the bar and continued diligently with her task.

He had to hand it to her, Reese thought as he headed for his office. She was putting up a really good front. If he didn't know better, he'd think she was actually having a good time. Which, of course, she wasn't. Chuckling to himself, he opened his office door.

"What the—"

An avalanche of peanuts flowed from his office.

Thousands, *millions* of peanuts consumed him, swept him up in a torrent and carried him along. He struggled to gain his ground, then went down and under, cursing and sputtering. Like lava flow, they kept coming, spilling into the narrow hallway outside his office and scattering across the hardwood floor.

When at last it stopped, he lay there, flat on his back,

staring up at the ceiling, wearing a blanket of peanuts. He narrowed his eyes.

Somebody was going to die.

When that somebody leaned over him, he stared up at her.

"I guess I forgot to mention I ordered a few more bags of peanuts." She raised her brows in mock concern. "You did say I should handle it, and since I wasn't sure where to put them I went ahead and—"

Sydney squeaked when Reese's hand snaked out and grabbed her down and on top of him. In one swift, fluid move, he rolled and had her pinned underneath him. Peanuts crunched and crumbled. Eyes wide, mouth still open, she looked up at him, saw the murderous glint in his eyes.

And the broken bits of peanut shells covering his head and clothes.

She couldn't help it. She started to laugh.

A muscle jumped in Reese's temple as he stared down at her. Revenge glistened in his deep green eyes. A slow, sinister smile touched his mouth.

Uh-oh.

Sydney struggled to stand, but Reese would have no part of it. He straddled her, then scooped up handfuls of peanuts and dumped them on her.

A peanut war ensued.

Lying on her back with Reese towering over her, Sydney had the disadvantage, but she held her own. Peanuts flew like popping corn. Sydney shrieked, ducked one large armful he attempted to throw on her, then scooped up two handfuls and flung them at him. They were both spitting out salty chunks of peanut shells, laughing and thrashing around on a thick, crunchy blanket of peanuts.

She snatched up another handful, but he grabbed her wrists and held her arms at her sides. She tried to break free, but his grip only tightened. He was much too strong to throw him off, and she knew she would only embarrass herself if she tried.

"Had enough?" she asked breathlessly.

He raised his brow at the absurdity of her question. Considering the current circumstances, she was hardly in a position to ask him that.

Reese shook his head and fragments of peanut shell floated down from his hair. "You want to tell me—" he drew in a deep lungful of air "—how you managed this little trick by yourself?"

"Lucian helped." She knew her smile was smug, but she didn't care. "We climbed in your office window, emptied all the bags from the delivery truck. Jessie helped, too, he's such a sweetheart—and then we went out the window again."

"My brother, my own flesh and blood, was part of this evil plot? And Jessie, too?" Reese's dark frown didn't make it to his eyes. "A triple murder in Bloomfield County. This will definitely be breaking news on the television tonight."

Her smile widened. "Lucian wanted to stick around for the show, but he had an appointment."

"Is that so?"

Reese's breathing had eased, but her chest still rose and fell sharply as she struggled for air. As he stared down at her, Sydney felt an imperceptible shift in the mood. She became increasingly aware of the fact that Reese was straddling her body. His large hands circled her wrists and held her captive.

Her heart skipped, then started to race. She blew a strand of loose hair from her eyes, reminded herself that they were simply having a little fun; it didn't mean anything.

But his body lying on top of hers was so intimate, so *sexual*....

"I—I'm supposed to give a detailed report to him later." She told herself that the breathless quality to her voice was merely a result of her struggling to escape, but at a very deep, instinctive level she knew it was much more than that.

"I'll give him a report," Reese said. "Right after he picks his teeth out of his tonsils."

"I claim full responsibility for my actions," she said emphatically. "I insist that all consequences be directed at me."

"You insist, do you?" His voice turned husky. "All consequences? You sure about that, Syd?"

She wasn't sure about anything at the moment. In fact, she was finding it difficult to think at all. She'd never been more aware of a man in her entire life. Reese's body was long and hard and muscular. The angles of his face were sharp now, his jaw clenched, his eyes narrowed and dancing with the devil. His strong mouth was pressed into a smirk, his dark hair tousled, dusted with flecks of peanut shells. A vein pulsed at the base of his throat, and for the life of her, she couldn't take her eyes off that spot.

The air shimmered around them. Grew taut.

She didn't want this. Didn't want to cross over any lines that she'd regret. She had enough regrets in her life at the moment, and she had no intention of adding Reese Sinclair to that list.

The pulsing in her body screamed at her to shut up and offer herself to Reese without question or protest.

Thank Heavens she still had a thread of good judgment left.

"So," she said lightly, desperately wanting to pull the mood back to playful instead of the dark, sensual tone that had suddenly closed in around them. "Had enough, Sinclair?"

He stared at her for a long moment, then his gaze dropped to her mouth. "Not even close, Syd," he said, his voice strained.

Her body still pinned underneath his, he lifted her arms over her head, then lowered his mouth to hers. At the first light touch of his lips on hers, she held very still, determined not to respond.

And then that last thread of good judgment she'd been so proud of snapped like a twig in a tornado.

His mouth was firm and strong, his lips gentle. Her heart slammed in her chest as he nibbled on the corner of her lips. Liquid heat rushed through her body; her skin felt tight and tingly.

"Reese," she whispered, her lips moving against his, "I don't think—"

"Me, either."

Then he completely destroyed her.

He crushed his mouth to hers. Her senses spun at the fierce demand of his lips, the press of his strong body over hers, the faint masculine scent that was Reese. She'd heard all those silly myths of bone-melting, exploding fireworks kisses, but she'd never believed in them. They simply had been romantic fairy tales and legends.

They were true.

She had no defenses against this, against him. His kiss stripped away every argument, every last remnant of reason and logic. Her mind was no longer in control; she could only feel.

And it felt wonderful.

He deepened the kiss, and a low, desperate moan rose from deep in her throat. She squirmed underneath him, frustrated that he still held her arms, yet excited at the same time. Intense pleasure sparked in her blood, then burst into flames. When his hands finally released her wrists, then slid down her arms, she trembled in anticipation.

Needing him closer, she wound her arms tightly around his neck. His mouth moved down her throat, his tongue, hot and wet, tasted and nipped. He murmured something against her ear and his warm breath sent ripples of delight through her. Skillfully he moved his hands down her sides, then lower still, gathering her skirt upward, exposing her calves, then her thighs. His callused hands were rough on her sensitive skin. She shivered at his touch. An ache settled between her legs, and she moved restlessly against him, wanting more.

Then his hands moved upward and slid under her blouse.

She gasped when he cupped her breasts, arched upward when his thumbs caressed her hardened nipples.

He nipped at the base of her throat, murmured her name, then moved lower....

"Hello! Anybody here?"

Both she and Reese jumped at the deep, booming voice that echoed from the empty tavern into the hallway where they lay on the floor, practically making love.

Muttering an oath, Reese moved off of her, then stood, reached out a hand to help her up. Shaking, she rose on watery knees, quickly smoothed her skirt and blouse.

"Sydney Marie Taylor!" the voice bellowed again. "Are you here, girl?"

She swallowed back the panic in her throat, then straightened her shoulders. Reese looked at her, his mouth pressed into a thin, hard line.

She sucked in a deep breath and called out, "In here, Grandfather."

Six

Judge Randolph "Duffy" Tremaine Howland, Bloomfield County's most prominent and most wealthy citizen, stood at the end of the hallway leading to Reese's office. His three-piece steel-gray suit matched the color of his keen eyes. Eyes now narrowed sharply as he took in the peanuts on the floor and the disheveled state of his granddaughter's and Reese's clothing.

Reese gritted his teeth and held back the groan in his throat. Dammit, dammit, dammit.

"Hello, Judge Howland." Reese nodded casually, though he felt anything *but* casual at the moment. His body still tight with need, his blood still simmering, it was all he could do not to snatch Sydney back into his arms, drag her into his office, then shut the door to finish what they'd started. To hell with her grandfather or anyone who dared interrupt them.

But as reality slowly crept into his dazed brain, as he

looked at the judge, then Sydney, with her flushed cheeks and tousled hair, he knew without a doubt that was *not* going to happen.

Duffy's gaze shot from Sydney to Reese, then dropped to the floor and the carpet of peanuts. "What on God's good earth is going on here?" the elderly man boomed.

Sydney smoothed her hands over the front of her skirt, then cleared her throat. "We were just, ah, cleaning up a bag of peanuts that spilled. Weren't we, Reese?"

Oh, yeah. Everyone cleans up spilled peanuts by thrashing around on the floor in a lip lock, Reese thought. "Right. Spilled peanuts," he muttered.

The judge's eyes narrowed as he studied them both. His mouth pressed into a thin line, Duffy raised one thick, silver brow and leveled a stern gaze at his granddaughter. "Sydney, if you needed money, why didn't you come to me?"

"If I needed money?" Sydney frowned, obviously confused by the sudden shift of conversation. "I don't need any money."

"Then why are you working here—in a tavern, of all places, if you don't need money?"

Reese crossed his arms and leaned back against the doorjamb. *Yeah, Syd, go ahead and tell your grandfather why you're working here....*

Sydney folded her hands primly in front of her. The pose was truly noble, but Reese thought that the empty peanut shell dangling from her hair spoiled the effect.

"I would hardly describe my position here as *working*, Grandfather," she said, her tone as regal as her demeanor.

"I was informed you were cleaning tables and serving food here yesterday.'' Duffy drew his thick silver brows together. ''What would you call that?''

She started to nibble on her bottom lip. ''Well…it's not, it's more like—'' She hesitated.

''Spit it out, girl,'' Duffy barked.

''It's more like a…business arrangement,'' she said carefully. ''I'm helping Reese out for a few days while he's shorthanded and—''

She paused, looked at Reese for back-up. He grinned at her. *Sorry, Syd. You're on your own.* As if she heard his thoughts, her lips pressed into a thin line.

She turned back to her grandfather. ''And in exchange he's, ah, consulting with me. Giving me his expert advice on the efficient management of a restaurant.''

''Is that so?'' Duffy narrowed a dubious gaze at Reese. ''Why would you advise the competition?''

Reese glanced at Sydney, considered giving her a break, then thought of all the peanuts he'd be cleaning up for weeks, probably months, to come. And besides, he couldn't possibly let this opportunity pass him by. In spite of that mind-boggling kiss they'd just shared, in spite of the fact he wanted to kiss her again, and more, he and Sydney were, after all, still adversaries.

''Well, sir, in all honesty, when Sydney first came to me, asking for my help, I have to admit that I did turn her down.'' Reese shook his head and sighed. ''But the sight of a woman's tears gets me every time. I just didn't have the heart to say no.''

''Sydney…tears?'' A look of sheer bewilderment shadowed Duffy's face. Sydney's face, on the other hand, had a look of sheer fury. Reese half-expected lightning bolts to shoot out of her eyes at him.

Let her put *this* in her report to Lucian, he thought smugly.

"And then I got to thinking," he went on smoothly. "And I decided that it was actually in my best interest to give Sydney my guidance. After all, it made sense to me that the wider the range of dining choices, the more customers that will be drawn to Bloomfield from neighboring towns and cities, including Philadelphia. So it also made sense that a little hands-on experience in the real world would improve Sydney's chance at success and in the long run, help us both."

"Actually, Grandfather," Sydney said through clenched teeth, "Reese is exaggerat—"

"Excellent thinking." Duffy nodded with approval. "Improved commerce in this town benefits everyone. Have you considered running for city council? This town could use a man with forward thinking like yours."

"I leave politics to experienced men such as yourself, sir." Reese knew he was laying it on a little thick, but the judge didn't seem to mind. Sydney, however, quite obviously minded a great deal. Her cheeks were flushed—this time not from kissing, but from anger—and he could swear he saw a twitch at the corner of her eye.

When Judge Howland's cell phone began to ring, he pulled it out of his pocket. While he spoke on the phone, Sydney turned her back to her grandfather and glared at Reese, silently mouthing a series of names that were extremely unladylike. Folding his arms, he leaned against the doorjamb again and smiled back at her.

When her grandfather finished his call, she snapped her mouth shut, spun around again and smiled at him.

Grumbling, the judge dropped his phone back into his pocket.

"Is something wrong, Grandfather?"

"I'm gone less than an hour and my office is already in chaos," Duffy said irritably. "The copy machine repair man blew a fuse and there's no power, and the dedication ceremony for Senator Johnson at city hall this afternoon has been moved to tomorrow morning."

Peanuts and Sydney forgotten, Duffy turned sharply on his heels. Reese could hear the judge muttering to himself until the tavern door clicked shut behind him.

Sydney stared after her grandfather, then very slowly turned back to Reese. "Tears?" she said, her voice rising an octave. "I asked *you* for help and *you* didn't have the heart to turn *me* down?"

She moved closer and jabbed one long, slender finger at his chest. "The only part of *that* you got right was the part about not having a heart. How dare you tell my grandfather that I cried to get you to help me!"

With her flushed cheeks and the blue sparks flying from her eyes, Reese thought that Sydney looked magnificent. He glanced down at her finger still poking into his chest, thought about kissing her again, but—thank Heavens—good sense prevailed.

"I saved your behind, Syd," he said evenly. "What would your grandfather say if he knew the truth, that you'd played poker with a lowly tavern owner, lost, and were paying off a bet? You should be thanking me."

"*Thanking* you?" She rolled her eyes and groaned. "After the two-hour lecture I'm going to get from my grandfather on my lack of professionalism in a business situation, then the one-hour lesson on the proper behavior for a young lady alone with a man, I'll tell you what you can do with any thanks you think you deserve.

You're the only one benefiting from this absurd bet we made, Sinclair, so don't go looking for any thanks from me.''

''Any time you want out, Syd...''

She pulled back when he reached toward her face. He plucked a peanut shell from her hair, and she frowned at him. ''I finish what I start,'' she said firmly.

He grinned at her. ''I'm glad to hear that, Sydney. Very glad.''

The sudden flush of pink on her high cheeks pleased Reese immensely. He leaned close, brought his mouth within a few inches of hers. Her eyelids lowered; she started to sway toward him. Then she blinked and jerked her head away.

''Oh, no.'' Peanuts crunched under her feet as she stepped back. ''*That's* one thing we won't be finishing,'' she insisted. ''Not gonna happen, Sinclair.''

She turned and quickly left.

He watched her go, heard the tavern door close behind her. He stood there for a long moment, staring after her.

''Don't bet on it, Syd,'' he said softly. ''Just don't bet on it.''

The beveled glass and oak doors welcomed customers to Le Petit Bistro—or at least it would welcome them when the restaurant had its grand opening in a little over three weeks. The dining area was small, room enough for only ten booths and seven tables, but that suited Sydney just fine. She preferred cozy and intimate, soft music, simple elegance. Her staff was small: a college student named Becky who went to school in the mornings would be her hostess; Nell, a single mother new to Bloomfield County who had been the first applicant to respond to the waitressing ad and had been so perfect that Sydney had hired her on the spot; and Latona, an assistant chef newly graduated from a cooking school in Philadelphia. Sydney had already developed and tested her menu, ordered her supplies in advance and placed her advertisements in all the local papers. Except for the granite countertop that Lucian would be installing for her next week, everything was in place and ready to go.

Excitement rippled through her.

Hands locked behind her back, she stood in the middle of the room and smiled. The tables were bare now, but come opening night, there would be fresh flowers on pink linen tablecloths, crystal votive holders, sparkling wine goblets. She could already hear the soft murmur of conversation, the faint clink of forks and knives on china. Smell the scent of fresh herbs and vegetables and melting butter.

From the time she'd been old enough to reach the kitchen counter, she'd wanted to learn how to cook, but her mother had never allowed it. The preparation of food was for the servants, her mother had always told her. As the granddaughter of Bloomfield County's Honorable Judge Howland, Sydney was expected to receive and entertain guests with conversation of current events or charming anecdotes of family history.

Occasionally, though, Sydney would sneak into the kitchen and watch Emily, the family cook, stirring a soup on the stove or chopping celery on the heavy butcher block island. Sydney could have watched, fascinated, for hours. But her mother would always find her and drag her back to the party, reprimanding her sternly on the proper etiquette and behavior for a Howland-Taylor.

Sydney's mother had been a first-class, stiff-necked, pretentious snob.

Sydney knew that everyone in Bloomfield County thought she was just as pretentious as her mother had been. And even though it hurt, she understood why they thought that. She'd spent a lifetime behaving the way her mother had expected of her.

But Sydney knew that she was worse than a snob. Much worse.

She was a coward.

Since she was a little girl, she'd always been frightened. Afraid she might receive a grade less than an A on a test, that she might get her dress dirty or say the wrong thing. That her parents would fight if she wasn't perfect. So she always did the extra credit, was always on time, always put her clothes neatly away and never made messes.

But it hadn't mattered that she'd done all those things. Her father had still left when she was twelve and never once come back. A day had never passed that her mother didn't spew anger and malice toward him.

Never a day, to this very day, that Sydney didn't wonder if maybe, just maybe, if she hadn't made so much noise, if she'd sat up straighter or never complained about eating brussels sprouts, her father would never have left.

And then, fourteen years later, maybe Bobby wouldn't have left, either.

She knew in her heart, of course, that marriage to Bobby would never have worked, but somehow that knowledge didn't quite cushion the embarrassment of standing in the church in her wedding dress, having Theresa, her maid-of-honor, come tell her that Bobby wasn't coming. Then having to tell all the guests that the groom had taken ill and the ceremony was called off.

He was sick, all right. Sick of her.

But then, slowly, over the next few weeks, her embarrassment turned to anger, her anger to determination. Determination to courage. The courage to do what she'd always secretly wanted. Her grandfather had argued that a restaurant was a foolhardy enterprise, most failed within the first year, the work was hard, the hours long. Nothing had changed her mind.

Let everyone feel sorry for her, or think she was a snob. Le Petit Bistro would be the best darn restaurant that Bloomfield County would ever see.

And that included Squire's Tavern and Inn.

She smiled at the image of Reese opening his office door three days ago to a sea of peanuts; the stunned look on his face. He'd been so smug when he'd come back from all his errands and found her at the counter, working so submissively at shelling all those nuts. So pompous.

Her smile widened. He certainly hadn't been so smug when he'd gone down in a deluge of peanuts.

Then he'd had to go and ruin it all by kissing her.

Nobody had ever kissed her like that. Not Bobby, certainly not Ken, the manager at Bloomfield County Trust and Loan she'd dated for a short time. Not even Jean-Paul, the French pastry chef she'd gone out with several times when she'd been in Paris. They'd all paled in comparison to Reese.

She'd never forgive him for that.

Before that kiss, it had been so easy to tell herself that she would never, in a hundred years, ever fall for a man like Reese. They were so completely opposite: He was a confirmed bachelor; she wanted to settle down. He never took anything seriously; she considered herself earnest and thoughtful. And she *liked* tablecloths and flowers, which he obviously didn't.

But in spite of all that, what really frightened her was the possibility—as remote as it was—of falling in love with him and knowing that he would never love her back. At a very basic level, she was afraid he had the power to break her heart. Not just a crack, like with Bobby, but complete annihilation. She'd moved on with her life, she had her restaurant. She wasn't willing to risk it with him.

And still, every time she thought of that kiss, every time she remembered the way his fingers had skimmed her leg, the way his palm had cupped her breast, her skin felt tight and hot, her pulse quickened and she had to remind herself to breathe.

Damn you, Sinclair!

Well, she'd just have to deal with it, she decided and snatched up a rag she'd been using to dust. She acknowledged her attraction, but she'd managed to keep her distance from him the past three days while she'd been working for him in the evenings. She could continue to do just that. And he'd kept his distance from her, too. He'd probably put the kiss out of his mind completely, she thought, pouring a little lemon beeswax onto the rag and rubbing furiously at the buffet table she'd placed in the entryway of the café. No doubt that sort of thing happened to Reese Sinclair all the time. One more woman, one more kiss in a long line of swooning females, she suspected. As long as she kept her feet on the ground and was sensible, she'd be safe.

"Sandpaper usually works better if you're trying to remove the stain."

With a squeak, she spun around at the sound of

Reese's deep voice behind her. Heavens! It was bad enough he infiltrated her mind, did he have to turn up in the flesh, as well?

"Reese!" Her voice was much too high-pitched and breathless. She cleared her throat. "You startled me."

"Sorry." Smiling, he nodded at the rag in her hand. "I wasn't sure if you were punishing that wood or polishing it."

She wasn't sure, either, since she'd been thinking about Reese. Afraid that he'd see it in her eyes, she kept her attention on the buffet and continued her buffing. "What brings you by?"

Why did he have to stand so close? she thought irritably. And why did he have to look so incredibly handsome wearing faded blue jeans and a moss green T-shirt that made his eyes look like a dark, mysterious forest?

Damn him.

"I brought you flowers."

Her heart skipped. He'd brought her flowers? Maybe he'd said flour, like for baking. Though that wouldn't make sense, either. She glanced up cautiously. "You what?"

"Flowers. I brought you flowers."

No man had ever bought her flowers. She felt a hitch in her chest. "You did?"

"Yeah." He gestured toward the open front door. "I don't know what they're called. The nursery guy said you could plant them now and they shouldn't die, at least not until we get a heavy snow."

She looked out the door and saw several colorful pots sitting next to the raised brick bed that Boomer was so fond of digging in.

He hadn't brought her flowers.

Well, he'd brought her flowers, she corrected, but he hadn't brought her *flowers*.

Of course he hadn't brought her flowers.

And the fact that she'd thought—for just an instant— that he had made her feel like a complete fool. An idiot.

"Thank you." She turned her attention back to her polishing. If she looked at him, she was afraid he'd see in her eyes what she'd been thinking and then he'd know what a little fool she was.

"My gardener from the tavern will be over later to plant them," he said. "I'd do it, but I'd probably cause more damage than Boomer trying to dig them up."

"Thank you, but I'd rather do it myself." She knelt in front of the buffet and began to polish the legs.

"It's my responsibility, Syd."

"I prefer to do it myself."

"Sydney. I think we should…well, we should talk."

He hunkered down beside her, stilled her hand with his. She cursed the thump of her heart. Cursed him. She knew she should stand, that she shouldn't let him this close, but she stayed where she was, her knees nearly touching his. "All right."

"I don't want you to come to the tavern anymore."

She doubted a physical slap would have hurt as much as the verbal hit he'd just given her. The cold gripping her chest made it hard to breathe. She tugged her hand out from under his and forced her attention back to the legs of the buffet. "All right."

He ran a hand through his thick hair and sighed. "God, that's not what I meant. I meant I don't want you *working* at the tavern anymore."

Oh, gosh, that made her feel *so* much better. Careful to keep herself composed, she continued polishing the wood, kept her strokes smooth and controlled. She *refused* to let him see her cry. "All right."

He took hold of her arms and turned her toward him. "Stop saying all right. It's not all right. And I'm not saying what I mean."

"Then why don't you?" she said coolly.

"Sydney, this isn't...I didn't..." He sighed. "Dammit, Syd, what I'm trying to say is I'm sorry. You had every right to be angry about Boomer digging up your flowers. I never should have made that bet with you."

"Then why did you?" She forced herself to concentrate on his surprise apology, refused to think about the feel of his strong hands on her arms and what had happened the last time he'd gotten this close and touched her. She knew if she did that every vow she'd made to keep her distance would fly out the window and she'd tackle him right here and now, and make him kiss her again. Touch her again.

And more.

"I don't know," he said, interrupting her wayward thoughts. "Maybe it was the way you flew into the tavern with Boomer in your arms. Your hair looking like you'd just climbed out of bed and your eyes flashing blue fire. The way you looked down at me with that arrogant little nose of yours, issuing ultimatums. I had to do something."

In spite of the heat rippling across her skin, she arched one eyebrow. "Oh?"

"See?" He smiled. "There it goes again. If I can admit I'm a jerk, you can at least admit you're a snob."

She sniffed. "I'm not a snob."

Now he raised a brow and looked at her doubtfully.

"Well, maybe it seems that way," she relented. "But I'm just...conscientious."

His brow went up higher.

She pursed her lips. "Oh, all right. Maybe sometimes I do set my expectations a little high. Maybe sometimes I am a snob. There. Are you happy?"

"It's a start." He smiled at her, loosened his hold on her arms and slid his hands up to her shoulders. "I just wanted to see you loosen up a little."

"Maybe I don't want to loosen up." Especially right now. If she loosened up now, the way he was touching her shoulders, she'd slide her arms around his neck and press her lips to his. "Maybe I like being just the way I am. And you like being the way you are."

"Oh?" He cocked his head. "And what way am I?"

Sexy as hell. Handsome. Rugged. Strong. She started to lean toward him....

Stop that.

"Frivolous."

He chuckled, slid his thumbs back and forth over her collarbone. "I'm not frivolous, Syd. I'm spontaneous. You should try it sometime."

It took every ounce of willpower to focus on his words, not on the way his thumbs were moving sensuously over her skin, or the warmth spreading like molten lava through her limbs. "You've obviously forgotten about Monday," she insisted. "If that wasn't spontaneous, then I don't know what is."

"I haven't forgotten anything. In fact, Sydney," he said with a slow smile, "I remember everything. In detail."

When his dark green gaze dropped to her mouth, her breath caught in her throat. "It—that—was a mistake, Reese. I was...we just—"

"Went a little nuts?"

She couldn't stop the smile on her lips any more than

the furious pounding of her heart. "Something like that. It was nice and all that, but I want you to know I realize it was just one of those caught-up-in-the-moment-things. You don't have to worry about it."

"You know, Syd," he said with a touch of exasperation, "I just might believe that if I hadn't been there. It was a hell of a lot more than nice, sweetheart. You were as hot for me as I was for you. If your grandfather hadn't walked in when he had, you would have been in my bed, begging me for more."

Her cheeks burned at the accuracy of his evaluation. She would have begged, dammit. Still, she started to protest until he slid his hands up the side of her neck and pulled her closer. "Go ahead and deny it," he said tightly. "Just say it one more time."

She snapped her mouth shut. It was a dare and she knew it. They both knew if he kissed her again what would happen. Where it would go.

And she couldn't go there with Reese. She didn't have the courage. She pulled away from him and stood, twisted the rag in her hand to keep from reaching for him.

"All right," she said, hating the little quiver in her voice. "I admit it. It was more than nice. But it's *not* going to happen again. A quick roll in the hay might be right up your alley, but sex is something special to me. It's more than an itch and more than a 'spontaneous' tumble into bed with the closest warm body."

He stood slowly, and the desire she'd seen in his eyes only moments before now turned to anger. She hadn't meant to, but she'd gone too far. She should apologize, she knew she should, but it was easier this way. This way, he'd walk away and stay away.

"You think whatever you like, Syd," he said tightly.

"But if you really believe all that bull, then you're going to spend a lot of lonely nights in a very cold bed."

She felt the tears gather in the back of her throat as he turned and walked toward the door.

"Reese?"

He stopped, but didn't turn around.

"There's no reason we can't be friends," she said carefully. "If you need help at the tavern, I don't mind."

"Thanks, Syd, but it won't be necessary. I'll manage just fine." He started to walk away again, but she called his name one more time. He waited.

"Thank you," she said. "For the flowers."

He nodded stiffly, then glanced over his shoulder at her. "I almost forgot. My sister wants you to call her. Something about a last-minute catering job for Gabe and Melanie's surprise engagement party tomorrow night."

He left before she could reply, and she stared at the empty doorway long after he was gone.

Seven

Sinclair family events were always noisy and the surprise party on Saturday night was no exception. Everyone was already waiting in the small private dining room at the back of the tavern when Gabe and Melanie showed up for what they thought was a typical get-together of "pizza and beer." They were not expecting an elegant celebration that included candles and white roses and a lavish five course French meal, prepared and served by Sydney Taylor.

Because the tavern was open for business, Reese split his time between the party and handling the busy Saturday night crowd. He'd rearranged schedules so he'd have a full crew, but at the moment he was filling in for Jimmy, his bartender, while he took a break. So far tonight there'd been no crises or problems that had demanded his attention.

Unless he considered Sydney in one of those categories.

Crises. No.

Problem. Yes.

He'd been angry when he'd left her place two days ago. Furious, even, with her assumption that he'd simply wanted a "quick roll in the hay" as she'd so delicately put it.

Not that he really knew *what* he'd wanted from her, or where their unexpected attraction would end up. He just didn't like her assessment of his morals, or lack of them. So maybe he had dated a lot of women. That didn't mean he didn't have scruples. And it certainly didn't mean he simply had an "itch," and she'd been the "closest warm body."

He clenched his jaw just thinking about her.

Lord, the woman made him crazy.

While he filled a pitcher of beer for Judy, one of his waitresses, he watched as Sydney came out of the kitchen carrying a tray loaded with steaming bread puddings. Since her kitchen wouldn't be fully operable until her oven was calibrated, she'd needed to use his to prepare the meal for this evening. When she'd come over yesterday during lunch to ask him if it would be all right, he'd said sure, then quickly turned his attention back to filling drinks for the thirsty noon crowd.

But even after he'd turned away from her, he'd been aware of her standing there, her shoulders stiff and chin lifted, looking as if she still had something to say.

Well, they'd said enough, he'd thought. More than enough. He wasn't about to waste his time thinking about Sydney Taylor night and day.

Thinking about how soft her skin was, wondering what it would feel like when he untied that knot of pretty hair at the top of her head and dragged his fingers through the loosened strands, what she would do when he slipped his hands under that pink silk blouse she had on tonight....

"Uh, I think that's probably full enough," Reese heard a woman say hesitantly.

"What?" Reese snapped his mind back to the present and looked at Judy, realized she'd been talking to him. She nodded toward the pitcher he was filling. Beer flowed over the sides.

"Damn," he muttered, releasing the valve and reaching for a towel. Damn, damn, *damn.*

Shaking her head, Judy poured off the excess, grabbed four cold mugs, then headed off to a table of construction workers that were currently on Sinclair Construction's payroll.

He glanced over as Sydney passed. He couldn't help but appreciate the sway of her slender hips under the crisp, white chef's apron she wore. Underneath the apron a pretty floral skirt skimmed those long legs of hers. He glanced back up at her face, noticed the flush of pleasure on her cheeks and the brightness in her eyes.

His throat turned to dust.

She'd looked like that right after he'd kissed her the other day, he remembered, only this time her pleasure was due to her excitement over Cara hiring her to prepare the food for the party. He hadn't seen what the big deal was all about, or even why Cara had hired Sydney at all. They could have celebrated just as well with pizza or hamburgers or Corky's famous chili. What was the point of all that fancy French cooking?

And then he'd tasted her ravioli stuffed with lobster and shrimp, drenched in a sauce. He'd actually moaned, it was so good. And so was the chicken and mushroom dish she'd made for a main course. That had been a taste of heaven, too.

So she could cook, he thought begrudgingly. Maybe she wasn't just some bored rich girl who thought owning a restaurant would be fun. He'd seen how hard she worked, and when Sydney set her mind to something, she was stubborn as a bulldog about it.

Too damn stubborn.

Well, he didn't need stubborn. And he sure as hell didn't need Sydney Taylor messing up his mind and his life. He'd been perfectly content before he'd locked horns with her, and he intended to go right back. She wasn't coming to the tavern to work anymore, and though he'd actually missed her the past two days, he didn't miss the aggravation. His life was back to simple and quiet, and he liked it exactly that way.

After tonight, he wouldn't give Sydney another thought.

Except for maybe every time he laid eyes on a peanut.

"Hey, Reese." A mug of beer already in her hand, Rhonda Waters sidled onto the bar stool across from him. "Where you been keeping yourself?"

"Right here waiting for you, honey," he bantered with the attractive brunette.

"You two-timing me, sugar?" Mary Lou Simpson, her new hair dye as red as a tomato, slid onto the bar stool next to Rhonda. "Shame on you. And here I voted for you in the Bloomfield County Best Butt contest. You could at least show a little appreciation."

Reese had always thought the whole business of that award had been good for a laugh. Suddenly it didn't seem so funny anymore. If anything, it was starting to annoy him.

He forced a smile, wished that Jimmy would hurry and get back from his break.

"So, Reese." Mary Lou leaned against the bar counter in an obvious attempt to reveal her ample bosom. "When we gonna go out driving? I've got a brand new convertible Camaro, and it's not too cold out yet to put the top down."

His smile still frozen in place, Reese cocked his head and raised a brow at Mary Lou's blatant innuendo. "Well, now, Mary Lou, soon as I have a full staff, maybe we'll talk about that." *Or maybe we won't...* Definitely won't, he decided.

Rhonda choked on her beer, then giggled. Mary Lou's eyes widened, then she purred, "I can hardly wait, sugar."

Oh, dammit! Reese groaned silently. That wasn't what he'd meant to say. He'd meant to say crew, not *staff.*

He glanced around the room, searching for any sign of Jimmy, then grabbed a towel and started wiping up an imaginary spill.

"I heard you been hanging around Sydney Taylor," Rhonda said, sipping on her beer. "You got something going with her?"

"Don't be ridiculous," Mary Lou said with a laugh. "What would Reese possibly see in someone like Sydney the Hun? What would *any* man see in her, for that matter?"

"True." Rhonda nodded. "Even Bobby got smart before he made the mistake of tying himself down to Sour Face Sydney."

"Hey, now," Reese said tightly, struggling to contain his anger, "just wait a—"

He stopped midsentence.

Sydney stood directly behind the two women. He'd been so distracted with Rhonda and Mary Lou's annoying insults regarding Sydney, he hadn't noticed her come up.

Maybe she hadn't heard.

"Hello, Rhonda. Mary Lou."

Oh, hell. Reese groaned inwardly. Based on the icicles dripping from her hello, she'd heard, all right.

Eyes wide, backs stiff, Rhonda and Mary Lou slowly turned and squeaked back a hello. *Ha,* Reese thought. *Serves you both right for being so nasty.*

"Sorry to hear about your job, Mary Lou," Sydney said, her cool gaze locked on the redhead. "I'm sure you'll find another employer who will appreciate your *qualifications* as much as John Sweeney did."

Everyone in town knew that Mary Lou had been sleeping with the owner of Sweeney's Sporting Goods. Well, everyone except Mrs. Sweeney, of course. Until she'd caught the two of them after hours, in the store's bass boat, wearing nothing but waders and surprised expressions. There were instant employment changes, which included an in-store, full-time position for Colleen Sweeney where she could keep a close eye on her philandering husband, and the boot for Mary Lou.

Sydney turned her attention to Rhonda. "And I'm sorry about Mike and you, too."

Rhonda narrowed her eyes. "Sorry about what?"

"That you broke up after such a long time," Sydney said, the sympathy heavy in her voice. "It must be hard for you."

"He's got a carpentry job in Ridgeway, that's all," Rhonda insisted. "That's why he's been gone so much. Even tonight he's working overtime on a job there and—" She stopped suddenly, doubt darkening her brown eyes. "Ah, well, I gotta run, Syd. Nice to see you."

Rhonda slid off the chair and headed for the pay phone by the restrooms. Mary Lou followed.

Reese stared at Sydney, a mixture of admiration and awe at the way she'd handled the two women.

"Your family would like you to come in and say goodbye when you have a minute," she said evenly.

"Thanks." He wasn't sure what else to say. She should be angry, he thought. Mad as hell. He knew *he* was. But Sydney stood there as calm as could be. As if nothing at all had just happened. As if it didn't matter to her in the slightest that these two women had insulted her.

"Thank you for letting me use the tavern's kitchen tonight, Reese," she said with a politeness that irritated him. "I'll just gather up my things from the back dining room and be out of your way."

"Okay." *But it's not okay. Dammit, Sydney, can't you just let yourself go and be mad? Yell or scream or hit something?* He sure as hell would. But not Sydney, he thought. Not cool, calm, collected Sydney. Nothing got through that thick skin of hers. And no one.

He watched her turn smoothly and head back through the thinning crowd in the tavern, then disappear down the hallway that led to the back dining room and his office.

Well, fine then, dammit. He wasn't about to waste his time worrying about Sydney. She could take care of herself. She didn't need him; she'd made that perfectly clear. As far as he was concerned, Sydney was ancient history.

Sydney felt Reese's gaze on her as she walked away from the bar, knew that he'd expected some kind of reaction from her after hearing Mary Lou and Rhonda's cruel comments. But Sydney had learned long ago to hide her feelings, to pretend everything was all right when it really wasn't. She'd learned to tuck every emotion into a tiny little spot inside of her, then wait until she was completely alone and no one would see the truth. That was the only time she'd let herself really feel.

She focused on her legs instead of the pain gripping her chest, ordered her knees not to buckle, to hold firm and carry her out of the tavern, down the hallway, past the dining room, past Reese's office, then to the back door that led to the outside garden.

Quietly she closed the door behind her, thankful that the night air was crisp and the garden dark, lit only from the soft light of a half-moon. She shivered, made it down two steps before her legs refused to listen to her anymore. She sank down on the steps, dropped her head into her shaking hands and let the tears come.

Sydney the Hun.

Sour Face Sydney.

She'd always known what people thought of her, that they didn't like her, but to actually hear those terrible things spoken aloud only confirmed what she'd always believed.

No one could ever love her. Not her father, not her mother. Not Bobby.

Certainly not Reese.

Mary Lou and Rhonda's words might have been cruel, but they were true. And the realization of that, the conscious acceptance of it as the truth, was like a dam breaking inside her. A tidal wave of hurt and pain rolled through her, and this time she was helpless to stop it. So she let it go.

In long, choking sobs and hot, endless tears, she simply let it go.

She felt the nudge on her arm, the cold, wet nose, and realized that Boomer had joined her on the step. He whimpered, then licked her face. Sydney slipped an arm around the dog, dragged her fingers through his thick fur and actually laughed at the irony of Boomer being the only one who seemed to really like her.

It had been such a wonderful evening. Preparing the meal, serving each course, seeing the pleasure on everyone's face when they tried each dish. She'd even heard Reese moan when he'd tried the lobster-and-shrimp ravioli.

And then she'd chosen exactly the wrong time to walk up and hear things about herself she'd never wanted to hear.

A fresh round of tears burst forth and she hugged the dog tightly to her.

"Sydney."

She heard her name called softly, then the touch of a hand on her shoulder.

Not Reese, she thought miserably. *Anyone but Reese.*

"Go away."

He didn't. Instead he sat down beside her and put his arm around her. He touched her wet cheek. "You're crying."

Humiliated, she turned her head from him. "No, I'm not. I never cry. Crying is for pathetic, helpless females," she managed to sob out through a fresh round of tears.

He chuckled, then pulled her closer. "Sydney, you are as far from pathetic and helpless as a person can get."

She shook her head to disagree, then laid her cheek on the shoulder he offered. When her tears eased and the shuddering finally ceased, she drew in a deep breath then let it out again.

"Better?" he asked quietly.

With a sniff, she nodded, then tried to sit up.

"Just be still for a minute," he said and drew her back into his arms.

Just for a minute, she told herself and let herself relax against his strong, warm body.

The sound of gurgling water from the fountain filled the cool evening air, and the scent of the last roses of the season drifted from the overhead arbor. In spite of her embarrassment, she couldn't remember when she'd felt such peace or tranquility.

They were quiet for several minutes, just listening to the sounds of the night and Boomer's soft panting.

"There were one hundred and fifty people in the church," she said, breaking the silence. "My maid-of-honor had just put my wedding veil on me and we were looking in the mirror, smiling at each other when the wedding director came in. I knew something was wrong. I thought maybe Bobby was sick or he'd had a terrible accident." She laughed dryly. "He had an accident, all right. With your cocktail waitress. The note he'd sent just said that he was sorry."

Reese swore under his breath. "I never could stand that guy. He was a jerk."

"I thought my life was over. I thought maybe I'd just move rather than face everyone again, knowing they were whispering behind my back." She closed her eyes, felt a single tear slide from the corner of her eye. "It hurt, Reese," she whispered.

"I know, baby."

"Almost as much as when my father left and never came back. Almost as much as when people call me Sydney the Hun or Sour Face Sydney."

She shivered when he brushed her cheek with his thumb and wiped away the tear. "Mary Lou and Rhonda are shallow, empty-headed bimbos. They couldn't hold a candle to you."

"You're just saying that."

"I'm saying it because it's true, sweetheart. You've got something no one can buy or fake. You've got spirit and integrity and an intensity about you that energizes the entire room whenever you walk in."

She blinked, then swallowed the lump in her throat. Had he really called her baby and sweetheart? And had he really said all those nice things about her?

And more important, had he meant them?

The moon shed enough light onto his face that she could see he *was* telling the truth. That he meant every word.

And through the pain she felt joy, a weight lifting off her chest and a swelling in her heart.

"I think you're wonderful with people." She straightened, looked into his eyes. "You know how to make people relax and have a good time. Laugh. I could never do that."

"Sure you could." He tucked a wayward strand of her hair behind her ear. "You just need to loosen up a little, Syd. Not take everything so seriously all the time. Let yourself go once in a while."

Everything in her entire life had been carefully planned, every sock neatly folded and put in the correct drawer, every slip of paper properly filed. Each "bunny in its own basket," as her mother used to say.

Could she let go?

She desperately wanted to do just that. To let herself go. Not think about anything but the moment and what felt good. Like the touch of Reese's fingertips on her ear, or the feel of his strong arm around her waist.

But she wanted more. Much more.

She didn't know how to tell Reese what she wanted, but she let instinct guide her. She touched his cheek with her hand; the strength she felt there gave her the confidence she so lacked.

"You were right, you know," she whispered.

He covered her hand with his, brought it to his mouth and gently kissed her fingers. "About what?"

His firm lips against her made her insides curl, gave her the courage to continue. "What you said about my grandfather interrupting us," she murmured. "If he hadn't, I would have been in your bed, begging you to make love to me."

Reese went very still. She felt a moment of panic that he wasn't feeling what she was feeling, that he didn't want her. If he pushed her away, she couldn't bear it.

But then she saw his gaze darken and narrow and the look of intensity in his eyes made her heart skip. She felt his jaw tighten under the palm of her hand. She leaned her body toward him, brought her lips close to his.

"Sydney, this might not be a good time—"

So she had been wrong. Pain ripped through her chest and she pulled her hand away and forced a smile. "Of course not. You're right. I—I don't know what I was thinking. I'm sorry."

"Dammit, Sydney." His voice was a soft growl as he took hold of her shoulders and forced her to face him. "Don't look at me like that. You're upset right now, you might not be thinking clearly."

She dared to put her hand on his chest, felt the rapid beat of his heart. It matched her own. "I'm thinking more clearly than I have in years." She kept her gaze level with his. "I know what I want. Do you?"

His hands tightened on her arms, and she felt a shudder move through him.

He nodded slowly, narrowed his eyes. "I want you, Sydney." His arms came around her, dragged her tightly against him. "I want you."

He crushed his mouth to hers, a demanding, forceful kiss that took her breath away. *I want you.* Sydney had waited to hear those words her entire life. She knew this was just about sex, not love, but still it didn't matter. For this moment, she was the happiest woman in the world.

His kiss thrilled her, made her mind spin and her pulse race. A lifetime of yearning spilled through her, yearning and desire, as hot as it was impatient.

She felt his impatience as well, his desire, as he deepened the kiss, slanting his mouth over hers again and again. She answered him, shivering with excitement, with anticipation.

His mouth still on hers, he scooped her up in his arms and stood. She wound her arms around his neck and clung to him, never wanting the kiss to end. The scent of his skin, as rugged as it was masculine, filled her senses. She felt safe and protected in his strong, steady arms.

As if she'd come home.

Not the home she'd been raised in. That had never been a home. But really home, a place where she belonged.

The realization frightened her, and the implications that came with it nearly had her pulling away. But she'd been a coward for far too long. She would not let this moment slip by her, would not let her fear deny herself this pleasure.

Just this once, she would let herself feel, just feel. No logic, no reason, no arguments. Just sheer, unfettered bliss.

Smiling softly, she laid her head on his broad shoulder.

Reese carried Sydney—not back into the tavern, which would be the wisest course of action—but to the front door of his cottage. Even if he'd wanted to take her back into the tavern, which he didn't, he didn't want anyone else to see her tearstained cheeks or red eyes. He felt strangely possessive of her at the moment, still angry at Rhonda and Mary Lou for their asinine remarks.

But he was the biggest idiot of all for not realizing how deeply the two women had hurt Sydney. He'd simply assumed—and that was certainly the appropriate word—that no one could hurt Sydney. That she was too tough.

Only she wasn't so tough, after all. What she showed on the surface wasn't what she really was at all. Underneath all that pluck and sass, she was soft and tender. Under that cool composure she was warm and vulnerable.

He'd known something was wrong when Gabe told him that she hadn't come back into the dining room to say goodbye. After his family had left, he looked in his office and she hadn't been there, either. And since she'd gone down the hall and hadn't come back, that had only left outside.

The sight of her tears, the sound of her small sobs, had ripped through his gut like a sharp knife. He'd watched her hug Boomer tightly to her and he'd never felt so damn helpless in his life.

He tightened his hold on her, reluctant to set her down as he stepped onto his porch. He fumbled awkwardly with the knob and Sydney reached down, pushed his hand away, then opened the door.

His living room was dark, but the soft glow from a bedside lamp shone through the half-open door of his bedroom.

"Sydney," he said hoarsely. "Are you sure?"

She smiled softly, pressed her lips to his.

Stunned by the force of the need pulsating through his blood, he carried her to his bed.

Eight

Sydney had never known that spontaneity could feel so wonderful. So liberating.

So exhilarating.

Reese crossed the distance to his big, beautiful four poster bed and it was all Sydney could do not to jump out of his arms onto the mattress and drag him down with her. She felt giddy with excitement and anticipation.

He lowered her not onto the bed, but let her slide slowly, sensuously down him until the tips of her feet touched the floor. She felt the tug on her apron strings behind her back, then the slide of the garment off her shoulders and down her body until it fell at her feet. Afraid that her knees wouldn't hold her, she kept her arms wound tightly around his neck. When she lifted her face to his, she saw the desire burning in his dark gaze, the need, and she shuddered from the force of it.

Yet he held back, waiting.

She smiled at him, brought her lips an inch from his. "You're going to make me beg, aren't you, Sinclair?" She brushed her lips lightly against his, whispered, "Make love to me, Reese. Please make love to me."

Her feet came off the floor as he dragged her upwards again, cupping her bottom as he lifted her, fitting her intimately against him. If there had been any doubt of his need before, there was certainly none now. His mouth all but consumed her in a hungry rush of frantic kisses.

And then, as if in slow motion, they were moving backward. As one, they glided down to the bed. Sydney sank into the soft mattress, easily took the weight of Reese's strong body on top of hers, thought it was the most glorious feeling in the world.

Until his open mouth moved down her neck. Oh, *that* was glorious, too. She felt the buttons of her blouse open one by one, then the slide of silk over her skin. He flipped open the snap at the front of her white lace bra, but instead of his hand, he used his teeth to tug the soft fabric aside. She felt the rush of cool air on her bare breasts, then the rush of his warm breath.

Gasping, she arched upward.

His mouth was hot on her soft flesh, his hands were gentle and kneading. And when he pulled the sensitive tip of one breast into his mouth and laved the nipple with his hot tongue, she moaned.

She'd been wrong. *This* was the most glorious feeling in the world. Intense pleasure rippled in hot waves through her, pooling between her legs. On a whimper, she raked her fingers through his thick, dark hair and moved against him.

He took his time, his hands and mouth giving equal

attention to each breast, until she felt like soft taffy, her insides pulling and stretching, over and over.

"Reese," she gasped, her hands moving restlessly over his back, his shoulders. "Please…"

He rose over her then and the soft light of the bedroom lamp shone in his dark, passion-glazed eyes. His face was hard and angular, his jaw tight, his hair rumpled as he stared down at her.

"You are so beautiful," he said hoarsely.

"Thank you," she said breathlessly, realized dimly that even in the heat of passion, a lifetime of impeccable manners could not be ignored. She also supposed that this was the proper pillow talk she'd only heard of, but never experienced. *You're beautiful, the only one. I love you…*. The things that people were supposed to say when they made love, even though they didn't mean them.

He shook his head slowly and sighed. "You don't believe me, do you? I can see it in your eyes that you don't. I want you to look at me, Syd. Look in my eyes."

Through the haze of desire humming through her body, she did as he asked.

"You're beautiful," he repeated softly. "You might make me crazy sometimes and confuse the hell out of me, but you're the most beautiful woman I've ever seen."

He *did* mean it, she realized. Her heart soared, and she had to quickly blink back the moisture in her eyes before she ruined the moment with silly tears. His words gave her courage, unleashed the last thread of inhibition inside her.

She rose up, slid her hands over his chest and rolled on top of him as she eased him onto his back. The surprise in his eyes delighted her almost as much as the sudden feeling of power she gained from this new position.

Her gaze held his as she slowly drew her blouse off her shoulders, then her bra, and tossed them onto the floor beside the bed. His eyes grew dark and intense as he watched her.

"Those clothes might get wrinkled," he teased. "Are you sure you don't want to fold them?"

"Nope." Smiling softly, she reached behind her head.

Reese's breath caught in his throat as he watched Sydney stretch her long, lovely arms up and behind her head in a seductive pose that made his blood boil. One at a time, she pulled the pins from the knot of hair coiled on top of her head and tossed them with her clothes. When the last pin was removed, her hair tumbled down around her soft shoulders like a curtain of gold silk. Her eyes had turned a smoky blue, her skin was smooth as the finest porcelain. His gaze traveled lower and his heart slammed in his chest at the beautiful sight of her soft, full breasts and the rosy, hardened peaks that he'd tasted only moments ago.

He wanted more.

He reached for her, but she shook her head and pushed his hands to his sides. "You have too many clothes on," she purred.

Her long, tapered fingers moved over his buttons until his shirt was open, then she slipped her hands inside and slid them over his bare chest, raking her fingernails lightly over his skin and through the dark hair on his chest. He sucked in a breath when she moved lower, over his belly, tugged his shirt from his pants, then reached for his belt buckle and pulled it open.

She glanced upward, met his gaze with hers, gave

him a slow, wicked smile that made his heart hammer furiously against his ribs. Gone was the proper Ms. Sydney Taylor: in her place was a siren. A temptress. And still there was an innocence that shimmered through those sexy eyes of hers that excited him more than any other woman had before.

Her hands moved lower; she leaned forward and blazed hot little kisses over his chest. He gritted his teeth, sucked in a sharp breath at the touch of her fingers slowly, methodically, deliberately inching down the zipper of his slacks.

When he couldn't stand it anymore, he took hold of her shoulders and flipped her onto her back, rolling with her. She gasped at the sudden movement, then just as quickly wrapped her arms around his neck. He crushed his mouth to hers while he kicked off shoes and slacks, then slid her skirt and underwear down her hips in one smooth move, taking her low-heeled black shoes with the garments and tossing everything into the pile she'd already created.

And then there was only skin touching skin.

He moved over her, kissed her temple, her cheek, the pulse at the base of her throat and an especially sensitive spot on her earlobe that made her moan. When he moved away for no more than a fraction of a moment to reach into the nightstand, she whimpered softly, called him back. Without missing a beat, he picked up where he'd left off at her earlobe and worked his way down again.

She writhed underneath him, murmured his name, whispered her pleasure while her hands moved over him, driving him as crazy as he drove her.

The heat burst into flames, consuming them. When they were both frantic with need, when he thought he would die if he waited another moment, he moved between her legs and thrust hard inside her.

Her nails dug into his back as she cried out softly.

He slammed to a stop.

"Sydney..." He struggled to speak, but it was difficult to think or form words since most of the blood from his brain had gone south. And the realization hit him like a Mack truck.

Sydney had never done this before. She was a *virgin*.

"Don't stop, Reese," she pleaded. "Please don't stop."

"But—"

"It doesn't matter." She tightened her legs around him and moved her body, confusing him, exciting him even in the midst of this unexpected revelation.

"Of course it matters," he said raggedly. "You never...you should have..."

She lifted her mouth to his and stopped his words, stopped any and all rational thoughts with her hands and her body. It was impossible not to move with the slow thrust of her hips, impossible to think of anything but the need clawing at his insides.

She set the pace and he followed, the urgency building and spiraling, coiling inside tighter and tighter.

He heard the sound of her gasp, felt the shudders ripple through her body into his, and he went over the edge with her.

She thought she would never move again. She would simply lie here forever on this big, wonderful bed, with her arms and legs twined around Reese, listening to the rapid sound of his heart beating against her own. Wanting the moment to last, she kept her eyes closed and held very still.

Her skin still tingled all over, right down to the tips of her toes. Her insides were the consistency of warm butter, and in spite of the weight of Reese's body on top of her own, she felt as if she were floating.

She now knew the *true* meaning of glorious.

"I'm too heavy for you," she heard him say. When he started to pull away, she mumbled a complaint and tightened her hold on him.

He compromised by raising himself on his elbows, then kissed her temple and cheek, then lightly brushed her lips with his. Slowly, reluctantly, she opened her eyes and looked up at him. His brow was knotted, his mouth set firm.

"Did I hurt you?"

She shook her head, smiled. "Is it always that wonderful?"

She didn't care how naive she knew she must sound. After a life-altering experience like that, what did it matter?

He smiled back at her. "No, Syd. It isn't always that wonderful."

Her smile dipped. "Does that mean it's usually better, or worse?"

Chuckling, he slid his hands up her arms. "It doesn't get better than that, Syd."

"Really? I mean, just because it was incredible for me, doesn't mean that it was—"

"Sydney. Shut up, will you?"

He covered her mouth with his before she could protest, kissed her hard and deep and endlessly.

Was it possible to want this again so soon? she wondered as his hand skimmed her waist then slipped up to caress her breast.

Obviously it was.

She let herself go, gave herself up once again to the kaleidoscope of sensations and couldn't remember once in her entire life when she'd ever been happier.

It was dark when he woke. His brain was still thick from sleep and the dream he'd had about climbing a tall, steep, snow-covered mountain, only to break through the clouds and discover a lush green meadow with wildflowers at the peak.

He scrubbed a hand over his face and thought of Sydney, then smiled. Geez, talk about symbolism.

He could hear her rustling close by, but when he reached for her she wasn't beside him. Frowning, he sat up and turned on the bedside lamp. She was dressed, on the floor beside the bed, on her hands and knees. Her head popped up when the light flooded the room.

"What are you doing?" he asked, his voice rough from sleep, or rather the lack of it. The clock on the nightstand said 3:00 a.m. They'd only gone to sleep maybe a half hour ago. At least *he* had. Apparently Sydney hadn't been asleep at all.

"I'm sorry I woke you." She had one shoe in her hand and was looking for the other.

"I asked you what you were doing?" he repeated, irritated that she was dressed and crawling around on the floor when she should be in bed with him.

"Well, it's so late and I didn't want to assume that I, well, that I should..." Her voice trailed off as she stared at the shoe in her hand.

"Spend the night?" he finished for her.

She nodded, but still wouldn't look at him.

She squeaked when he reached out unexpectedly and dragged her back into bed, then rolled her underneath him.

"Love 'em and leave 'em, huh?" He stared down at her, saw the tinge of pink on her cheeks. "Sydney Taylor, you are heartless."

"I'm sorry." Her thick lashes fluttered downward. "I just wasn't sure...I didn't know what I should do."

"Sydney." She looked so damn tempting, he thought. After making love with the woman half the night and only thirty minutes of sleep, all he had to do was look at her and he was hard again. "One of us has too many clothes on."

"I suppose that would be me." She smiled demurely.

"Looks like we have to start all over again from the beginning." He began to unbutton her blouse, then slid the soft fabric open. "This might take a few hours."

"Promise?" she asked, wrapping her arms around his neck and pulling him down to her.

He smiled against her warm, willing lips. "Promise."

Early morning light filtered in through the wooden blinds on Reese's bedroom windows. Sydney listened to the quiet, the distant sound of birdsong, and the steady, secure beating of Reese's heart.

She lay snuggled in the crook of his arm and watched him sleep. A dark shock of hair fell forward onto his forehead and she resisted the urge to slip her fingers through the errant strands and comb them back. Resisted the urge to press her cheek to his and feel the rough, short stubble of his morning beard against her smooth skin.

Resisted the urge to slide her hands over his broad, muscled chest and arms, his flat stomach and lean hips.

And more.

Smiling, she watched him instead. The slow rise and fall of his chest, the light flutter of his thick lashes, the occasional twitch of his strong jaw. He had the muscled, hard body of an athlete and though she'd experienced firsthand that strength last night, she'd also experienced his tenderness. He'd been a wonderful lover, forceful at times, yet gentle and thoughtful, too.

Lover. The word danced through her head, then rippled like warm waves over her skin. At twenty-six years old, Sydney Marie Taylor was no longer a virgin.

Her smile widened.

"When a woman smiles like that," Reese said in a sleep-roughened voice, "she's got something wicked on her mind."

Startled, Sydney felt her cheeks warm. It surprised her that after last night she would feel any embarrassment at all with Reese, but she was glad to see she still had at least some sense of propriety left.

"Certainly not," she said primly. "My thoughts are pure and chaste and—"

She gasped softly as he rolled her onto her back and covered her mouth with his. It wasn't a gentle kiss, it was possessive and insistent. Her hands slid up the warm skin on his back. When he pulled his mouth away, she kept her eyes closed and continued, though more breathlessly this time "—benevolent. The epitome of goodness and piety—"

His mouth swooped down again and she wrapped her arms around his neck, drawing him closer still. This time when he pulled away from her, his hands slid up her waist and cupped her breasts. She sucked in a breath. "Virtuous—" she arched upward when his mouth replaced his hands "—saint-like—" she heard him chuckle at that one, then pay careful attention to her hardened nipple with his tongue "—wholesome…"

Unable to think any pure thoughts with Reese's hands

and mouth doing such exquisite things to her, unable to think at all, she simply joined him.

Streaks of light from the swiftly rising sun warmed the rumpled sheets by the time they collapsed in each other's arms, flushed with passion and breathing heavy.

He held her close, kissed her temple and cheek. "Who would have ever thought," he said, his voice husky and rough, "that Sydney Taylor was such a wanton woman?"

"Don't forget wicked," she murmured against his neck. "And loose and—"

"Sydney…"

She heard the shift in his voice from playful to serious, felt her heart stop, praying he would at least wait until later, or tomorrow, even, to tell her that last night had been a mistake.

"Tell me how a beautiful woman gets to the ripe old age of twenty-six without…well, why is it you never…that you were still…" He hesitated, obviously unsure how to phrase such a delicate question.

"A virgin?" she finished for him while relief poured through her that he hadn't said what she'd been thinking, and at the same time wondering why she wasn't mortified having this conversation with Reese. "Dating was never easy for me like it is for other women." She skimmed a restless finger over his chest. "And the longer I waited for the right man, the more difficult it became."

"You were engaged, Syd," Reese said gently. "To Bobby, of all people."

"I always thought that was why he asked me to marry him, because I wouldn't jump into bed with him the way most women did. Well, and because my family had money, too. Then after he did ask me to marry him,

I figured if I slept with him, he wouldn't want me any-more, money or not. I wanted to believe that, maybe just a little, Bobby really did love me.''

Reese decided that if he ever saw Bobby again, he'd punch him in the nose. Just walk up and lay one on him, then walk away without so much as a second glance or thought. Thank God he hadn't married Syd-ney. She deserved much better than that muscle-brained moron.

And thank God she hadn't slept with the jerk, too. She definitely deserved better than Bobby in *that* de-partment, as well. She deserved someone like...well, like himself, Reese thought. He cared about Sydney, respected and appreciated her. Which was more than Bobby had ever done.

And the fact that he'd been her first, Reese thought, made Sydney all the more special to him. Made him want to, well, beat his chest, as ridiculous as that sounded. She'd made him feel...virile. Powerful. Ro-bust.

He had no idea how to tell her any of that, but sud-denly he wanted to try. "Syd—"

She sat, pulled the sheet up to cover herself and shook her head. "Reese, the last thing in the world I want from you is pity. You don't have to tell me how absurd it was to believe that Bobby really wanted to marry me, or that he loved me. I know perfectly well how pathetic I was.''

When he opened his mouth to protest, she put her fingers on his lips to silence him. "But that was the old Sydney Taylor," she said firmly. "I'm a new woman. In two weeks my restaurant will be open and now, thanks to you, I have an entirely different outlook on relationships.''

"Which is?" The touch of her fingers on his mouth distracted him for a moment and he couldn't resist kissing each delicate fingertip, delighted at the shiver he felt ripple through her.

"You've been right all along, Reese. I'm much too serious about everything. Too analytical and uptight. It's time I learned how to relax and enjoy life more. Have more fun."

He smiled, moved his lips to the palm of her hand and kissed her there. "Atta girl, Syd."

"I have so much time to make up for." Her voice was breathless, her eyes bright. "So many new things to experience."

He was liking the sound of all this more and more. And he was just the man to help her out with all those new experiences, Reese thought cheerfully. Who was he to discourage such energetic enthusiasm?

Smiling, she let her head fall back and stretched her arms wide. "I feel so incredible."

She *looked* pretty damn incredible, too, Reese thought as the sheet slipped away from Sydney's breasts. He was reaching for her when she suddenly jumped out of bed. He took a moment to enjoy every naked curve, then realized she was pulling her clothes on.

"And just what do you think you're doing?" Lying on his side, he bent his elbow and propped his head in the palm of his hand. She looked tousled and sexy with her hair falling over her shoulders and her skin flushed from their lovemaking. He watched her pull on her bra and blouse, still amazed at the night they'd spent together.

The first of many, he thought with a smile.

"Have you seen my shoes?" She dropped to the

floor, and Reese's heart jumped at the momentary sight of her pretty lace-covered bottom thrust upwards as she looked under the bed. "Here they are."

That did it. He wanted her back in his bed. Right now. He reached out and dragged her up onto the mattress with him, then rolled her onto her back as he kissed her. "And just where do you think you're going?" he murmured as he nuzzled on her ear.

Her arms came over his shoulders. "Home, silly. It's getting late. You've got to get to work."

"What happened to all that talk about enjoying life and having more fun?" He trailed kisses down her neck, delighted in the soft little moan he heard from deep in her throat.

"Well, I wasn't just referring to making love, though that—" she sucked in a breath and arched upward as his hand cupped her breast "—is certainly pleasurable, too."

"So what did you mean?" He started to unbutton her blouse again.

"I meant life in general," she gasped softly, closed her eyes as his hand slid under her silk blouse. "Enjoying every moment. I've worried my entire life what people would think and say about me. I'm not going to do that anymore."

"Good." He frowned when she stilled his hand and pushed upward on his shoulders until they were both sitting. Okay. She wanted to talk, that was fine. He made a mental note where he'd left off, so he could be sure and come back to the right spot.

"You were right about me being a snob, Reese." She took his face in her hands and smiled. "But not anymore. I'm going to take the time to meet different kinds of people and do things I've never done before. Listen to rock music. Cut my hair. Buy a short skirt. Eat breakfast in bed. All the things I never allowed myself to do before.''

That all sounded great, especially the short skirt part. And she could eat breakfast in bed with him anytime. He'd even make it for her.

She didn't need to cut her hair, though. He liked it just the way it was. And come to think of it, if she wore a short skirt, other guys would be looking at those great legs of hers. He decided he didn't like that at all.

And what the hell did she mean about meeting different kinds of people?

Before he could ask her, she'd slipped out from underneath him, then grabbed her skirt from the floor and pulled it on. ''I don't want to make you late for work and I'm sure you wouldn't want to have to explain Sydney Taylor sneaking out of your place early in the morning looking like she'd slept in her clothes.''

He frowned at her. ''You just said you didn't care what people thought.''

She tugged on a shoe. ''I don't care what they think about me, but I wouldn't want you to have to endure any rib-poking or jokes because of me.''

''And you think *I* care what people think?'' Shaking his head in exasperation, he sat on the edge of the bed. ''And if just one person pokes my rib or even hints at making a joke, they'll be wearing their teeth.''

She went still, then looked at him with tear-filled eyes. ''That's the nicest thing anyone has ever said to me.'' She moved toward him, then lightly pressed her lips to his and said softly, ''Thank you, Reese. That was the most wonderful night of my life. You've been kind and honest and incredibly sweet. You made my first time special and I'll never forget that.''

Kind, honest and *sweet?* Never forget? What the hell was she talking about? He narrowed his eyes and frowned. "Is this a brush-off, Syd?"

"Of course not." She turned away, spotted her other shoe and reached for it. "But we're both responsible, mature adults, and I don't want you to think that I have any expectations regarding a continuing relationship. What happened last night just happened. I don't want you to feel any sense of...responsibility."

Responsibility? Would this woman ever cease to make him crazy?

Probably not.

"So what you're saying," he said carefully, "is that you just want to be friends. Is that it?"

Her cheeks flushed pink as her gaze met his. "Well...yes."

He didn't believe a word of what she was saying.

"Sure, Syd," he said easily. "We'll just be friends."

"Great." Smiling, she moved toward him. "These next few days are going to be busy getting ready for the café's opening, so I may not see you for a while."

"Okay."

"Bye." She brushed his cheek with her lips.

"Bye, Syd."

"Bye." She brushed his other cheek.

"Syd?"

"What?"

"Come back to bed."

He saw the relief in her eyes, then, with a laugh, she threw her arms around his neck and sent them both falling back on the mattress. "I thought you'd never ask."

Nine

"Oh, Lucian, it's so beautiful."

Sydney ran her hand over the new granite countertop that Lucian had just installed in the café. It would separate the dining area from the wine and beer and cappuccino machine on the back wall. If her tables were full, then customers could wait here on bar stools and have drinks or hors d'oeuvres until they were seated.

"It's strong enough to hold an elephant, too." Screwdriver in hand, Lucian knelt behind the countertop and gave the last screw head on the supporting cabinet a solid twist.

"I don't suppose I'll get too many elephants for customers," Sydney said lightly.

Lucian stood, slipped his screwdriver into the tool belt around his waist. "I suppose not. But there are Henry Offman's two teenage sons. Don't think I'd want those boys to come in any restaurant I owned. Some say they single-handedly shut down Barney's Buffet. Just be sure you don't have any All-You-Can-Eat nights or they'll clean you out.''

Laughing, she shook her head and joined him behind the counter. "How would you like to be my first cappuccino customer? Or maybe an espresso?''

"That's straight-up black, right? Whipped cream and foam on coffee is for wimps.''

"Espresso it is.''

He leaned against the counter and watched while she prepared the coffee. "Looks like you're just about ready to open.''

"Six days, four hours and thirty-two minutes.'' She handed him the aromatic dark coffee in a demitasse.

Lucian raised a skeptical brow at the miniature mug, then took a sip. "Not bad, Syd. By the way, I like your hair like that.''

"Thanks.'' Her cheeks warmed at the compliment. "I just got it cut this morning.''

Lucian's cell phone rang and while he spoke to his foreman regarding a building permit on a job site outside of town, Sydney glanced into the ceiling-high mirror behind the cappuccino machine. She still couldn't believe the woman looking back at her was Sydney Taylor.

It had taken her an entire week to work up the courage to go to the salon. She touched the sides of the shaggy, layered cut that Frederico had insisted was created just for her. He'd also talked her into adding a few highlights to her already blond hair, and while she had those silly pieces of foil in her hair, he handed her over to Marie, the esthetician, who'd tweaked and plucked, plastered mud on her face, then applied a light touch of eye make-up. By the time her hair had been blown dry, Sydney looked and felt like a new woman.

Marie had oohed and ahhed and nodded with approval.

Frederico had called her Sexy Sydney.

Sexy Sydney.

She smiled. No one had ever called her sexy in her entire life. She liked it.

She'd gone straight from the salon and bought that short skirt she'd told Reese last week she was going to buy, plus a few other items of clothing that she'd always admired on other women, but never thought right for herself.

She couldn't wait until Reese saw her in them.

Or not in them.

She felt her skin heat up at her lurid thoughts of Reese, what it felt like to have his hands on her, his mouth. They'd seen each other several times since they'd made love that first time. On Monday, when the tavern was closed, they'd gone for a drive through the back roads of the country to a lake where he told her that he and his brothers used to race cars and drink beer. Just thinking about how she and Reese had made love in a secluded glen by the lake made her heart quicken. Never in her wildest dreams would she have ever thought that she'd make love outside, surrounded by trees and bushes and the sky overhead.

With Reese Sinclair.

A woman couldn't ask for a more skilled, generous, thoughtful lover. One minute he was gentle, the next wild and rough. These past few days had been the most exciting time of her life. He'd come to her apartment one night after the tavern had closed, a bottle of wine in his hand. They drank it in her bed. And just yesterday afternoon he'd shown up while she was unpacking an order of bread baskets and dragged her over to his cottage. She'd been breathless, excited that he'd wanted to make love with her so much that he couldn't wait until that night.

But he hadn't wanted to make love. He'd wanted to show her his brand-new, just arrived off the UPS truck, first edition, signed copy of Hemmingway's *For Whom the Bell Tolls*.

The pleasure and excitement in his face had made her heart stutter. There was so much more to Reese Sinclair than she'd ever imagined, and the fact that he'd wanted to share something so special with her made her eyes tear.

Then she'd been the one kissing him, tugging his clothes off as she pulled him to his bed with an urgency that startled herself.

With a sigh, she turned back to the cappuccino machine and made herself a cup. She refused to think beyond the moment. She'd be a fool to think that there was any kind of future for her and Reese. She understood that their relationship—whatever it was—was not permanent. They were…dating. Sort of. Enjoying each other's company. Definitely. They took each day as it came. No commitments, no plans, no explanations.

And if she started to dream for a moment, let herself think for even a millisecond that there could be more, all she had to do was remember standing at the front of the church, forcing her knees not to give and her voice not to shake as she looked at all those people and made her excuses. The pity in everyone's eyes had nearly done her in. They'd seen all along what she'd been too blind to see. That Bobby had lied to the very end, made promises, told her he loved her and wanted her to be his wife. She didn't ever want to see that look in anyone's eyes again. She wouldn't be a fool again. This time she'd be realistic. No expectations.

But Reese was honest. He'd made no promises, and he'd certainly never told her that he loved her. As long as she didn't make a foolish mistake and fall in love with him, then she would survive when he decided to move on to the next woman.

She swallowed the sudden lump in her throat. She didn't want to think about that now. She wouldn't.

She turned suddenly and bumped into Lucian who'd just finished his call. He steadied her with one hand, then frowned at the coffee that had splashed over the side of her cup onto the front of her blue cotton sweater.

"Did it burn you?" he asked with concern.

"No, no, I'm fine." She grabbed a bar towel from a hook under the cappuccino machine and dabbed at the spot. "I've got it."

"You sure? I'd help you out, but then you might have to slap me. Course," he said, grinning at her with that same Sinclair smile that made women melt, "it might be worth it."

Laughing, she shook her head. The Sinclair men were all hopeless flirts, charming, but deadly. And Lucian, well, there was something under the surface with Lucian, something under that Sinclair smile and eyes that appeared wounded. She recognized that look. She'd seen it in her own eyes.

But she already had her hands full with one Sinclair male. She wasn't remotely interested in another.

That wasn't how it appeared to Reese, however, when he chose that moment to walk into the café. At the sight of his brother standing so close to Sydney behind the new countertop, with his hand on her arm, smiling at her and her smiling back, Reese's blood started to simmer.

"Can I get in on the joke, too?" He kept his gaze carefully on Lucian as he crossed the room. "Or is this just between you two?"

Startled, Sydney jumped, but Lucian turned smoothly and grinned.

"Hey, Reese." Lucian dropped his hand away from Sydney's arm and leaned back casually against the small counter that held the coffee machine. He took a slow, deliberate sip of his espresso. "What's up?"

"Not much." His gaze slid to Sydney, who had just enough guilt in her eyes to make his jaw tighten. And just what had she done to her hair? He looked back at Lucian. "What's up with you?"

"Just putting in the counter for Syd," he said easily, then raised the little cup in his hand. "I'm her first espresso customer."

"Is that right?" A muscle twitched in the corner of Reese's eye. He didn't want Lucian to be Sydney's first anything. Or any other guy for that matter. And he sure didn't like his brother standing behind that counter getting so cozy with his girl.

"Would you like a cup?" Sydney asked quickly and turned toward the machine. "It will just take a minute."

"Maybe if you put it in a real cup," Reese said evenly. "That little thing Lucian's got there won't do much to get the heart pumping."

Lucian raised a brow at his brother's dig. To say his name and "little thing" in the same breath were fighting words and they both knew it.

While Sydney worked the machine, Reese glared at his brother. Lucian grinned right back, sipping his coffee.

Reese took the cup that Sydney offered, was irritated that she seemed to be avoiding his gaze. "Ah, I've got to go soak this or the spot will never come out," she said hesitantly as she glanced down at the front of her sweater. "I'll be right back."

Reese noticed the coffee stain between her breasts, then narrowed his eyes as he realized that Lucian was looking at the same spot. When Sydney turned and walked out from behind the counter, Reese nearly spit out the coffee he'd just drank. She was wearing a tight, black skirt that didn't have enough fabric to wipe a tabletop dry. Her legs went on forever. So did Lucian's stare.

"Put your eyeballs back in your sockets and close your mouth," Reese growled after Sydney was gone.

"Did you get a look at those legs?" Lucian whistled softly. "Lord have mercy, I think I'm in love."

"Unless you want to eat that little cup in your hand," Reese warned, "don't say another word."

"Why, Reese," Lucian said with a smile, "I do believe you're jealous. Just say the word, Bro, and I'll back off."

"I'm not jealous," he snapped. "I never get jealous. But just touch her again, keep looking at her like that, or thinking what you're thinking, and you die."

"Well, well." Humor lit Lucian's eyes. "So you *do* have a thing for Sydney, don't you? We were all wondering where you'd been keeping yourself when you weren't at the tavern."

Reese had never come out and exactly announced that he and Sydney were seeing each other, but he had a right to a private life, didn't he? Who he saw or what he did was nobody's business but his own. "Sydney

and I—'' he hesitated, trying to think of the right words
''—have an understanding.''

''Which is?''

''We like each other, enjoy each other's company.''
He took a sniff of the strong coffee, then sipped, decided he liked the strong, rich flavor. ''That's it.''

''Right.'' Lucian gave a snort of laughter. ''That's
why you started barking and growling when you walked
in and saw me with her. Because you *like* her.''

''That's right.''

''When I dated Susie Hutton at the same time you
did, you never even blinked,'' Lucian said, obviously
enjoying every minute of Reese's irritation. ''Or Mary
Walinkski. She dumped you to go out with me and you
didn't care. You liked them, didn't you?''

''I liked them *different*,'' he insisted. ''And Mary
didn't dump me. I got busy and she got bored sitting
around waiting for me to call. Anyway, Sydney is different, that's all.''

''Different from what?'' Sydney asked as she came
back into the room, still wearing that little black skirt
that had raised his blood pressure twenty notches and a
V-neck pink sweater. It was all Reese could do not to
grab the chef's apron laid over a bar stool and cover
her up with it. Instead, he narrowed his eyes at Lucian,
warning him off.

''Or should I say, different from who?'' Sydney
handed a check to Lucian. ''Thanks, Lucian. The countertop is perfect.''

''Anytime you need anything,'' Lucian said
smoothly, ''anything at all, Syd, just give me a call.
You have my home number?''

Reese understood perfectly well that Lucian was
goading him, but it still didn't ease the desire to grab

his brother by the scruff of his neck and shove him out the door.

"That shouldn't be necessary." She smiled. "I'm sure I can find you if I need you."

Reese gritted his teeth, decided to rough his brother up later for setting him up like this.

"Thanks for the coffee." Lucian handed Sydney back the cup, slid a grin at Reese as he passed him. "See ya."

Reese nodded stiffly, watched Lucian stride casually out the front door, whistling as he stepped out into the cool November air.

"What did you mean, 'I'm different'?" Sydney asked, dragging Reese's attention from his brother back to her.

He moved toward her, backed her against the countertop and braced one arm on either side of her. He covered her mouth with his, felt a surge of hot satisfaction at the soft moan he heard rise from deep in her throat.

"Mmm," he murmured. "You taste like coffee and cream."

"Stop trying to distract me," she said, then slid her hands up his chest and gently nudged him away. "How am I different?"

"Your hair, for one thing. You cut it." He knew enough about women to never say you didn't like a new hairdo, but in this case he did like it. It made her eyes look bigger, her face softer. "Very sexy."

Pleasure shone in her blue eyes, and he felt something shift and move inside him, an unfamiliar tilt to his equilibrium that had him tightening his grip on the countertop to steady himself. Lack of sleep, he decided.

He hadn't had much of that this past week, between making love at night with Sydney, or wanting to.

"That's what Frederico said," she said, her voice breathy.

"Who?"

"The stylist who cut my hair."

"Oh." He felt the tension ease from his shoulders. "I was beginning to think I was going to have to beat up every guy in town, including Lucian."

Especially Lucian, he thought, remembering the way his brother had drooled over Sydney's legs.

"Reese, Frederico is a happily married man, with two children." She laughed at the surprise on his face. "And *Lucian?* You're actually jealous of your own brother?"

There was that damn word again. "Protective," he said, deciding he liked the neutrality of that word.

"Of me?" She stared at him in wide-eyed wonder. "Why?"

"Why wouldn't I be?" he asked irritably, uncomfortable with the shift this conversation had taken. Why did women have to make things so complicated? Pick every thought and word apart and analyze it?

"Well…" Her gaze dropped to his chest while she busied one fingertip circling a button on his denim shirt. "I realize that we're sleeping together, but I never—"

"Just stop right there."

He took hold of her arms, narrowed his eyes as he looked down at her startled face.

"We're not just *sleeping together,*" he said through clenched teeth, then eased up on the tight grip he had on her. "I think I deserve better than a comment like that, and so do you."

"Okay. I'm sorry." Her fingers stilled, then she

asked carefully, "So what are we doing, then?" she asked carefully.

Oh, hell. Too many damn questions, when all he wanted to do was drag her upstairs to her apartment and make wild love with her all afternoon. "We're...seeing each other, Syd. Exclusively. In spite of what you may have heard about me, I'm not with a different woman every night and while I may not be a saint, I sure as hell haven't slept with all the ones I have gone out with. Not even close. Got that?"

He'd never explained himself to any woman before, Reese realized with annoyance. It surprised him, as much as it aggravated him, that he felt the need to do so now.

"All right." She spread her fingers on his chest, her expression thoughtful. "So you like my new haircut?"

His annoyance dissolved, in its place a heat built where her fingers had begun to move over his chest. "Yeah, I do. And you know what else I like?"

"What?" She leaned forward and pressed her lips to his throat.

"This skirt." His pulse quickened when she nipped lightly at the base of his throat. "I especially like this skirt."

His hands slid the fabric up and slipped underneath to reveal the tiniest sliver of black satin. He moaned softly, reached behind her and cupped her firm buttocks, lifted her up to fit snugly against the growing ache in the front of his jeans.

"I was hoping you would," she murmured, slipping her arms around his neck and pressing herself even closer, moving her hips in a way that made his heart slam like a fist in his chest.

He'd never wanted a woman the way he wanted her,

didn't understand the need that rocked him to his very core. Didn't want to understand it.

Right now, he only understood the urgency racing through his veins to possess her completely, thoroughly, mindlessly.

He scooped her up in his arms and carried her upstairs to her tidy, organized apartment, laid her down on her feather mattress, felt the last of his control snap when she held out her arms to him and pulled him down beside her.

"Just for the record," she said, gasping when he pushed her skirt up around her waist, "I'm not interested in Lucian."

"Sydney—" he skimmed the edge of her panties with one curious fingertip, felt masculine satisfaction at the sound of her sharp intake of breath and the upward thrust of her hips "—I don't want to talk about my brother right now."

"Okay." The blue of her eyes darkened with desire when he palmed the soft mound between her legs. She moved against his hand, closed her eyes on a moan. "What shall we talk about? The weather?"

"I heard there's a storm coming in." Just watching her squirm underneath him set Reese's blood boiling. He moved over her, inched her sweater upward with one hand while he caressed her intimately with the other. "You might want to stay inside to keep warm."

"Maybe I should light a fire." She sucked in a breath when his hand closed over her breast.

"I'll do it."

He slipped his hand under the band of elastic on her panties, then slid into the damp heat of her body and moved in a time-old rhythm, letting her set the pace. She arched upward when he leaned down and kissed her belly, raked her hands through his hair, grasping at his shoulders while his mouth moved lower.

"Reese," his name was ragged on her lips, a frantic plea.

He took his time, nuzzling the sensitive flesh on the inside of her thighs, softly biting, teasing with his mouth, stroking, loving her.

When she surged upward, gasping, then melted bonelessly back onto the soft mattress, he quickly slid her panties off, still kissing her while he tugged his jeans down. She opened to him, drew him to her. He heard her name on his lips as he drove himself deep inside her, heard the sound of his own hoarse breathing and her soft encouragement.

Insanity, he thought, as his body coiled tighter and tighter. What her hands did to him, her mouth. He looked at her, thought her the most beautiful, exciting woman he'd ever seen. Her eyes, glazed with passion, met his hard gaze; her lips, softly parted and swollen from his kisses, whispered his name.

Pure insanity.

And then he did go crazy, completely, and took her with him.

Ten

The snowstorm hit exactly as Reese had predicted, only three days later. Three days after that and twelve inches later, snow was still falling lightly on Bloomfield County; a pretty picture of white that covered roofs and cars and roads. On any other day Sydney would have appreciated the softly falling flakes and peacefulness. She might have put on her boots and gone for a walk, sat in front of a fire and sipped a hot brandy. Read a good book.

Any other day but today.

Today was the grand opening of Le Petit Bistro.

She stood at the window of the café in her new white silk suit, stared out at the snow-covered roads and walks. Her heart sank at the sight of the empty streets. Very few people came out on an evening like this, those that did had a purpose or a need. They didn't usually go out to dinner, especially to French restaurants with pink linen tablecloths and cappuccino machines.

Turning from the window, she scanned the restaurant; candles flickered softly from crystal-cut votives, one fresh pink rose bud on every table, strains of Mozart floating from the sound system. The scent of garlic and herbs filled the room. Everything looked exactly as she'd pictured in her mind.

Well, not exactly. In her mind, there'd also been customers.

The few reservations that had been made had been cancelled earlier in the day, but she'd still hoped until the last minute that the snow would stop and bring people out of their homes. When it hadn't, she'd simply hoped that people would come out anyway. The roads were still drivable, and the temperature wasn't as cold as it had been the past two days.

But she'd been open for business exactly twenty-two minutes and so far, her front door hadn't opened once. Her own grandfather wasn't even coming. He'd been snowed in at Baltimore airport and wouldn't be back until tomorrow. And Reese had his own business to run, with a short staff to run it. He had told her he'd come by, but he hadn't said when. If his place was as slow as hers was, she guessed he'd be by in an hour or two, but she knew that in this weather, people would be much more inclined to go out for a casual dinner and a beer than a fancy French meal.

There would be other days, of course. People would come once the snow stopped, she was certain of that. But this day, the first day, was special. A person always remembered firsts, she thought, and touched one soft petal of the pink rose on the table beside her. In spite of everything, she felt herself smile.

When she thought of firsts, Reese instantly came to mind.

But then, he was on her mind most of the time. She'd been too busy this past week taking care of all the last minute preparations to see him. Well, except for two nights ago, when he'd called late at night just to say hello, and the conversation escalated into a scintillating discussion of what she was wearing. As she'd laid back in her bed to describe her pink satin nightie in detail, a knock at her door interrupted her. It was Reese, out of breath from his sprint across the street. The second she'd opened the door he'd pulled her into his arms and made love to her right there, standing against the door he'd kicked closed.

Just thinking about the intensity in his dark eyes, the way he'd lifted her off the floor and she'd wrapped her legs around his waist, made her pulse quicken and her skin heat up.

"Ms. Taylor? Is there anything else you want me to do while we're waiting? I already folded the napkins."

Sydney glanced over her shoulder at Becky, her hostess, and smiled. "Why don't I show you how the cappuccino machine works? When Nell and I get busy with orders and serving, we may need you to fill in for us." *Hope springs eternal,* she thought with a sigh.

"Did I hear my name?" Nell popped her head out from the kitchen and glanced around. "Please tell me we've got customers. Latona has made a crab cake in some kind of sauce that could bring a grown man to his knees."

Sydney had worked all week with Latona fine-tuning all the recipes for the café. Most were Sydney's creations, but what her chef could do with pasta and chicken bordered on genius.

At the sound of the front door opening, all three heads turned expectantly.

Sydney's heart sank. It was a man wearing a mechanic's uniform and a baseball cap. "Anybody here call for a tow?" he barked.

Sydney shook her head, considered dragging the man inside and forcing him to sit at one of her tables. He was a lot bigger than her, but she was determined enough she could probably wrestle him into a chair.

Fifteen minutes later, with the snow still softly falling and not one customer in sight, she smoothed the corners of each table for the tenth time while Becky practiced making cappuccinos and Nell received an impromptu cooking lesson in the kitchen from Latona.

The door opened again.

A customer. A living, breathing customer.

Well, at least, sort of. It was Griswald Mantle, who'd had his eightieth birthday party last week at the tavern. His wife had passed on last year, and he spent most of his time at the tavern now.

For a moment Sydney thought maybe he was confused and had mistakenly walked into the wrong place, but he shuffled directly to a table without even waiting for a flustered Becky to seat him, handed her his coat, then sat, tucked his napkin into his shirt and asked for some bread.

Well, it was a beginning, Sydney thought and started toward his table to welcome him. Then the door opened again. This time it was Margaret and Jimmy Metzer, who owned the dry cleaners three stores down. Sydney seated them while Nell brought a basket of bread for Griswald.

Pandemonium struck five minutes later when the Sinclair-Shawnessey clan arrived. Cara and Ian, Callan and Abby, Gabe and Melanie and Kevin.

"Sorry we're late." Cara unwrapped the scarf from around her neck and shook the snow from her hair. "The roads slowed us a bit. Oh, Sydney, this is so beautiful."

"You shouldn't have come out in this weather." But she couldn't help being pleased that they all had. While Sydney hung their coats on the rack inside the door, Becky and Nell hurried about with breadbaskets and water glasses.

Lucian showed up next with Louise Wittmeyer on his arm, the pretty brunette office manager from Do-Right Lumber; Ken and Jan Stockton, local horse ranchers came in after them.

And so it went. They trickled in, shrugging out of coats and hats, filling the tables that had been empty just a short time ago. Sydney offered free samples of hors d'oeuvres and champagne, while Nell took orders and Becky helped serve.

For the first time in her life, Sydney felt completely alive. Whole. As she bustled about, she watched her customers enjoy the food she'd prepared, smile and roll their eyes with approval, and her chest swelled with joy.

And then Reese walked in.

Her hand tightened on the unopened bottle of wine she'd just removed from the rack under the countertop; she sucked in a breath at the sight of him. Flakes of snow dusted his dark hair and the shoulders of his brown leather bomber jacket. His gaze scanned the room, then stopped when he saw her.

He smiled.

Her heart skipped, then raced.

Never mind the room was crowded, filled with the

sounds of people talking and enjoying a meal, and that she was supposed to be serving her customers. Suddenly the only two people in the world were Reese and herself.

And then she simply knew.

She loved him.

She supposed at some level she'd known that she loved him since that first time he'd taken her to his bed. No, before that, she admitted to herself. When she'd hit him in the nose with that door then held his face in her hands and looked into those amazing eyes of his, that's when she'd really known.

But she'd refused to accept it, and even after they'd made love, she'd told herself she could handle their relationship without letting her heart get involved. The "new" Sydney wasn't looking for a commitment, she'd convinced herself. A man like Reese didn't play for keeps, he simply played, enjoyed the moment and the woman he was with at the time.

Well, the "new" Sydney was just as big a fool as the "old" Sydney. She'd fallen in love with a man who would never love her back the way she wanted. The way she needed.

Or could he?

The way he looked at her right now, as if she were the most beautiful woman, the *only* woman in the room—in the world—made her hope for things she shouldn't hope for. That she didn't dare hope for.

His gaze slid away then, looked at Becky who was staring at him as if he were a giant ice-cream cone she'd like to gobble up. He had that affect on women, Sydney knew, herself included. Only she thought of him as a potato chip and she wanted the whole bag. Every last, tasty morsel.

He shrugged out of his jacket and moved toward her then, still smiling, his intense gaze locked on hers. He looked incredibly handsome in a dark blue dress shirt, new jeans and—good Heavens, she never thought she'd see it—a tie.

"Congratulations, Ms. Taylor. Le Petit Bistro is a hit." He took her hand, brought it to his mouth. His compliment, as well as the touch of his warm lips on her suddenly cold fingers made her breath catch.

"You made it." She smiled at him, pushed away all the worry and doubt and just let herself enjoy. "Can you stay for a while?"

"The burners are out at the tavern, and we were slow anyway because of the storm. I decided to close down."

She should feel bad that he'd had to close down his business, but she was thrilled. "You mean I have you for the night?"

He kept her hand to his mouth, discreetly touched the tip of his tongue to her knuckle. "All night," he whispered, his voice heavy with promise.

"*All* night?" She raised a brow. "That's an ambitious endeavor, Mr. Sinclair. Are you sure you're feeling up for it?"

He gave her a wicked grin. "I'm certain I will be."

Heat shivered up her arm. "I set a place for you at your family's table, just in case you made it," she said softly. "But I'm busier than I expected so I may not be able to give you as much personal attention as I'd hoped."

"You can make up for it later, darlin'. In fact—" he kissed her hand again, nibbled this time "—I'm counting on your *very* personal attention."

The glint in Reese's eyes made Sydney's heart pound. With a wink, he walked away and joined his family. She stared after him, reminded herself to breathe. Lord, but the man was a distraction, she thought with a smile. A wonderful, sexy, exciting distraction.

"Table four would like a glass of Merlot," Nell said as she breezed by with an order. "A diet soda at six and more bread at seven."

Sydney snapped her attention back to her work, poured the wine and soda, filled a new breadbasket, then carefully composed herself. After all, she thought with a grin, a full-grown woman skipping around an elegant restaurant serving food and drink would hardly be considered dignified, now, would it?

"Get the wheelbarrow now and wheel me out." Cara sat back in her chair with a satisfied groan, but still had her eyes on the last bite of chocolate éclair on her husband's dessert plate.

"Good thing you've got those expanding pants," Ian said playfully. "I wouldn't want our son to get too crowded in there."

Cara placed a hand on her stomach and smiled. "Look who's talking. You ate an apple tart *and* an éclair."

"I couldn't very well hurt Sydney's feelings when she brought me an éclair on the house, could I?" And to make sure he didn't, he finished the last bite, then sighed with delight.

"We'd all be as big as houses if we ate like this every day." Melanie pushed her own plate away. "I couldn't force another bite."

"Maybe that's because you don't have another bite left," Gabe teased, then pulled a sleepy Kevin onto his lap and smoothed his rumpled sandy-blond hair.

"Sydney says she's open for lunch on Thursdays and Fridays," Abby said, still working on her own éclair. "Why don't we come here after our dress fittings on Thursday?"

The ladies all agreed, then Cara looked at Reese. "By the way, one of the males sitting at this table hasn't gone in for their tux fitting yet."

Callan, Ian and Gabe all looked at Reese. Good grief, he thought, sinking in his chair, it was bad enough he'd put this noose called a tie around his neck tonight. Just the thought of wearing that monkey suit made his neck itch.

"Monday," he promised reluctantly, though he'd already planned on spending his day off with Sydney. Somewhere quiet and extremely private.

When the conversation between the ladies shifted to talk about the wedding, seats were rearranged, separating ladies from men. While Gabe and Ian argued over the last Eagles-Cowboys game, Reese only half-listened as he scanned the café, hoping for a glimpse of Sydney. He narrowed his eyes at the sight of her serving wine to Mary Lou and Rhonda, who had come into the café with Emmett and Dean Farley, brothers who owned twenty acres of farmland just outside of town. Reese didn't like the idea of Sydney waiting on the women after what they'd said about her. But Sydney was smiling and talking to them as if nothing had ever happened, so she must have let it go. Or was at least pretending that she had.

His gut still twisted every time he remembered how she'd cried that night. He'd rather walk barefoot over broken glass than see her cry like that again.

He didn't know what she was doing to him, but he didn't like it one little bit.

When he wasn't with her, he spent hours thinking about her. When he was with her, all he could think about—other than making love to her—was when he would see her again.

He'd never done that with a woman before. Never wondered what she was doing when he wasn't with her, or if she was thinking about him. If she was listening to the same song on the radio, maybe looking at the phone thinking she should call.

She was driving him absolutely crazy.

Maybe he should back off, he thought. Let things cool a little between them. Get his head on straight so he could think more clearly about them, about their relationship. Just the thought of that word and what it might mean had him slipping a finger under the knot of his tie and loosening it.

Still, he watched her move about the restaurant, this new Sydney, who was softer, sweeter, more approachable. This was her night to shine and she was, literally. Her face glowed with pleasure, her eyes sparkled; it was all he could do not to drag her upstairs right now and make love to her. He glanced at his watch, figured he'd have to wait a couple of hours before he could manage to entice her away. And when he did, he was going to slowly strip that pretty silk suit off her, take his time as he opened every pearl button on her jacket, slide his hands inside—

Realizing where his thoughts had gone and where he was, he caught himself, blinked, then turned back to the table.

Gabe, Ian, Callan all stared at him, grinning like idiots. "What?" He wiped at his mouth.

"Either he's got a bad case of indigestion or he's in

love." Callan draped his arms over the back of his chair.

"They're pretty much the same," Gabe said knowingly. "But the way he's looking at Sydney, I'd put five bucks down that says it's love."

Reese shook his head and grinned right back at them. "Don't count me in your little club of hearts and flowers, boys. This Sinclair is made of tougher stuff than that."

"He's hooked." Ian slapped a five-dollar bill on the table.

"Big time." Callan did the same.

After the amazing meal that Reese had just eaten, he was too relaxed and satisfied to argue with anyone. Besides, it required patience when dealing with fools. "We're two adults enjoying each other's company, that's all," he said easily.

"Well, we know Sydney is one of the adults," Callan said. "So who's the other?"

"Didn't you guys know?" Lucian slipped into the chair where Kevin had been sitting. "Reese told me that he and Sydney have an understanding."

Reese frowned at his brother, deciding he would definitely have to beat him up later. "I thought you had a date. She get scared off already by that ugly face of yours?"

"She's in the powder room." Never one to let an opportunity pass to rile up a brother, Lucian leaned back in his chair and grinned. "You married guys all know the understanding. Whatever the woman says is the way it is, they insist you pick out rings and china together, only she decides what you'll buy, that—"

"What are you men talking about?" Frowning, Cara cut in. All the women were listening now.

"Lucian was just giving us his opinions on marriage," Reese said easily. "I'm sure he wouldn't mind repeating them for you."

The women all looked at Lucian, who was smart enough about the female gender to know it was time to get outta Dodge. "Oops, my date's back. Gotta go."

Enjoying himself, Reese reached for the beer he'd been working on for the past hour, keeping an eye on the kitchen door that he'd seen Sydney go through a few minutes ago. The crowd had thinned out and he knew that she would be closing soon. He'd already decided he'd help her clean up and shut down so they could have their own private celebration of her opening night success.

In fact, no reason not to get started now, he thought, anxious to get Sydney alone. He mumbled a goodbye to his family, then headed for the kitchen.

"Reese Sinclair. There you are, you little devil."

Groaning silently, Reese found himself face-to-face with Mary Lou. Coming from the restroom, she wobbled toward him on four-inch heels, her eyes glazed over. Rhonda was with her, but she held back, obviously uncomfortable.

He looked for a way out, but the women were between him and the kitchen. He glanced back over his shoulder at his family, hoping for some help from that corner, but they were all busy talking.

Damn.

"Mary Lou. Rhonda." He didn't smile, but good manners kept him from ignoring them completely. "Excuse me."

"Anytime you wanna play poker with me, honey," Mary Lou said, slowly running one long red fingernail down the front of his tie, "just call. I won't even care if you cheat to win."

Reese went very still, refrained from slapping her hand away. "You better get back to your table, Mary Lou. Emmett and Dean are waiting."

Rhonda tugged on her friend's arm. "Let's go, Mary Lou."

"Oh, come on, Reese," Mary Lou said, slurring her words. "Don't pretend you don't know what I'm talking about. Marilyn told me she heard you tell Lucian that you and Sydney Taylor played poker because of your dog digging up her stupid flowers, and that you cheated to win just to knock her off that high horse of hers."

Reese glanced at the kitchen door, thankful that Sydney hadn't come back out, then looked over his shoulder at Emmett and Dean, relieved when he saw them getting out of their chairs, looking embarrassed by Mary Lou's rising voice. "You're drunk," he said tightly.

"What a man won't do to get a girl in bed." Mary Lou laughed, and her voice rose even higher. "So, you into charity work these days, Reese? I'm sure Sydney was grateful for your philanthropic service, but—Hey!"

Emmett grabbed hold of Mary Lou's arm and practically dragged her toward the front door, while Dean and Rhonda hurried behind, gathering jackets.

Reese drew in a slow breath to calm the anger pumping through him, then realized that the restaurant had gone quiet.

The few customers who were still in the restaurant were staring, not at him, but past him. *Oh, God, no.*

He saw her standing behind the countertop, where she'd been kneeling. A wine bottle still in her hand, she stared blankly at him, her face pale. She'd heard every damn word.

"You cheated?" she whispered so softly he could barely hear her. "Just to teach me a lesson?"

Panic slammed in his chest. "No, Syd, it wasn't like that—"

"You made me work for you, shell those stupid peanuts, then you actually let me believe that you—" She stopped, sucked in a breath, then smiled stiffly. "That's a pretty good one, Sinclair. You must be some kind of hero around here, playing a joke like that on me, of all people. I gotta hand it to you, you are smooth."

"Dammit, Sydney, will you just let me—"

"No, Reese." Carefully, she set the wine bottle down. "I won't let you."

She turned smooth as silk and walked back into the kitchen. He started to follow, but Nell blocked the doorway, her eyes narrowed and accusing. He considered picking her up and moving her, but realized if he touched the woman, he'd probably have assault added to his already long list of evil doings.

He'd give her a little time to calm down. She'd understand once he explained what had really happened. That it hadn't been the way Mary Lou said.

At least, not exactly.

Knowing that every female in the room would probably like to stick their butter knife in his back—including his own sister—he opted for retreat.

On an oath, he grabbed his jacket, stalked out of the restaurant and didn't look back.

Eleven

———

"**T**en pounds of shrimp...twenty pounds of white fish...ten filets..."

Pen in hand, Sydney sat at the counter and entered the items Nell recited onto her shopping list, pausing here and there to make adjustments on quantities. She'd be opening at eleven-thirty today, and she'd offered discounts, plus free desserts to all the employees of local businesses to come in at lunchtime.

Her dream had come true.

She'd been in business exactly six days, not counting Monday when she'd closed, and the café, so far at least, was a success. Her customers loved the food and atmosphere, not to mention the reasonable prices, and she was already booked for the weekend prime dinner hours.

She should be dancing on this countertop Lucian put

in, swinging from the chandelier, swigging champagne and laughing.

She wanted to cry.

She wouldn't, of course. Not even for Reese would she let herself crumble into a pathetic little pile and bawl like a baby. She wanted to, but she refused to let the pain take control. Refused to let a broken heart turn her into some weepy, maudlin female. She would despise herself, and Reese, too, if she fell apart. In spite of what he'd done, the fool he'd made out of her, she couldn't hate him. It would only be another lie to deny that she loved him, that she always would.

She hadn't answered any of the messages he'd left every day on the answering machine in her apartment, and when he'd called the café, she'd been polite, then told him she was busy and she'd call him back, but didn't.

Over time the pain would ease, she'd been there enough times to know that. She might take longer to heal this time, but she would. She had to.

At least she had the café to keep her busy, occupy her mind and hands so she wouldn't think about him every minute of every day…every night…

"—six thousand pounds of pickled porcupine, five thousand pounds mongoose medallions, ten tubs of turtles—"

"What?" Sydney glanced up. "Turtles?"

Nell folded her arms and leaned across the counter. "Sydney, why don't you call him?"

"Call who?" She glanced back at her list and studied it as if it were a difficult algebraic problem.

Nell pulled the list from Sydney's stiff hand. "He's called and sent flowers every day, Syd."

Sydney glanced at the huge vase of red roses that had

just arrived. She allowed herself a moment to appreciate their beauty, then shook her head. "These are going back, just like the others," she said firmly.

A man had finally sent her flowers and she was sending them back. Funny how life worked out that way. Hilarious.

Nell shrugged. "Maybe you should just listen to what he has to say."

"Maybe you should."

Reese.

Her heart jumped at the sound of his voice. *Slow breaths,* she told herself. Slow, calming breaths.

Shoulders squared, she glanced over her shoulder at him.

He stood at the open door, watching her, his expression dark and somber. It pleased her that he looked a little ragged around the edges, but she supposed a guilty conscience did that to a person.

She'd known that she'd have to face him sooner or later. They lived and worked on the same street, in a town that wasn't all that big. "Good morning, Reese." She offered a stiff smile. "What can I do for you?"

Reese slid a look at Nell, who sighed, then shook her head as she headed back to the kitchen. "I'll go place this order, Syd. You still want those turtles?"

"That won't be necessary."

Reese frowned at the strange request, but he obviously had other things on his mind than Nell and turtles. He moved toward her, his jaw clenched tight. "You haven't called me."

"I apologize." Needing distance between her and Reese as much as needing something to do with her hands, she slid off the stool she'd been sitting on, moved behind the countertop and reached for the container of coffee she'd ground fresh a little while ago. "I've been busy here."

"We need to talk about this, Syd."

"All right." She scooped the grounds into the basket, but lost count. She'd be damned if she'd recount in front of Reese. "I have about five minutes before I have to set up for lunch today."

"Dammit, Sydney." He raked a hand through his dark hair. "You owe me more than five minutes."

She arched one brow, looked coolly at him as she flipped on the coffee machine. "We don't owe each other a thing, Reese. We had fun for a few days, that's all."

Like a caged cat, he began to pace. "Look, I know you're upset because of what Mary Lou said the other night. I'm sorry about that. If you'll just let me explain, we can—"

"Did you—" she cut him off "—or did you not cheat when we played poker, with the intention of, and I quote, 'knocking me off my high horse'?"

"Well, sort of, but—"

"I suppose there were side bets going on how long I'd tough it out working at the tavern." She reached for a towel, wiped at the counter. "Then, of course, there'd certainly be bets on how long it would take you to get me into bed. You must have made a pretty penny there."

He moved on her so fast she didn't even see him coming. One second she was wiping up some spilled grounds on the counter, the next second he had his hands on her arms and was holding her up against his body.

"Don't say that." His face was tight with anger.

"Don't ever say that. What happened between us wasn't planned, and it sure as hell was mutual."

His anger surprised her, but she refused to let him intimidate her, or get through her defenses ever again. "You're right, of course. Just because people like Mary Lou believe it's true, well, what difference does it make what they think? So what if they have a few laughs at my expense? I can live with that." She had lived with it for years. She'd survive.

Somehow, she'd survive.

A muscle jumped in his temple, but he slowly loosened his hold on her. "Other than I'm sorry, I don't know what to say. Tell me what to say, Syd."

Knowing he would never say the words she wanted to hear, she simply sighed. "A few flowers and 'I'm sorry's' won't make it okay, Reese," she said softly, then drew in a breath to steady herself. "But I would like to put all this behind us and still be friends."

"Friends?" Startled, he dropped his hands away from her. "You want to be friends?"

"If that's all right with you."

A glint of something dark and primal shone in his eyes, then it was gone, as if a shade had been drawn. "Sure," he said tightly. "Friends."

"Good." She managed to force a smile, even though her heart was shattering slowly into tiny, jagged little pieces. She turned away from him and wiped at the counter again. "If you'll excuse me now, I've got a hundred things to do. You know how it is in this business."

"Yeah. I know how it is."

He turned, started for the door.

"Reese?"

He stopped, glanced over his shoulder.

"Did...did your family all know about what happened, I mean, before?"

"Just Lucian, only because he guessed."

She closed her eyes with relief. She didn't know how she would have managed, how she'd ever face them again, if they'd all known and had been laughing at her.

She nodded, but didn't say anything. She felt his hesitation, and it frightened her. If he didn't leave, she was certain she would crumple up into a little ball.

But then she heard the door close behind him. She let out the breath she'd been holding, then leaned against the counter for support. She hadn't thought it possible to hurt any more than she already was.

But once again, she'd been wrong.

So very, very wrong.

A wedding was just as good a reason as any to get drunk, Reese decided. And since it was his own brother's wedding, so much the better. Nobody would question him if he got plastered and made a fool out of himself.

Something he seemed to be very good at these days.

Frowning, he stared at the beer in his hand, then took a big swig and leaned back in his chair to watch the reception guests dance to "Livin' La Vida Loca." Normally he'd be out there, too, celebrating and having a good time, but tonight the only celebrating he intended to do was with a bottle. He'd pay for it tomorrow, but for a few hours tonight, at least, he could forget about a curvy blue-eyed blonde with skin like silk and a mouth that could make a man groan out loud. He listened to the music and decided the number should be his theme song.

Living the Crazy Life. That was him all right.

Only Sydney could make a man crazy like that, he thought and threw back another slug of beer. Make a man wake up in the middle of the night, his sheets tangled and damp with sweat. Intrude into every tiny corner of his life, every thought, until there wasn't anything else but her. The sound of her laugh, the smell of her skin, the feel of her body against his.

His hand tightened on the bottle.

Dammit, he couldn't even get drunk without her invading his mind.

What else could he say to her that he hadn't already said? Before he'd finally gone over there to talk to her last week, he'd apologized a dozen times, sent flowers. He didn't know what else to do.

A few flowers and I'm sorry's won't make it okay, she'd told him.

So what the hell would?

Well, fine, then. He certainly wasn't going to crawl after her. He'd get over it, get over her.

He took another long pull on his beer. He would, dammit.

"Well, well, what have we here? Somebody looks lonely."

Reese frowned at Lucian and Callan, who'd just come off the dance floor and grabbed a beer on their way to harass him. When they turned two chairs around and straddled them, he knew they were settling in for a while. He'd get up and leave, but since they'd just follow, he didn't much see the point.

"He's still pining for Sydney," Callan said to Lucian.

"I'm not pining for anyone," Reese growled.

Lucian laughed. "Right. That's why you've been

holed up in the tavern for two weeks and you've been snapping at everyone who even looks at you.''

"I haven't snapped at anyone," Reese snapped.

"It's not as if we don't understand, Bro." Lucian tipped his beer to his lips. "I mean, Sydney's a fine-looking woman, especially since she did that thing to her hair and started wearing those short skirts and sweaters. I saw her yesterday at the post office and she had on the hottest little—"

"Shut up, Lucian." Reese slammed his bottle down on the table. Dammit, his brothers had even spoiled his taste for beer. "Just shut up."

The beer bottle that had been halfway to Lucian's mouth stopped. "'Course, she looks fine in a slinky black dress and high heels, too. Damn fine."

Reese followed Lucian's gaze across the crowded reception room. His heart stopped, then slammed against his ribs.

Sydney.

Her dress had a scoop neck, long sleeves and flared softly around her knees. Legs that never seemed to end were encased in black stockings; her high heels were spiked; her hair pulled up in a fountain of curls that cascaded down her slender neck. She stood with Melanie and Gabe, smiling as she congratulated them on their marriage. When Gabe kissed her, Reese felt his insides twist.

"Wow."

It took Reese a moment to realize that Lucian had said the word out loud and not himself. "Wow" definitely described her.

"What's she doing here?" Reese asked, surprised that his tongue still worked.

"Melanie asked her to come." Callan sat back with

a grin on his face. "When the women went into her café for lunch the week before last, they all bullied her until she promised to at least come to the reception for a little while."

It figured that no one would tell him. He'd been a pariah with the females in his family since the Mary Lou incident. Cara had chewed him out big time for his stupidity; Melanie and Abby had been silent, but the accusation in their eyes stung. As if he needed anyone to tell him what an idiot he'd been.

Lucian set his beer down and started to rise. "Since you're not pining for her, Bro, then I'm sure you won't mind if I—"

"Take one step toward her and you'll be wearing that cummerbund around your neck."

Lucian sighed, then shrugged and sat back down. "Let me know if you change your mind."

Keeping his eyes on Sydney, Reese stood and made his way across the room. He was probably just making a bigger fool out of himself than he already was, if that were possible, but what the hell?

"Dance?" he asked from behind her.

Her red lips thinned as she turned. "No, thank you, I—"

"We're friends, remember? Friends can dance together."

Ignoring her resistance, he pulled her into his arms and led her out onto the floor. He said a silent prayer of thanks when the music changed from fast to slow, a popular song by a current group about needing someone tonight. He pulled her close, felt her stiffen.

"You look good, Syd." She felt good, too. And her perfume was different tonight, he realized. Something exotic and sexy, intended to drive a man crazy. Not that she needed perfume for that. He was already there.

"Thank you." She placed a hand between them, eased back. "You look nice, too. If you'll excuse me, I really need to go see—"

"How did you manage to get off work?" He figured if he kept the conversation more business oriented, she wouldn't run off as quickly.

"I hired one new waitress and Nell's sister is in town for a few days. She manages a delicatessen in New York and offered to help out at the café tonight."

He hated the cool, disinterested tone in her voice. She wasn't disinterested, dammit. He *knew* she wasn't.

Or, fool that he was, maybe he was just hoping.

"That woman Lucian is dancing with," she asked casually, "who is she?"

If she was trying to twist the knife in his gut, she was doing a hell of a job, Reese thought as he narrowed his gaze at his brother, then back at her. "That's Raina, Melanie's maid-of-honor," he said tightly.

"I thought she looked familiar," Sydney said thoughtfully. "She came into the café on Thursday night with Melanie."

A tiny bit of the tension that had gathered in his shoulders eased as he realized she wasn't thinking about Lucian, but Raina. Reese had met the pretty brunette last night at the rehearsal dinner, but had been too caught up with thoughts of Sydney to even consider wandering into that territory. He'd thought at first that Lucian had been interested in Melanie's friend, but the way she and Lucian had avoided each other after their initial meeting, Reese figured that he'd been wrong about any attraction between the two. If anything, he thought, watching the stiff way they moved around the dance floor together and the expressions on their faces, they looked as if they'd rather dance with an axe murderer than each other.

Reese made a mental note to tweak Lucian's pin later over the woman's rejection. Payback's a bitch, dear brother, Reese thought with a smile.

Ian and Cara danced past them at that moment and said hello to Sydney, then Callan and Abby came by next. Reese wanted to be alone with Sydney, away from this crowd and the prying eyes of his family. He was certain she hadn't meant what she'd said about being friends with him. If she would just talk to him, he could change her mind. He knew he could. He just had to keep her in his arms long enough for her to relax a little, to remind her how good it had been between them.

Weather was a neutral subject, he decided. She didn't have to run from that topic. "It's supposed to snow again tonight."

"That's what I heard."

"Maybe tomorrow, too."

"Should be lovely."

Okay, well, maybe weather wasn't the best topic, after all. He tried another tactic. "Boomer got a thorn under his paw. I had to take him to the vet to remove it."

Bingo. That got her attention. Concern wrinkled her brow as she looked up at him. "Is he all right?"

"It was a pretty big thorn." Under a microscope maybe. "He's been limping around, looking for sympathy and a little extra attention."

Kind of like me, Reese thought.

"I'm sure he'll be fine." She smiled at Melanie and Gabe, who danced by holding Kevin in their arms.

"I don't know," Reese mused. "Sometimes when

something gets under the skin like that, it can turn into something serious.''

"He's a tough little dog,'' she said evenly. "He'll bounce back in no time.''

"He misses you.'' Reese pulled her closer, felt her stiffen. "I miss you.''

"Reese—''

"Tell me what to say, Syd.'' When she put her hand on his chest, he felt panic grip his throat. "Please, just tell me what to say.''

She looked up at him then, and for a split second his pulse jumped; he was certain he saw something in her eyes: a need, longing. But then it was gone. Once again her eyes were cool and blank, and he knew it had just been wishful thinking.

"We've said everything already, Reese,'' she said quietly, then stepped out of his hold. "Excuse me, I need to say goodbye to Melanie and Gabe before I leave.''

The song turned to a fast beat again, a Donna Summer disco song. Sydney disappeared into the throng of jumping bodies on the dance floor. He started to follow her, then stopped. Like the beat of the music, her words pounded in his brain.

I'd like us to be friends, if that's all right.

A few flowers and I'm sorry's won't make it okay.

We've said everything already.

Eyes narrowed, hands balled into fists, he turned and made his way back to his beer.

Six inches fell during the night, a white blanket of fluffy snow that sparkled in the early-morning light. From her bedroom window, Sydney watched the sun peek over the tops of John Gelson's maple trees. The branches were bare now, the brilliant colors of fall already yielded to the white of winter.

Like those branches, she felt stripped bare, cold. Empty.

Good Heavens. She turned away from the window and laughed at herself, shook her head at the absurdity of her thoughts. She'd promised herself she wasn't going to think about Reese today. She'd thought about him all night; dreamed of him even when she'd finally managed to fall asleep sometime in the wee hours of the morning.

She'd known better than to go to the reception last night, but Melanie and Cara and Abby had all been so insistent that she hadn't been able to refuse them. She'd thought that she could avoid Reese, mix with the other guests and keep her distance from him. He'd caught her off guard by dragging her out onto the dance floor like he had.

When he'd pulled her into his arms, it had taken every ounce of willpower not to give in to him. When he'd told her he missed her, she'd nearly thrown her arms around him and kissed him right there, in front of everyone.

But he hadn't said the words she needed, and she knew he never would. The mistake had been hers, trusting him, falling in love, foolishly believing, if only for a moment, that he might love her back.

Marry her.

Well, enough of feeling sorry for herself. She reached for her robe. A streusel muffin would take her mind off Reese, she decided. She'd bake up, oh, say, ten or twelve dozen, then maybe whip up a couple of hundred chocolate chip cookies, then a few dozen oatmeal raisin or—

She jumped at the sound of the ringing phone. No one called at seven-thirty on a Sunday morning. Her heart beat furiously as she stared at the phone.

Reese might.

She reached for the phone, then pulled her hand back. She wouldn't talk to him. She waited, breath held, when her machine clicked on, listened while her announcement played....

"Sydney, this is Cara...please, if you're there, pick up...there's been an accident...."

Twelve

"Sydney, I'm so glad you're here."

Cara hurried down the hospital corridor toward her, and the women hugged briefly.

"How is he?" Sydney asked, glancing worriedly at the hospital door Cara had just stepped out of.

"Lots of scrapes and bruises, and a mild concussion. The doctors said he can go home in a couple of hours and he should be fine in a few days. Lord, he scared the bejesus out of all of us. Come on—" she took Sydney's arm and dragged her toward the room "—one smile from you ought to cheer him up. He's been very cranky with everyone since they brought him in an hour ago."

"Do you really think I should go in?" Sydney didn't want to intrude on a family gathering. "He might not feel like having company, especially so soon, and I could—"

But Cara was already pulling her through the door. Callan and Ian stood beside the bed, laughing as if someone had just told a joke, and Abby was shaking her head at them while she filled a glass with ice water.

Lying in bed, dressed in a blue hospital gown, one large bandage on his temple, was Lucian.

Everyone went quiet when she entered the room; Sydney shifted nervously, then looked at Lucian, felt her stomach twist as she took in the scrapes and bruises covering his arms and left side of his face. "How are you feeling?"

A smile touched his mouth, but the pain in his blurry eyes was evident. "I'm sure a kiss would make it all better," he suggested.

Abby rolled her eyes and handed the glass of water to Lucian, then moved toward Sydney and gave her a hug. "That's what he said to the nurse fifteen minutes ago, just before she stuck him in the butt with a needle."

Sydney moved beside the bed and placed a gentle kiss beside the bandage on Lucian's forehead. He closed his eyes and sighed. "Now I can die a happy man."

"He said that to another nurse when she fluffed his pillow a few minutes ago," Cara said dryly.

The Sinclair men, Sydney thought with a smile. There wasn't a woman who was safe around them. She knew firsthand. Her smile faded as she glanced around the room. "Reese isn't here yet?"

"I finally got hold of him about ten minutes ago," Cara said. "He'll be here any minute."

When Cara hadn't been able to reach Reese at the cottage or the tavern to tell him about Lucian's accident, she'd called Sydney, thinking maybe he'd spent the night at her place. Sydney didn't want to know where

Cara had finally found Reese. Didn't want to know if he'd spent the night with someone. She was still too fragile to think about him being with another woman, holding her, kissing her. Making love to her.

Pain squeezed her chest at the thought. She wouldn't think about Reese now. She was here for Lucian. Lightly she covered his hand with her own. "What happened?"

Lucian shook his head, then winced at the movement. "Damned if I know. The last thing I remember is toasting Gabe and Melanie at the reception. Next thing I know I'm lying in this bed with the Headache from Hell."

"They found him at Jordan's Junction, unconscious in his truck," Ian said. "It appears that he skidded on some ice and went over the side of the road."

"What in the world he was doing at Jordan's Junction at six-thirty in the morning remains a mystery." Cara folded her arms, trying to look stern and reprimanding, but the worry in her eyes was plain, as was the relief that her brother was going to be all right.

"Do Gabe and Melanie know?" Sydney asked.

Cara shook her head. "They left after the reception for a red-eye flight out of Philly. Right about now I figure they're having breakfast on a beach in St. Thomas."

"Sure they are." Callan looked at the other men, who all grinned knowingly.

Cara rolled her eyes. "So okay, they're having breakfast in their room. In any event, we all decided, since Lucian is all right, not to tell them until they get back in two weeks."

"Gabe's not gonna like it."

All heads turned at the sound of Reese's voice from the doorway.

At the sight of him standing there, Sydney's throat went dry as dust. He still wore his tuxedo, minus the cummerbund and bow tie. His hair hadn't been combed; he hadn't shaved and his eyes looked glassy.

He looked as if he'd been out all night.

Sydney swallowed, followed his gaze down to where her hand was still touching Lucian's. She noticed a twitch at the corner of one weary eye, but when he moved into the room, he had his attention on Lucian, not her. She slipped her hand from Lucian's and moved away from the bed.

Reese nodded at his brother. "You all right?"

"Pretty nurses to fluff my pillow and beautiful women at my bedside." Lucian lifted one brow, then winced at the movement. "Maybe I did die and go to Heaven."

Reese frowned. "Not funny, Bro. I saw your truck as it was being towed away. It looks about as pretty as your face right now."

"Damn," Lucian growled. "I liked that truck, too."

As the banter continued, Sydney inched her way toward the door and slipped out. She was halfway down the hallway, struggling not to break into a run. Emotions were running too high right now. For her, for Reese. He'd been out all night, she knew. It was obvious. It could just as easily have been him lying on the side of an icy road somewhere. Only maybe he wouldn't have been as lucky as Lucian. When he'd walked into the hospital room, she'd wanted to throw herself in his arms and kiss him, tell him that she loved him.

Thank God she hadn't.

"Sydney. Wait."

She stopped at the sound of Cara's voice, closed her eyes on a sigh, then opened them again as she turned.

"Come have a cup of herbal tea with me. After all this excitement, my child and I need a little something to calm us down." Cara smiled and pressed a hand to the slight bulge on her stomach. When Sydney hesitated, Cara took her arm. "Please."

They walked to the hospital cafeteria and sat down with two steaming cups of hot water and tea bags. Cara stared at hers while it steeped, then said, "You know he loves you, don't you?"

Sydney glanced up sharply. "What?"

Cara raised her cup, blew on the hot liquid. "Men can be such...well, men. They want to believe that they're the dominant creature and no one can ever control them, so they beat their chests and jump around like a bunch of monkeys. But when they're all done acting ridiculous, they come around and roll over like puppies."

Somehow Sydney didn't quite see Reese as a monkey or a puppy. When she'd been furious with him, though, she *had* thought of him as a donkey's behind. "You're wrong, Cara. He doesn't love me. What we had was—" she hesitated, felt the tears at the back of her throat "—was about sex," she whispered. "That's all."

"Don't kid yourself, Syd. I've never seen him look at a woman the way he looks at you. And believe me—" she smiled "—I've seen him look at a lot of women."

Sydney raised a brow. "I suppose that's intended to make me feel better?"

Cara laughed. "It's no secret that Reese has dated a lot of women. But it was always casual, never serious. And never, ever was he jealous. According to Lucian,

Reese nearly took his head off when he saw you two alone in your restaurant. And these past two weeks, Lord help us, sweet, never-let-anything-or-anybody-get-to-him Reese Sinclair has been a bear. A big, grumpy bear. And that, my dear, is *not* just about sex.

"There is something else," Cara said and leaned closer. "But he'd kill me if he knew I told you this. The night of the café's opening, the burners weren't down at the tavern. He sent everybody over from his place to yours, told them that their meals were on the house next time they came in, then he closed down. Believe me, there isn't another woman alive Reese would do that for."

"He did *what?*" Wide-eyed, Sydney stared at Cara.

"He doesn't think anyone knows," Cara said, sipping her tea. "But I suspected, so I ran a stealth operation and checked out his story. Every single burner was in perfect working order."

He'd done that? Lied about his burners being out and offered incentives to anyone who came over to her place? There *had* been an odd assortment of customers that night, she remembered, but she'd been too excited to consider that they hadn't come in on their own.

She pressed a shaky hand to her temple. She didn't know what to think, what to believe. It was possible that the burners had simply started working again. Maybe Corky or someone had fixed them. Cara could be wrong about everything.

Sydney couldn't believe any of it: the burners being out, that Reese was in love with her. She wanted to, but she couldn't. Couldn't risk the pain of letting herself believe that Reese loved her, only to learn the truth.

"Cara." Sydney sighed, shook her head. "Thank you. I know you're just trying to help, but it won't work between Reese and me. We had a…nice time together, but we're completely different people.''

"You really believe that?" Cara asked.

"Absolutely." She would, Sydney told herself. She would believe it. "He'll go his way and I'll go mine. It's better that way for both of us.''

"Okay, Syd." Cara shrugged, tucked a loose strand of blond hair back behind her ear. "Well, I'd better get back to check on Lucian. Thank the good Lord hard heads run in this family," she said as she stood. "It's the only thing that saved that boy.''

Sydney stared at her tea long after Cara had left, long after the steam ceased to rise. She no longer felt like baking cookies or muffins, but she had pastries to make for tonight's desserts at the café, plus tables to set up, bread dough to prepare and an herb dressing for one of tonight's special salads.

She rose slowly, hugged her jacket tightly to her as she stepped out into the cold and headed back home.

"Tonight we have a pan-roasted white fish with garlic mashed potatoes and sautéed green beans, a grilled filet mignon with Yukon Gold potatoes…''

Sydney recited the evening's specials to Max and Eileen Brenner, who had already been to the café three times since the opening. In only two weeks, Sydney already had several repeat customers for dinner, plus several regulars at her lunch dining: ladies out for a social afternoon and businessmen and women who wanted to impress their clients with something a little nicer than a sandwich or hamburger from a coffee shop or Squire's Tavern.

Even her grandfather had conceded to her that she'd done a good job, though Sydney had nearly fallen over at his praise. Tonight he was at the café with a group of lawyers and their wives from Ridgeway, and she could hear him bragging about his granddaughter's cooking while Nell opened a bottle of wine for the table.

And all she wanted to do was sit down on the floor and cry.

She was thankful that the café was unusually busy this evening. Work was the only thing that kept her mind off Reese and what Cara had told her this morning at the hospital.

He loves you.

He didn't. She'd had all day to think about it, reason it out in a logical manner. In spite of what Cara said, Sydney was certain that the physical aspect of their relationship had been what attracted him to her, that's all. And she wanted more than that. A happy-go-lucky bachelor like Reese Sinclair didn't settle down and have kids with the uptight, snooty granddaughter of the Honorable Judge Randolph Howland. She would like to think that she'd relaxed a little, and that she didn't take life quite as seriously as she had, but she was basically the same person she'd always been. Whoever she *did* marry would have to love her exactly the way she was, with all her flaws and faults.

"I made an artichoke ravioli today with you both especially in mind," Sydney told Max and Eileen when she noticed Cara and Abby come into the café. "I'll have some sent over, on the house, while you decide what you'd like for dinner."

Sydney excused herself and made her way toward Cara and Abby, who waved at her, then seated themselves at a table that Sydney called her "last chance" table. It not only had a direct view of the main kitchen door, it was in the path of the servers coming in and out of the kitchen. She offered to move the women, but they just smiled and insisted they were fine.

"How's Lucian?" Sydney asked.

"They sent him home at noon," Cara said with a smile. "Probably to stop him from coming on to the nurses. Based on one cute little brunette he'd been flirting with, I have the feeling that he'll be receiving some at-home nursing care."

"Ian and Callan will be along shortly." Abby smoothed her napkin on her lap. "Before they get here, we were hoping we could talk to you about something."

"Well—" She glanced around the restaurant. Becky was at the front, and Nell and her new waitress, Susan, seemed to have everything under control. For the past twenty minutes, Sydney had been busy talking to customers and serving drinks, but Nell had reassured her— several times, in fact—that everything was fine in the kitchen and she wasn't needed there.

"I have a couple of minutes." She sat at their table, suddenly nervous what they might want to talk to her about. "But I've got to help serve as the orders come up."

"This won't take long," Cara said. "We need to talk to you about Reese."

Sydney felt her insides twist. "Cara, Abby, this really isn't—"

"It's serious," Abby whispered. "He's gone crazy."

"Crazy?" Sydney blinked. "What do you mean?"

"Right over the edge." Cara made a diving gesture with her hand. "We think he needs to be committed before he hurts himself."

"That's ridiculous." Sydney laughed, then frowned when both women stared at her, their expressions sober.

This was absurd. Ludicrous. She shook her head, then

went still when Reese opened the front door of the café and stepped in. He was wearing a tux, not the one from last night, but a clean, fresh one.

"Sorry I'm late, Syd," he said, moving toward her.

"Late?" She had no idea what he was talking about, or why he was wearing a tuxedo.

He turned away from her then and looked at Cara and Abby. "Good evening, ladies. Is there anything I can get for you this evening? A glass of wine, sparkling cider?"

What in the world?... Dumbstruck, all Sydney could do was stare.

"I'll have the cider, Abby will have the wine," Cara said smoothly.

He pulled an order form and pen out of his pocket and wrote it down. "Anything else? I made a lovely quiche tonight, with goat cheese and just a kiss of basil."

"Just the drinks for now." Cara casually picked up her menu and stared at it.

"Very good, then," he said in a most proper, stuffy waiter manner.

He turned away, headed for another table, when Sydney jumped up and tugged on his arm. "What do you think you're doing?" she growled between her teeth, though she had a smile frozen on her lips. He *had* gone crazy, she thought. Cara and Abby were right.

"Wasn't that the bet?" He looked at her with a puzzled expression in his green eyes. "I'm supposed to wear a tux, wait on tables and make quiche if I lost?"

The bet. He was owning up to losing. And *now,* of all times. "Reese, this isn't funny."

"We think it's hilarious," Cara muttered from behind

them, but Reese merely lifted a bored brow at her comment.

"I'm not trying to be funny," he said quietly, and gazed at her so intently she felt her chest tighten. "You should have won that game, Syd. I did cheat to teach you a lesson, and it got out of hand. I'm sorry. And now I'm holding up my end of the deal. What's right is right."

The determined look in his eyes told her that he wasn't going anywhere, and she hardly wanted to make a scene now. When he turned away from her again and moved to another table to take their order, she could only stare in disbelief.

Callan and Ian came in through the front door then and glanced at Reese. She noticed one corner of Ian's mouth twitch, but the men turned their attention to their wives, then joined them at their table.

This had to be one of those weird, doesn't-make-any-sense dreams, she decided. Nothing else could possibly explain the bizarre behavior going on around her. Certainly she'd wake up any minute, her heart racing, her palms sweating, gasping for breath.

Except she *was* awake, and her heart *was* racing, her palms sweating, her breathing labored.

She realized that everyone was looking at her, as if waiting for something to happen.

Well, she had a restaurant to run, she thought as she glanced at the kitchen and realized that it had been a long while since the door had opened and any orders had been brought out. Quite a long while, as a matter of fact. The last thing she needed was a problem in the kitchen. At the moment, she had more than she could handle out here.

She certainly didn't have time to stand around and

play this game with Reese, she fumed as she started toward the kitchen. If he wanted to wait on tables, fine. Let him wait on tables. But it wasn't going to change anything between them, not one thing at—

She stopped, then frowned when she pushed on the kitchen door and it didn't give. Wondering what else could go wrong tonight, she yanked the door open instead.

Roses.

Dozens and hundreds and *thousands* of roses of every color poured out from the kitchen. Startled, she stepped back, but lost her footing and went down on her bottom onto a soft blanket of petals and thornless stems.

When the river of roses stopped, she stared up at Reese, who stood over her, looking down.

Her eyes narrowed slowly. "You—you—" She grabbed a handful of roses and threw them at him. "You *are* crazy!"

"Certifiable." He knelt beside her, an amused grin on his face.

"Cara is right," she sputtered and threw another handful of flowers. "You should be committed."

"Okay." His grin faded. "I will if you will."

"Will what?" She blew a strand of hair out of her eyes, knew that everyone was looking at her.

"Be committed," he repeated. "To you, Syd. Only to you."

She stilled as he reached into his pocket and pulled out a black velvet box. His hand was as steady as his gaze as he handed it to her.

Her heart, which had stopped only a second before, now pounded furiously as she took the box. Her hands shook as she opened it.

A beautiful diamond solitaire sparkled on a shiny

gold band. The swelling in her chest made it impossible to speak.

"Will you marry me?" he asked in front of everyone there, including her staff, who'd all stopped in their work to come over and watch the show. Even Latona stood by, her chef's hat on, a spatula in her hand and her big brown eyes all dewy.

When Sydney didn't answer him, Reese felt his throat turn to dust. The thought that he might have lost her forever ripped at his insides. He was on shaky, unfamiliar ground here, and he could only let instinct and his heart guide him.

"I love everything about you, Syd," he said quietly. "The way your eyes light up when you smile, the sound of your laugh, your enthusiasm for life and for—" he paused, glanced around the room and thought he really shouldn't mention their lovemaking in front of all these people, especially her grandfather, who was staring very hard at him at the moment.

He swallowed hard and turned back to Sydney. "I even love that snobby little way you lift your nose at me when you think you know more than me."

"I do know more than you," she said, but there was no challenge in her words. She was still staring at the ring, her lips softly parted.

"Then you know I love you, that I need you more than my next breath," he said and took her hand in his, slipped the ring out of the box onto her finger. "Please marry me, Syd. Please."

The scent of roses filled the silent café. Reese held his breath; it seemed as if the entire room held its breath. She glanced up at him, stared with wide, tear-filled eyes.

"Yes," she whispered. "Yes, yes."

Her arms came around him as a cheer went up with the room. Whistling and clapping, silverware clinking against glasses. He scooped her up off the floor into his arms, kissed her deeply.

"Tell me you love me, too," he said against her lips. "I need to hear it."

Her arms tightened around his neck. "Of course I love you, you idiot."

He grinned at her. "Ah, the words every man longs to hear, other than, 'dinner's ready.'"

Smiling, she brought her lips to his. "I love you," she whispered. "It frightens me, I admit it, but I do love you. With all my heart."

Her words were like bubbles of champagne bursting in his chest. He'd never felt anything like this before, this *elated*. He wanted to laugh, go outside and dance in the snow, make love to her all night.

He kissed her again, thinking that a lifetime with this woman wouldn't be enough. He'd fought against his feelings for her from the first night she'd walked into the tavern, covered with mud, holding Boomer in her arms. He now realized he hadn't lost the battle, he'd won.

"We've got it covered here," Nell said, and the rest of Sydney's staff all nodded. "Why don't you two go celebrate?"

Applause went up from the room again. Reese looked at Sydney, who smiled, then nodded. Amidst more cheers and applause, Reese carried her outside, then up the back stairway that led to her apartment.

When he had her inside, alone, he set her down and drew her into a kiss. Long and slow, he tasted the sweetness of her, knew that she was what he wanted. What he would always want.

"You know that by tomorrow, the whole town will

be talking about you and me,'' he murmured between kisses.

''Let them talk.'' She eased back, looked up into his eyes. The love he saw in her steady gaze took his breath away. ''As long as you love me, nothing can ever hurt me again.''

When she touched his cheek, he turned his head and kissed the palm of her hand, smiled when he felt her shiver.

''So tell me how you got all those roses in there without me knowing?'' she whispered, her voice breathless.

''It's a secret.'' He pulled her closer, loved the feel of her heart against his. ''Maybe in fifty or sixty years, I'll tell you.''

Smiling, she stepped out of his arms and backed toward the bedroom. ''I'll bet I could get you to tell me now.''

''Sweetheart,'' he said with a grin and followed, knowing that life with Sydney would never be dull, ''that's definitely a bet I'd lose.''

*   *   *   *   *

THE TEMPTATION OF
RORY MONAHAN

by
Elizabeth Bevarly

ELIZABETH BEVARLY

is an honours graduate of the University of Louisville and achieved her dream of writing full-time before she even turned thirty! At heart, she is also an avid traveller who once helped navigate a friend's thirty-five-foot yacht across the Bermuda Triangle. Her dream is to one day have her own yacht, a beautifully renovated older-model forty-two-footer, and to enjoy the freedom and tranquillity sea-faring can bring. Elizabeth likes to think she has a lot in common with the characters she creates, people who know love and life go hand in hand. And she's getting some first-hand experience with motherhood as well—she and her husband have a six-year-old son, Eli.

For all the wonderful librarians who made the library
a truly magical place for me when I was a kid.
And for all the ones who keep it magic
for me as an adult.
Thank you all so much.

One

Miriam Thornbury was testing a new Internet filter for the computers in the Marigold Free Public Library when she came across hotwetbabes.com.

She experienced a momentary exhilaration in her triumph at, once again, foiling a filter system—score one for the anticensorship campaign—but alas, her victory was short-lived. Because in that second moment she saw what, precisely, the Web site claimed as its content.

And she began to think that maybe, just maybe, censorship might have its uses.

Oh, dear, she thought further, alarmed. What was the world coming to when librarians began to advocate such a thing as censorship? What on earth was she thinking?

Of course Miriam knew librarians who did, in fact, support censorship. Well, maybe she didn't quite *know* any; not personally, at any rate. She was, after all, one of only two full-time librarians in all of Marigold, Indiana, and

Douglas Amberson, the senior librarian, was as vehemently opposed to censorship as she was herself.

But she knew of colleagues like that out there in the world, few though they may be, fortunately. Librarians who thought they knew what was best for their patrons and therefore took it upon themselves to spare the poor, ignorant reading public the trouble of weeding through all the icky things in life, by doing the literary gardening—so to speak—themselves.

· Worse, Miriam knew mayors like that. Mayors of towns like, oh, say…Marigold, Indiana, for example. Which was why she was sitting in her office at the library on a sunny July afternoon, trying to find an Internet filter that would effectively screen out things like, oh, say…hotwetbabes.com.

It was a task Miriam had undertaken with mixed feelings. Although she by no means approved of some sites on the Net, sites such as, oh, say…this one, she had a hard time submitting to anyone who deemed him—or herself so superior to the masses that he or she would presume to dictate what was suitable reading and viewing material for those masses. Anyone like, oh, say…Isabel Trent, Marigold's mayor.

Miriam glanced down at the computer screen again and bit back a wince. Hotwetbabes.com, however, did rather give one pause. All those half-naked, glistening female bodies right there on the Internet, for anyone to stumble across. That couldn't possibly be a good thing, could it? Especially since these particular half-naked, glistening female bodies were so inconsistent with what real women looked like, even wet.

Inescapably, Miriam glanced down at her own midsection, well hidden—and quite dry, thank you very much—beneath her standard librarian uniform of crisply ironed cotton blouse—in this case, white—over crisply ironed straight skirt—in this case, beige. Then, inevitably, she glanced back up at the screen. Not only was her midsection sadly lacking when compared to these women, but the rest of her suffered mightily, too.

Where the women on the computer screen had wildly billowing tresses—even wet, they billowed, she noted morosely—in hues of gold and copper and ebony, her own boring blond hair—dishwater, her mother had always called it—was clipped back at her nape with a simple barrette, performing no significant billowing to speak of. And instead of heavily lined, mascaraed eyes of exotic color, Miriam's were gray and completely unadorned.

No, the women on this particular Web site certainly were not what one might call usual, she thought with a sigh. Nor were they what one might call realistic. Of course, she reminded herself, the site *was* called hotwetbabes.com, so she supposed she shouldn't be surprised to find all those photos of, well, hot, wet babes. Still, she did wish *some*one would try to impose *some* measure of…of…of *accuracy* on existing Internet businesses.

There. That wasn't advocating censorship, was it? Who in his or her right mind would object to accuracy, after all? Accuracy was a very good thing. The world needed more accuracy. And in Miriam's opinion, it was high time the Internet became more accurate.

Yes, indeed.

She positioned the mouse to close the program with a convenient click—clearly this filter *wasn't* the one the Marigold Free Public Library would be using, if sites such as these found their way through—but her hand, and therefore the mouse, must have just missed the mark. Because she accidentally—and she was absolutely certain it was indeed an accident—clicked instead on an announcement. An announcement which read, of all things, *Visit our brother site! Hotwetbods.com!* And before she had a chance to correct her mistake—drat these fast new modems, anyway—a different screen opened up. And she suddenly found herself looking at—

Oh, my.

More half-naked, glistening bodies appeared on the screen, only this time they weren't female bodies. And this time they weren't naked from the waist up. Instead they were—

Oh, dear.

"Ah. Miss Thornbury, there you are."

Oh, no.

The only thing that could have possibly made Miriam's current state of abject embarrassment any more complete would have been to be discovered by a second party while she was gazing—however involuntarily—at hot, wet bods on the Internet. Even worse—which one might have thought would be impossible, all things considered—the second party in question was none other than Professor Rory Monahan, one of Marigold's most upright, forthright, do-right citizens.

And also one of Marigold's cutest citizens.

And one of the most eligible, too.

Not that Miriam was necessarily in the market for an eligible man. But she was only human, after all. And she did rather like cute ones. In fact, she rather liked Professor Rory Monahan. But everyone in Marigold—even a newcomer like Miriam—knew that Professor Monahan was far too involved in his scholarly pursuits to ever show an interest in anything, or any*one,* else.

More was the pity. Because Miriam would have very much liked to pique his interest. Though, she had to admit, not while she was gazing at half-naked men on the Internet. It could, after all, only lead to trouble.

Guiltily, she shot up from her chair and positioned herself in front of the computer monitor, just as Professor Monahan strode through the door to her office. He looked even cuter than usual, she noted—and even more eligible, drat him—with his round, wire-rimmed glasses enhancing his pale-blue eyes, and his black hair tousled, as if he'd run restless fingers through it as he perused *The Encyclopaedia Britannica* with wild abandon. He was dressed in a pair of dark-brown, baggy trousers, a cream-colored dress shirt with sleeves rolled back over surprisingly muscular forearms—no doubt from carrying around all those heavy tomes, she thought—and a much too outdated, and not particularly attractive, necktie.

All in all, he looked adorably rumpled and delightfully disheveled. He was the kind of man a woman like her just wanted to take home with her at night and…and…and…

And *feed,* she realized with much annoyance. Because truly, that was what she wanted to do, every time she saw Rory Monahan. She wanted to take him home and *cook* for him, for heaven's sake, then present him with a homemade pie for dessert. And Miriam wasn't even a *good* cook. She was an even worse baker. Nevertheless, after she'd plied him with her dubious culinary creations, she wanted to linger over coffee with him, then take a walk through the neighborhood with him—hand in hand, of course—then pop microwave popcorn with him, and then watch a rented copy of an old romantic comedy like *The Thin Man* or something with him.

In fact, what Miriam wanted to do with Professor Monahan was so sweet and so quiet and so harmless, it scared the bejabbers out of her. The last thing she needed in her life was more sweetness, more quietness, more harmlessness. She was already the safest, most predictable, most boring woman on the planet.

If she was going to dally with a man, not that she had *any* intention of dallying with *any* man—even Rory Monahan, honest—then, she told herself, she should at least have the decency to seek out someone who was dangerous and thrilling and outrageous, someone who might, possibly, stir dangerous, thrilling, outrageous responses in her. Because she was truly beginning to worry that she wasn't capable of a single dangerous, thrilling, outrageous response.

Worse, her desire to pursue such sweet, quiet, harmless activities with Professor Monahan smacked much too much of domesticity, of settling down, of matrimony. Not that Miriam had anything against matrimony. *Au contraire*. She fully planned to marry and settle down and be domestic someday. Someday, she hoped, in the not too distant future.

But she wouldn't be settling down and being domestic with Rory Monahan, alas. Because Rory Monahan was, quite simply, already married—to his work as a history professor at the local community college and to his studies and to his research and to his quest for knowledge. When it came to women, he had the attention span of a slide rule. In the six months that Miriam had lived in Marigold, she had never once seen him out on a single date with a woman.

Then again, she herself hadn't been out on a single date with a man since she'd moved to Marigold, had she? And what was her excuse? She certainly had a longer attention span than a slide rule. And she had been asked out on a few occasions. She just hadn't accepted that was all. And she hadn't accepted, because she hadn't been interested in the men who'd asked her out. And she hadn't been interested in the men who'd asked her out because...because...because... She gazed at Professor Monahan and tried not to sigh with melodramatic yearning. Well, just *because*. That was why. And it was a perfectly good reason, too.

So there.

"Miss Thornbury," Professor Monahan said again now, taking a step forward.

Recalling what was on the screen behind her, Miriam shifted her position to the right a bit, to compensate for the angle at which he had placed his own bod. Uh, body, she hastily corrected herself.

"Yes, Professor Monahan? Can I help you?" she asked, innocently, she hoped. Because the thoughts suddenly parading through her head were anything *but* innocent. No, they were more of the hot, wet variety.

"I'm in a bit of a bind," he told her, "and I suspect that you're the only one who can help me out."

Well, that sounded kind of promising, Miriam thought. "Oh?" she asked.

He nodded. "I've looked high and low for volume fifteen of *Stegman's Guide to the Peloponnesian War,* but I can't locate it anywhere. And if there's one person who knows this library backward and forward..." He hesitated, arrowing his dark brows down in consternation—and looking quite adorable when he did so, Miriam couldn't help but notice. "Well, I suppose it would be Mr. Amberson, actually," he said. "But he's not here right now, and I know you're familiar with the system, too, and I was wondering if you could help me."

Well, she *could*, Miriam thought. It was, after all, her job. Not to mention it would offer her the opportunity to be close to Professor Monahan, and she could see if he smelled as wonderful today as he usually did, of that tantalizing mix of Ivory soap and Old Spice aftershave—he really was so adorable. But that would mean moving away from the computer monitor, and that would leave him looking at what she had just been looking at—namely, hot, wet bods—and that wouldn't be a good thing at all, would it?

So she did the only thing she could do. She pointed frantically toward the door behind him and shouted, "Oh, look! Isn't that the Artist Formerly Known as Prince?"

And when Professor Monahan spun around to see if it was, she hastily turned and, even more hastily, clicked the mouse to shrink the screen. Which left visible on the monitor nothing but the "Great Metaphysical Philosophers of the Eighteenth Century" wallpaper that she'd downloaded herself earlier that morning.

When she straightened again, it was to find that Professor Monahan was still craning his neck to gaze out the office door, toward the circulation desk. "I don't see any artist," he said. "Or any prince, for that matter." He turned back to face Miriam, his expression puzzled. "In fact, I don't recall any prince who *is* an artist. Not in this century, at any rate." He brightened. "Now, during the Renaissance, you had any number of—"

"Professor Monahan?" Miriam interjected lightly. She'd seen before how his scholarly tangents could go on for a long, long time, and she knew she had to nip this one in the bud, or else she'd never have time to complete all the work she had on her agenda today.

"Yes, Miss Thornbury?" he asked.

"Volume fifteen of *Stegman's Guide to the Peloponnesian War,* wasn't that what you wanted?"

He appeared bewildered again for a moment, as if he couldn't quite remember who or where he was. Then, suddenly, his expression cleared, and he smiled. "Why, yes.

That's exactly what I was looking for. How did you know?''

She smiled back. "You just told me."

"Ah. I see. Well."

He blushed at his display of absentminded professorship, and Miriam's heart did a funny little flip-flop in her chest. Oh, he was just too adorable for words.

"Do you know where it is?" he asked.

"As a matter of fact, I do," she told him. "I guess it's true that great minds think alike. Because as providence would have it, I was reading it myself over lunch earlier." She turned again, this time hefting the fat, leather-bound book from her desk. Then she spun back around to stride toward him. "I always like learning about new things," she said as she went. "And I found the fifth chapter in particular to be quite interesting."

Professor Monahan grinned a bit shyly as he adjusted his glasses. "I know," he told her. "I've read it three or four times myself. It's quite outstanding. Thank you, Miss Thornbury," he added as he took the book from her.

Somehow, though, during the exchange—and Miriam had no idea how it happened, truly—their fingers became entangled, and as they vied for possession, the book went spilling to the floor. It landed on its back with a loud *thwack*, and both she and Professor Monahan stooped at the same time to pick it up. But as each of them reached for it—and Miriam had no idea how it happened, truly—their fingers wove awkwardly together again, and before she knew it, her hand was linked completely with his, and a dangerous, outrageous thrill was dashing through her body.

And all she could do was think that if this was the reaction she had to simply holding hands with the man, then what would happen to her if the two of them joined more intimately?

And then all she could do was blush—furiously. Because she glanced up to find that Professor Monahan's light-blue eyes seemed warmer somehow, and his cheeks were flushed with what *might* be embarrassment, but which could very well be something else entirely. His expression suggested that his own reaction to their light touch was none too sweet. Nor did it seem quiet. Nor did it seem harmless.

Oh, dear.

Immediately Miriam let go of both the book and Professor Monahan's hand, then she pushed herself quickly back to standing. She tucked behind her ear a stray strand of blond hair that had escaped her barrette and did everything she could to avoid his gaze. She realized quickly, though, that such an effort was unnecessary. Because no sooner had she stood than Professor Monahan bolted. Right through the office door, out to the circulation desk, with a *very* hasty, "Good day, Miss Thornbury, and thank you again," tossed over his shoulder.

And then Miriam was left feeling oddly dazed and disoriented, as if someone had just— What was the phrase they used in historical romances? She tried to remember. (Well, one couldn't exist on a steady diet of *Stegman's Guide to the Peloponnesian War,* could one?) Ah, yes. Now she recalled the phrase. She felt as if someone had just...tumbled her. Quite thoroughly, too. It was an odd sensation. But not altogether unpleasant.

No, not unpleasant at all.

She smiled what was almost certainly a wicked smile. She was almost certain of that, because she *felt* wicked at the moment. And speaking of wicked...

She remembered then that there was still a window

open on the computer screen which she very much needed to close. She returned to her desk and had just brought the screen back up, when she was interrupted yet again in her effort to get rid of the, um, hot…wet…bods.

"Miriam, I need a word with you right away," Isabel Trent, Marigold's mayor, said as she entered.

Hastily Miriam spun back around, positioning herself in much the same way she had done earlier, when she'd been trying to spare Professor Monahan's tender sensibilities. Because Ms. Trent's tender sensibilities would go absolutely ballistic if the mayor saw what the town librarian had been inspecting prior to her arrival, even if the mayor was the one who was responsible for the town librarian's finding it in the first place.

"Yes, Ms. Trent? Can I help you?" Miriam asked innocently, feeling a wave of déjà vu.

"It's of utmost importance," the mayor told her.

Of course, *everything* was of utmost importance to Isabel Trent, Miriam thought with a sigh. Nevertheless she adopted her expression of utmost gravity as she replied, "Oh? I'm all ears."

Ms. Trent, too, wore a standard uniform for her job, Miriam had noted some time ago, a uniform of tightly buttoned, very conservative suits. Today's selection was dark-blue in color—almost the same dark-blue as her eyes—but it was as closely bound as all the others. Her spun-gold hair was closely bound, too, wound up in a terse knot at the back of her head. Huge, tortoiseshell glasses were perched on the bridge of her nose, giving the mayor the appearance of someone trying to hide from something. Like the world, for instance.

Honestly, Miriam thought, lifting a hand to her own dishwater—drat it—ponytail. Isabel Trent was an even blander-looking person than Miriam was herself. And that was saying something.

"It's about all those copies of *Metropolitan* magazine scattered about in Periodicals," the mayor said.

Miriam nodded. "Those are checked out and read very frequently. I apologize if there's a mess. I'll have someone tidy them right away."

Ms. Trent straightened to her full—and very militant—five feet four inches. "No, you'll have someone get *rid* of them right away."

Miriam's dishwater-blond eyebrows—drat them—shot up beneath her dishwater-blond—drat them, too—bangs. "I beg your pardon?" she asked.

"I said you'll get rid of them," the mayor echoed. "Completely. Cancel the library's subscription."

"But...but why?" Miriam asked. "As I said, *Metropolitan* is one of the library's most popular periodicals."

"Yes, well, it's also one of the library's most unacceptable periodicals."

"Unacceptable? In what way?"

"Don't tell me you haven't noticed some of those headlines that appear on the cover of the magazine," the mayor stated in a cool, clipped tone.

"Well, no, I haven't," Miriam said honestly. "I don't read *Metropolitan* myself." She braved a halfhearted smile. "I'm not much of a *Metro* Girl, I'm afraid."

"Well, I should hope not," Ms. Trent said. "That magazine is about nothing but sex, sex, sex."

Which went a long way toward explaining why Miriam never read it, she thought, and why she wasn't much of a *Metro* Girl. Sex, sex, sex wasn't exactly a big part of her life, life, life. Or *any* part of her life, for that matter. Not her real life, anyway. As for her fantasy life, well...

There *were* those occasional daydreams in which she

indulged, daydreams about herself and Professor Rory Monahan, even though his preference for the reference section of the library far outweighed his interest in the librarian herself. In fact, the reference section of the library also played a significant role in Miriam's daydreams, come to think of it. More significantly, the tables in the reference section played into her daydreams. Because it was on one of those tables in the reference section that she and Professor Monahan were invariably engaged in—

Oh, dear. She was doing it again. Or, rather, fantasizing it again. *Doing it,* after all, didn't actually show up on her agenda anywhere—more was the pity. Why schedule something that wasn't going to happen?

"And on top of all that…" she heard Ms. Trent say, clearly concluding what had been a long diatribe against the mass media that Miriam had thankfully missed because she'd been too busy daydreaming about—oh, never mind. "…those women who appear on the cover of *Metropolitan* are, quite simply—" Instead of voicing a word to illustrate her feelings, the mayor made quite the sour face. "Suffice it to say," she then continued, "that *Metropolitan* is completely inappropriate reading material for our library. As are these other magazines that I want you to remove from the periodical section."

The mayor strode forward, pausing within arm's length of Miriam, and extended a hand-written list, which Miriam accepted in silence—mainly because she was so surprised by the gesture that she didn't know what to say. She was even more surprised when she glanced down at the list to find that some of the other journals and magazines that Ms. Trent deemed inappropriate for the library patrons were, like *Metropolitan,* wildly popular with the library patrons.

Evidently mistaking Miriam's stunned silence for complete agreement, the mayor hurried on to her next point. "There are some novels in the browsing section that I'd like to see removed, as well," she said. "*Love's Burning Ecstasy,* for instance…" Her voice trailed off, but its tone held enough chilly disapproval to generate a new Ice Age.

"But *Love's Burning Ecstasy…*" Miriam began.

"Don't tell me *it's* popular with the library patrons," Ms. Trent said, clearly incredulous.

"Well, no," Miriam conceded reluctantly. *Not with the library patrons, necessarily,* she added silently to herself. But Miriam had enjoyed it immensely. Several times, in fact.

"I want it gone," Ms. Trent concluded simply. "Along with these others."

She extended another list toward Miriam, who took it automatically, still having no idea what to say with regard to this blatant attack of censorship.

"And I want to make a more thorough inspection of the British literature section, too," the mayor continued. "It was purely by chance that I stumbled upon *this.*" She held up a slender, bound tome as if it were exhibit A and continued, "I'm shocked to find something entitled *The Rape of the Lock* in our facility. I don't think it's at all appropriate. Do you, Miriam?"

For a moment all Miriam was able to manage in response to the mayor's question was a series of quick, incoherent—and none too polite—expulsions of air. But she quickly recovered enough to say, "*The Rape of the Lock* is a virtuoso piece of writing, Ms. Trent, arguably Alexander Pope's crowning achievement."

The mayor gaped at her. "A man named *Pope* wrote that piece of trash?" she gasped. "I can hardly believe it."

This time Miriam was the one to gape. "Piece of *trash?*" she sputtered. "It's one of the poet's most luminous performances!"

She took a giant step forward to snatch the book from the mayor's hand and to read her a few verses, because clearly Ms. Trent had not taken the time to do that herself. Otherwise she would have realized the work was a social satire of completely inoffensive—and quite riotous—humor. Unfortunately, Miriam never achieved her goal, because she had barely completed her giant step when Ms. Trent's face went white, and the book slipped right out of her fingers.

"Good heavens, Miriam," the mayor cried in a hoarse whisper. "*What* is *that?*"

Miriam squeezed her eyes shut tight when she remembered what had been displayed on her computer screen when Isabel Trent entered her office. Unable to quite help herself, however—the mayor was such a…such a…such a *prude*—Miriam pretended not to be affected by the scene herself. Feigning bland indifference to the subject matter of hotwetbods.com, she glanced swiftly, once, over her shoulder, then back at Ms. Trent.

"Actually, seeing as how there are considerably more than one displayed there, I believe the correct phrasing of your question should be, '*What* are *those?*' And really I'm rather surprised you have to ask, Ms. Trent. But if you must know, the correct term for them is peni—"

"*Shhhh!*" the mayor shushed her before Miriam could fully pronounce the word. "Don't say it." She narrowed her eyes. "And don't mock me, either, Miriam. You haven't been working for the Marigold Free Public Library very long. You are by no means inexpendable."

Miriam narrowed her eyes right back at the mayor, but said nothing in response. It was true that her job wasn't exactly secure. She'd only moved to Marigold six months ago, specifically to accept the position. Douglas Amberson was senior librarian, even though Miriam was assigned the most hours and completed the most work. And although there was an unspoken agreement between her and Douglas that when he retired next spring, she would move directly into his position, Douglas and Miriam were, unfortunately, the only two people in Marigold who knew about that agreement. And the mayor of Marigold had the authority to accept or reject Douglas's recommendation for his replacement, when that time arose.

So, for now, Miriam remained silent and waited to see what Isabel Trent was going to object to next.

"I see our latest attempt at finding an effective Internet filter has failed. Again," the mayor said.

"This one won't meet with your approval, no," Miriam agreed. "But truly, Ms. Trent, I don't think it's necessary for us to use filters in the library. It is a form of censorship, you know."

Ms. Trent gave her an icy glare. "And your point would be?"

"That since the computers in the children's and young adults' sections aren't hooked up to the Internet," Miriam said, "then a filter isn't necessary. The people who use the Internet at the library are adults, Ms. Trent. They don't need policing."

"Of course they need policing," the mayor immediately countered.

"Why?"

Ms. Trent waved awkwardly at the sight on Miriam's computer screen, but at no time did she steer her gaze in that direction. "So that they don't find themselves looking at something like *that*."

Miriam sighed. "Ms. Trent, it's none of our business

if they find themselves looking at something like that,'' she said softly.

''It is if they're using computers purchased with the taxpayers' dollars.''

Miriam wasn't sure how to reply to that, mainly because she knew Isabel Trent had already made up her mind that the Marigold Free Public Library *would* be using a filter system, and there would be no reasoning or arguing with her on that score. And, truth be told, having viewed the contents of hotwetbabes-and-bods.com, Miriam was hard-pressed to launch much of a defense, anyway.

''At any rate,'' she finally conceded, ''this particular filter isn't effective in the way you demand that it be effective.''

Isabel Trent lifted her chin a fraction. ''Well then, try the next one on the list.''

Miriam inhaled a deep breath and expelled it slowly. ''Whatever you say, Ms. Trent.''

In one swift, graceful gesture, the mayor scooped up the book she had dropped on the floor and tossed it onto Miriam's desk. Then, averting her gaze, she felt around awkwardly until she found the button to switch off the computer monitor. Miriam bit her lip to prevent herself from pointing out that, in her effort to avoid seeing all those male members on the monitor, Ms. Trent brushed her fingers inadvertently over quite a few of them in her pursuit of the power button.

After finally succeeding in switching the monitor off, the mayor spun back around. ''I'm going to start inspecting the children's section this weekend,'' she said starchily. ''I'll make a list of everything I want removed from there.''

Once again, Miriam gaped. ''But that's—''

"Don't argue with me, Miriam," the mayor interrupted. "I have the approval of the majority of members on the board of aldermen behind me on this. I want this library to be a facility where families can feel comfortable."

Miriam chose her words carefully. "Families have felt comfortable in this facility for more than a hundred years, Ms. Trent. The Marigold Free Public Library can take care of itself. And so can all the Marigoldians who use it. They don't need someone else telling them what they are and are not allowed access to."

She might as well have been talking to a brick wall, because the mayor offered no indication that she'd heard a word of Miriam's admonishment. "Keep looking for an effective filter," Ms. Trent said. "And get rid of those magazines on the list I gave you. Today. When I come back this weekend, I want to see that this library reflects the decency and family values of all who use it."

And without awaiting a reply, the mayor of Marigold, Indiana, spun on her heel and exited the office. Miriam watched her go with a sinking heart. It wasn't the decency and family values of the library patrons that Isabel Trent wanted reflected here, she thought. No, what Isabel Trent wanted the library to reflect was the decency and family values of Isabel Trent. Period.

Miriam decided to take the matter up with Douglas when he returned from his vacation the following week, but for now she had no choice but to do as the mayor had instructed. She glanced down at the list of periodicals she still held in her hands and shook her head with much disappointment. It appeared her afternoon was going to be quite full now, what with all the censoring and blacklisting she had to do.

My, my, my, she thought. A librarian's work was never done. With a sigh of defeat Miriam went to work.

TWO

Rory Monahan was, as usual, far too absorbed in his work to notice that the library was closing—until he was plunged into almost total darkness. He sighed as he glanced up at the extinguished lights overhead and waited for his vision to adjust. Then he carefully inserted an index card to mark his place in the heavy tome he'd opened on the table before him, and flipped it closed. Damn. Just when he'd found exactly what he'd been looking for, too.

But Rory didn't mind leaving his work where it lay. It would be here waiting for him tomorrow afternoon when he returned, as he invariably would. He was confident that no one would come along and reshelve all the work and trouble he'd gone to tonight, because the table at which he sat was, unofficially, Professor Monahan's domain. Everyone who worked in the Marigold Free Public Library, from Mr. Amberson, the head librarian, right down to Gladys Dorfman, who cleaned up after hours, knew not to touch a thing on this particular table.

After settling his wire-rimmed glasses back on the bridge of his nose, Rory launched himself momentarily into a full-body stretch. Upon completing it, he shoved a restless hand through his black hair, noting, without much surprise, that he was long overdue for a trim. He made a halfhearted—and only partly successful—effort to straighten the knot in his tie but didn't bother rolling the cuffs of his shirt back down to his wrists. He collected his tweed jacket—which was really much too warm for July, but Rory couldn't imagine going anywhere without it—then scooped up his notes and filed them meticulously in his leather satchel. Then he neatly stacked, in volume order, all the reference books he'd used that evening, and he rose to make his way out.

He was confident that whichever librarian was on duty, either Mr. Amberson or Miss Thornbury—though, for some reason, he was thinking Miss Thornbury was working today, but he couldn't remember now just *how* he knew that—would be waiting for him by the main exit, just as he or she was always inevitably waiting for Rory by the main exit when they were closing the library. Whichever librarian it was would greet him warmly, ask him how his research was going, accompany him through the front door and lock up behind them.

It was, after all, a routine. And routine was a very good thing, as far as Rory Monahan was concerned. Routine was exactly the way he liked things. Well planned. Predictable. Secure. Safe. Life, to his way of thinking, was good.

It got even better when he saw that it was indeed Miss Thornbury waiting by the doors this particular evening, and Rory recalled then why he had known it would be her. They'd had an interlude of sorts in her office that afternoon, hadn't they? The details of that interlude escaped him now, swamped as they had been over the last several hours by great, hulking chunks of *Stegman's Guide to the Peloponnesian War*. But for some reason, he recalled the interlude with a feeling of fondness. In fact, for some reason, he recalled it with a warm flutter of something rather intense skipping through his midsection, a warm flutter of something that felt very much like… desire?

Oh, surely not.

Ah, well. No matter, Rory thought. All that mattered was that his mind had retained the important things, the details he'd garnered and analyzed and recorded from numerous volumes of *Stegman's*.

As he drew nearer Miss Thornbury, though, those details began to fade a bit, and something warm and easy and indolent wound through him. Involuntarily, Rory smiled. She always had that effect on him for some reason, every time he saw her. He had no idea why. But invariably, when he encountered her, something that had previously felt off-kilter seemed to shift right into place.

Not that Rory felt as if anything in his life was currently off-kilter. On the contrary, everything was going surprisingly well. But Miss Thornbury had a way about her, a way of making a person feel…right. Steady. Complete. And somehow, whenever he saw that it was Miss Thornbury standing there waiting for him at night, the discovery was infinitely more appealing to Rory than finding Mr. Amberson there instead.

Not that he didn't like Mr. Amberson. On the contrary, Mr. Amberson had been one of Rory's idols since he was a child. The man knew virtually *everything*. What few things the elder librarian wasn't entirely sure about, he knew exactly where in the library to look, to discover the answers. And because Rory had always craved knowledge above all else, even as a child, Douglas Amberson had always seemed something of a god to him. Rory had admired and respected the older man that much—certainly above everyone else in Marigold.

Which, he supposed, meant that he should see Miss Thornbury as something of a god*dess*. Because she, too, was well read, well educated, well spoken, well everything. She, too, was utterly familiar with the library and knew exactly where to find anything, even having worked there for such a short time. He admired and respected her as much as he did Mr. Amberson. For some reason, though, her distinction as *goddess* carried a significantly different connotation than Mr. Amberson's status as *god*. Yes, Miss Thornbury was every bit as smart as Mr. Amberson, but for some reason the feelings she roused in him went well beyond admiration and respect. Rory just wasn't quite able to identify exactly what those "beyond" feelings were.

Furthermore, for some reason when he thought of Miss Thornbury as a goddess, it always evoked a mental image of her wearing some flowing, gossamer—really almost translucent—gown, the kind that dropped off one shoulder and dipped low over lush breasts, draping seductively against an elegant waist, with the side slit high enough so that one firm, naked, creamy thigh was exposed, and—

Ahem.

Where was he?

Oh, yes. The translucent, goddess-like garment. Rory *never* envisioned Mr. Amberson in something like that when he thought about him as a god. It was something of a paradox, really.

Tonight, however, Miss Thornbury's translucent garment was nowhere to be seen, something about which, Rory discovered, he had mixed feelings. Still, her smart white blouse and straight beige skirt were practical and not unattractive, even if there was nothing even remotely goddess-like about the attire. Coupled with the dark-blond hair caught at her nape and the deep-gray eyes unadorned with cosmetics, she was by no means a remarkable-looking woman. But her mouth was rather good, he noted, not for the first time, wide and full and lush, and the sight of it now roused deep inside him something hot and wanton and demanding and—

Ahem.

Where was he?

Oh, yes. He was leaving the library to go home. Alone. Where there wouldn't be anyone with a full, lush mouth, dressed as a goddess, waiting for him.

"Good evening, Professor Monahan," Miss Thornbury greeted him warmly at his approach.

"Hello, Miss Thornbury," he replied, as was his custom.

"How's the research going?"

"Very well, thank you."

As was likewise the custom, they chitchatted as they passed through the main entrance—evidently she'd forgotten the details of their earlier interlude, too, because she made no reference to it at all as they spoke—and then she locked the doors behind them. As was not customary, however, she juggled a large, unwieldy box under one arm as she performed her nightly routine. Rory was about to offer her some assistance when the box pitched forward, dumping its entire contents onto the walkway just outside the entrance. An assortment of glossy magazines fanned out between the two of them, and immediately he stooped to help her pick them up.

"I didn't realize you were such a fan of *Metropolitan*," he said when he noted what the majority of the magazines was.

Somehow, Miss Thornbury just didn't seem the *Metro* Girl type, even with the translucent gown thing going. On the contrary, the models depicted on the covers of *Metropolitan* were much more scantily dressed than even his goddess-vision of Miss Thornbury, and they wore cosmetics that had evidently been applied with trowels and other such garden implements. But even at that, not a single one of them had a mouth that was as lush and as ripe and as erotic and as hot and as—

Ahem.

Where was he?

Oh, yes. None of them had a mouth that could compare with Miss Thornbury's.

She expelled an exasperated sound as she, too, dropped to her knees to join him in gathering up the scattered periodicals. "I'm not such a fan of *Metropolitan*," she said, sounding a bit breathless for some reason, though what that reason might be, Rory could scarcely imagine. "But our illustrious mayor," she continued, "has decided these are inappropriate for the library, and she's ordered them removed."

Rory nodded, finding the revelation not at all surprising. "I did get the impression upon meeting Ms. Trent that she was something of a...of a...a, um..."

"A prude?" Miss Thornbury offered helpfully—and not a little acerbically.

Rory smiled. "Well, yes, I suppose that would be a suitable enough word for her."

"Mmm," the librarian murmured. "I can think of a few others for her, as well. Ultraconservative. Right winger. Dictator. Fascist."

Rory chuckled. He'd never seen Miss Thornbury so passionate about something. And now that he did see her so passionate…

Well, he hastily decided that it might be best not to dwell upon it.

"I think Ms. Trent is just trying to make a good impression on the community," he said instead. "She is, after all, Marigold's first woman mayor. And she's also the youngest mayor we've ever had. And she did run on the family-values platform."

"I don't think it has anything to do with making a good impression, or even family values," Miss Thornbury said. "I think it has to do with her being completely terrified of her own sexuality."

Miss Thornbury reached forward for a magazine at the same time Rory laid his own hand on it, and in the ensuing volleying for possession, their fingers somehow tangled together. That scant physical contact, coupled with hearing the word *sexuality* emanating from Miss Thornbury's luscious lips, made something go tight and hot and urgent inside Rory. And suddenly he remembered very well the details of their earlier interlude. He remembered, because that same tight, hot, urgent sensation had shot through him then, too, the moment his hand had touched hers.

Good God, he thought as the sensation shook him for a second time. What on earth *was* that?

He glanced up at the same time Miss Thornbury did, only to find her blushing. And somehow he knew—he just *knew*—it was because she had experienced a similar reaction herself. How very, very odd.

And how very, very interesting.

"I am so sorry I said that," she apologized, her cheeks going even pinker. He couldn't help but note, however, that she did nothing to untangle their fingers. "I spoke out of turn," she added quickly, huskily. "I never should have said such a thing about Ms. Trent. I don't know what I was thinking."

Well, clearly, Rory thought, she'd been thinking about sexuality. The mayor's, if not her own. Though how one could think about someone else's sexuality without at least giving one's own some little consideration was beyond him. Not that he himself spent any gratuitous amount of time thinking about anyone's sexuality, he quickly reminded himself, but on those few occasions when he did, he could never think about someone else's sexuality without allowing his own a quick run. Which meant that at the moment he was pondering not just the mayor's sexuality but his own sexuality, too, and also, since she was the one who brought it up in the first place—if one could pardon the incredibly tacky pun—Miss Thornbury's sexuality, as well.

And that brought him right back to the translucent goddess gown again, only this time it was infinitely more translucent than it had ever been before, and it was dropping far too seductively off one shoulder, and it was dipping dangerously low over her lush breasts, and as for that one firm, naked, creamy thigh, well—

Ahem.

Where was he?

Oh, yes. Miss Thornbury's sexuality. *No!* His own sexuality. *No, not that, either!* The mayor's sexuality. Ah, yes. That was something he could think about safely. Essentially because Isabel Trent, as far as Rory was concerned, anyway, had no sexuality to speak of. And still Miss Thornbury had not freed her hand from his, and somehow Rory found himself reluctant to perform the task himself.

"I...I...I..." Miss Thornbury stammered. But she seemed not to know what else to add, so she clamped her mouth shut tight.

Which was a shame, Rory thought, because in doing so, she ruined the sensual line of those full, ripe, rosy lips, lips that just begged for a man to dip his head to hers and cover her mouth with his and taste her deeply, wantonly, demandingly—

And good *God*, where was his head this evening?

Quickly Rory released her hand and surrendered the magazine to her—but not before he caught a headline that screamed, Love Your Man Orally TONIGHT! which just brought back that translucent-gown thing yet again and, worse, the ripe, luscious-mouth thing again, both with much more troubling explicitness than ever before.

"I really must be going," he said suddenly, rocketing to his feet. "I have to get home and prepare an oral sex— I mean an oral sexam, uh...oral *exam*—for my students tomorrow."

And before Rory could further humiliate himself, he spun on his heel and fled.

Miriam carefully sipped her hot Sleepytime tea, snuggled more deeply into the cool, cotton pillows she had stacked between her and her headboard, listened to the soothing strains of Mozart that drifted from the stereo...and squirmed a bit on the mattress as she read about loving her man orally TONIGHT! Honestly. The things they printed in magazines these days. She'd seen college girls reading *Metropolitan* magazine and hadn't thought a thing about it. Now...

Well, now Miriam was thinking that the girls growing up in Marigold today knew a lot more about things than she'd known as a girl growing up in Indianapolis. So much for big-city sophistication.

She sipped her tea again and closed the magazine—after finishing the article, of course, because librarians never left an article unfinished—then she arced her gaze over the other issues of *Metropolitan* that were scattered about her bed. She hadn't known what else to do with all the magazines she'd confiscated that afternoon, except bring them home with her. Naturally, she hadn't wanted to discard them, because she was sure that eventually she—or else Douglas Amberson—would be able to talk Isabel Trent out of her misguided notion that the Marigold Free Public Library needed policing. And then Miriam could return the issues of *Metropolitan* to their rightful place in periodicals, along with the issues of the half dozen other magazines she'd been required to remove.

For now, though, all of those magazines would be living here at her apartment with her. And since she was a librarian with a love for the written word, Miriam was naturally drawn to the magazines. Especially the issues of *Metropolitan*, though she was absolutely certain that the *only* reason for that was because of the bright colors and simple composition the covers seemed to uniformly present, and *not* because of all those scandalous headlines with the proliferation of capital letters and exclamation points. At any rate she had found herself sifting through the magazines and had eventually started to read them.

Which was how she came to be in her current position, encircled by the glossy journals on her bed. Now scantily clad, heavily made-up women gazed back at her with much boredom, their images surrounded by headlines that screamed instructions like, JUST DO IT—in Every Room in the House! and Find His Erogenous Zones—and Help

Him find YOURS! and Call of the Siren—BE the Devil with the Blue Dress On!

Miriam shook her head in bemusement. Did women truly read these articles? she wondered. Did they genuinely find them helpful? Did they honestly put their "tips" to good use? Because she herself couldn't imagine the magazine actually offering any information that the normal, average—i.e. *not* a nymphomaniac—woman might be able to actually apply to her normal, average— i.e. *not* oversexed—everyday life.

Miriam set her tea on her nightstand and was about to collect the assortment and return them to the box in which she'd originally placed them, when her gaze lit on one headline in particular.

Awaken Your Inner Temptress! it shouted at her. And below it, in smaller letters, You Know You Want to!

Hmm, thought Miriam.

And in the same issue: Go from Invisible to Irresistible in Just Seven Seductive Steps!

And somehow Miriam found herself reaching for the issue in question, telling herself, *Well, it won't hurt to look, now, will it?*

She flipped to the Inner Temptress article first, and read all about how she was suppressing a very natural part of her psyche by refusing to admit that she could turn any man of her acquaintance into putty with her bare hands— all she had to do was uncover the secrets of what those bare hands could do. And as she read further, she discovered that her bare hands, the very ordinary-looking ones with the short, clipped nails, the ones that sorted efficiently through the card catalogue everyday, the ones that capably sliced fresh, nutritious vegetables for her regular evening repast, could also, very easily…

Oh, my.

Oh, my goodness, *no.* They couldn't do *that.* Could they? Well, *perhaps* they could, she finally conceded as she read a bit further. Maybe if she *did* awaken her Inner Temptress.

Miriam blushed furiously when she realized the avenue down which her thoughts had traveled. Oh, no, her bare hands could *not* do that, either, she told herself sternly. They couldn't even do it if they had on gloves. Which, when one considered such a scenario, actually added a rather naughty dimension to the potential, all things considered, especially if they were latex gloves, and—

No, she insisted more firmly. She was *not* going to indulge in such...such...such *wanton* behavior, Inner Temptress or no Inner Temptress. Miriam Thornbury simply was not that kind of girl. The very idea. Honestly.

So what else did the article have to say...?

As she continued with her reading, Miriam also learned that she wasn't putting her store of repartee to effective use at all. No, where she had always been under the impression that good repartee was generally used more for, oh, say...conversation, she now discovered that it was widely used, particularly in Europe, as a tool for sexual enticement. She'd had no idea, truly. How she had lived her life for twenty-eight years without such knowledge was beyond her.

Reading further, she also learned how one's very wardrobe could be used as a weapon of seduction. This actually came as no surprise, because Miriam did, after all, receive the Victoria's Secret catalogue, even if the only thing she had ever ordered from it were those wonderful flowing, white Victorian nightgowns that took up only two pages of the publication. She had at least *looked* at the rest of the catalogue. And she'd been reasonably certain that most of those other undergarments were *not* worn for the sake of comfort and functionality. Mainly because they looked in no way comfortable or functional, what with all their squeezing and lifting and expanding of a woman's—

Well. At any rate the undergarments weren't what one might call *practical*. Which meant they were worn for some other purpose than to be, well, practical. And it didn't take a genius to realize what that purpose was. *S-E-X*. 'Nuff said.

Still, it had never occurred to Miriam that she *herself* might don one of those sexy fashions. One of the cute little black ones, say. Made of that delicious-looking, see-through lace. With those brief, naughty demi-cups. And garters. Oh, yes. According to *Metropolitan* magazine, one must wear garters if one was to proceed successfully with awakening one's Inner Temptress. And now that Miriam *did* think about donning such…accoutrements…

She blushed furiously, that's what she did.

How on earth could she even *think* of such a thing? Miriam Thornbury was not the black-lace, demicup, garter-belt type. No, ma'am. Flowing, white, ankle-length, embroidered cotton was much more her style. Still, she might make some headway in the repartee department, she told herself. She'd always been very good at repartee. She'd just never tried to use it for…temptation. Now that she did give some thought to the possibility of doing so…

She blushed furiously *again*.

Absolutely not. There was no way she would be able to walk up to Professor Rory Monahan at the library and say something like, "Hello, Rory. Is that volume fifteen of *Stegman's Guide to the Peloponnesian War* you have in your pocket, or are you just happy to see me?"

Oh, no, no, no, no, no. That would never do.

She sighed fitfully as she tossed the magazine back onto

the bed. Clearly, her Inner Temptress was sleeping quite soundly. Clearly, her Inner Temptress was out like a light. Clearly, her Inner Temptress was buried much too deep inside to ever show her face in Marigold, Indiana. It was ridiculous to even think about becoming such a thing. She was practical, pragmatic Miriam Thornbury. Capable, competent Miriam Thornbury. Staid, sensible Miriam Thornbury.

Drab, dull Miriam Thornbury, she concluded morosely. No wonder Rory Monahan scarcely paid her any heed.

Ah, well, she thought further. Even if she was a devil with a blue dress on, Rory Monahan still probably wouldn't pay her any heed. He was a man on a quest. A quest for Knowledge with a capital *K*. Not even a devil with a blue dress on would have a hope of swaying him from his chosen course. Not unless that devil with a blue dress on was holding volume fifteen of *Stegman's Guide to the Peloponnesian War,* or some such thing.

Hmmm, Miriam thought again, brightening.

Just how badly did she want Rory Monahan to notice her? she asked herself. And immediately she had her answer. Pretty badly. After all, she'd spent virtually the last six months wanting him to notice her. She'd spent virtually the last six months *wanting* him, period.

For six months she'd been walking into the Marigold Free Public Library in her usual fashion, to find the good professor sitting at his usual table in the reference section, performing his usual research in his usual manner. And she'd always melted in her usual fashion at how his blue eyes twinkled in their usual way, and how his mouth crooked up in his usual shy smile, and how his fingers threaded through his jet hair in his usual gesture of utter preoccupation. And she always responded to him in her usual way—by becoming very hot and very confused and very flustered.

And she'd spent the last six months, too, doing things and thinking about things that no self-respecting librarian should ever do or think about. Not in a public facility like a library, anyway. Because Miriam had spent the last six months *fantasizing* about Rory Monahan. Naturally, she'd also spent the last six months trying to reassure herself that the *only* reason she fantasized about him was be-cause...because... Well, because...

Hmmm. Actually, now that she thought more about it, she wasn't sure why she'd been fantasizing about him. Suddenly, though, now that she thought more about it, she realized that she very much wanted to find out.

Because suddenly, after reading all those articles in *Metropolitan* magazine, Miriam found herself armed with new knowledge. And she began to wonder if maybe all this new knowledge—whether she applied it the way *Metro* suggested or not—might just have some use. Al-though Professor Monahan had always been pleasant to her, had even gone so far as to smile warmly at her on occasion, he'd never shown any indication that he recip-rocated her, um, interest. In fact, he'd never shown any indication that he reciprocated anything about her. Except, of course, for volume fifteen of *Stegman's Guide to the Peloponnesian War*.

Knowledge, she reiterated to herself. That was all Rory Monahan wanted from life. Knowledge, knowledge and more knowledge. And as much as Miriam admired knowl-edge in a person...

She sighed fitfully. She'd like to show Rory Monahan knowledge. Boy howdy, would she. And as she thought more about it, she began to think that maybe, just maybe, there might not be any harm in putting her own newly acquired knowledge to good use.

Not *all* of it, necessarily, she hastily qualified when she remembered the gist of some of those articles. Not even a lot of it, really. But some of it, perhaps. A little. Surely there had been one or two things in that Inner Temptress article, for example, that might prove useful. Provided, of course, she could use them without completely humiliating herself.

Because if Miriam did manage to use one or two of *Metro*'s suggestions to capture even a tiny bit of Professor Monahan's attention, then she might just be able to garner a bit more of his attention all by herself. And if she did that, then she might very well win a nice prize for her efforts. She might very well win Professor Rory Monahan.

As prizes went, that was a pretty good one, as far as Miriam was concerned.

Now, where to begin? she wondered. Hadn't there been another article of interest in that Inner Temptress issue? Something about going from invisible to irresistible in seven seductive steps? Not that Miriam would use all seven steps—heavens, no. She didn't want to overwhelm the good professor, did she? Not yet, anyway. But surely one or two of those steps might be helpful, she thought. She hoped.

Reaching for the issue in question, she settled back against the pillows again to read.

Three

Rory was quite vexed. He was utterly certain he had left volume fifteen of *Stegman's Guide to the Peloponnesian War* sitting right here on his table in the reference section the night before, when he'd left the library at closing time. Yes, indeed, he was positive he had done so. Because he recalled very clearly stacking volumes twelve through eighteen in numerical order, and not one of them had been missing. Now, however, fifteen was gone.

It was quite the mystery, to be sure. No one—absolutely *no one*—at the Marigold Free Public Library had *ever* had the audacity to remove a reference book from his table. Everyone knew his research was far too important to him for anyone to ever interfere with it. Yet at some point between closing last night—he glanced down at his watch to discover that it was nearly 3:00 p.m.—and roughly 2:52 p.m. today, someone had used stealth and heaven only knew what other means to confiscate his book.

All right, all right, so it wasn't *his* book, per se, Rory admitted reluctantly. Technically it belonged to the library. The transgression was no less severe as a result.

Let's see now, he thought further. Who could possibly be the culprit? Gladys Dorfman, the custodian? It was entirely possible. Not only was she here alone at the library during the dark hours of the night, able to commit, unobserved, whatever mayhem she might want to commit, but she'd also been a student in one of Rory's morning classes last spring and had shown an inordinate amount of interest in the Peloponnese.

It could be significant.

Mr. Amberson? Rory pondered further. Possible, but unlikely. Although Mr. Amberson had keys to the library and lived alone—a condition that would make an alibi difficult to either prove or disprove—the elder librarian's preferred area of history lay decidedly further west and a good two millennia ahead, most notably in the New World at the time of its colonization.

Besides, Rory vaguely recalled, Mr. Amberson hadn't been working the night before, and he doubted the man would make a special effort to come to the library for that particular volume, unless it was an emergency, which, Rory had to admit, was also entirely possible. He himself had experienced such crises of research from time to time, and they were by no means pleasant. They could conceivably drive a man to commit an act which, under normal circumstances, he would never consider committing.

Still, Rory doubted Mr. Amberson would have had reason to be in the library last night. No, it had been Miss Thornbury who had worked the previous evening, Miss Thornbury who had closed the li—

Miss Thornbury, Rory thought with a snap of his fingers. Of course. She must be the culprit. Not only had he caught her red-handed with volume fifteen of the *Stegman's* yesterday afternoon in her office, but she was a relative newcomer to Marigold, having lived here only... Well, Rory wasn't sure how long she had lived here, but it wasn't very long.

At least, he was fairly certain it hadn't been very long. Although he remembered—surprisingly well, actually—the day she had started working at the library, he couldn't quite pinpoint when, exactly, that day had occurred. It had been snowing, though. He did recall that much. Because she had just come in from outside when he first made her acquaintance, and her nose had been touched adorably with red, and her eyes had glistened against the cold, and her mouth had been so full and so red and so luscious, not that that had necessarily been caused by the elements, but Rory had noticed it, and...and...and...

Where was he?

Oh, yes. The missing volume of *Stegman's*. At any rate, there was a very good chance that Miss Thornbury didn't even know about the unofficial don't-touch-Professor-Monahan's-table rule that everyone else in town held sacred.

Of course, that didn't excuse her violation, Rory told himself. Ignorance was never an excuse. And he was confident that Miss Thornbury herself would agree with him on that score. He was going to have to make clear to her that his research was of utmost importance in and to the community at large. He owed it to her. And once he explained the situation, he was certain she would never commit such an egregious error in judgment again. He was also certain that she would thank him for setting her straight.

Sufficiently convinced now of the nobility of his errand, Rory went in search of Miss Thornbury, and, consequently, volume fifteen of the *Stegman's*. But he didn't have to search far. Because he located her almost immediately, standing on a ladder, two stacks away from his table in the reference section, where she was in the process of shelving—

Good heavens, it was volume fifteen of the *Stegman's!* Rory realized triumphantly. He'd caught her red-handed *again!* He prepared himself for battle, hiked up his dark gray trousers, pushed back the rolled cuffs of his white dress shirt, straightened the skewed knot in his plaid—but it was a tasteful plaid, truly—necktie, and raked both hands through his shaggy black hair. Then, after settling his glasses intently on the bridge of his nose, he bravely entered the fray. Or, at the very least, he bravely entered the stacks. And he didn't stop entering until he stood at the foot of the ladder upon which Miss Thornbury had perched herself.

As he halted before her, though, Rory, well…halted. Because he vaguely realized that she was standing on a rung at such a height as to put her thigh directly at his eye level. And, less vaguely, he realized that there was a side slit in her straight, black skirt. It was conservative enough to be acceptable for a librarian's wardrobe, but open just now—thanks to her position on the ladder—in such a way as to make a professor of history take notice. And somehow, this particular professor of history found the sight of Miss Thornbury's leg to be strangely… arousing?

Oh, surely not.

Rory shook off the sensation and forced his gaze higher, toward her face. But his gaze got held up at her torso, because on top of her slim skirt with the intriguing, though conservative, side slit, Miss Thornbury was wearing a rather snug, rather red, knit top. A snug, red top that had no sleeves, he noted further, offering him just the merest glimpse of a bare shoulder, a glimpse that he'd never had before, a glimpse that was strangely...arousing?

Oh, surely not.

Rory steered his gaze away from the glimpse of shoulder, intent now on finding Miss Thornbury's face, only to have his attention get held up elsewhere on her torso, this time on the elegant swell of her breast, which pushed against the taut fabric of her sweater in such a way as to make the vision strangely...arousing?

Oh, surely—

It was then that a burst of recollection shot the memory of his previous night's encounter with Miss Thornbury to the very forefront of his brain. They had been outside, in front of the library, Rory remembered, and something had kept making him envision her in that goddess get-up that he caught himself thinking about her wearing every now and then. But not very often, truly. Only once, or maybe twice, a week. Three times *at most*, honestly. Like when he happened to see her, oh... Rory didn't know. Perched on a ladder, for instance. Like now.

Uh-oh...

And last night, he hurriedly rushed on, dispelling the realization, they'd been holding hands for some reason, too, hadn't they? But why...? Oh, yes. Now he remembered. For a purely innocent reason. He'd been helping her gather up an assortment of periodicals that she'd dropped on the ground. What had they been...? Oh, yes. Now he remembered. *Metropolitan* magazine, which he'd thought an odd choice for her. Especially when he pondered what some of those headlines had contained. Hadn't there been one, in particular, that had caught his attention? Something about loving one's man orally to—

Oh, yes. Now he remembered. Now he remembered very, *very* well. *Too* well. He remembered how Miss Thornbury's mouth had been so full and luscious. And he remembered wondering if her other body parts would be as full and luscious as her mouth. And he remembered wondering—well into the night, in fact—how it would be to have her mouth, not to mention her other body parts, being full and luscious alongside his own body parts. Preferably while they were both alone. And horizontal. And naked.

Uh-oh, indeed...

"Miss Thornbury," he called out quickly, hoping to distract himself enough that the memories—not to mention the sudden discomfort in his lower regions—might disappear. And he called her name out quietly, too, of course—he was in the library, after all, and didn't want to disturb anyone.

However, it wasn't, evidently, quiet to Miss Thornbury. Because when he uttered her name, she gasped in surprise and started visibly, then immediately lost her balance on the ladder. As she began to fall backward, Rory instinctively stepped forward, extending his arms before himself in an effort to steady her. But to no avail. Because she fell from the ladder, at an angle which, upon impact, created enough propulsion to send them both stumbling back. And then, before Rory could say *Stegman's Guide to the Peloponnesian War,* he had landed hard on his fanny, and Miss Thornbury had fallen quite literally into his lap.

For a moment neither of them seemed to know what had hit them, and neither reacted in any way. Rory sat with Miss Thornbury seated across his thighs, and having the weight of her body pressing against that particular part of him was a surprisingly appealing sensation. And that sensation, coupled with the memories he had just been entertaining—not to mention her slim skirt and snug top—left him feeling more than a little dazed.

He glanced down to see if they both still had all their parts in place, only to discover that he could see one of her parts still in place quite clearly. Probably more clearly than was actually prudent—or, at the very least, socially acceptable. Because, at some point during their tumble, Miss Thornbury's slim skirt had ridden up on one side, and now the slit that before had offered only a hint of the leg beneath, suddenly offered a view that went way, *way* beyond the hint phase.

And Rory saw that his goddess-vision of Miss Thornbury's creamy thigh simply had not done justice to the reality of Miss Thornbury's creamy thigh, that the silky skin beneath her skirt was as smooth as satin and as flawless as a sheet of glass, and as warm and welcoming as a summer afternoon. And then he wondered hazily how he could possibly know that her thigh was smooth and warm, and to his astonishment—nay, to his utter *horror*—he realized he could know that because he had his hand placed firmly on that smooth, warm thigh, his fingers curling into her bare flesh as if they had every right to be there.

Immediately Rory snatched back his hand, mumbling an incoherent apology for having placed it where it was to begin with. For a scant, delirious second, Miss Thornbury gazed back at him with lambent—yes, *lambent* was most definitely the word he was looking for—eyes, and for one brief, dizzying moment, he thought she was going to ask him to put his hand right back where it was, if he pleased. And Rory realized then, with much amazement, that it would have pleased him, very much, to do that very thing. He even felt his fingers begin to curl slightly and creep forward again, as if they'd already decided to take matters—or, at the very least, Miss Thornbury's thigh—into their own hands.

Or something like that.

But before his fingers could complete their journey, Miss Thornbury, in a jumble of movement, scurried off Rory's lap, pushed herself up to standing and struggled to return her slim skirt and that snug, red top back to their original positions. Which, quite frankly, did nothing to dissuade Rory's fingers from wanting to pursue their original quest to find her thigh, because the skirt and top were considerably more...more...*snug,* and more...more...*red,* than the clothing Miss Thornbury normally wore to work.

And her hair, Rory noted further. There was something different about it today, too. She wasn't wearing it the way she usually wore it. At least, he didn't think she'd ever worn it down loose that way before now. Because he'd never realized before now how long it was, how it could cascade over both her shoulders, curling softly into perfect, elegant *U*s right above her breasts. Nor had he realized how silvery highlights shimmered so abundantly amid the silky mass. Nor had he ever had the urge to reach out and clutch a fistful of her hair in his hand and lift it to his nose to see what it smelled like, and then rake the long tresses back and forth over his mouth and then...and then...and then...

And *good heavens,* what had come over him today? Rory wondered. He'd all but forgotten about...about... What was it he had been about to do? Why was it he had gone searching for Miss Thornbury? Surely it couldn't have been to ponder her hair. Could it? Oh, surely not. Still, he couldn't quite remember now *why* he had been seeking her out. In fact, he couldn't remember much of anything.

He shook his head fiercely, once, as if trying to dislodge some unpleasant thought, but he hadn't had any unpleasant thoughts today, only thoughts about Miss Thornbury and Miss Thornbury's thigh and Miss Thornbury's hair and Miss Thornbury's mouth and—

No, wait a minute. He hadn't thought much about Miss Thornbury's mouth today, had he? But now that he *did* think about her mouth, now that he turned his attention to that part of her forthwith, he realized her full, ripe, luscious lips were even fuller, riper and more luscious than they usually were—he knew that, because he *had* noticed her mouth on several other occasions—and also much more…red…than they usually were. And suddenly his fingers began to curl again, because his fingers—and, all right, the rest of him, too—suddenly wanted very badly to go to that mouth and…

Rory growled under his breath, squeezed his eyes shut tight, fisted his hands resolutely at his sides and began reciting dates of great historical significance, to pull his mind back to where it belonged. *The Magna Carta was signed in 1215,* he thought. *The Protestant Reformation began in 1517. The U.S. Bill of Rights was ratified in 1791. The Emancipation Proclamation was made in 1862. Miss Thornbury's mouth was fuller and riper and redder and more luscious than usual in 2001.*

Damn, he thought further, opening his eyes. He'd almost made it.

"Miss Thornbury," he said softly, driving his gaze to some point over her shoulder—anywhere but her ripe, red mouth. Or her lambent gray eyes. Or her silky, silvery hair. Or her creamy, warm thigh.

Good God, man. Get a hold of yourself.

"Are you all right?" he asked further, still focusing on

the books behind Miss Thornbury, instead of Miss Thornbury herself.

"Um, yes, I believe so," she replied a bit breathlessly.

And there was something about her being a bit breathless, and something about the fact that Rory had been responsible for her breathlessness—even if it had only been because he had knocked her off of a ladder—that made his own breathing skip a few necessary stages.

"I apologize if I...caught you off guard," he added. Still, it was only fair, he thought further to himself. Because she had caught him off guard, too.

"That's all right," she said, her voice still sounding low and husky. "No harm done."

Oh, that was what she thought.

"Was there something you wanted, Professor Monahan?" she asked further.

Oh, he really wished she hadn't phrased her question quite that way. Because Rory suddenly realized, too well, that there was indeed something he wanted. Something he wanted very badly. And he wanted it specifically from Miss Thornbury. And it was something he hadn't had for a long, long time, from any woman. Something that suddenly seemed of utmost importance, something which, if he didn't get it very, very soon, might just make him spontaneously combust.

And no, it *wasn't* volume fifteen of *Stegman's Guide to the Peloponnesian War*, either.

"I, uh," Rory began eloquently. "That is, um... What I meant to say was... Ah..."

As he stammered and stumbled over his words, Miss Thornbury bent to retrieve the book that had fallen on the floor between them when they'd taken their tumble. But, polite woman that she was, she didn't stop looking at Rory as she completed the action. And, automatically,

Rory allowed his gaze to follow her movements. And as she bent down, he accidentally—truly, he did *not* do it intentionally—found himself…well, um, looking down her snug, red top, which wasn't so snug that it didn't fall open a bit at the low neckline, to reveal the pearly swells of her breasts encased in—

Good heavens.

He was shocked and scandalized to see that Miss Thornbury was wearing—even Rory's mental voice dropped to a lower volume as he realized it—*pink, lacy underthings.*

He'd had no idea.

Not that he spent an inordinate amount of time thinking about what Miss Thornbury might be wearing under her clothing—well, not *too* inordinate an amount of time, not until today, anyway, because it was usually that goddess thing he had in his thoughts where she was concerned—but somehow, now that he did think about it, she simply did not seem like the pink-lacy-underthing type. No, she'd always seemed more like the white-unadorned-cotton-underthing type. Functional. Practical. No frills. To the point. At least she had seemed that type before. Before he'd seen her in the slim skirt and snug top and red lipstick. Now, however—

And why was Rory standing here speculating about a woman's underthings in the first place? What was the matter with him? He had infinitely more important things to be pondering. If he could only remember what those more important things were…

He lifted a hand to his forehead, rubbing fiercely at an excruciating ache that erupted out of nowhere. And he wondered if it might not be possible for him to simply turn on his heel and exit the library, then reenter and start all over again. Maybe then Miss Thornbury would be wearing her usual type of clothing, and her hair would be in its usual ponytail, and Rory's pulse would return to its usual steady rate.

Because with her looking so unusual today—and with him feeling so unusual today—Rory got the distinct impression that he was going to be preoccupied with thoughts of Miss Thornbury, and her mouth and her thighs and her underthings, for quite some time to come. Certainly for the rest of the afternoon. Maybe even for the rest of the day. And Rory couldn't afford to be preoccupied by anything other than his studies, for any length of time. Least of all by a woman.

Because he *had* been preoccupied by a woman once before, many years ago. In fact, he'd been so preoccupied by her he'd nearly married her. He'd been that far gone in his preoccupation. Of course, that woman had been nothing like Miss Thornbury. Miss Thornbury was practical and pragmatic, and capable and competent, and staid and sensible. At least, she had been before the slim-skirt, snug-top, red-lipstick episode. Rory's fiancée had been anything but practical or capable or sensible. No, Rosalind had been, well...

In hindsight Rory supposed the best way to describe Rosalind was well formed, but empty-headed. Not that she had been stupid—well, not *too* stupid, though she'd never been able to remember the date of the Battle of Hastings, which had always annoyed him to no end, because it had been the PIN number for their bank account—but she rarely thought of anyone but herself. In fact, so self-involved had Rosalind been, that she'd dumped Rory without a second thought the moment something she'd perceived to be better came along. Worse, she hadn't bothered to tell Rory she had dumped him until she'd married the something better, three months later.

Of course, had Rory been more observant, he probably would have noticed long before that three months was up that Rosalind had, well, dropped off the face of the planet. There had been signs, after all, which he'd recognized once he'd received her telegram informing him that she wouldn't be returning. There had been the fact that her clothes had disappeared from their closet, something he hadn't noticed until he received her telegram. And he'd been forced to acknowledge then, too, that what he had thought was her coming to bed late and rising for work early every morning had in fact been her, well, not being there at all.

But that was beside the point.

The point was that Rory couldn't afford to get that preoccupied by someone again. Because it would only serve to disrupt his wonderfully routine existence. Rosalind's departure had disrupted his routine for weeks—once he'd realized that she had, in fact, departed. And he didn't want to suffer such a disruption again.

He simply was not the kind of man who could invest heavily in a relationship. He was too interested in other things. He felt no lack in his life, romantically speaking, and it wouldn't be fair to get involved with a woman who would expect him to do things like pay attention to her from time to time. Rory was perfectly content on his own. Or, at least, he had been. Until a few minutes ago.

Besides, he didn't need a woman in his life, he told himself. Who did? What purpose could a woman possibly serve in his life that wasn't already being met?

When Miss Thornbury straightened, Rory's gaze fell on the plump swell of her breasts again, then dropped to the knee revealed by the side slit in her skirt once more. And way, way, *way* deep down inside him, very close to what felt like his libido, something stirred to life that hadn't been stirred for quite a long time.

All right, all right, he conceded. Perhaps there was a purpose Miss Thornbury might meet in his life that wasn't already being met. Was it really such an important purpose? And was it worth sacrificing his peace of mind?

That something close to his supposed libido stirred again, jumping and dancing this time as if it had been touched by a live wire. All right, so maybe it *was* an important purpose, he conceded. And maybe his peace of mind right now was moot. Because it wasn't his mind that was responding to Miss Thornbury. No, it was something infinitely more primitive and intrinsic and uncontrollable. It was that essence inside him which made him a man, something from which he absolutely could not separate himself, even if he'd wanted to.

She was very attractive, he thought as he studied her more thoroughly. And her hair did look to be very soft. And her eyes were quite lovely. And her mouth... Well, best not to ponder that one again. Best not to ponder any of the rest of her again, he told himself. Somehow, though, he didn't think he'd be able to heed his own advice.

"Actually, Miss Thornbury," he said, "I can't remember now what it was that I wanted."

And he hoped God would not strike him down for uttering so blatant a lie. Because he knew very well what he wanted. He wanted Miss Thornbury. There was no way, however, that he was going to tell her—or anybody else—about that. Because it wouldn't last. Of that, he was certain. The moment he remembered whatever it was he had intended to do... The minute he began studying and researching whatever it was that he was supposed to be studying and researching... The second he remembered that… He sighed inwardly. Then he would forget all about Miss Thornbury. And her hair. And her thigh. And her mouth.

"I apologize again for startling you," he added.

She smiled, and that something inside him that had stirred to life began to quiver and hum like a finely strung wire. "Think nothing of it," she told him, clasping the heavy book possessively to her breasts.

The book, Rory thought vaguely as he watched her complete the gesture. There was something about that book… That was what he had wanted to ask her about initially, wasn't it? Volume fifteen of the *Stegman's?* Yes, of course. Now he remembered. Miss Thornbury had been about to shelve it. And now she had it clasped to her breasts. Clasped affectionately to her full, ripe—

Oh, he was never going to be able to look at *Stegman's Guide to the Peloponnesian War* the same way again.

"Is that volume fifteen?" he asked softly, dipping his head toward the book in question.

She glanced down at it, then back up at Rory. "Why, yes. As a matter of fact, it is. I was reading it on my lunch hour again and was about to put it back where it belongs."

"Actually, Miss Thornbury, where it currently belongs is on my table."

She offered him a faintly puzzled expression. "Your table?" she asked.

He nodded again, more resolutely this time. "You see, I was using it last night for my research, and I placed it with the other volumes I'd consulted, on my table, because I knew I would need it again today. I'm sure that's where you found it in the first place."

She seemed to give his remark thorough consideration. "Yes, I did find it on a table, now that you mention it," she said, "but I didn't realize you were using it."

"Well, now you do," he replied mildly.

He told himself to remind her that the table from which she'd taken the *Stegman's* was Professor Rory Monahan's table, and to reiterate how essential it was that she never, ever touch a single volume of any book she might find there. He told himself to stress most forcefully how important his research was, and how it was imperative that he have a place where he might be able to pursue that research unhampered.

Unfortunately, Miss Thornbury chose that moment to extend the book toward him, and when she did, the faint scent of lavender seemed to come at him from out of nowhere, and Rory could no more form words in that moment than he could have changed lead into gold.

So he only took the book from her and tried not to notice how warm it was from being pressed against her, or how rosy and plump the upper swells of her breasts were where she had held it. Somehow, he managed to mumble his thanks under his breath. And then, without a further word, he spun on his heel to return to his desk. To his studies. To his research.

He told himself he was *not* fleeing in terror from an attractive woman. And he assured himself that there was *nothing* more important than the work that he needed—and intended—to pursue that afternoon.

Nothing.

However, Rory very much feared that for the rest of the afternoon he would be able to think of little other than Miss Thornbury's...assets. And suddenly the word *research* took on an entirely new meaning.

Four

Well, that had gone *very* well, Miriam thought as she watched and marveled at Professor Monahan's speedy retreat. Very well indeed. She'd had no idea about the power one could wield with no more than a slim skirt, a snug top and a tube of really red lipstick. Had she realized how easy it was to turn the tables on a man, she might have tried to do it a long time ago.

Then again, there hadn't been many men in her life upon whom Miriam had actually wanted to turn the tables. Oh, certainly there had been the occasional romantic interest—one or two of them had even become somewhat serious over time. But eventually, all of those romantic interests had fizzled out and wandered off. And in the long run Miriam had been left feeling surprisingly unhurt by the failure of any of them. Really, she supposed she'd just never felt for any of those men the kind of…well, whatever it was she found herself feeling for Rory Monahan.

And just what precisely *was* she feeling for Rory Mon-ahan, anyway? she asked herself. Before today she had thought she was just more or less infatuated with him. She had thought she was experiencing a crush on him, albeit a rather substantial one. Though, granted, she had hoped she might broaden that infatuation, that crush, into something more, for both of them.

After the interlude they'd just shared, however, she was beginning to think that her feelings for the good professor already went much, much deeper than simple infatuation or a mere crush. Recalling the way he had looked upon her just moments ago, with such heat and such fire build-ing in his eyes... Remembering the way he had clenched his fingers tighter on the bare flesh of her thigh...

Well, something equally fiery and hot had sparked to life inside of Miriam. Something very significant. Some-thing totally unrecognizable. Something she'd never come close to feeling before.

And she very much suspected that it was her Inner Temptress awakening.

Goodness, she thought. *Metropolitan* magazine was right. Where Professor Monahan was concerned, she had indeed gone from invisible to...well, something *visible*, she told herself, if not irresistible. And she had done it in fewer than ''seven seductive steps.'' Because she'd only used two seductive steps so far—the one about opting for brighter, snugger clothing, and the one about donning re-ally red lipstick. And look at the results she had already achieved. At this rate it might not even be necessary for her to go as far as seductive step number seven, which involved—

Well. Miriam would just as soon not ponder what se-ductive step number seven involved right now. Not here, in a public place. A public place that was supported by the tax dollars of hardworking citizens.

Instead she pondered the amazing results she had already achieved with regard to her...temptressing...of Rory Monahan. Because she had definitely become visible to him, she thought with much satisfaction. He had definitely seen her. He'd also felt her, she recalled as a rush of heat raced through her. And the article had said nothing about going from invisible to malleable, in *any* number of steps, so that was *really* an accomplishment.

And she congratulated herself, too, for using her own ingenuity to supplement seductive steps number one and two. After all, she had been the one to theorize that if a woman wanted to draw a man's attention, then she must have something that the man in question wanted. And what could Rory Monahan possibly want more than volume fifteen of *Stegman's Guide to the Peloponnesian War,* hmm?

Well, if things worked out the way she hoped, Miriam thought, there would indeed be something that Rory Monahan wanted more than volume fifteen of the *Stegman's.* He would want *all* the volumes of Miss Miriam Thornbury, along with all assorted indices, appendices, tables and charts.

She smiled as she began rehearsing in her head how she would go about applying seductive step number three with regard to her temptressing of Professor Monahan. That particular step involved repartee, so she knew she would have to do some practicing before she actually put the step into motion. And truly, there was no reason why she had to rush into repartee today. She had already made herself visible to Rory Monahan this afternoon. If she used repartee now, it might very well be too much for him. She didn't want to overwhelm the poor man, after all.

Plus, she needed to prepare *herself,* in case the results of that foray ended up being as successful as her results today had been. Should Rory decide he wanted to...oh, grip her thigh—or some other part of her—again, Miriam wanted to be ready for it.

My, my, my, she thought with a smile—and a nervous stomach. She had never been much of a magazine reader in the past, but suddenly she couldn't wait to get home to see what words of wisdom *Metropolitan* had to impart to her today.

Miriam gave Rory Monahan as little time as possible to recover before she launched into the next phase of her plan. And it wound up being a very good next phase, too, one she should have thought of undertaking a long time ago, and as much more than just a next phase. Because two days after Miriam had awakened her Inner Temptress, she read in the Marigold *Messenger* that the final section of summer adult extended education classes would be starting at the Marigold Community College. And one of those extended education classes just so happened to be an intensive five-week session taught by Professor Rory Monahan, a session called "Introduction to Classical Civilizations II."

Miriam could not believe her good fortune upon reading the announcement. Not only could she enroll herself in a class that Rory Monahan would be teaching, but she'd always wanted to learn more about classical civilizations, anyway. It was a definite win-win situation. She stopped by the community college on her way to work that very afternoon to register for the class that, very conveniently, began the following Monday night. Then she rearranged her workload at the library so that Lucy Chin, one of the assistant librarians, could cover some of her hours.

Intensive, Miriam reiterated to herself now, as she strode toward the classroom where her session would be meeting. That was what the course description had called Professor Monahan's class. *Intensive.* Oh, yes. She hoped it would be very intensive indeed.

She ducked into a nearby ladies' room before entering the classroom, to drag a brush through her hair and reapply some of the really red lipstick that had worked so successfully on the good professor the week before. She also ran a hand over the snug, sapphire-blue Capri pants she'd purchased over the weekend to compensate for her wardrobe's current—and profound—lack of perky, peppy, fun fashions, which was what *Metropolitan* magazine assured her she must wear. Miriam contemplated her sleeveless, sapphire-blue blouse, too, as she studied her reflection in the mirror, and, very daringly, decided to unfasten the top button before heading off to class.

My, but she was audacious. She hoped Professor Monahan wasn't *too* awfully overcome by her taunting behavior. Or, rather, by the taunting behavior of her Inner Temptress. Because that was who was behind the unbuttoning, Miriam told herself. Normally Miriam would never do such a bold thing. Her Inner Temptress, however, had no such qualms.

Only as Miriam was turning away from the mirror did she begin to have second thoughts about what she was doing. Did she really want to come across as such a…such a…such a taunting temptress? Especially since that wasn't her natural state at all? What if she did finally manage to snag Rory's attention, and more, only to realize that he had fallen for her Inner Temptress, instead of her Real Self?

It was entirely possible that such a scenario might occur, she thought. After all, he'd never paid her much heed before the day she'd awakened her Inner Temptress. Oh, certainly he had always greeted her politely when he encountered her at the library, and he had always paused long enough to make small talk with her. He had also usually, and very chivalrously, walked her to her car on those evenings when the two of them left the library together alone.

But that had probably just been because his car was invariably parked close to hers, she told herself now. Or simply because he was a gentleman who would perform the same service for any solitary woman. It wasn't necessarily because he was interested in Miriam specifically.

Though she was confident that he did like her. At least, he liked her when he gave her some thought, she amended with a heavy sigh. Unfortunately, he didn't seem to give Miriam Thornbury much thought once she was out of his direct line of vision. He had certainly seemed to like her Inner Temptress much better. Certainly he had noticed her Inner Temptress more.

Then again, Miriam argued to herself, it was *her* Inner Temptress, wasn't it? Therefore, it must be a part of *her*. Somehow. Somewhere. Some way. Right?

Right?

Ignoring, for now, the sick feeling that was squishing around in the pit of her stomach, she squared her shoulders and lifted her chin and hoped that she appeared more confident than she actually felt. Then, throwing caution to the wind, and her hair back over her shoulders, Miriam reached up to unfasten a *second* button on her blouse.

Well, what could she say? she asked herself. Her Inner Temptress made her do it.

* * *

Rory had just completed his first time line on the chalk-board when he turned to face the students in his intensive, five-week, "Introduction to Classical Civilizations II" session. He didn't normally teach night classes during the summer—that was time he liked to reserve for his research—especially the classes in the adult extended-education program. But the regularly scheduled professor had, at the beginning of the summer, been presented with an opportunity to spend a full three weeks at the end of July studying Hippodamus of Miletus—in Piraeus, no less. How on earth could Rory have refused to fill in for her, by teaching her class, so that she could take advantage of such an amazingly fortuitous circumstance? Provided, of course, she shared all of her notes and photographs with him upon her return.

Now as Rory spun around to face his class, he realized it might not be such a bad thing to teach this session. It was one of his favorites in spite of its lack of in-depth analysis, and nothing brought him greater joy than imparting the fascinating details of Classical life to people who were unfamiliar with those details.

Teaching, Rory thought, was almost as gratifying and fulfilling as learning was, and he always looked forward to both. Especially when the faces gazing back at him from the classroom were so rapt and eager and focused...

And luscious and tempting and ripe and red and...

And good God, was that Miss Thornbury and her ripe, red, tempting, luscious mouth sitting there in the very front row? With her calves showing? And two buttons of her blouse unfastened? Was it?

Oooh, it was going to be a long five-week session, Rory suddenly thought. And intensive, too. Very intensive indeed.

He sighed as he tossed the stub of chalk into the tray

behind himself, then pushed away from the blackboard to take his place behind the dais he'd set on the table between him and his class. Not that a dais was going to do him any good with Miss Thornbury looking like... like...like *that*.

He gripped the dais fiercely, anyway, cleared his throat and said, "Good evening, class. I'm Professor Rory Monahan, and this is 'Introduction to Classical Civilizations II.' I hope you've all come to the right place."

One person, Rory noted, stood and gathered her things together, having evidently realized she was indeed in the wrong place. But it wasn't Miss Thornbury. And that, Rory discovered, was a development about which he had mixed feelings. On one hand, it would make his going infinitely smoother if he didn't have to be distracted by Miss Thornbury's mouth—or, rather, by Miss Thornbury, he hastily corrected himself—seated there in the center of the front row. On the other hand, an oddly pleasant sensation spiraled through him at seeing Miss Thornbury's mouth—or, rather, Miss Thornbury, he hastily corrected himself—seated there in the center of the front row.

What to do, what to do...

Well, what could he do? Rory thought. He must teach the class, as he normally would teach it. He couldn't exactly ask one student to leave because she was too ripe and luscious and tempting, could he? No, that would be frightfully impolite. Not to mention it would open up the community college to a sexual harassment lawsuit the likes of which Marigold, Indiana, had never seen. And Rory didn't want to harass Miss Thornbury sexually. No, what he had planned for Miss Thornbury, sexually speaking, was in no way harassing. Fun, by all means. But not harassing.

And good heavens, where was his mind tonight? Certainly not on anything classical—that was clearly evident. He had *no* plans for Miss Thornbury, Rory reminded himself, sexual or otherwise. She was far too distracting. Among other things. He'd never be able to focus on his studies and his research if he began planning things with her.

Then again, would that necessarily be such a bad thing? he asked himself.

He was utterly shocked by the question when it unrolled in his head. Of *course* it would be a bad thing to be unable to focus on his studies and research. Why, the very idea. Rory's studies and research were *every*thing to him. Life without the quest for knowledge would be...would be...

Well, it would be meaningless. What other reason was there to exist, if not to seek and gain more knowledge?

Inescapably his gaze wandered back to Miss Thornbury, over her shins, her calves, her arms, her two unfastened buttons and, inevitably, her mouth. And he began to think that there might be one or two things besides the quest for knowledge that would give his life meaning, and make it more enjoyable.

Nevertheless, he cautioned himself, he wasn't the sort of man who could make the kind of commitment to a relationship that a woman like Miss Thornbury would demand and deserve. It wouldn't be fair to promote a liaison with her, because regardless of how...incandescent...such a liaison might be, in the long run Rory would need more than just a ripe mouth and tempting calves. He would need knowledge. That would override any potential relationship that might develop between him and the luscious librarian. And that, Rory thought, simply would not be fair to Miss Thornbury.

He cleared his throat again, and tried to proceed in his

usual fashion once more. "I'm Professor Monahan," he began again on behalf of his eight remaining students. "And in this particular session, we'll be covering the period between 735 B.C.—we'll begin with the Messenian wars between Sparta and Messenia—and 554 A.D., with Emperor Justinian's attempts to reclaim the Roman Empire from the Byzantines. Yes, it's a lot to cover, and very exciting stuff to boot," he said with a smile, "but if we all work very hard, pay attention and complete our assigned reading, we shall all be better people for it by the end of the term. Now then. Let's get started."

Rory plunged immediately into his lecture—they only had three hours, two nights a week, after all, and much to cover—losing himself completely in the lesson. Whenever he glanced up to gauge how his students were faring, his gaze inevitably fell first on Miss Thornbury, who, invariably, seemed to be wholly absorbed in every word he uttered. That wasn't necessarily true of some of his other pupils, though, which was why, Rory was certain, his gaze fell more and more often on Miss Thornbury, and less and less often on her classmates.

At 7:25, exactly eighty-five minutes into class, Rory told his students to take a ten-minute break. "But only ten minutes," he admonished them carefully. "We shall reconvene at 7:35 and continue with the lesson. Hurry back. As I said, we have much to cover over the next five weeks."

All but one of his students abided by his instructions—some more quickly than others, he couldn't help noting—filing out of the classroom to see to whatever needs they might have. Miss Thornbury, however, apparently didn't have any needs. Or, at least, she seemed not to have any needs outside the classroom. Because she remained seated exactly where she had been sitting for the last hour and a half. And she continued to look every bit as delectable as she had been looking for the last hour and a half. And Rory found that he was in no way immune to her appeal. Nor, God help him, could he think of any way to tactfully escape.

"So," he said suddenly, surprising them both, if the jerk to Miss Thornbury's entire body was any indication of her reaction. "I'm puzzled to find you in class, Miss Thornbury. Your name wasn't on my original class list. I just now noticed it was penciled in at the end."

"I only enrolled on Friday," she replied. "They told me in admissions it wasn't too late."

"No, no, of course not," he assured her. "After all, it's never too late for knowledge."

Oh, hell, had he actually just said that? Rory groaned inwardly. To an attractive woman? An attractive woman whose calves were exposed, and whose blouse had two— count them, *two*—buttons unfastened? He fought off a cringe.

However, Miss Thornbury didn't seem to be put off by his inane comment, because she smiled at him in response. "No, you're absolutely right, Professor Monahan," she agreed. "It's never too late for...*knowledge*."

For some reason Rory couldn't comprehend, she dropped her voice a bit on that last word, fairly purring it the way a cat would. In fact, she was speaking in a voice that bore no resemblance whatsoever to her usual voice. It was huskier somehow, lower, more throaty.

"Miss Thornbury, do you have a cold?" he asked.

Her eyes widened in something akin to panic. What an odd reaction, he thought.

"No," she replied, still in that same, rather hoarse, voice. "Um, why do you ask?"

He pointed to his own neck. "You sound like you have a frog in your throat."

If he didn't know better, he'd swear he had just said something to embarrass her, because her cheeks were suddenly tinted with red. But he couldn't imagine why she might be embarrassed. Then another thought struck him. He hoped she wasn't running a fever, as well as having a sore throat.

"I'm fine," she told him softly, her voice sounding much more normal now.

But her cheeks were still red, and Rory had to battle the urge to place his open palms against them. Just to see if she was indeed feeling feverish, he hastily qualified. Not for any reason other than that. It was a simple concern for her health, that was all.

"Well, that's good," he said, still not quite convinced.

He was disconcerted by the intensity of her gaze, too. She had her attention fully fixed on his face, as if she were preparing to ask him something very, very important. Rory waited to hear what that question might be.

And waited. And waited. And waited.

For, truly, a full minute must have passed with Miss Thornbury doing nothing but stare at him, as if she were trying to unravel a particularly troublesome riddle. Finally, though, she opened her mouth to speak. But what emerged was really the oddest thing.

"Professor Monahan," she said. "Do you mind if I call you Rory?"

He arched his brows in frank surprise. Really, the request was unprecedented. Had she asked him such a thing in her capacity as librarian, it might not have been quite so unexpected—though, even then, he would have been surprised. But in her capacity as his student, it was really rather unusual.

"I mean, we are colleagues of a sort, aren't we?" she asked further. "We both work in jobs that contribute to the education of people."

Rory opened his mouth to respond, but found that he honestly had no idea what to say.

"And we're contemporaries of a sort, too, yes?" she asked. "I mean, how old are you?"

This time Rory gaped slightly in response. He'd never been asked such a personal question, point-blank this way, by anyone outside his family. Although, now that he thought about it, he'd never been asked such a question by his family, either. Of course, he reminded himself, they all already knew how old he was, so asking him something like that would have been unnecessary, not to mention silly. Still, coming from Miss Thornbury, it was a peculiar request.

He suddenly wondered if she had been drinking. That would explain her hoarseness, and even the blush on her cheeks. Nevertheless, she didn't seem intoxicated....

"I-I-I'm thirty-two," he heard himself reply. Though he didn't recall making a conscious decision to do so.

She smiled, a smile that was quite dazzling. "There, you see," she said. "I'm twenty-eight. We're practically the same age."

"Yes, well, that's true, but I—I—I—"

"And we do seem to share all kinds of interests in common, don't we?" she hurried on. "Not the least of which is Classical Civilizations."

"I—I—I suppose, but I—I—I—"

"So it only makes sense that I should call you Rory."

"I—I—I—"

"And you should call me Miriam."

Oh, now wait just a minute, Rory wanted to say. In-

stead, what he heard come out of his mouth was, "I—I—
I suppose it would be all right."

"Especially now that I'm one of your...*students*," she
added, her voice once again pitching to that strangely
husky timbre as she uttered—nay, *purred*—that final
word.

How very, very curious, Rory thought. Perhaps she *had*
been drinking.

"And I've always wanted to *learn* more about...what
you have to *teach*," she continued in that same husky,
peculiar, emphatic tone. Then, even more huskily, even
more peculiarly, even more emphatically, she added,
"*Rory.*"

"I—I—I see," he managed to reply. Somehow.

My, but it suddenly seemed warm in the classroom.
Was the custodial staff turning the air conditioner off at
night now, to conserve energy and save money? he wondered. With a quick twist of his head, he shook the observation off quite literally.

"Well then," he said. "You've, um, you've come to
the right place, haven't you?" Just to be polite, he concluded, "Miriam."

"Oh, I do hope so," she said with a smile.

A smile that was even more puzzling than what she
had been saying, a smile that Rory could only liken to...
wicked? Oh, surely not. She just wasn't feeling well, obviously, in spite of her assurances to the contrary.

Or perhaps she really had been drinking.

He was about to say something else—though, truly, he
knew not what—when a pair of his students ambled back
into the classroom, having concluded their break. Within
moments, a few others joined them, until, at precisely the
time Rory had indicated, everyone was back in his or her
designated seat, ready for the last half of class.

He breathed a sigh of relief to see it. For several moments there, his wonderfully steady, predictable existence had felt a bit...skewed. As if the Earth had somehow tilted, just the tiniest bit, on its axis. Now, though, with everyone seated back in their earlier places and prepared for his lecture, he felt as if everything had reverted back to normal again.

Until, involuntarily, he turned his attention to Miss Thornbury again. Or, rather, he corrected himself, to... Miriam. Because...Miriam...still sat at rapt attention, her hands folded daintily on her desktop, her legs crossed, her calves exposed, her two buttons unbuttoned, her mouth luscious. And the moment Rory's attention lit on her, damned if the Earth didn't do that tilting thing all over again. In fact, damned if the Earth didn't threaten to go spinning right out of its orbit.

He sighed heavily. It was going to be a long—and intensive—five weeks.

Well, seductive step number three—repartee—hadn't gone well at all, had it?

Miriam drew her conclusion with a sigh of defeat as she watched Rory Monahan erase the elaborate time line he'd drawn on the chalkboard behind himself, and as the rest of her classmates paraded by her and out the door. He'd barely noticed her during class, she thought. Only when she'd remained behind for the break to deliberately waylay his attention had he spared her little more than a glance.

Still, the evening hadn't been a total waste, she tried to reassure herself. Because Professor Monahan's—or, rather, she corrected herself, *Rory's*—lecture had been utterly fascinating. The man was amazing. His store of knowledge was, she was certain, limitless. And so casual about it he was, too. Why, he'd pulled dates and locales and names from thin air, facts with which Miriam hadn't even had a nodding acquaintance. Had she not already found him thoroughly attractive, she would be half-gone on him now.

In fact, she realized with some trepidation as she gathered together her own things, she *was* half-gone on him now. She had been half-gone on him for nearly six months, since the first day she had laid eyes on him at the library. And she feared it would take very little to make her fully gone. The problem was, of course, that once she *was* fully gone, she would be there by herself. Because Rory Monahan certainly wasn't going anywhere with her.

Ah, well, at least she'd managed to convince him to address her by her first name, she consoled herself. That was something, wasn't it? She still grew warm at the recollection of how he had voiced it, too. Miriam. She'd never considered her name to be a particularly beautiful one. No, she had always thought it too sedate. Too plain. Too functional. Much like the woman upon whom it had been bestowed. But when Rory said it, *Miriam* became the stuff of legends.

It had been rather exhilarating, really. And it was just too bad that hearing him say her name was evidently going to be the high point of their relationship.

She rose from her desk to make her way out of the classroom just as Rory stepped around the table upon which he had placed his dais. As a result, their bodies collided, her right shoulder connecting with his left arm, and the action jostled her just enough to send her book and notebook flying to the floor. Immediately she bent to retrieve them, but when she did, her oversize straw purse fell from her opposite shoulder and likewise dropped to the floor. In doing so, it spilled much of its contents, including a six-month old issue of *Metropolitan* magazine that cried, in big red letters, How to Seduce a Man—and Keep Him Coming Back for More!

Naturally, Rory, being a gentleman, fell to his knees beside Miriam in an effort to help her collect her things, lightly offering the observation that they just *had* to stop meeting like this. And naturally, Rory, being a searcher of knowledge, reached first for the written word. And naturally, closest to him was the issue of *Metropolitan*. and, naturally, he read the headlines upon it.

When he realized what they said, though, and what sort of knowledge he held in his hands, he blushed, hastily stuffing the magazine back into her bag. Then he scooped up her book and notebook and handed those to her, as well. Miriam was left to chase after an errant pen, a runaway roll of breath mints, a purse-size atomizer of Chanel No. 5, and her much-celebrated tube of really red lipstick.

Oh, what a girly-girl she had become, Miriam thought as she stuffed all her feminine accessories back into her bag, alongside the copy of *Metropolitan*. Really, until today, all she'd ever carried in her purse were her wallet, her sunglasses, a package of tissues, and, it went without saying, a good book—usually one of the classics, but sometimes it was a well-thumbed paperback from the browsing collection with words like *temptation, seduction* and *irresistible* in the title. Much like *Metropolitan* magazine, she couldn't help but think. And now, suddenly, thanks to *Metropolitan* magazine, Miriam had discovered that she had needs she'd never realized she had before.

She was fast becoming, she suddenly realized—oh, dear—a *Metro* Girl.

Good heavens, she thought. How could this be happening? Although she'd been reading the magazine and taking the articles to heart, she hadn't actually intended to become one of...*them.* One of the sultry, sexy, sleepy-eyed temptresses who appeared on the front cover. Of course, all of those temptresses, she reminded herself, had considerably more tools of temptation to work with than Miriam had herself. Still...

"This seems to be becoming a habit with us," Rory said as he straightened, extending her book and notebook toward her.

Grateful for his remark, because it scattered her troubling thoughts, Miriam took her belongings from him and slid those, too, into her big purse. "Yes, it does, doesn't it?" she replied.

Replied inanely, she couldn't help thinking. Too bad she'd used up all of her repartee during the class break. Not that her repartee then had been particularly stellar, she amended when she recalled the dubious results of her earlier conversational endeavors. Nevertheless, she could really use some repartee now, regardless of its questionable quality.

But words truly did escape her. Because Rory Monahan was standing right next to her, close enough to touch, close enough for her to turn him around and drape her arms over his shoulders, close enough for her to thread her fingers through his dark hair, close enough for her to push herself up on tiptoe just the slightest little bit and touch her mouth to his, and—

Well, he was just standing very close, that was all, she thought with some shakiness. Much too close for her peace of mind. Among other things.

"Once again, your choice of reading material surprises me, Miss—I mean, Miriam," he said, smiling.

But his smile seemed a bit nervous somehow, she noted, and she couldn't help wondering if maybe he, too, was just now realizing how very close the two of them were standing.

"Well, I don't know why you should find it surprising, Prof—I mean, Rory. This may come as a surprise to you, but librarians do, on average, rather enjoy reading. A variety of things, as a matter of fact."

"Oh, of course," he readily conceded. "I didn't mean… I mean, I wasn't trying to… That is, I hope you don't think me…" He sighed heavily. "Oh, never mind. Can I walk you to your car?" he added, seemingly impulsively. His expression, she noted, suggested that he was as surprised by the sudden offer as she was. Even so, he dipped his head toward the door as he continued, "Everyone else seems to have deserted us."

So they had, Miriam realized when she trained her gaze in that direction. "Thank you," she said. "I'd appreciate it. I had to park farther away than I normally would."

Not that Marigold, Indiana, was in any way dangerous, she knew. Even a newcomer like her could easily see that the place was as safe and secure as a Disney film. Still, she thought further, every now and then, those Disney films had surprisingly heinous villains, didn't they? So it was doubtless best not to let oneself get complacent.

Besides, Miriam really did want to spend as much time with Rory as she could. And he really was staying very close to her. And he really did look and smell so nice.

The night sky outside was black and clear and limitless, the near-full moon spilling silver light over the couple as they walked toward Miriam's car. She strove to find some kind of light, meaningless conversation that might make the stilted silence of the quick trip less awkward, but truly, all that was going through her mind at the moment was how nice it felt to be walking with Rory, even if it wasn't hand in hand, and how warm his body seemed to be next to hers, and how very much she wanted to touch him, and how wouldn't it be so wonderful if he just leaned right over and kissed her.

And then, too soon, they were standing beside her car, and Rory was waiting politely for her to unlock it and climb inside and drive away, out of his life, at least until he encountered her in the library the following afternoon. And it hit Miriam then that if she wanted Rory Monahan to ever become anything more to her than her teacher or an escort to her car, she was going to have to do something drastic—something even more drastic than enrolling in Classical Civilizations II.

Oh, what the heck? she asked herself. She might as well just skip right over seductive step number four and proceed onward, to seductive step number five: making the first move.

After unlocking and opening her car door, she tossed her purse and books over the driver's seat, into the passenger seat, to make room. Then, her hands freed, her stomach churning with nervousness, she spun back around. She gripped the car door fiercely with one hand, then lifted the other to push back—seductively, she hoped—a stray length of her hair.

And then, before she lost her nerve, "Rory," she said, "would you like to have dinner with me tomorrow night?"

Her question seemed to hit him the same way a two-by-four upside the head would. For a moment he only gazed at her blankly, as if he didn't understand the language she was speaking. Then, abruptly, he shook his head once, as if to clear it.

"I—I—I beg your pardon?"

"Dinner," she repeated. "Tomorrow night. With me." Maybe by keeping the sentences short, she thought, they would gel more quickly in his—admittedly crowded with knowledge—brain.

For another long moment he only gazed at her face— or, more specifically, she noted, at her mouth—without replying one way or the other. Miriam held her breath, preparing herself for his rejection of her offer, and waited to see what he would say.

And waited, and waited, and waited...

Five

No matter how many times or how many ways he replayed the previous evening's events in his head, Rory still couldn't quite figure out how he had come to agree to have dinner with Miriam Thornbury. He only remembered that one minute he had been walking beside her, enjoying the comfortable silence that had settled over them and the tantalizing fragrance of her that seemed both familiar and exotic, and then in the next minute he had been gazing down into her clear gray eyes, noting how they reflected her smile as well as her mouth did, and marveling again at the lusciousness of that mouth.

And *then*, in the *next* minute that mouth had opened and formed some words, mesmerizing Rory with their subtle movement and soft sound. And although he could vaguely remember eventually replying in the affirmative to Miriam's request, he couldn't remember precisely *why* he had replied in the affirmative. Because he had been promising himself for days that he would stay as far away from her as possible.

It would, he was certain, remain one of history's greatest unsolved mysteries.

In spite of his confusion, though, he now stood poised to rap his—rather damp, he realized—fist lightly on Miss—on *Miriam's* front door. His other—rather damp, he realized further—hand clutched a cellophane box that contained a pink corsage. Truly. A corsage. A pink corsage, at that. He couldn't recall ever buying such a thing for a woman, not even for his date to the senior prom in high school.

His date that night had been… Oh, let him think for a moment… The girl's name was right there on the tip of his tongue…Daphne. That was it. Or perhaps Danielle. Or maybe Denise. Anyway, he'd taken Daphne/Danielle/ Denise Somebody to his senior prom—after she had asked him to—and although he did recall her wearing a wrist corsage, he was reasonably sure that the girl had purchased it, and donned it, on her own.

It wasn't that he was thoughtless, Rory hastened to reassure himself. It was just that he was… Well, he supposed he *was* thoughtless, when he got right down to it. About things other than his studies and his research, anyway. But it wasn't an intentional sort of thoughtlessness. It was a negligent sort of thoughtlessness. Rory's brain, for all its vast store of knowledge, was a simple organ. He just didn't think about things he didn't care about. Ergo, thoughts of corsages didn't normally make appearances in his crowded cranium.

Tonight, however, he had honestly had the foresight to stop by a florist on the corner near his apartment building and ask the proprietress what would be appropriate for a first date. Even though the phrase *first date* had suggested that there would be a *second* date, and perhaps even *more* dates, to follow it, and that was something Rory really didn't want to get into right now. Which was why, when the phrase *first date* had initially unrolled in his head, he had shoved it back to the furthest recesses of his mind and focused on orchids instead.

Orchids, he marveled now. Never in his life had he thought of orchids, until this night. Somehow, though, the moment he had beheld one of the splendid, extraordinary, intoxicatingly fragrant flowers, he had known it would be perfect for Miriam. He just hoped she didn't misinterpret the gesture. He hoped she wouldn't think he'd done it out of something like thoughtfulness. Because, truly, he was only doing it to be polite. If she misconstrued his gesture to be a thoughtful one, then it would only lead to trouble.

He knocked on her front door with a trio of deft, confident raps before he even realized he had intended to complete the action, and within moments he heard a soft shuffle of sound from the other side. Instinctively he lifted his free hand again, this time to straighten the knot in his tie and smooth out any wrinkles that might be lingering in the fabric of his best navy-blue suit. He hoped his attire was appropriate, as he had no idea where Miriam was taking him tonight. Which, in itself, signified a host of oddities.

First, that he was allowing a woman to call the shots, an idea at which Rory would have thought his masculinity, however unmacho it was, would balk—but it did not. Besides, he had compensated by insisting that *he* would pick *her* up in *his* car, and not the other way around.

Second, that he was allowing himself to be led into the unknown, something he normally would never do, because he always insisted on very detailed advance knowledge about any outing—but this time he had not.

And third, that whatever their outing involved, it almost certainly did not include the quest for knowledge or the performance of research, and he couldn't remember the last time he had engaged in any activity that didn't include those things, at least in part—and tonight, he didn't care.

It was proving to be a most educational experience all the way around.

The realization had just unwound in his head when the door to Miriam's apartment opened completely, and he saw her standing on the other side. And, oh, what a sight she was. She'd left her hair loose again, and it fell in a silky, dark-blond cascade over one shoulder. One *bare* shoulder. At least, Rory assumed it was bare. Because the one he could see, the one that didn't have silky hair cascading over it, was bare, and it only made sense to conclude that such would be the case with the other one, as well. Miriam Thornbury was nothing if not symmetrical.

And her shoulders were bare, he noticed further, because her dress had evidently run out of the silvery, satiny fabric from which it was made not far above her breasts. Not that Rory minded, really. He just noticed, that was all.

And there *was* a good bit of the dress above her breasts, because it nearly met with the necklace she wore, a silvery wisp of filigree that matched the earrings dangling from her ears. And the garment dipped well below her knees, too, at least on the right side, because her stance provided him with a very nice view of her leg extending from another one of those intriguing slits on the left side, a slit much like the one that had intrigued him in the library that day, except that this one wasn't nearly as conservative as that one had been.

Or something like that.

My, but his thoughts were run-on this evening, Rory

mused. What could possibly be the cause of that? Normally his thoughts were very well ordered and to the point. Then again, normally his thoughts focused entirely on historical data. Normally his thoughts didn't include things like legs and side slits and silky hair and silvery dresses. His thoughts had sometimes included the goddess-gown thing, of course, he conceded, but even that reflection had generally tended to be well structured. Probably because he rehearsed it so frequently.

At any rate, Miriam's attire tonight indicated to Rory that he had, in fact, dressed appropriately by donning his best navy-blue suit. However, he couldn't think of a single place in Marigold where *her* attire would be appropriate.

"You look, ah...lovely," he said with profound understatement after greeting her.

She smiled, her cheeks pinking with the gesture. "Thank you," she said shyly.

Shyly, he marveled. In that dress. Amazing. "Here," he said, extending the cellophane box of orchid toward her. "This is, um, for you."

She blushed even more as she took the corsage from him, and something inside Rory hummed to life at seeing it. A blush, he marveled. In that dress. Amazing.

"Thank you," she said softly. She glanced up demurely and asked, in that same soft voice, "Would you help me put it on?"

Rory swallowed hard. Well. He hadn't anticipated this at all. When he'd purchased the corsage, it hadn't occurred to him that she might want help donning it. It hadn't occurred to him that he might be required to...touch her. All in all, though, touching Miriam Thornbury didn't seem like such a bad deal.

"Of course," he said.

He reclaimed the cellophane box from her, deftly

flipped it open, and carefully removed the fragile blossom from within. After handing the box back to Miriam, he lifted her hand and, very slowly, nearly hypnotically, slipped the elastic band over her fingers and hand, settling the flower resolutely on the back of her wrist. Immediately she lifted the delicate bloom to her nose, closing her eyes as she inhaled deeply its sweet aroma. Rory, too, could discern the fragrance from where he stood, a powerful, exotic scent that seemed, somehow, wholly appropriate for her.

"So...where are we going to be dining?" he asked.

"I thought we could drive into Bloomington," she told him as she held her hand before her, gently fingering the fine petals of the orchid.

Something about the gesture captured Rory's complete attention, making his heart race frantically in his chest as he noted the way she so gingerly traced each thin vein in each delicate petal. For one long moment he only watched the slow, precise, mesmerizing motion of that finger, his body temperature rising with each meticulous revolution it made.

Then the gist of her comment hit him square in the brain, and he arched his eyebrows in surprise. "Bloomington?" he repeated. "But that's a half hour's drive, at least."

"More like forty-five minutes," Miriam corrected him as she returned her attention to his face. "But it's a beautiful drive," she added. "And it will give us a chance to chat."

Chat? Rory echoed to himself. She wanted to *chat* with him? In that dress?

"I-I-I..." he began.

"And there's the most wonderful restaurant in Bloomington called Winona's," she continued blithely, oblivious to his distress. "It only opened a few months ago, and it's very popular. And I don't mind telling you that I had to pull some pretty big strings with the owner to secure reservations for us this evening on such short notice. Usually one has to call weeks in advance to get a table at Winona's."

"I—I—I—"

"Fortunately, the owner happens to be my sister, Winona, so it worked out very well. She frequently does me favors like this, because she still feels guilty for beheading my Malibu Barbie when we were young."

"I—I—I—"

"Not that it was an intentional beheading," Miriam rushed on, still apparently unmindful of Rory's state. "No, it was most definitely an accident. Winona had no idea Barbie's head would explode that way when she attached a missile to her back and sent her rocketing down the clothesline."

"I—I—I—"

"It was an experiment Winona was performing for her physics class—all very scientific, I assure you. She's ten years older than me, you see. Which, now that I think about it, makes one assume she would have known better than to attach a missile to Barbie's back and send her rocketing down the clothesline." Miriam shrugged, a gesture that did wonderful things to her dress, Rory couldn't help noting. "But there you have it just the same," she concluded. "Well then. Are you ready to go?"

"I—I—I—" he stammered again, still preoccupied with the comings and goings of her dress.

"We're driving in your car, yes?" she asked. "You did sound so insistent about that, after all."

"I—I—I—"

"Well then," she said again. "Let's be off, shall we?

Our reservation is for seven, and it's just past six now. Thank you for being on time, by the way. It's always so gratifying when a person is punctual.''

"I—I—I—''

Rory realized then that it would probably be best for him to just keep his mouth shut for the next several minutes—or, more accurately, for the next forty-five minutes—because, clearly, Miriam Thornbury could run rings around him in the chat department. Still, there was something about her loquacity that gave him the impression she herself was more than a little nervous about the evening ahead.

Hmmm...

"Drive," he said. "My car. Yes. Let's.''

Oh, well done, Rory, he congratulated himself. Women were always impressed when a man was as articulate as a famous literary character. Unfortunately, in Rory's current state, the literary character in question would be Frankenstein's monster.

He bit back a growl. "I'm ready when you are," he said.

Though, truly, where Miriam Thornbury was concerned, he was coming to suspect that he would *never* be ready.

Winona's, Rory noted upon entering the establishment, was a very busy place, and he could see why Miriam had been forced to take advantage of her sister's decades-old guilt in order to ensure a table for the two of them. Winona's was also, he noted further, a very *nice* place. The decor resembled a turn-of-the-century luxury hotel, very elegant, very opulent, very abundant.

He was immediately reminded of the set for that movie that had been so popular a few years ago.... What was the name of it again? His ex-fiancée, Rosalind, had dragged him to see the film, oh…ten or twelve times, at least. Some blond prettyboy had appeared in the starring role…. What was the actor's name again? *Titanic,* that was it. Not the blond prettyboy, of course. The movie Rory remembered because of the film's historical significance.

At any rate, the set for *Titanic* was what the restaurant reminded him of. But even he could see that the beauty and splendor of the place wasn't the focal point of the decor. No, the focal point of the decor would have to have been the antique-looking telephones, one of which was perched at the center of each of the tables. They must be the focal point, he reasoned, otherwise, they wouldn't have been perched there.

Miriam must have noticed where his attention was directed as their hostess—whose outfit and hairstyle likewise resembled something from *Titanic*—seated them. Because she immediately told him, "The telephones are very popular here at Winona's. Those, along with the food, which is quite excellent, are what keep bringing people back."

"Yes, but why are they sitting on the tables that way?" Rory asked.

Miriam smiled. "So that people can call each other from the tables. It was Winona's idea. The telephones have made for a very successful gimmick to bring people into the restaurant." Her smile broadened. "And they've been rather effective matchmaking tools, as well."

"Matchmaking tools?" Rory repeated, not liking the sound of that *at all.*

Miriam nodded. "Winona told me she's hosting a wedding reception at the restaurant next month for a couple who met here on opening night, via the telephones on the table. There's a number above us," she added, pointing upward.

Rory turned his attention in that direction, only to discover that the two of them were indeed numbered with an ornately scrolled sign—sixteen, to be precise. And, sure enough, as he arced his gaze around the rest of the room, he saw that every other table had a similar sign, complete with number, floating above it, as well.

"Are you telling me," he said, gazing back at Miriam, "that I can pick up this telephone, dial one of those numbers, and the phone on the corresponding table will ring?"

She nodded again. Then, as if cued to do so, the telephone on their own table rang with a delicate whir. They glanced at each other in surprise, but Miriam was the one who answered the phone.

"Hello?" she said into the receiver. Then she chuckled. "It's Winona," she told Rory. "She's up at the hostess stand."

Rory turned toward the door where they had entered and saw a startlingly beautiful woman speaking into a telephone there. She had pale-blond hair and pale eyes, as well, though he couldn't quite discern the color from this distance. She did, however, most definitely resemble Miriam, though he could see that she was a bit older. Her attire was in keeping with the rest of the restaurant's mood, right down to her Gibson Girl hairstyle.

"Yes, the table is perfect," Miriam said into the receiver. "Thank you again for making room for us. It was very nice of you. No, honestly, Winona, I'm not mad about that anymore. Really. Yes, I know Malibu Barbie was my favorite, but all good things must come to an end. No, please don't beat yourself up over it anymore. I grew as a person thanks to the loss. I did. Really. Yes, I did, too. Oh, Winona…"

The woman at the hostess stand looked gravely distressed now, and Rory couldn't help wondering why she didn't hang up the phone and approach the table to address her sister in person. Perhaps she felt too guilty. Evidently, these childhood traumas ran deeper for some people than others, he mused.

Then again, Rory himself recalled his own tragic loss of Sir Stuart, the Silver Knight of the Noble Knights, when he was seven. After all, all thirty-three pieces of armor had disappeared with Sir Stuart. Not to mention the twenty Medieval scale weapons. It had been heartbreaking. But, as Miriam had just told her sister, he, too, had grown as a person for having dealt with his grief afterward.

After a few more minutes of reassurance from Miriam, her sister, Winona, began to look appeased. Then the hostess signaled for her employer's attention, so the sisters broke off the conversation, and each hung up her phone.

"Your sister seems very devoted to you," Rory observed as Miriam completed the action.

She nodded gravely. "I'm beginning to think that Winona was more traumatized by the Barbie beheading than I was." She brightened, smiling again, and Rory was, quite simply, dazzled. "Still, it did get us a nice table, didn't it?" she asked.

He was about to agree with her when his gaze lit on a man who was seated by himself at another one of the tables behind her. What on earth was his brother Connor doing here? Rory wondered. Instinctively, he picked up the phone and dialed the number 27, which was what was hanging over Connor's head.

"Who are you calling?" Miriam asked.

"I just saw someone I... Hello, Connor?" Rory said

when his brother picked up at his end...or, rather, at his table.

"Who's this?" came Connor's gruff reply.

"It's Rory, your big brother," he told his sibling, "and don't you dare use that tone of voice with me, young man. What are you doing here in Bloomington all by yourself? Does Mom know you're out? Alone?"

Connor began to gaze frantically around the room until his eyes lit on Rory, wherein they narrowed menacingly. "I can talk to you any way I want to, Rory," he said tersely. "And I can go anywhere I want to, anytime I want to, and it doesn't matter if I'm alone or not. I'm twenty-eight years old, in case you've forgotten. You're not my keeper."

"What are you *doing* here?" Rory asked again, side-stepping, for now, the fact that he was going to give his little brother a good talking to the next time he saw him back in Marigold. How dare Connor use that tone of voice with him?

"I'm *working*," Connor said, fairly hissing the words. "Now hang up the phone and don't call me again."

"Working?" Rory repeated. "You're a police detective. And a brand-new one, at that. Why would you be working here?"

"Shhh," his brother cautioned him. "Will you pipe down? Don't say another word about me to *any*one. And hang up the damned phone, will you?"

Connor immediately followed his own instructions, slamming his receiver back down in place. Rory gazed in silence at his receiver for a moment, then, feeling more than a little puzzled, replaced it.

"Your brother is here?" Miriam asked. She began looking around the room. "Where is he? I'd love to meet him. I want you to meet Winona, too, before we leave."

Rory shook his head lightly. "Well, I *thought* it was my brother," he said. "He certainly didn't sound like himself, though. Perhaps I was wrong."

She shrugged her—deliciously bare—shoulders, and a thrill of something warm and dangerous shot through Rory. "They say everyone has a double in the world," she remarked. "Maybe it's just someone who looks like your brother."

"Actually, Connor does have a double in the world," Rory said. "His twin brother, Cullen. But that didn't sound like Cullen, either."

Because it wasn't Cullen, Rory told himself. It was Connor. Still, he'd respect his brother's wishes—or, rather, his brother's edict—and not divulge his identity. The nature of Connor's work as a detective—however new he was at the job—often called for such discretion. Nevertheless, Rory couldn't help wondering what his brother, a Marigold, Indiana, police detective, would be doing working here in Bloomington.

Oh, yes. He would definitely be having a talk with Connor the next time he saw him at home.

Six

Miriam still couldn't believe she was sitting in a four-star restaurant, in a town forty-five minutes away from her home, with Rory Monahan. She couldn't believe she'd had the nerve to ask him out in the first place, and she couldn't believe she'd had the audacity to suggest a restaurant this far away. Most of all, though, she couldn't believe she'd donned the dress she had for the occasion, regardless of how insistent *Metropolitan* magazine had been about her attire.

But she had followed the magazine's instructions to the letter tonight. Because tonight, one way or another, she was determined to capture Rory's interest. And keep it.

She couldn't believe she'd managed to keep her wits about her this long, either—not to mention keep up reasonably intelligent chitchat, not to mention keep from flinging a coat on over her dress—as they'd made the long drive together alone.

Although, considering the heightened state of her nerves, Miriam supposed she should be grateful that she'd been able to *stop* talking long enough to catch a few breaths along the way. Otherwise, she might have passed out from oxygen deprivation. And it would have been frightfully embarrassing to have had to make the bulk of the trip with her head lolling awkwardly against her shoulder and—horror of horrors—drooling.

But she was here with Rory now—fully conscious and drool-free—and her nerves did seem to be settling down. A little. Of course, when she noted again just how yummy he looked in his navy-blue suit, how the color made his eyes seem even bluer and more expressive than usual behind his wire-rimmed glasses, how it brought out blue-black highlights in his hair…

She bit back an involuntary sigh. Even Winona was impressed, she thought. Because Miriam had seen the look in her sister's eyes when she and Rory had first entered the restaurant, and Winona most definitely approved. Now Miriam just hoped she could carry off the rest of the evening as well as she had so far.

Their server had come and gone and returned with a bottle of white wine, which Rory had selected from the extensive wine list, assuring Miriam that she would enjoy it and that it would go beautifully with the pecan-encrusted chicken dish that she had ordered. Honestly, though, she could be drinking lighter fluid as an accompaniment to a rubber chicken, and as long as Rory Monahan was her dinner partner, the meal would taste like ambrosia.

Nevertheless, she thought, after an experimental sip of the pale yellow wine, it was a very choice good. Clearly, his store of knowledge did indeed extend to things other than historical facts. Somehow she was relieved to discover that.

And somehow, before she could stop herself, she found herself wondering, as a warm rush of anticipation washed through her, that she couldn't wait to find out what else, *precisely,* he was knowledgeable about. Perhaps, she thought further, if she was very, very lucky, then later in the evening she might possibly find out.

Oh, my, she immediately thought, shocked by the new avenue down which her thoughts had just turned. Where on earth had *that* idea come from? She hoped her Inner Temptress wasn't awakening. She had hoped her Inner Temptress needed her beauty sleep. That could only lead to trouble. Because Miriam was quite certain she could handle Rory perfectly well tonight *without* her Inner Temptress's interference.

Oh, boy, could she handle Rory tonight. And she couldn't *wait* to do it.

Hush, Miriam told the Temptress inside her. *Go back to sleep. Ro-o-ock-a-bye, Temp-tress, in the tree to-o-ops...*

Lovely, Miriam thought. This was just lovely. It was going to be all she could do now to restrain the little vixen for the next few hours. Surprisingly, though, she did manage to keep her Inner Temptress unconscious for the duration of their meal. In fact, she and Rory dined quite companionably for the next hour or so, their conversation never once straying into dangerous waters.

More was the pity, Miriam couldn't help thinking, in spite of her efforts to keep her Inner Temptress at bay. Though, once or twice, she couldn't help but think that her and Rory's gazes did connect in a way that might be construed as, oh, perilous, perhaps.

A girl could dream, couldn't she?

And a girl could not only dream, Miriam realized some time later, but a girl might actually realize those dreams, too. Because after bidding goodbye to Winona—with their compliments to the chef, of course—Miriam and Rory spent another hour strolling through the neighborhood where the restaurant was located. It was a charming little historic area in Bloomington, filled with tiny boutiques and antique and curio shops, canopied by mature trees and lined by old brick town houses and wrought-iron railings and cobbled sidewalks.

And at one point, as she and Rory strode side by side under the twilit sky, their hands and arms occasionally bumping, it occurred to Miriam that she was indeed realizing one of her dreams where Rory Monahan was concerned. Not that she had taken him *home* and fed him, as she often thought about doing, but she had taken him *out* and fed him—even if he *had* insisted, quite vehemently, on paying for that meal himself. And now they were walking—almost hand in hand—through the neighborhood, even if it wasn't her *own* neighborhood. And she discovered, not much to her surprise, that the reality of the dream was even better than the dream itself.

And then she wondered if maybe some other dreams might turn to reality soon.

"It's lovely here," Rory observed at one point. "Although I've been to Bloomington on several occasions, I've never seen much of the town." Hastily, he added, "Outside the IU library, of course."

Miriam nodded. *Of course,* she thought. "This part of Bloomington is a lot like Marigold," she said. "Winona and I grew up in Indianapolis, but we both attended IU and fell in love with the place. She decided to stay here after she graduated, oh…fifteen years ago, I guess. In fact, I lived with her while I attended college. Winona just oves it here. Almost," Miriam added, glancing over at Rory now, "as much as I love Marigold."

"But you haven't lived in Marigold very long, have you?" he asked.

"Six months," she told him. "Before that I worked and lived in Indianapolis."

"You've been in Marigold that long?" he asked, seeming surprised by the information. "Funny, but it doesn't seem as if any time at all has passed since you came to own."

She smiled as she asked, "You noticed when I came to town?"

He colored faintly and glanced away. "Yes, well... I, am, I couldn't tell you the exact date of course, but, ah, actually... Yes," he finally confessed. "I noticed when you came to town." He continued to gaze straight ahead when he finished his admission, as if he would be uncomfortable under her scrutiny. "It was snowing that first day I saw you in the library, and you hadn't yet shed your coat when I came down to the circulation desk looking for Mr. Amberson."

Suddenly he stopped walking and then, surprisingly, turned his body to face her. Miriam, too, halted beside him and likewise turned to face him. Her breath caught in her chest as she studied him, because he had fixed his gaze on hers, his blue eyes piercing and intense. She watched, stunned, as he began to lift a hand toward her hair, but when he realized what he was doing, he must have reconsidered, because he hastily dropped it back to his side. Nevertheless he continued to hold her gaze steady as he spoke.

Very softly he said, "Snow had melted in your hair, and it looked like little fairy crystals scattered about your head. And I thought your eyes were the most unusual shade of gray. And they seemed to be filled with intelligence and kindness and gentleness. I couldn't help but notice you.''

His confession set off little detonations of heat throughout Miriam's midsection. She realized suddenly that she was still holding her breath, so, slowly she released it and slowly she filled her lungs again. But she had no idea what to say to him now. Not unless she told him the truth. Which, ultimately, was precisely what she decided to do.

''I, um, I noticed you, too,'' she said. ''That first day at the library, I mean.'' But she couldn't think of a single thing to add to the statement.

Rory continued to gaze at her for a moment, as if he were mesmerized by something in her eyes. Then his gaze fell to her mouth, and he swallowed visibly. He parted his lips, presumably to say something in reply to her own confession, but not a word emerged to identify his thoughts. Instead he leaned forward and, after only one small, eloquent hesitation, covered her mouth lightly with his. He kissed her gently, tenderly, very nearly chastely. And then, a breathless moment later, he withdrew.

When he pulled back, Miriam realized her eyes were closed and her heart was racing and the entire world was spinning out of control. Then she opened her eyes again to find that Rory was watching her, smiling softly, and...blushing.

He said nothing to explain his action, simply turned forward to stare straight ahead again. And then he started walking, very slowly, and all Miriam could do was follow. Amazingly, in spite of her muzzy-headedness, her steps never faltered. She scrambled for something to say, then worried that speaking might somehow spoil the magic of the moment. Rory seemed to share her sentiments, because he, too, remained silent.

Miriam, optimist that she was, decided to take it as a good sign. She'd left him speechless, after all. That had to be good, didn't it?

Eventually they both found their voices again, even found the wherewithal to make chitchat as they completed their evening constitutional, making a full circle back to Winona's parking lot and Rory's car. For some reason Miriam found herself both looking forward to and dreading the ride back to Marigold. Although the trip guaranteed they would have a little more time together alone, she wasn't sure what awaited them at the end of it. Tonight had been full of uncommon revelations and unexpected surprises, but she feared the enchantment would end once they returned home.

Worse, she worried that by tomorrow Rory would have forgotten everything he'd said and done—everything *she'd* said and done—tonight. Or, worse still, she would awaken in her bed in the morning, only to discover the whole evening had been nothing but a dream.

But dreams came true sometimes, she reminded herself. One of her fondest had come true tonight, only moments ago. Rory Monahan had kissed her. Of his own free will. And although it hadn't been the kind of passionate embrace she often found herself fantasizing about, it had certainly been very pleasant and very promising.

And the evening wasn't even over yet, she reminded herself. They still had the long drive home....

They were almost exactly midway between Bloomington and Marigold—traveling on a deserted two-lane state road that was infrequently used after work hours during the week—when a loud gust of sound alerted them to the fact that there was something terribly wrong with Rory's car.

Well, the loud, gust of sound alerted them to that, along with the way the car suddenly jolted and jerked and slipped and swerved and then nearly ran right off the road. That, Miriam concluded as the car fishtailed dangerously and its tires squealed ominously, was most definitely a key clue that something was amiss.

"Damn," Rory muttered, once he had the vehicle under control again and crawling to a stop on the narrow shoulder of the road. "I do believe I have a flat tire. Again."

"This happens to you often?" Miriam asked, her heart still pounding, thanks to the rush of adrenaline that had shot through her during the momentary vehicular commotion.

"No, not often," Rory told her. "But I had another flat tire not long ago. About, oh… Let me think… Well, I forget now. I'm not sure exactly how long ago it was, but it wasn't very long ago. Certainly it was long enough to give me time to buy a new tire and stop driving on the spare."

Miriam breathed a silent sigh of relief. "Well, thank goodness for that," she said.

He glanced over at her, and even in the dim, bluish light that emanated from the car's dashboard, she could see that his expression was…sheepish? *Oh, dear.*

"I, um, I said it was long enough to *give me time* to buy a new tire and stop driving on the spare," he repeated. "I, ah, I didn't say that was what I had actually done."

"Oh, dear," Miriam said aloud this time.

"Because what's lying in the spare compartment right now, is I'm afraid," Rory said, "my old tire."

"Oh, dear," she said again.

"My old tire with a whopping great hole in it."

"Oh. Oh, dear."

"I rather forgot to buy a new one."

"Oh. Dear." With a good, swift, mental kick, Miriam roused herself off that riff, and tried to look on the bright side. "Well, then," she said. "We'll just call Triple-A. You *are* a member of Triple-A, aren't you?"

Rory hesitated a moment, then slowly shook his head. "I've always meant to join, but I, um… I keep forgetting."

"Not to worry," she reassured him. "I've been a member since I first got my driver's license. They're wonderfully efficient and should be here in no time at all. Do you mind if I use your cell phone?"

Again Rory looked worried. "Well, of course I wouldn't mind you using my cell phone," he said. "If, that is, I had a cell phone for you to use."

She gazed at him blankly. "You haven't a cell phone?"

He shook his head again. "I've always meant to get one. They do seem like they'd be so convenient. Especially in circumstances such as these. But I just—" he shrugged again "—I keep forgetting to get around to it."

This time Miriam wasn't quite so reassuring. Because although she *did* normally carry a cell phone, tonight, her tiny little handbag—the one *Metropolitan* magazine had promised her she absolutely must have to carry off this particular dress with any amount of success—was far too small for necessities like cell phones. Oh, there was room enough for necessities like identification, lipstick, hanky, money, *Triple-A card,* breath mints and um…a condom, she recalled with a blush—well, she *was* a *Metro* Girl now, wasn't she, and *Metro* insisted that she *always* carry one, just in case, didn't it?—but no room for anything as practical and important as a cell phone.

Not that Miriam had any desire to diminish the importance of fresh breath, mind you. Or of safe sex, either. But at the moment if she'd had a choice between good oral hygiene, sexual preparedness or a link to the outside world on a dark, isolated, potentially dangerous stretch of road, she was fairly certain she would opt for the last. Especially since it was looking like the sexual preparedness wasn't going to be an issue with Rory Monahan for quite some time.

"Well then," she said again, striving for an optimistic tone, even as her optimistic attitude bit the dust. "I guess we'll just have to make the best of a bad situation, won't we? Surely some Good Samaritan will come by and render aid soon, if you turn on the emergency flashers. Besides," she added with an—albeit forced—smile, "it could be worse, you know."

"Could it?" Rory asked wearily, sounding nowhere near convinced of that.

She nodded. "Oh, yes. It could definitely be worse. It could be raining."

And then, as if cued by her remark, a rumble of thunder sounded overhead.

"Oh, dear," Miriam said—yet again—when she heard the inauspicious echo.

"Then again…" Rory muttered at the same time.

And as if by speaking as one, they'd uttered a magical incantation, the dark skies opened up above them, dumping what sounded like buckets of water over the midsize sedan. Rain sheeted the windows and windshield, completely obscuring the view—what little view there had been, anyway, considering the fact that it had been pitch-dark on the road when they'd been forced to stop.

For long moments neither Rory nor Miriam said a word, only sat there waiting to see if maybe, just maybe, this was nothing but a bad dream. Then, just when it seemed as if those long moments—not to mention the

ain—might go on interminably, Rory had to go and ruin
t.

"Well, it could still be worse," he commented. "It
could be hailing."

"Oh, don't say it, Rory," Miriam cautioned him, "because if you do—"

Sure enough, before she could even complete the ad-
monition, she heard a rattling *nick-nick-nick* from somewhere beyond the sheets of rain. After a moment the *nick-
nick-nick* was followed by a louder and more threatening
thump-thump-thump that beat relentlessly against the hood
and roof of the car with much maliciousness. The rain
abated for a moment, just long enough for Miriam to see
marble-size bits of ice pinging—nay, bulleting—off the
hood of the car, then the downpour seemed to triple in
severity, blocking her view with a watery curtain again.

She sighed in defeat. "Usually," she said softly, "the
arrival of hail heralds a dip in the temperature." And even
as she uttered the comment, little goose bumps erupted
on her arms. Without consulting Rory, she reached for the
car's air conditioner and switched it off, then crossed her
arms over her midsection in a completely useless effort to
ward off the chill.

"Here," he said as he noted her actions, struggling to
remove his jacket.

He turned off the car's ignition completely, then flicked
on the emergency flashers—not that Miriam thought for
a moment that anyone would be able to see the blinking
lights through this downpour. Not that she thought there
would be anyone out there *to* see them in this downpour.
After all, who in his or her right mind would be out driving on a night like this, unless they were returning home
after a truly lovely interlude with someone about whom
they cared very deeply?

"It looks as if we're going to be stuck here for a while," Rory added. "And I'm afraid to run the engine any longer, even the heater, in case we need the battery for something later. You just never know. But this should keep you warm," he told her, generously extending his jacket toward her, holding it the same way a gentleman would hold a lady's wrap for her.

"How gallant," she couldn't keep herself from saying as she smiled and took the garment from him.

And when she did, Rory blushed. Even though Miriam couldn't see his face very clearly, now that the car's interior lights had been extinguished, she still somehow sensed intuitively that he was indeed blushing. And realizing that only endeared him to her that much more.

Honestly, she thought. One would think she was in love with the man. Which of course wasn't true at all. What Miriam felt for Rory, she was sure, was simply an intense attraction and a powerful longing and a soul-deep need. That was all. Certainly she wasn't denying the possibility that love might occur later in their relationship. But first, she told herself, they must *have* a relationship. She wasn't in love with him. Not yet. Heavens, no.

"This deplorable weather shouldn't last long," he said as she awkwardly thrust her arms through his suit jacket and wrapped it snugly around herself. "These summer storms seldom do. We can wait it out."

Although she knew what he said about summer storms was normally true, Miriam was also certain that Rory had just jinxed it completely the moment he'd spoken the observation aloud. Now it was doubtless going to rain for another forty days and forty nights.

Drat, she thought. They were going to be stranded out here, on this dark, deserted strip of highway, with nothing to keep them warm, all night long, all alone. Immediately upon forming the realization, though, Miriam suddenly brightened. Because now they were going to be stranded out here, on this dark, deserted strip of highway, with nothing to keep them warm, all night long, all alone.

Well, well, well. Maybe this date wasn't going to end up being so disastrous after all. If nothing else, the two of them would now have an opportunity to talk, and perhaps an opportunity to get to know each other better. And maybe, if she was very lucky, they'd even have an opportunity to get to know each other intimately.

Oh, dear, Miriam thought as that last idea unrolled in her head. Her Inner Temptress must be awakening again. And right on time, too, she couldn't help remarking. Sleep all day, and then wake up to carouse all night. That was her Inner Temptress, all right. The little minx.

Miriam snuggled more comfortably into the jacket she had wrapped around herself, inhaling deeply the familiar scents of Rory Monahan and enjoying the warmth of his body that still clung to the inside of the garment. She smiled. Wearing Rory's jacket was almost as nice as being touched by Rory himself, she thought. Then he reached across her for something, and, in the darkness, his arm brushed lightly over her breasts.

And she realized as a thrill of electric heat shot through her that wearing Rory's jacket was absolutely *nothing* like being touched by Rory himself.

"I'm sorry," he immediately apologized as he jerked his arm back again. "I was reaching for the glove compartment. I think there's a flashlight in there."

"That's all right," Miriam said genuinely, if a little breathlessly. "No harm done."

All right, so that last part of her statement hadn't been quite as genuinely offered as the first part. Although it certainly had been all right for Rory to touch her, he'd actually just done plenty of harm—to her thoughts, to her well-being, to her sense of propriety and to her libido.

"Perhaps you could look for the flashlight," he suggested. "You're in a better position to find it than I am, anyway."

Obediently she felt around the dashboard until she located the knob to open the glove compartment. And when she reached inside, she wasn't surprised to discover how tidy and well organized were the contents. It took her no time at all to find the flashlight. But when she withdrew it and switched it on, no light flashed forth. She shook it gently, hoping to rouse some scant illumination, but to no avail.

"I think the batteries must be dead," she said.

She heard Rory's frustrated sigh part the darkness between them. "They are," he told her. "I recall now that they ran out while I was changing my last flat tire. I meant to put new ones in, but—" he shrugged apologetically "—I forgot."

"Oh, Rory," Miriam said as she replaced the flashlight and closed the glove compartment. In spite of their difficult situation, she couldn't quite halt the smile that curled her lips. "You need someone to look after you."

She felt him stiffen in the seat beside her. "I beg to differ," he said curtly. "I've been looking after myself for my entire adult life."

"Have you?" she asked, still smiling.

"Of course I have."

"Well, I do apologize then," Miriam told him. "And I do stand corrected."

Now that her eyes were adjusting better to the darkness, she could distinguish his features fairly well, and she saw him relax some. But there was no way she would ever believe that Rory Monahan looked after himself. Not with any degree of success, anyway.

"Well, then," she continued after a moment, "as you said, we may be stuck here for a good while. What on *earth* shall we do to pass the time? What could there *possibly* be available to two people—two consenting adults, I might add—who are stranded alone together on a dark and stormy night, with absolutely no hope of discovery for hours and hours and *hours* on end?" She leaned toward him a little and cooed softly, "Hmmm, Rory? What would *you* suggest we do?"

Seven

At no time had Miriam intended for her questions to be in any way suggestive. Somehow, though, even as she was uttering them, she realized they sounded exactly that. Not just suggestive, but...*sexually* suggestive. How on earth had that happened?

Probably, she thought, it was because the voice in which she had uttered the questions hadn't been her own voice at all. No, the voice that had spoken just then had most definitely belonged to her Inner Temptress, no two ways about it. Because the voice had been very low and very throaty and very, well, tempting.

Rory must have noticed that, too, because he turned to face Miriam fully and said, with much surprise lacing his own voice, "I—I—I— What did you say?"

She opened her mouth to make amends, not to mention an explanation, for having created such an awkward situation—presumably by making a light jest, somehow, of what she had just said. But she realized fairly quickly that, what with her Inner Temptress being awake and all—drat the little firebrand—she wasn't about to be corralled anytime soon. No, in fact, Miriam's Inner Temptress—little vixen that she was—made matters even worse.

Because what came out of Miriam's mouth, instead of being a hasty, jesting explanation for her previous, dubious, suggestion, actually wound up being a throatily—and temptingly—offered, ''Oh, come on, Rory. Surely, an educated man like you can think of *some*thing for two consenting adults to do that would pass the time in an…interesting…fashion.''

Heavens, had she actually said that? Miriam marveled. Well, of course, she could argue that no, she *hadn't* actually said that, that her Inner Temptress—the little tigress—had been the one behind it. But Miriam had been forced to conclude some time ago—shortly after awakening her Inner Temptress, as a matter of fact—that she alone was responsible for the little rabble-rouser. Ergo, the little rabble-rouser was a part of her makeup, and no amount of denying that would change anything. So when her Inner Temptress spoke, Miriam had no choice but to listen. And to take responsibility.

And she would have to take the initiative, too, she thought further, if she didn't want to completely humiliate herself now by backing down and apologizing profusely for her Inner Temptress's questionable behavior and shrinking back into her seat like a docile little lamb. Then again, taking the initiative with Rory Monahan wasn't such a bad prospect, she decided. Because maybe if she took the initiative, then he might take something else. Like liberties, for example. That might be fun.

After all, he had kissed her not long ago, she reminded herself as a warm, wanton little curl of anticipation unwound inside her. Granted, it had been a nice, simple, harmless kiss, but it didn't take much effort to turn a nice, simple, harmless kiss into a seething, passionate, relentless embrace. Not according to *Metropolitan* magazine, anyway. All Miriam had to do was give her Inner Temptress free rein.

So, without allowing herself time to think about what she was doing, Miriam surrendered herself to her Inner Temptress. And immediately after doing so, she found herself lifting a hand toward Rory's face and threading her fingers through his hair.

Oh, my, what a vamp that Inner Temptress was.

Then, very softly and very seductively, Miriam heard herself telling him, "Do you realize how incredibly handsome you look this evening? Honestly, Rory, Winona would never forgive me for saying this, but all through dinner, all I could do was think about how our meal couldn't possibly be any more delicious than you must be."

He gaped hugely at her, but Miriam couldn't quite blame him. She felt like gaping hugely at herself. Goodness. She must have taken those articles in *Metropolitan* magazine closer to heart than she realized.

Finally, and not a little nervously, Rory said, "Miss...I mean...Miriam...I—I—I think maybe, perhaps, possibly you may have had a little, small amount, tiny bit too much to drink tonight."

"I only had two glasses of wine," she reminded him, weaving her fingers through his hair again. And as she did, she couldn't help noticing that, for all his verbal objecting, Rory had done nothing to remove her hand.

"Yes, but those two glasses were more than three-fourths full," he pointed out. "Which actually goes against the proper pouring procedure for any fine dining establishment.''

"Winona is a generous hostess," Miriam said, twining one dark lock of his hair around her index finger. She pushed her body to the edge of her seat, as close to Rory as she could, and still he did nothing to physically dissuade her physical advances.

"Yes, well, if she gets any more generous," he said, "she may just compromise her profits and drive herself right out of business. Not to mention compromise the virtue of her patrons."

"Is that what I'm doing?" Miriam asked innocently as she leaned further over, to push herself closer to him still. She lifted her other hand to join the first, threading those fingers, too, through his hair, and she marveled at the satiny softness of the dark tresses as she sifted them through her fingers. "Am I compromising myself?" she asked further, hopefully.

Rory's discomfort seemed to compound, but he still made no move to halt her brazen actions. "Oh, I never meant to suggest that you're compromising yourself," he told her. "It's the wine that's compromising you. I'm sure of it."

She waited one telling moment, then said huskily, "I'd rather it be you compromising me."

To punctuate the statement, she reached for his glasses and gently removed them, then set them on the dashboard, her eyes never leaving his. Then she pushed herself to the very edge of her seat and dipped her head to his, nuzzling his nose softly with her own.

Her heart rate quickened as she performed the gesture, her body temperature rocketing into triple digits, she was certain. He smelled spicy and well-scrubbed and manly, an intoxicating combination that dizzied her, dazzled her, dazed her. The storm blustering outside the car was nothing in comparison to the one that was suddenly raging inside her. Miriam had no idea where it had come from, and she was astonished by its utter potency, but there it was all the same. She felt Rory's heat surrounding her, wrapping her, enclosing her completely. And she wanted him. Badly. More than she had ever wanted anything before in her life.

"Miss Thornbury," he began to protest. Though she couldn't help thinking his objection sounded more than a little halfhearted. "I—I—I—"

"Miriam," she immediately corrected him. "Call me Miriam."

"Miriam," he repeated obediently. "I—I—I—"

"I like the way you say my name," she interrupted him. For good measure, she added, "Rory. In fact," she continued, still in that low, husky voice that she couldn't help thinking sounded much more convincing now than it had before, "I like you, period. I like you very much."

As Miriam urged her body closer to his, Rory couldn't, for the life of him, figure out what had come over her. Or him, for that matter, because he certainly wasn't doing what he should to put a stop to her advances. Odder still was the fact that he didn't *want* to put a stop to her advances. In fact, he felt like making a few advances of his own. He was just too startled at the moment to know where to begin.

In spite of his suggestion that Miriam had had too much to drink, he didn't think wine was what had generated her current actions. Not only had they each only had two glasses, as she'd said, but they'd topped them off with coffee over dessert. Then they'd fairly well walked off what scant inebriation may have remained while exploring the neighborhood around the restaurant.

All right, so when he had kissed her, there may have been some kind of intoxication involved, he conceded, but even that, he was sure, hadn't come from a bottle of wine. Where it *had* come from, Rory couldn't quite say at the moment, but he and Miriam both had been as sober as the proverbial judges by the time they'd returned to his car. Until a few moments ago, she'd seemed fine.

And then, suddenly, a few moments ago…

Well, Rory still couldn't figure out exactly where or when things had begun to go awry. One minute they'd been settling in to await the end of the storm, and the next minute…the next minute…

Well, the next minute another sort of storm entirely had begun to brew.

Because suddenly Miriam had been sitting close enough for Rory to fill his lungs with the faint scent of lavender that clung to her, close enough for him to feel her nearness, her heat, her desire. And she'd begun to run her fingers through his hair, and nuzzle his nose with hers, and all of it had just been so overwhelming, all of it had simply felt much too good to ask her to stop any of it, not that he wanted her to stop any of it, even if he knew it would definitely be a good idea to ask her to stop it, but asking her to stop it might make her stop it, and he didn't want her to stop it because…because…because…

Where was he?

Oh, yes. Miriam's nearness. And her scent. And her heat. And her touch.

It was all coming back to him now.

And it was no less confusing now than it had been a few moments ago, when it all began. Even more confusing, though, was his own reaction. Because instead of pushing Miriam away, which Rory assured himself any self-respecting gentleman would do when faced with an amorous—and surely inebriated, right?—escort, he found himself wanting to lean right back into her and thread his fingers through her hair, and wind one or two tresses around his hand to bring her closer still, close enough for him to cover her lips with his and kiss her more deeply.

And suddenly Rory realized that that was exactly what he was doing. His hands, half-filled with her silky hair, were cupping her jaw, and he was tilting her head slightly to one side so that he could press his mouth more intimately against hers. And never in his life had he tasted anything as sweet as she.

Forget about the wine, he thought vaguely. Miriam Thornbury was infinitely more intoxicating.

His eager return of her kiss was, evidently, all the encouragement she needed. Because the moment Rory conceded even that scant surrender to her, she looped her arm around his neck and crowded her body even closer to his. He felt the soft crush of her breasts against his chest, felt her palm open wide over his shoulder before gripping it with much possession. And in that moment all Rory knew was that he wanted—needed—to be closer to her. Even though the two of them were already as close as two individuals could be in the narrow confines of an automobile.

So, ignoring those close confines, he hauled her from her seat into his lap as he deepened the kiss, reaching awkwardly to the side of his seat to release the lever that would glide it back as far as it would go. Then he skimmed the tip of his tongue along the plump curve of her lower lip and moved one hand from her jaw to her neck, strumming his fingertips lightly over the slender column before dipping them into the elegant hollow at its base.

Miriam murmured something incoherent—but incredibly arousing—against his mouth, and Rory moved his fingers sideways, tucking them beneath the opening of his jacket, to trace them along the graceful line of her collarbone. Back and forth, back and forth, back and forth he drew his hand, her skin growing hotter and hotter beneath his touch, her breathing growing more and more rapid, more and more ragged, with each pass he made.

The soft fabric of her dress skimmed along his wrist as he completed each movement, creating a surprisingly erotic friction. Without even thinking about what he was doing, Rory moved his hand down over that soft fabric, so that he might explore more of it. Once there, though, he realized that what lay beneath the dress was infinitely more interesting than the garment itself. Because his hand was suddenly cupped over one full, soft breast, a breast that fit perfectly in his earnest grasp.

Without thinking, acting purely on instinct, he reached for the top of the dress and urged the fabric lower, until, much to his delighted amazement, that soft, perfect globe lay bared to him. Miriam gasped in surprise when he placed his palm over her warm, naked breast, and he took advantage of her reaction by thrusting his tongue into her mouth and tasting her more deeply still. She melted into him with a sigh, and even as he located the tantalizing, and quite aroused, peak of her breast beneath the pad of his thumb, he told himself he should remove his hand immediately, that he shouldn't be taking such liberties with Miriam, because she was far too nice a girl.

Really, though, removing his hand was the last thing Rory wanted to do. So he hesitated, rolling the tight bud beneath his thumb again. Miriam arched her body toward him, pushing that part of herself more completely into his possession, and that was when all thoughts of stopping anything fled his brain completely. Instead he flexed his fingers tighter, and he rotated his palm so that he could grasp her yielding flesh more flagrantly. In response she curled her fingers over his biceps and squeezed hard.

And in a very rough, very aroused voice she said, "Oh, *Rory*. Oh, *please...*"

And then, before he realized what was happening—and although he truly didn't know which one of them released the lever this time—the driver's seat was reclining at a 180-degree angle, with Rory flat on his back and Miriam flat on top of him. Their legs got tangled beneath the steering column, so he adjusted their bodies as well as he could until they lay slantways, though still awkwardly, with their legs in the passenger seat. The press of Miriam's body along his then was...oh. Simply too delicious. And she in no way discouraged their position, either, because she fairly crawled on top of him once the seat was fully back, her body touching his now from chest to knee.

For a moment all Rory could do was gaze up at her face, noting the way her breathing was as ragged as his was, and how she seemed to be gazing back at him with a hunger that only mirrored his own. Her hair cascaded down over them, creating a silky privacy curtain—not that either of them seemed to be particularly concerned with privacy at the moment—and he wrapped a great fistful of it around one hand before cupping that hand over her nape. Then he urged her head lower, down to his own, and kissed her once again. Thoroughly. Completely. Utterly.

This time, though, Miriam was the one to seize control of the kiss, parting Rory's lips with her tongue and plunging inside, to taste him as deeply as he'd ever been tasted before. He looped his other arm around her waist, opening his hand at the small of her back, urging his fingers lower, over the soft swell of her derriere. Miriam gasped at the liberty, and when she did, Rory reclaimed the kiss as his own. This time he was the one to taste her, cupping his free hand now over the crown of her head to facilitate his penetrating exploration.

She uttered a wild little sound at the contact, opening one hand over his chest before moving it down over his rib cage and his torso, to his hip and back up again. He felt her fingers skimming along the length of his belt, back and forth, back and forth, back and forth, in much the same way he had caressed her collarbone only moments before. And, just as he had done moments before, she dipped her fingers lower, then lower still, until she, too, had claimed with her hand an intimate part of his anatomy.

Rory sprang to life at her touch, his member swelling and stretching against his suddenly too-tight trousers. He curved his fingers more resolutely over her bottom and pushed her hard against himself, bringing her pelvis into more intimate contact with his own as he arched his body upward to meet her. She cried out at the contact, pushing her upper body away from his, far enough to move her hand to his belt buckle. And then, almost ferociously, she began to tug the length of leather free.

As she wrestled with his belt, Rory dipped his head a bit and captured her breast again with his mouth, tantalizing the taut nipple with the tip of his tongue. Her fingers faltered in their quest for a moment, then, when he drew her more fully into his mouth, sucking her hard, she moaned, a long lusty sound, and went studiously back to work. As she loosed the length of leather from its buckle and began to unfasten his pants, Rory pushed the fabric of her dress up over her thighs, her hips, her fanny. And he was shocked—truly, shocked—to discover that, beneath her dress, Miriam was wearing skimpy little panties over an even skimpier little garter belt to hold up her stockings.

Oh, Miss Thornbury, he thought as he dipped his fingers beneath the silky panties to cup his palm over the sweet curve of her bare bottom beneath. *The things I never knew about you...*

Her fingers fell to the zipper of his trousers then, and she clumsily tugged it down as their bodies continued to bump each other in the restricted boundaries of the car. Before Rory could say a word—not that he necessarily had any idea what to say at that moment—she, too, tucked her fingers inside the garment, curling them intimately over his hard shaft. Rory closed his eyes at the sharpness of the sensation that shot through him. Really, it had been much too long since he'd indulged in this sort of thing. And something about indulging in it with Miriam just made the whole experience...

Oh, God, he thought as she squeezed him briefly in her hand. *Extraordinary.* That was what the experience was. That was what the woman was, too, he couldn't help thinking further. Extraordinary.

And then he couldn't think at all, because Miriam moved her hand upward, curving her palm over the ripe head of his shaft, rolling it beneath the heel of her hand before steering her fingers lower again. The hand he had placed on her derriere dipped lower, too, scooting her panties along with it. Miriam must have known what he had in mind, because she arched her bottom higher, so that he could move the garment down over her hips and thighs. Then she lowered herself again, bending one knee this time, in a silent bid for Rory to remove her panties completely.

And although he couldn't quite manage that, thanks to their restricted position, he did manage to free one of her legs, thereby granting him enough access to... Well. Thereby granting him enough access, he thought dazedly. His hands skimmed upward again, over the backs of her knees and thighs, to crease the elegant cleft in her firm bottom with one long finger.

"Ohhh...*Rory,*" she said again. But her voice was thicker now, and the words were slower than they had been before.

By now, she had opened his trousers and urged down the waistband of his briefs in front, far enough to free him completely. She wrapped her fingers possessively around him, claiming him manually again and again, trailing her fingers up along his heavy length, circling the firm head before moving oh, so leisurely back down again, until he was nearly insensate with wanting her.

Oh, things really had gone much, *much* too far, he thought. If they didn't stop this *immediately,* they were going to...

"Make love to me, Rory."

Too late.

The realization occurred to him vaguely, through a red haze of very urgent desire. And although his rational, thinking mind told him he absolutely must cease and desist *now,* his irrational, unthinking mind—which he would have sworn was not nearly as powerful as it currently seemed to be—insisted he follow her instructions to the letter. Rory was about to do exactly that when his thinking mind interceded again, this time with a very good argument as to why he must put a stop to things *now.*

"I don't have any..." he began roughly. "I mean, I'm not prepared for... That is, I haven't a, um..."

"Check my purse," she told him breathlessly.

"I—I—I beg your pardon?" he replied.

And vaguely it occurred to him that he would be begging for something soon if she didn't stop doing that thing she was doing with her hand.

He knew he must sound like the most inane human being on the planet, begging her pardon—of all things—at the moment, but truly, Rory had no idea what else to say. How could she have possibly known? he wondered. Not just what he'd been talking about when he was making absolutely no sense, but that there would even be a need tonight for that thing he was making no sense about?

Right now, he thought further, dizzily, was probably not the time to ask her.

Before he could say another word, anyway, Miriam shifted her body slightly on his and reached back toward the seat she had vacated—or, rather, the seat he had helped her vacate by pulling her off it and onto his lap himself—what seemed now like hours ago. And he watched with astonishment as she opened her purse and withdrew a small plastic packet from within. He watched with even more astonishment as she hastily tore the packet open and withdrew the prize from inside, holding it aloft as if it were a trophy.

And then she said something *so* astonishing as to be nearly unbelievable: "I'll help you put it on."

"I—I—I beg your pardon?" Rory stammered again before he could stop himself.

"Oh, it's all right," she assured him. "I've been doing some reading."

As if that would explain all of this, Rory thought. Reading. Honestly. He hated to think what.

But before he could ask, Miriam nestled her body atop his again, and, as she had just promised him she would do, she, um…helped him with it. In fact, she took matters completely into her own hands. So to speak. And no sooner had she completed her task than Rory surged to life again—not that he'd ever really fallen much—his member disagreeing quite vehemently now with his brain, insisting that what she was proposing was a very good idea indeed.

"Now then: Where were we?" she asked.

Immediately, though, she answered her own question, by positioning herself in exactly the same place she had been before. Now if Rory could only remember what she had been saying to him at the time…

"Make love to me, Rory."

Oh, yes. It was all coming back to him now.

"Please," she added, her voice low and husky and tempting…and, well, demanding.

"Are you sure this is what you want?" he asked breathlessly, still feeling hazy and flustered. "This is all happening so quickly," he pointed out.

"Is it?" she asked him. "Funny, but it feels to me as if it's taken forever."

For some reason Rory didn't disagree with her. He only repeated, "Are you sure, Miriam?"

"I've never wanted anything more than I want you right now," she said.

And something in her voice assured him that that was true. In spite of her utter certainty about her avowal, though, Rory could tell she was as confused and surprised by this new development as he was. Then again, he supposed it shouldn't come as a surprise. He had been dreaming about her for months now—nearly since her arrival in Marigold—and in his dreams, the goddess gown had, on occasion, disappeared.

And there had been that odd, sexually charged interlude in the library only days before, where she had fallen, quite literally, into his lap. And there had been those moments in the classroom when the two of them had seemed to connect on a level that went far beyond the scholarly. And there was that kiss that he had stolen from her—and which she had so freely given—earlier this evening. Even though that kiss had seemed relatively harmless at the time, Rory's intentions behind it, he knew now, had been anything but.

He wanted Miriam. Only now did he realize that he had wanted her for a very long time. Never had anyone so...so...so *distracted* him the way she did. Why, there had been times over the past six months when he hadn't even been able to concentrate on his studies, because Miriam Thornbury had walked by his table at the library, scattering every thought he had except the ones involving her.

So maybe he shouldn't be surprised at all, he told himself now as he dropped his hands to her waist again and covered her mouth with his. Maybe he should have seen this coming a long, long time ago...

And then he stopped thinking about what he should or should not have seen, what he should or should not have known, what he should or should not be doing. He bunched her dress in his hands again and shoved the garment back over her hips, then urged her body up a bit, so that he could position himself beneath her. Then he lowered her again and settled his straining shaft at the entrance to the innermost heart of her.

There was one taut moment when he wondered if they were both having second thoughts, then Miriam grasped him in her hand and moved him toward herself. She lowered her body to his, and began to draw him inside herself, encasing him in her damp heat.

She felt... Oh. So fine. So sweet. So perfect. So right. Rory didn't think he had ever welcomed a sensation as eagerly as he did this one. They both sighed their satisfaction as, slowly, he parted her, opened her, entered her, going deeper and deeper, taking longer and longer, until he was buried inside her totally. For a moment they only lay still, allowing their bodies to grow accustomed to the newness of their joining. Then Rory pushed his hips upward, once, thrusting himself deeper still.

Miriam cried out at the extent of his penetration, and for one frantic moment he feared he was hurting her. Then she lifted her hips up a bit, allowing him to glide slowly out of her, before lowering herself over him again. Rory closed his eyes, held tight to her hips and let her set the pace. And the pace she set was slow at first, almost leisurely, a steady, repetitive parry and thrust that nearly turned him inside out.

Gradually, though, her rhythm increased, quickened, deepened. Again and again she covered and released him, pulling him in and out, further with each motion. Rory cupped both hands over her bare bottom and pushed her harder, thrusting his own hips up to meet her. He felt a hot coil beginning to compress inside him, pulling tighter and tighter with every movement they made, until it finally exploded in a white-hot rush of relentless response. Miriam cried out her own climax at the same time, then her body went limp atop his, and, vaguely, Rory wondered if the two of them would ever be the same.

He buried his face in the fragrant curve where her neck met her shoulder and pressed an urgent kiss to the heated flesh he encountered there. He was about to tell her something very, very important, wondering just how he should phrase the complicated sentiment that was spiraling frantically through him, when a trio of—very loud—raps rattled the driver's side window.

Eight

Between the rapid raging of his heartbeat and the dizziness ricocheting around in his brain, Rory somehow realized that it had stopped hailing outside and that the rain had lessened to a mere pitter-pat against the roof of the car and the windshield. He also noticed that every single window his car possessed was fogged up enough to make the glass completely opaque.

And then he noticed that someone was rapping against the driver's side window again.

Miriam must have noticed that, too, because as quickly and as feverishly as the two of them had come together in the darkness, they now sprang apart. She retreated to her seat and began to hastily rearrange her clothes, while Rory fumbled to remove and discard that convenient sexual accessory that was suddenly anything but convenient.

After a long, awkward moment—wherein another trio of raps, louder this time, came at the driver's side window—he had managed to rearrange himself well enough to suit, his shirttail spilling over the waistband of his pants to hide the fact that they were unfastened. Miriam, he noticed, had managed to get her dress back down over her hips and held his jacket closed tightly over her torso.

Gingerly he lifted his arm and used his shirtsleeve to wipe away enough of the fog on the window to reveal a dark figure standing on the other side. A dark figure who was cast briefly into red light, then blue light, then red again, then blue again. Rory could only see the figure from the chest down, but he could tell it was a man wearing a raincoat, a raincoat that appeared to be part of some kind of uniform.

Coupled with the red-and-blue-light business, Rory, scholar that he was, deduced that the figure was, most likely, a policeman.

And for one brief, delirious moment, he wondered if the policeman had come to arrest him, because the activity in which he'd just engaged with Miriam must certainly be illegal. His response to her, after all, had felt more than a little illicit. Then he remembered that he and Miriam, in addition to being consenting adults—oh, boy, had they been consenting—were also stranded on a deserted stretch of road with a flat tire and the emergency flashers were turned on.

Of course, Rory thought further, inevitably, the emergency flashers weren't the only things that had been turned on over the last who-knew-how-many minutes....

Hastily he thumbed the button on the steering column to turn the flashers off. Then shook his head once fiercely, in an effort to dislodge the confusing, confounding conflagration of thoughts that were parading through his head. Then he snatched his glasses from the dashboard and settled them on the bridge of his nose, and somehow found the presence of mind to roll down the car window. The moment the glass began to descend, the police officer tilted his body to the side a bit, to gaze into the car's interior.

"Is, um, is there a problem, officer?" Rory asked. Funny, though, how his voice bore absolutely no resemblance whatsoever to its usual, even timbre.

"You tell me," the policeman said. "You're the one parked here on the shoulder of the road with your emergency flashers turned on."

Among other things, Rory couldn't help thinking. "Ah, yes," he said. "We, um, we were driving home, you see, when we suffered a flat tire, and with the weather being so severe and all..."

He left the explanation unfinished. Not so much because he knew the policeman would be able to infer the rest of the story himself, but because Rory suddenly felt too fatigued to go on. As if he were completely physically spent. As if every cell in his body had just breathed a collective sigh of release and then decided to lie back and light up a cigarette.

It was the strangest sensation. He'd never experienced anything like it before. And he and Miriam hadn't even done what they had done in the most ideal setting. They'd just made love in his car, for heaven's sake. He hadn't even done that when he was a teenager. Probably because he'd never had sex when he was a teenager, he couldn't help thinking, but still.

And if he felt this spent after a quick interlude in his car—fiery and intense though that interlude might have been—then how would he fare with Miriam in a more intimately friendly situation? Like a bed, for example. Where they wouldn't be confined by a steering column or bucket seats? Where they wouldn't be interrupted by a police officer and could prolong their encounter for hours and hours and hours on end?

Good heavens, Rory thought. He might never be able to speak coherently or get around under his own speed again.

"Need any help changing the tire?" the policeman asked, rousing Rory from his troubling thoughts.

He started to shake his head, then remembered that he did, in fact, need some help—at least to alert someone who could bring them a new tire. "Actually, the spare tire I have is useless," he told the policeman. Then he gestured toward Miriam. "But my, um…my, uh…my…"

He turned his full attention to Miriam and found her sitting in the passenger seat staring straight ahead, clutching his jacket fiercely around herself and saying not a word. Her cheeks were flushed, her hair was a mess, and her chest still rose and fell with her rapid respiration. She looked, Rory thought, like a woman who had just been thoroughly tumbled. Which, of course—all modesty aside, he thought modestly—was precisely what she was. And he wondered just how he should classify her to the police officer who was waiting for his reply.

Just what was Miriam now? he wondered. Well, let's see now. She was his…his…his…

His *friend,* he told himself. That was what Miriam was. Wasn't she? That was what he had considered her to be before. Before she'd lain prone atop him with her breast in his mouth and her bottom fitted lovingly into his palm. Before she'd taken him into her body and glided herself along his length, over and over and over and…

Okay, so perhaps *friend* wasn't quite an appropriate term for her anymore. Because Rory had never done any of those things with any of his other friends.

Companion? he wondered. But no, that didn't seem like

a fitting label for her, either. It conjured up an image of one of them being old and frail and infirm, and as they'd just realized, that wasn't the case with either of them at all.

Escort, too, seemed like an inappropriate designation for her, because it was too impersonal, too formal. And with Miriam wearing the dress that she was wearing—not to mention looking as if she'd just been thoroughly tumbled—a man of the law might very well misinterpret the word *escort* to be something that went way beyond inappropriate.

Significant other? Rory wondered further. Oh, absolutely not, he immediately told himself. That indicated that the two of them had the kind of relationship he wasn't about to enter into again. Well, probably not, anyway, he amended reluctantly for some reason.

Lover? he asked himself. Although that was technically true after what had just happened—in the connotative sense, at least—Rory was uncomfortable applying that tag to her, as well. For one thing, it offered the policeman insight into their relationship that Rory had scarcely had time to consider himself. For another thing… Well, for another thing, he wasn't sure just how much *love* actually entered into things.

So then what, exactly, he asked himself again, *was* Miriam to him now?

"My, um…" he began again, still gazing at her as he tried to find the right word to give the police officer. "My, uh… My, ah…"

"Your wife?" the policeman offered helpfully.

"Oh, God, *no,*" Rory replied vehemently, jerking his head back around to look at the police officer. "She's not my *wife.*"

"Oh, it's like that, is it?" the policeman asked with a knowing nod.

Rory arrowed his eyebrows down in confusion. "Like what?" he asked, genuinely puzzled.

The policeman shrugged carelessly. "You're out with your girlfriend instead of your wife," he said blandly. "You get a flat, you get home late, you get in big trouble... Hey, I know how it is. I got two ex-wives. And two ex-girlfriends."

"No, no, no," Rory said quickly, adamantly. "Absolutely *not*. She's not my *girlfriend*, either." Because that word, too, seemed utterly inadequate in describing what Miriam was to him. She was much more to Rory than a girlfriend. She was...she was... Hmmm...

He tried again to pinpoint her role in his life, aloud this time, for the policeman's sake. "She's my... She's my...my..."

"I'm his librarian," Miriam said softly from the other side of the car. "That's all I am."

And even though that, technically, was true, somehow Rory knew he was going to have a lot of trouble thinking about Miriam Thornbury as only that in the future.

The police officer dipped his head lower, looking past Rory this time, deeper into the car's interior, at the woman seated beside him. And Rory could tell by the expression on the other man's face that there was no way—*no way*—he would ever believe that all Miriam Thornbury was to Rory was his librarian.

Which was just as well, Rory supposed. Because that wasn't all she felt like to him anymore, either.

"Yeah, well, whatever," the policeman said as he straightened again. "So do you need a hand changing the tire or not?"

Rory backpedaled to where they had been before in

their conversation. "As I was saying, my, um, my librarian, is a member of Triple-A, but we don't have access to a telephone at the moment, so—"

"You don't have a cell phone?" the policeman asked. "But they're so convenient. Especially in circumstances like these."

Rory bit back a growl. "Yes, well, I'll take it under advisement," he said. "In the meantime, if you could be so good as to place a call to Triple-A for us, telling them we'll need a new tire in addition to help changing it, we'd very much appreciate it." He forced a smile and hoped it didn't look as phony as it felt. "And then," he told the policeman, "you could...carry on."

Oh, Rory really wished he'd come up with a better phrase than that one to use. Because he knew right away that the policeman was going to respond with—

"And, hey, then you two could carry on, too."

Somehow Rory managed to refrain from indulging in a knee-slapping guffaw and a riotously offered *Oh, hardy-har-har-har.*

"I'll just go back to my car and make the call for you," the policeman said as he turned and strode away. "I'll get the emergency number off my own card. I'm a member, too, of course. You shouldn't have to wait long. Just to be on the safe side, though, I'll hang around until the wrecker shows up. Wouldn't want you and your... librarian...getting home *overdue*," he added with a wink. "Wives hate that."

"But I'm not—" Rory began. But he halted when he saw that the police officer was out of earshot. And as grateful as he was for the other man's departure, he realized with a silent, heavy sigh that now that the policeman was gone, Rory was once again all alone with Miriam. And he had no idea what to say to her.

Except maybe for "I apologize for my abominable behavior a few minutes ago."

She nodded halfheartedly but said nothing.

"It really was unforgivable," he added.

"Yes," she concurred quietly. "It was."

He was surprised to hear her agree with him so readily. Although his behavior *had* been unforgivably careless—and at the risk of sounding like a tantrum-throwing child—Miriam had started it. Not that that gave Rory an excuse to go along with her so willingly—after all, if she jumped off a bridge, would he jump, too?—but he didn't think he should be forced to shoulder the bulk of the responsibility for what had happened. She was the one who'd purred out such intimate suggestions about consenting adults in the first place. Just because he hadn't done anything to stop what had happened—and just because he had enjoyed it so immensely—that didn't let her off the hook.

In spite of his mental pep talk, however, he said, "Truly, Miriam. I am sorry for what I did."

She lifted her shoulders and let them drop, a small shrug that seemed in no way careless. "It's all right," she told him softly. "It's not like you said anything that was untrue. And I am your librarian, after all."

He opened his mouth to say more, then realized how badly she had misunderstood him. She thought he was apologizing for something totally different from what he was actually apologizing for—though he wasn't entirely sure what she thought he *was* apologizing for. In any case, her response suggested that she *wasn't* upset by their sexual encounter, which was what Rory had actually been apologizing for.

"No, Miriam," he said gently, "I meant I'm sorry for...for...for pouncing on you the way I did." He dropped his voice to a softer pitch as he spoke, even though there was no one to overhear him. "For taking advantage of you the way I did. Sexually, I mean."

She glanced over at him, her expression puzzled. "You didn't pounce on me," she said. Then, very matter-of-fact, she added, "I pounced on you."

"Well, perhaps so," he conceded, guarding his surprise that she would so freely admit her part in what had happened. "But I did nothing to stop you. I went right along with it."

"And you're apologizing for that?"

"Of course I am."

She gaped at him in disbelief for a moment. Then, "Oh," she said in a very small voice. "I see."

"Well, don't you think I should apologize?" he asked. After all, he thought, she certainly deserved better than a quick tumble in his car. She deserved satin sheets and candlelight and soft music and a man who took his time with her, loving every luscious inch of her body. Several times over, in fact.

"Are you sorry it happened?" she countered.

"Of course I'm sorry," he told her again.

Their first time together should have been much nicer than what the two of them had just had, he thought. Though, mind you, what the two of them had just had had been very nice. Oh, yes. Very nice indeed.

"Oh. I see," Miriam repeated in that same small voice.

"Well, aren't *you* sorry it happened?" he asked.

She inhaled a deep breath and released it slowly. "I wasn't before," she told him. "But I suppose I am now."

Well, then, he thought triumphantly. Somehow, though, his triumph felt in no way victorious.

Miriam said nothing more in response—not that any-thing more seemed necessary—so Rory, too, remained silent. In a few moments the police officer returned to say that a wrecker was on the way to the scene with a new tire, and should be there shortly. And less than twenty—totally silent—minutes after that, the tumble of yellow lights in the darkness heralded its arrival.

The police officer left after a knowing smile and a casually offered, ''Good luck to you both,'' and then Rory and Miriam stood outside the car—in silence—as the mechanic deftly changed the tire, and recorded her AAA information, and said good-night.

And then, in what seemed like no time at all, Rory and Miriam were sitting alone—and silent—in his car once again.

''Well, I suppose it would be best to get home,'' he finally said as he turned the key in the ignition.

She nodded slowly, but said nothing.

''Unless you'd like to stop somewhere for coffee,'' he added, surprised to hear himself make the offer.

He was even more surprised to realize how much he wanted her to take him up on it. They really did need to talk, he thought. Then again, maybe now wasn't the time. There was a definite awkwardness in the air. Perhaps once they both had time to reflect upon what had happened, they would be better able to figure out what was going on.

''No,'' Miriam told him. ''That's all right. Thank you.'' But the words were flat, mechanical, emotionless. She didn't sound at all the way she usually did.

Still feeling as if he should say *some*thing—but having no idea what that something might be—Rory reluctantly guided the car back onto the road, and they continued on their way back to Marigold. In silence. Somehow, though, he didn't quite feel as if they were going home. Because somehow he suspected that when they got there, nothing was going to be the same.

And when he pulled up to her apartment building a little while later, and turned off the engine to accompany her to the door, only to have her tell him in a very soft, very wounded voice, that it wouldn't be necessary... As he watched her walk slowly and wearily up the walkway to her front door and enter her building alone... When he recalled how wilted and crushed had been the corsage still affixed to her wrist...

Well. Then Rory was sure nothing was going to be the same.

When Miriam unlocked the front doors to the library the morning following what was to have been a momentous date with Rory Monahan, she felt none of the usual zest or élan she normally experienced when she arrived at work. And not just because it was raining, either, although the rain did rather hamper her mood, because it only served to remind her what had happened the night before with Rory.

Oh, God, she thought as she entered the library with one explicit image after another replaying itself in her muddled brain. Her stomach pitched with a mix of anxiety and desire with each recollection. What *had* happened the night before with Rory? she wondered. In spite of her efforts to tempt him last night, at *no* time had Miriam intended for things to go as far as they had gone. *Metropolitan* magazine may have talked her into carrying a condom around, but not once had she honestly thought she would ever have cause to use the silly thing. Not until after she and Rory had gotten to know each other *much* better.

Then again, she told herself, she knew him as well as

she knew anyone. Better than she knew most people, actually. At least, she knew all the things about him that were important. And she knew that the feelings she had for him were anything but casual.

But she still couldn't believe she and Rory had actually made love last night, in his car, no less, like two hormonally unstable teenagers. She still couldn't imagine what had come over her to make her lose control the way she had. As much as she wished she could blame her Inner Temptress, Miriam knew that she alone was responsible for her behavior. Even if her behavior had been completely alien to her.

She simply had not been able to help herself. The moment Rory had kissed her so deeply, when he'd covered her bare breast with his hand… Something had exploded inside of her, unlike anything she'd ever felt before. She'd just been so overcome with wanting him, with needing him. She'd assumed that whatever it was that was building between them, it was unique, and it was special, and it was eternal. She had been so sure that he must feel the same thing for her that she felt for him. She had been so certain that he must…that he must…

She sighed deeply. That he must…love her the way she loved him. There was no way she could have stopped what had happened the night before with Rory. Because it had felt so natural, so perfect, so right.

But it wasn't what had *happened* the night before with Rory that caused her to feel so melancholy today, she knew. No, the reason she felt so melancholy today was because of what she had *learned* after what had happened the night before with Rory. Because she had learned that he didn't want her. Not the way she wanted him to want her, at any rate. Not the way she wanted him. She only wished now that she had learned it before things had gone too far.

Oh, certainly he had *wanted* her last night. In exactly the way *Metropolitan* magazine made clear that a man *should* want a woman. Why, what she and Rory had experienced together was exactly the stuff that *Metropolitan* headlines were made of: Roadside Attractions Your Mother Never Told You About! Or Finding His Gearshift When He Goes into Overdrive! Or Make-Out Blowouts: What to Do When the Tire's Flat, but He's Not!

Oh, yes, Miriam thought wryly, sadly. She would have to write a letter to the editor immediately and suggest that the next issue of *Metropolitan* magazine be the car and driver issue. She herself could be a major contributor.

So, yes Rory had *wanted* her last night, but only in a sexual sense. Not that it would normally bother Miriam to have him wanting her sexually—not in the least. Provided he wanted her in other, less tangible ways, as well.

Oh, God, no. She's not my wife.

Absolutely not. She's not my girlfriend, either.

But he didn't want her in other, less tangible ways, she thought as the echo of his unmistakable aversion reverberated in her brain. Judging by the way Rory had spoken the night before, the prospect of having a wife, or even a girlfriend, was about as appealing as finding a dead slug in his dinner salad—after he had added a liberal amount of salt.

Only now did Miriam realize—too late—the difference between *tempting* a man and having him *fall in love* with her. Because she realized now that what she had really wanted all along—what this whole, silly *Metro* Girl fiasco was supposed to have achieved—was for Rory to fall in love with her. And although he certainly had been tempted and had certainly wanted her, loving her evidently wasn't part of the bargain. Not to his way of thinking, anyway.

And just what was *Metropolitan* magazine going to do about that, hmmm? Miriam wondered as she strode behind the circulation desk and began flicking the rows of switches that would illuminate the first-floor lights. Because no matter how furiously she had searched the night before, sifting through the box of magazines that still occupied her bedroom, there hadn't been a single headline on a single issue that had mentioned the word *love*.

As she entered her office and struggled out of her raincoat, she realized she had fallen into the same trap that so many women fall into—equating sex with love and love with sex, and completely forgetting about the fact that the presence of one didn't necessarily include the presence of the other.

Au contraire.

People could certainly have sex without love, she reminded herself, as evidenced by Rory's reaction to her the night before. And people could have love without sex, too, as witnessed by her own reaction to Rory.

Because she did love him. She admitted that to herself freely now. She had loved him for months, probably since her arrival in Marigold. Certainly long before she had experienced sex with him. And she knew she would continue to love him for some time to come. Perhaps for all time to come. And she would feel that love despite her plans to *not* have sex with him again. Because there was no point to pursue such a thing when he so readily dismissed the idea of having her for his wife or his girlfriend.

Miriam was an intelligent woman, after all. She knew better than to have sex with a man who didn't love her. She just wished she had been smart enough to identify that lack of love before she had gone too far.

She sighed heavily again as she tossed her damp rain-coat onto the hook affixed to the back of her office door. Would that she had been smart enough not to fall in love with Rory in the first place, too, she couldn't help thinking further.

Inescapably her mind wandered backward then, to that single, sweet kiss the two of them had shared while walking through the neighborhood near Winona's after dinner. Miriam still wasn't sure what that had been all about. Rory had taken the initiative for that one, but his initiative had been so innocent, so solicitous, so tentative then. How had they gone from a simple, chaste kiss during their promenade, to a raging conflagration of need only an hour or so later?

Miriam feared she had a response to that, but it wasn't one she cared much for. While walking with Rory, she had been Miriam Thornbury, librarian. Later, in his car, she had been a Temptress. And where Miriam the librarian might have stood a chance with Rory, had she just let things move forward at their own pace, Miriam the temptress had gone and ruined everything by jumping the gun. Among other things.

And now here she stood, Miriam the librarian again, dressed once more in her standard attire of straight gray skirt and pale-pink blouse, her hair caught at her nape with her standard tortoiseshell barrette. And where was Rory? she wondered. Probably at home sleeping, dreaming about the temptress who had seduced him the night before.

Damn *Metropolitan* magazine anyway, Miriam thought. Someone should put a warning label on the publication.

So bleak was her mood by now that if Mayor Isabel Trent had come striding into her office at that moment and asked her to hold a public book-burning in the town square for *Metropolitan* magazine, Miriam could very well have seen fit to bring the marshmallows.

"Oh, wonderful, Miriam, you're here early. I knew you would be. You're so dependable."

As if conjured by her thoughts, Mayor Isabel Trent did, in fact, come striding into Miriam's office at that moment. But she carried neither *Metropolitan* magazine nor gasoline can nor propane torch, so although Miriam's hopes of igniting the publication were dashed, she at least had hopes that she might have a reasonable conversation with the mayor for a change.

At least, she had hopes of that until Mayor Trent told her, quite adamantly, "Miriam, I want you to dance for me."

Miriam tried very hard to keep her eyes from bugging out of her head—that was such a frightfully impolite thing to do—but wasn't sure she was able to manage it as she replied, as courteously as she could, *"Huh?"*

"Oh, nothing difficult, I assure you," Ms. Trent said with a negligent wave of one hand. "Just a little foxtrot. Maybe a waltz or two. Surely you took lessons when you were a girl. You have that look about you."

Miriam tried to maintain her courtesy as she repeated, a bit less impulsively this time, "Huh?"

"All right, if the waltz is too challenging, then perhaps it would be all right if you stuck to a simple box step," Ms. Trent told her magnanimously. "But I do want you to dance for me."

This time Miriam made no bones about it. Quite forcefully now, she demanded, "Huh?"

Ms. Trent seemed to finally notice her discomfort, and she must have realized how strangely she was articulating whatever it was she wanted to articulate. Because she laughed lightly and lifted a hand to nervously twist the top button of the charcoal blazer that topped her straight, charcoal skirt.

"Well, I suppose that sounded rather odd, didn't it? I should offer you a little more by way of an explanation, shouldn't I?" she asked.

Miriam nodded enthusiastically. "That would be most helpful, Ms. Trent, yes."

"The local Kiwanis Club is holding its annual fund-raiser this weekend, at Tony Palermo's Stardust Ball-room," the mayor said. "They do this every year, which, of course, you couldn't possibly know, because you're a relative newcomer to Marigold. But everyone in town looks forward to it, and everyone comes, and the Kiwanis always need extra dancers, because Tony Palermo never has enough for this sort of function. And this year there's a shortage, because Tiffany Parmentier broke her ankle, and Debbie Sherman is on her honeymoon, and Shannon Epstein just had twins. So you're up, Miriam."

Miriam's head was fairly spinning with the wealth of information—little of it coherent—that was buzzing around in her brain. "I...huh?"

"We Marigoldians always chip in when a helping hand is needed," Ms. Trent admonished her. "I myself have offered to trip the light fantastic in Debbie's place." She sniffed a bit haughtily. "I would *never* ask one of my constituents to do something that I wouldn't do myself."

Of course not, Miriam thought. Which was why she had no trouble asking the local librarian to ban books. She fixed her gaze levelly on the mayor's. "I'm afraid I don't understand, Ms. Trent. Just what kind of fund-raiser is this, anyway?"

"I told you. It's the Kiwanis Club's annual 'Trip the Light Fantastic Night' at Tony Palermo's Stardust Ball-room. The money raised goes to their scholarship fund.

It's the social event of the summer. And it usually earns enough to send several students off to IU in the fall.''

"But…dancers?" Miriam asked.

"Well, that's what tripping the light fantastic is all about, isn't it? Ballroom dancing?''

"I suppose, but…why me?''

Mayor Trent smiled warmly. Miriam recognized it as her "family values" smile. "Well, it's always nice to have attractive young men and women present at this event, to dance with the elderly widows and widowers.''

"Um, why can't the elderly widows and widowers dance with each other?" Miriam asked.

Isabel Trent gazed at her blankly. "Because they'd rather dance with attractive young men and women, that's why.''

"Oh.''

"It costs fifty dollars per person to attend, and that doesn't include refreshments,'' the mayor added, as if that explained everything.

And, Miriam supposed, in a way, it did. Even with the family-values thing going. "But this is such short notice,'' she protested. "I'm not sure I can take the night off. I was going to have my car worked on this weekend. I don't have anything to wear.''

Let's see now, she thought further. Were there any other lame excuses she'd forgotten about?

Not that it mattered, because Isabel Trent clearly wasn't buying any of the lame excuses she'd already offered. "Find the time,'' the mayor decreed. "You can have the car worked on another time. And Lola Chacha, Tony Palermo's top dance instructor—which, of course, isn't her real name, but it's appropriate nonetheless—has plenty of ballroom-type dresses she'll be glad to loan out for the occasion. She's already told me she has one for me that's perfect.

"So that settles it," the mayor concluded with a satisfied smile. "I'll see you Saturday night at Tony Palermo's. Wear comfortable shoes. I'm sure you'll be dancing all night."

And without even awaiting a reply, Isabel Trent swept from the office, doubtless off to recruit another unsuspecting dancer.

Miriam shook her head ruefully and wondered if she should call the mayor back, to tell Ms. Trent that for generations the entire Thornbury family had been notorious for having two left feet, and none of them could dance to save his or her life.

Oh, well, Miriam thought further. She'd only be dancing with elderly widowers. And they probably wouldn't even notice or care how many feet she had, or of what variety. She tried not to feel too morose when she realized that Rory Monahan fell into that category, too.

Then again, Rory Monahan wouldn't be at the dance, she reminded herself. Because in spite of Mayor Trent's assurance that the fund-raiser would be the event of the summer and that everyone in Marigold looked forward to it, Miriam knew that one citizen, at least, wouldn't be in attendance. Because while she was tripping the light fantastic with a retiree in a borrowed ball gown—Miriam, of course, would be the one in the ball gown and not the retiree...she hoped—Rory Monahan, scholar, would doubtless be sitting at his usual table in the library, carousing openly with volume fifteen of *Stegman's Guide to the Peloponnesian War*.

And somehow Miriam couldn't help thinking that he would be having a much better time than she. Because Rory, at least, would be with the one he loved.

Nine

Rory entered his classroom on Wednesday night for the second session of his evening Classical Civilizations II class, feeling nervous and anxious and totally unprepared. Not that he felt this way because of his lecture, mind you. No, he knew his history backward and forward and inside and out. But—and this was a *most* remarkable development—history was the last thing on his mind tonight. Because all Rory had been able to think about all day was Miriam Thornbury.

Surprise, surprise.

When he'd awoken that morning—from a very restless sleep—he'd been convinced that he had only dreamed the episode of the night before. There was no way, he had told himself, that he and Miriam Thornbury could have possibly made love in his car. Not just because of the limitations of the physical logistics involved, but because they were both rational, intelligent, thinking adults, far above being controlled by their basic, instinctive, irrational natures.

Yes, surely, he had told himself all morning long, he had only dreamed about the smoothness of Miriam's soft skin and the sweetness of her silky hair and the luscious taste of her breast in his mouth and the exquisite sensation of himself inside her. Only a dream, he had repeated to himself over and over again. Only a dream. Only a dream. Only a frantic, hot, erotic dream.

Then he had gone out to his car to drive to work, and had discovered a bit of champagne-colored silk sticking out from beneath the passenger seat. And when he had tugged on that bit of silk and discovered it to be a complete pair of panties, he had realized that what he had thought was a frantic, hot, erotic dream had actually been frantic, hot, erotic reality.

He *had* made love to Miriam Thornbury. In his car. On a dark stretch of highway. As if he'd had no more control over himself and his body than a sixteen-year-old boy would have. Then again, that was precisely how Miriam made him feel—like a rank adolescent, in love for the first time.

Wait a minute, he told his scrambled brain now as he settled his briefcase on the dais at the front of the empty classroom. *Hold on. Back up. Repeat.*

In love for the first time… In love… Love…

Love?

Could that possibly be what lay at the crux of his current preoccupation with Miriam? Because, truly, no one had ever distracted Rory to the point where he didn't think about his studies or his research. To the point where he didn't even *want* to think about his studies or his research. Come to think of it, his distraction with Miriam didn't feel anything like his distraction with Rosalind had felt

It didn't even feel like his *preoccupation* with Rosalind had felt. In fact, it didn't feel like preoccupation at all. What it felt like went way, way beyond preoccupation. What it felt like was...was...was...

Well. He very much suspected that this was, in fact, what it felt like to be in love with someone. Because suddenly the only thing Rory wanted in life was to be with Miriam.

What a startling development, he thought. But, surprisingly, it wasn't at all unpleasant.

Then again, maybe that wasn't surprising at all. Because for some time now, Rory's thoughts—and fantasies—about Miriam had been fast usurping his intellectual pursuits. And even Rosalind, although certainly distracting, hadn't invaded his thoughts or his life to the extent that he had disregarded his intellectual pursuits. Neglected them, yes. He had indeed neglected his studies when he'd been involved with Rosalind. But he hadn't forgotten about them entirely. He hadn't even assigned them to second place. That was the place Rosalind had held. Which, he supposed, was why she had left him. Not that he could blame her.

Since last night, however, Rory hadn't given his lessons or his research a second thought. Hell, he hadn't given them a *first* thought. Because the only thing he'd been able to think about was Miriam. The only thing he had *wanted* to think about was Miriam. In fact, thoughts of Miriam made thoughts of everything else pale. Even thoughts about his studies. Even thoughts about his research. Even thoughts about history. Even thoughts about the Peloponnesian War.

Good heavens. He *was* in love with her, he realized suddenly. That could be the only explanation for why he felt the way he did. Because although he was as excited as usual to be coming to class tonight, although he wa anticipating the sharing of information with as much plea sure as he always did...

It wasn't teaching and learning that captivated him so at the moment. No, it was the prospect of seeing Miriam again. The thought of seeing *her* again excited him. And he anticipated with pleasure the opportunity to share in formation with *her*. Though, if he were honest, it wasn' information about classical civilizations that he wanted to share with her. It was information of a much more inti mate nature.

His heart began to race wildly in his chest when he finally realized what was going on. Rory Monahan. In love. Who would have ever suspected such a thing? Cer tainly not Rory Monahan.

Well. He supposed now that he *really* should have called her today. This was something, after all, he wa going to want to tell her about.

And he had actually thought about calling her earlie that morning, after he'd discovered her panties in his ca and realized he hadn't, in fact, been dreaming about wha had happened between the two of them the night before But he'd been so stunned by the realization that he quite frankly hadn't known what to say to her.

Hello, Miriam? Did you know you left your panties in my car last night? Yes, I had a nice time, too. We'll have to do it again very soon.

No, somehow that just didn't seem quite right.

What Rory needed to say to Miriam, he needed to say in person. But he hadn't wanted to interrupt her at her work, at the library. And he'd wanted to have some time to prepare. And he'd known he would be seeing her to night, in his class. So he'd assumed, or at least hoped that afterward the two of them might go someplace—

someplace quiet and private and conducive to intimate discussion—and talk about what had happened. About what it all might mean. About how they were going to approach the future.

Because Rory very much wanted a future with Miriam. A future that involved infinitely more than research and knowledge and intellectual pursuits. He could only hope she felt the same way.

He inhaled a deep breath to steady his heart rate, but the moment he exhaled, his pulse began to beat erratically again. It quickened even more when he heard the classroom door creak open, and he jerked his head in that direction, hoping with all his might, and all his heart, that the person who strode through would be Miriam.

But the person who entered wasn't she. Nor was the next person who entered the classroom. Nor was she the third or the fourth or the fifth. And fifteen minutes later, even after Rory had done something completely unprecedented—holding off starting his lecture until the rest of the class arrived—there was still no sign of Miriam.

And he told himself this couldn't possibly be a good development.

Where was she? he wondered as his students began to grow restless—as if they could be any more restless than he was himself. Certainly Miriam might feel a little awkward about things, just as Rory did himself. But he had thought she would still come to class tonight, if for no other reason than that *she* wanted to talk to *him* afterward, too.

Why hadn't she come? he wondered again. Unless, he thought morosely, after what had happened, she simply didn't want to see him again.

Could that be possible? he asked himself. Although she had seemed as enthusiastic and overwhelmed as he had been last night, perhaps her reasons for being so didn't mirror his own. Where Rory's heart had been engaged with his behavior—even if he hadn't realized it at the time—maybe Miriam had only been driven by her physical needs. And now that those needs had been met—at least he hoped he'd met them—then perhaps her interest in him was waning.

Still, he couldn't see that being the case. Miriam Thornbury didn't seem like the kind of woman who could divorce her physical needs from her emotional ones. Not needs like the ones they'd shared the night before, anyway.

No, Rory was certain—well, fairly certain—that Miriam had feelings for him, too. He just wished he knew the depth of those feelings. What if, having made love with him now, in a situation that had been anything but ideal, she was having second thoughts? he wondered. What if she thought him a heel because he had taken advantage of her on a dark, deserted strip of road? Granted, she had told him she thought *she* was the one who'd taken advantage, but still. What if, now that she'd experienced the next level of emotion with Rory—the most intimate level of emotion—she'd decided she didn't want any part of it?

In other words, what if he'd disappointed her last night? What if she didn't like him, didn't want him, anymore?

Oh, he definitely needed to talk to her, he told himself. Tonight. After class, this very evening, he would stop by her apartment for a chat. He had to know where he stood with her. And he needed for her to know where she stood with him. He only hoped they both stood in the same place. Or at least on the same level. He didn't think he could stand it if Miriam told him she didn't want to see him anymore.

And not just because the library was his favorite place
on earth, either. No, it was because Miriam was his favorite librarian on earth. Among other things.

With a heavy heart and a total lack of enthusiasm, Rory
began his lecture. But there was none of the joy in teaching that he usually felt, none of the contentment that came
with sharing his thoughts and observations about classical
culture. History held no appeal. Nor did anything else.
Because Miriam wasn't here to share it with him.

And somehow that just didn't feel right at all.

Unfortunately, when Rory went to Miriam's apartment
that evening, she wasn't home. At least, she didn't answer
her door. Not any of the ten times he knocked upon it.
Which was odd, because he knew she wasn't working,
either. She would have had to arrange for the night off so
that she could attend his class. And she would have made
that arrangement *before* they had gone out to dinner, *before* the two of them had made love. So it was unlikely
she was at the library.

In spite of that, after scribbling a quick note telling
Miriam he had stopped by to say hello—Well, what was
he supposed to have said? That he had stopped by because
he was obsessed with thoughts about her? What, and scare
her even more?—and slipping it beneath her front door,
Rory checked the Marigold Free Public Library, too. But
she wasn't there, either, not much to his surprise. And the
assistant librarian confirmed that. So Rory wrote her another note, saying he had stopped by to see her—Well, it
wasn't like he could write *I love you, I want you, I need
you, come back to me please, sweet Miriam,* and then
hand it over to a stranger, was it?—and then he left.

And he felt strangely bereft as he exited the library to
return home. Honestly. It almost felt as if Miriam had

dropped off the face of the planet. If she wasn't in class and she wasn't at work and she wasn't at home, where else could she be? And how was he supposed to talk to her if he couldn't find her? And what if it was her intent to avoid him forever?

No, he decided. She couldn't do that. He knew where to find her, knew she would be at the library tomorrow, just as he would be himself. And the library was a quiet place, a peaceful place, a place full of potential and possibility. Granted, one wasn't supposed to talk in a library, but he was sure the librarian would make an exception in this case.

At least, he thought the following afternoon, the librarian would make an exception if he could *find* her. But once again Miriam was nowhere to be found. Although she was indeed working—one of the students manning the circulation desk had confirmed that for Rory—she was never where she was supposed to be. Her office was empty, she was nowhere in the stacks, and volume fifteen of *Stegman's Guide to the Peloponnesian War* was right on his table, where he had left it.

Funnily enough, though—or maybe it wasn't so funny, at all—Rory had no desire to peruse the *Stegman's* today. No, what he wanted to peruse today—and, more than likely, every day for the rest of his life—was Miriam Thornbury. Evidently, however, Miriam had no such desire to peruse *him.*

Fine, he thought sullenly as he left the library again. If she didn't want to see him or talk to him, he couldn't very well force her, could he? Maybe she just needed some time, he told himself. Time to make sense of what had happened between them. Time to adjust to what he hoped were some newfound feelings for him. Time to decide how they should proceed.

Soon, he promised himself. Soon she would come round. Surely she would. He only hoped that when she did she would still want Rory Monahan. Because he was beginning to suspect that there would never come a time when Rory Monahan wouldn't be wanting her.

By Saturday night Rory still hadn't seen hide nor hair of Miriam, much to his discontent. And he couldn't remember agreeing to attend the local Kiwanis Club's fundraiser at Tony Palermo's Stardust Ballroom with his brother Connor, either. But Connor had assured him most adamantly that afternoon that Rory had, indeed, agreed to go, if for no other reason than to help Connor further his romantic pursuit of one Miss Erica Heywood.

Though, as Rory stood now at the fringe of the crowded dance floor, eyeing the swirling, twirling, gaily dressed dancers with much wariness, he couldn't imagine how he might be helpful in Connor's romantic pursuit. In fact, at the moment Rory couldn't even remember who Miss Erica Heywood was or why Connor was romantically pursuing her in the first place.

Well, he'd formed one or two *ideas* why Connor was pursuing her...especially after Rory had received his first glimpse of Miss Erica Heywood shortly after entering Tony Palermo's Stardust Ballroom earlier that evening. Because Miss Erica Heywood was... Well, she was quite stunning, actually, Rory had thought when he'd seen her. If one went for statuesque redheads with full breasts and hips, that was. And, he recalled, that was generally the type of woman that Connor went for.

Somehow, though, Miss Erica Heywood wasn't what Rory himself considered an ideal woman. No, to his way of thinking, the ideal woman wasn't quite so showy. In fact, to his way of thinking, the ideal woman wasn't statuesque or redheaded or even full in breast and hip. No, to his way of thinking, the ideal woman had darkish-blond hair and storm-gray eyes and a slender build and a mouth that just begged to be nibbled and a goddess outfit that was cut down to and up to *there*, and—

Oh, not again, he thought. Honestly, for an educated man he was certainly having some flights of fancy lately. Then again, seeing as how he was able to ponder little other than Miriam, he supposed he should be happy he could think at all. Because thoughts of Miriam only bewitched, bothered and bewildered him. Mostly because he still had no idea what was going on between them or what the future held in that regard—if anything at all.

In spite of the notes he'd left at both her apartment and the library, she hadn't contacted him once. And although he'd made another foray to the library in an effort to find her, she had eluded him again. He was beginning to think she really did want nothing to do with him. And that was the most heinous thought of all.

So he quickly stopped thinking and brought himself back to the matter at hand…and promptly realized that he couldn't remember, exactly, just what the matter at hand was. Something to do with dancing, obviously, considering his current location was Tony Palermo's Stardust Ballroom. But what precisely to do with dancing, Rory couldn't remember.

Now, the *history* of Tony Palermo's Stardust Ballroom, Rory knew quite well. It had been a Marigold fixture since 1937, and, from all accounts, had changed not one iota in the last six-plus decades. It was even still owned by Tony Palermo, though the current Tony Palermo was a junior version of the original owner, Tony, Sr. Oh, there had been a scare in the late seventies, when it was said that Tony, Jr., intended to turn the place into a discotheque but that, thankfully, had ended up being nothing more than a particularly nasty rumor. And with the resurgence of swing music during the nineties, Tony Palermo's Stardust Ballroom was seeing new life. There were even a couple of members of the current in-house band who were the offspring of members from the original swing ensemble who had performed there in the thirties and forties.

And although Rory also knew all about how the local Kiwanis Club held their annual ballroom dancing fundraiser here at Tony Palermo's every summer and how, each year, virtually the entire adult population of Marigold turned out for it, this was, surprisingly, Rory's first encounter with the event. Because until tonight it had never once occurred to him to attend.

It wasn't that he had anything against fund-raisers or swing music or ballrooms—or the local Kiwanis, for that matter. He just usually forgot that the event took place. He'd only remembered it this year because Connor had shown up at his front door just as Rory was sitting down to dinner and had reminded him of the promise Rory still couldn't recall making.

But even that wasn't the real reason Rory had come. No, Rory had come because *everyone* in Marigold generally turned out for this event. Including, he hoped, Miriam Thornbury.

At any rate, the two brothers were here now, and Rory was dressed in his very best navy-blue suit again, along with his very best tie—an inoffensive burgundy silk he couldn't recall purchasing himself—and his very best shoes—black tasseled loafers of Italian design, though he couldn't recall the precise manufacturer without removing one and reading the instep.

All in all, he felt very dapper indeed, and he rather wished he'd had the foresight to bring along an escort.

Which of course, he would have, had he been able to locate Miriam. She would have been infinitely more fun than his brother was. Although, technically, since Connor was the one who had dragged him here, Rory supposed that he himself was the one who was actually playing the role of escort. And since Connor had abandoned him the moment he'd seen Miss Erica Heywood standing on the other side of the room, Rory further supposed that he himself was playing the role of wallflower now.

Of course, Rory thought further still, had he had the foresight to bring along an escort—even Miriam—it might have posed a slight problem. And not just because both of them would have been playing the role of escort, something that rather skewed the workings of the universe in a way, even if Rory wasn't sure, exactly, what way it might skew the universe.

Or something like that.

But worse than any skewing, if Rory had brought along an escort—even Miriam—that escort would, no doubt, have wanted, even expected, to dance. Tony Palermo's Stardust Ballroom was, after all, a ballroom, just as its moniker indicated. And Rory, quite simply, didn't know how to dance. Worse than that, he had two left feet. Even if he knew enough steps to fake it, he'd probably get them all mixed up and make a fool of himself.

Ergo, he thought now, it was a good thing he hadn't brought along an escort. Even if he was feeling rather like a wallflower at the moment.

He really should have brought a book with him.

No sooner had the thought formed in his head than something even better than a book—imagine that—materialized in the crowd, in the form of the local librarian. And *not* Mr. Amberson, either. But Miriam Thornbury herself.

At least, Rory *thought* it was Miriam. Though he began to wonder as the woman spun around and disappeared into the crowd again. Because she had been dancing with an elderly gentleman who was at least three times her age and a good six inches shorter than she. And judging by the way the man was hobbling about, either he was terribly infirm, or else Miriam was an even worse dancer than Rory was. And having had just a glimpse of the woman's attire, he grew even more doubtful. Because he was fairly certain he'd never seen Miriam dressed in a ball gown before. Certainly not a ball gown like that one.

Then he remembered what she had looked like the last time he'd seen her—like a silver cloud bursting with good tidings. And he remembered what she had smelled like— like a garden full of ripe purple lavender. Better still, he remembered what she had *felt* like the last time he'd seen her—soft and warm and sensuous.

He really should have tried harder to get in touch with her, he told himself again. And when he hadn't been able to locate her physically, he should at least have tried to call her. And although he *had* intended to call her—had, in fact, picked up the telephone to do so on a number of occasions over the last few days—something had always stopped him. Not just because he wanted so badly to speak to her in person. And not just because she had so clearly been trying to avoid him. But because he couldn't stop thinking about how awkwardly their last evening together had ended. And because he still honestly wasn't sure if she even *wanted* him to call her.

Still, he really should have called her, Rory told himself again.

And he really should have eaten something for dinner, too, he thought further. Connor had purchased a handful of drink tickets at the door and had stuffed half of them into Rory's pocket before abandoning him, so Rory had taken advantage by having a couple of glasses of a surprisingly nice red, thinking he would feel better if he had something on his stomach. And the wine *had* felt good on his stomach. It felt even better zinging through the rest of his body, as it was now.

Hmm…

Yes, it probably would be best to have something to eat, he told himself. By then Miriam should be finished dancing—or whatever—with the elderly gentleman who currently had her attention, and then maybe Rory could draw her aside for a little conversation.

Naturally, though, the band struck up an even livelier, even louder, number just then, assuring Rory there would be little opportunity for conversation—not as long as he and Miriam remained inside. The crowd on the dance floor shifted along with the music, and he caught another glimpse of the woman he'd been certain was Miriam. Yes, that was most definitely her, he told himself. And before the night was through, he *would* talk to her. Among other things.

Not sure when he even chose to move forward, Rory suddenly found himself approaching the place on the floor where he'd last spotted her. He halted again, though, when she disappeared, feeling profoundly disappointed by her disappearance. He spent several minutes more trying to locate her among the throngs of people on the dance floor, then finally gave up in frustration.

But when he turned to make his way back to the wall, where a wallflower should be, he found himself gazing instead at a vision—for truly, a vision was what Miriam was—in blue.

"Rory?" she said softly.

"Miriam," he replied, just as softly.

She gazed at him gravely, appearing in no way happy to see him. In spite of that, though, she took a step toward him. And when she did, a side slit in her dress parted, revealing a length of slender, creamy leg from ankle to thigh. And oh, what memories that glimpse of leg roused inside him.

Somehow he managed to pull his gaze away from her thigh and return his attention to her face. And, oh, what a face, he thought. What a lovely, splendid, beautiful face. How had he resisted her for so many months? he wondered. She was even more breathtaking than had been Miss…Miss— Oh, whatever the name of Connor's romantic pursuit was. At the moment Rory couldn't have cared less about *her*. Not when Miriam was looking like…like…like…

Well. Like a devil with a blue dress on. That was what she looked like.

And it had most definitely been Miriam whom he had seen earlier in the evening dancing—or whatever—with the elderly, either-infirm-or-in-pain gentleman. But strangely, where from a distance he had identified her fairly well, up close he scarcely recognized her.

Her dark-blond hair was wound up the back of her head in an elegant twist and held in place by what appeared to be two chopsticks. Except that the chopsticks were decorated with bright blue enamel paint, something that led Rory to conclude that they were, in fact, *supposed* to be stuck there in her hair, and weren't the result of some practical joke a friend had played over dim sum earlier in the evening. Her gray eyes were shaded by a silvery-white tint, making them appear larger somehow and more compelling. Her cheekbones, which he had admired on a number of occasions, seemed more prominent tonight, thanks to the presence of a darker color that shadowed them. And her mouth...

Oh, good God, her *mouth*. That mouth that had caused Rory *so much* preoccupation over the past six months was, once again, as plump and as glistening and as tempting as a ripe, red raspberry. And all he could do was wonder if those full, damp lips tasted as sweet and as luscious as they looked—as sweet and as luscious as he recalled them tasting only a few nights before.

He squeezed his eyes shut tight, hoping that this vision of Miriam Thornbury, this...this...this devil with a blue dress on...might disappear in a puff of lavender-scented smoke. Because although he had assured himself he could have a rational discussion with her about what had happened the last time they were together, seeing her this way now, Rory was confident that *rational* was the last thing he could hope to be, and *discussion* was the last activity in which he wanted to engage.

Alas, however, when he opened his eyes again, he saw that she was still there, still luscious, still a devil with a blue dress on. She also seemed to be standing closer to him than she had been a moment ago. And she appeared to be preparing to move closer still.

"What brings you to the fund-raiser?" she asked innocently. Innocently. In that dress. Imagine. And, just as he had suspected she would do, she took a step toward him.

"I—I—I," he stammered. Immediately, he closed his mouth again, fearful that he would ridicule himself even more than he already had, especially when she completed *another* step toward him.

"Rory?" she asked as she approached.

"I—I—I came with my brother," he managed to get out. "Connor."

She nodded, seeming relieved for some reason. "I see. I thought maybe you'd come with a date."

A date? he repeated to himself. Why on earth would he have come with a date? Why, the only date he'd had in the past two years had been with Miriam, so how could he possibly be here with anyone other than—

Then again, he was here with her now, wasn't he?

"Actually, I'm glad to see you here, Miriam, because—" he began.

But before he could finish, he and Miriam were joined by a third person, another woman dressed in attire similar to Miriam's, except that her dress was, impossibly, even *more* revealing than Miriam's was, and screaming-red in color to boot. Even more shocking than either of those two observations, however, was the one Rory made when he gazed at the woman's—rather overly made-up—face.

"Mayor Trent?" he asked, aghast. How could she be dressed like that? he marveled. She'd run on the Family Values platform.

She blushed at Rory's unmistakable astonishment—at least he thought she was blushing; it was hard to tell for sure under all those cosmetics—but said nothing to comment. Instead, she turned her attention to Miriam.

"I've been looking for you all night," she said in a clipped tone. "I wanted to apologize for the dress."

"Oh, but it looks lovely on you, Ms. Trent," Miriam assured the other woman, sounding utterly sincere.

And although Rory was inclined to agree that Isabel Trent did indeed look more fetching than usual, *lovely* wasn't the adjective that came to mind when he considered the mayor's red, revealing dress again. No, in keeping with the rock 'n' roll metaphors—which Rory normally wouldn't do, except that Miriam *was* such a devil with a blue dress on—Isabel Trent, he supposed, rather resembled a hunka hunka burnin' love. Yes, that analogy, he thought, would be very appropriate.

"No, I'm apologizing for *your* dress," Mayor Trent said, her voice a fair hiss, even with the music blaring. "There can be no apologizing for mine," she added, clearly distressed.

Why on earth she would be apologizing for Miriam's dress, though, Rory couldn't imagine. There was absolutely no need to apologize for something so goddess-like, after all. Well, goddess-like save the glittering sapphire sequins and the sweep of marabou that trimmed the bottom.

Miriam, however, seemed to share the Mayor's anguish, however, because she, too, glanced down at her garment rather apologetically. "Yes, well, Miss Chacha's idea of a ball gown and my own idea of a ball gown were a tad at odds, but..." She shrugged philosophically, a gesture, Rory couldn't help noting, that did wonderful things to her dress. "She insisted this was the best she could do."

Mayor Trent nodded. "Yes, well, her idea of appropriate attire and my idea of appropriate attire were likewise at odds. But it's too late to do anything about it now. I just wish I hadn't taken her up on her offer to do my makeup, as well." She sighed heavily as she considered Miriam's face. "I see she did yours, too."

"I'm afraid so, yes," said Miriam.

Honestly, Rory thought, he couldn't imagine what the two women were objecting to. Although he'd never really been the kind of man who liked heavily made-up women, he had to admit that there was something rather, oh...appealing...about how Miriam and the mayor looked. Why, they rather resembled the models on that popular women's magazine, he thought further. What was the name of it again? Something about city living, wasn't it? *Urbanite? Metropolis? Municipality?* Something like that. It would come to him eventually.

"At any rate, when I saw you out there dancing and realized what you had on, I felt I should apologize to you," the mayor was telling Miriam again, "since this was my idea in the first place. If I'd had any idea Miss Chacha would be dressing us up as...as...as..." She made a sour face. "Well, I'd rather not say what I feel as if I'm dressed as right now," she finally concluded. "But had I known I'd end up this way..."

"Just remember that it's for the scholarship fund," Miriam told her. "It's for the children, Ms. Trent."

The mayor didn't look much appeased by the reminder, Rory noted. But she did still look rather fetching.

Suddenly, however, when something over Rory's shoulder caught her attention, her expression changed to one of utter panic. "Omigosh," Ms. Trent said, ducking quickly behind him. "No one told me Cullen Monahan was going to be here tonight."

"Cullen?" Rory echoed.

He glanced at the entrance and, sure enough, saw that his younger brother, Connor's twin, had indeed arrived. But why that should make Isabel Trent panic, Rory had no idea. After all, Cullen worked for the mayor. He was, in essence, her right-hand man. Why would she be concerned to find him here at the fund-raiser? Especially since, in his capacity as a public servant, Cullen *always* attended functions such as these.

"I thought he was going to be out of town," the mayor said, still hiding behind Rory. "If Cullen asks, tell him you haven't seen me."

Rory gaped in disbelief. A woman who'd been voted into office on the Family Values platform, encouraging her constituents to tell a falsehood? Dishonesty in a politician? Now *that* was a shocking development.

"Ms. Trent, I'm afraid I can't do—" Rory began.

But before he could say another word, Isabel Trent spun on her heels and fled, disappearing onto the crowded dance floor like so much stray marabou. And all Rory could do was shake his head in wonder at what could possibly be going on with the mayor and his brother.

The music kicked up again, another lively tune, just as Cullen joined them and might potentially offer an explanation. He, too, was wearing his best suit, Rory noted. Plus, his black hair was combed expertly—perhaps even recently cut—and his blue eyes reflected something akin to…anticipation? How interesting.

Really, Rory thought, Cullen looked much better than he usually did. As if he were trying to impress someone. In a word: Hmmm…

Naturally, after greeting them with "Hey, Rory. Hi, Miss Thornbury," the first question out of Cullen's mouth was, "Have either of you seen the mayor? I overheard her saying she was going to be here tonight. And I really need to talk to her about something."

Rory opened his mouth to respond, even got so far as to say, "Actually, she just…" when Miriam circled firm fingers around his wrist and began to tug him away.

"Hello, Mr. Monahan," she said to Cullen as she dragged Rory off. "I'm sorry, but we can't chat right now. Rory promised me this dance, and I intend to collect."

Dance? Rory repeated to himself. *Dance?* With her? In that dress? She must be out of her mind.

"But…" he began.

And again, he was forced to halt midsentence, because Miriam began to jerk on his arm more forcefully, propelling him out toward the dance floor, whether he liked it or not. And Rory couldn't say another word, because he had to pay very close attention to where he was going, otherwise he would have gone barreling right into her, sending them both toppling to the floor. Which, upon further reflection, he decided, might not be such a bad thing.

Then again, he asked himself, why topple to the floor in a place where the two of them would be surrounded by onlookers, not to mention an entire swing band on the stage? No, no, no, he told himself. *Much* better to topple later, when the two of them were alone, and the swing band was on the stereo.

Fortunately for Rory—where the dancing part was concerned, at any rate—there were far too many people on the floor for him and Miriam to have any room to move about, so his horrific lack of knowledge, dancewise, would no doubt be left undiscovered. *Un*fortunately for Rory, however—where *other* parts were concerned, at any rate—there were far too many people on the floor for him and Miriam to have any room to move about, so the moment they came to a stop near the center of the crowd, their two bodies were immediately squashed together. Close together. And as the squashing occurred, inevitably he recalled how the two of them had been squashed the last time they'd been together.

Oh, yes. It was all coming back to him now.

And suddenly the last thing Rory wanted to do was dance. So he told his partner, a little breathlessly, he couldn't help noting, "Really, Miriam, I'm not much of a dancer."

To his surprise she replied, just as breathlessly, he couldn't help noting, "Oh. Good."

He arched his eyebrows in surprise. "Why is that good? I thought you wanted to dance."

She shook her head. "Oh, no," she told him. "In fact, *dancing* is the last thing I want to do with you."

Ten

Oh, dear, Miriam thought as soon as she uttered the statement. She probably should have phrased her last remark a little differently. Because, judging by the expression of utter shock etched on Rory's face, there was a good chance he might have mistaken her intent.

Oh, she *knew* she should have just stayed away from him tonight, she told herself. But when she'd left the dance floor after ending her wrestling match with ninety-five-year-old Leonard Federman, whose hands, at least, hadn't quite made it out of puberty, and had seen Rory standing at the edge of the crowd, she hadn't been able to resist him. She'd felt as if someone had pulled taut an invisible thread that was attached to her, winding it tighter and tighter, pulling her closer and closer, until she stood within a few feet of Rory. And once she was that close to him, well... She could no more have pulled herself away than she could have pushed the moon out of the Earth's orbit.

She should have known it would be futile to try to keep avoiding him. Marigold was a small town. They were bound to run into each other sooner or later. Especially since her place of employment was, in effect, his home away from home. Still, she hadn't known what to say or how to act around him. The notes he'd left her had been so casual, so impersonal. And he hadn't once tried to call her on the phone. Although he'd made clear his desire to talk to her, to see her, she had feared he would only tell her that what had happened between the two of them had been a mistake, one he couldn't risk repeating.

He had, after all, regretted making love to her immediately after it had happened. Why would he want to repeat it?

She wished she hadn't pulled him onto the dance floor, because being this close to him again was a such a sweet torture. But she'd felt it was essential to get him away from Cullen, because Rory had been about to tell his brother exactly where Isabel Trent was.

And there was no way Miriam was going to let him do that, because Isabel Trent had obviously been uncomfortable with the idea of Cullen seeing her dressed the way she was—not that Miriam could blame the other woman for a moment, because Miriam wasn't any too comfortable herself being dressed like a...like a... Well. Like a devil with a blue dress on. Even if *Metropolitan* magazine assured her that men went for such a thing, because Miriam had vowed days ago that she would never, ever, be a temptress—inner *or* outer—again. The sooner she could remove this ridiculous get-up, the better.

At any rate, in spite of her frequent disagreements with the mayor, Miriam didn't want to see Isabel Trent put on the spot with Cullen Monahan the way Rory had been about to put her on the spot. Not when Isabel was a kindred spirit. Not when Isabel was clearly suffering from the same affliction Miriam herself was suffering from these days.

Because Miriam had seen the look on the mayor's face when Cullen Monahan had entered the Stardust Ballroom. And it had been a look with which Miriam was very well acquainted—after all, it was the same look she saw on her own face every time she glanced in the mirror. Because Isabel's expression had been the expression of a woman who wanted a man—a special man. A special man who didn't want her in return.

Oh, my, Miriam thought. Mayor Trent had a major thing for the man who was her former campaign manager and current assistant—Cullen Monahan. And Cullen Monahan evidently didn't have a clue.

Goodness, she thought further. What was wrong with the Monahan men, that they couldn't see the most obvious things in the world? Really, for being so popular and so prominent in the community, the Monahan boys had a lot to learn about life. And love. And women.

In spite of having just told Rory that she didn't want to dance with him, Miriam did nothing to stop the swaying of their bodies. Not just because she was too preoccupied by thoughts of other things, but because, thanks to the overpopulation of the dance floor, she had no choice but to keep moving. People were crowded around them, and everyone seemed to be moving in perfect time with the music.

Well, *most* of the people were moving in perfect time, she thought when someone bumped into her from behind, thrusting her forward, more resolutely into Rory's embrace. She tried her best to extricate herself from the awk-

ward situation, then realized that Rory was doing absolutely nothing to help her disengage. For a man who had
so recently made clear his reluctance to embrace any
woman—in more than a physical sense, anyway—it was
an interesting response. Then again, she thought, the embrace *was* awfully physical…

Then again…again she thought further, perhaps Rory
hadn't pushed her away simply because there was no
place to push her. Because in spite of the physicality of
their current clinch, she still remembered, too well, how
utterly he had assured the police officer the other night
that Miriam was neither his wife nor his girlfriend,
thereby ensuring that he didn't entertain any thoughts—
or any enthusiasm—of having her assume either role.

This in spite of the fact that Miriam had assigned the
role of boyfriend—and even husband—a time or two to
Rory, if only in her dreams. This in spite of the fact that,
despite his assurances to the police officer, Rory had done
nothing that night to halt the passion that had erupted
suddenly between the two of them. This in spite of the
fact that he had, on the contrary, pulled Miriam closer and
kissed her just as deeply as she had kissed him, something
that rather negated the whole premise of wanting neither
a girlfriend nor a wife, she thought.

Or maybe it didn't negate that, she further pondered.
Maybe it only served to illustrate what Rory *did* want in
his life—a sex partner.

Men had physical needs, after all, Miriam reminded
herself. Then again, women had physical needs, too,
something to which she herself could attest. *Oh, my,* could
she attest to that. And maybe that was all that had been
on Rory's mind that night when he had denounced the
girlfriend/wife idea—his physical needs and perhaps even
her own. That was why he had so eagerly embraced her

physically while mentally and emotionally repelling the idea of her involvement with him in any other capacity. He had wanted to assuage a physical need. And he may have thought that was all she wanted, too.

And perhaps that was exactly what was on his mind tonight, as well—their physical needs. Perhaps that was why he was embracing her physically again right now. After all, she was dressed as such a temptress. And if he *was* only thinking about their physical needs at the moment, then there was a very good chance he would once again repel her mentally and emotionally later.

Then again, Miriam's physical needs *had* been on her mind that night, too. And they were on her mind tonight, as well. *Oh, my,* were they on her mind tonight, she thought as she splayed her hands open over Rory's chest and felt the firm expanse of muscle beneath. And now that she thought more about it, seeing to one's physical needs, even if it meant neglecting one's emotional needs, might not necessarily be such a terrible thing....

She sighed heavily her frustration, and she reminded herself of what she had been telling herself for the past few days—that she should get over Rory Monahan and put him out of her mind and move on to live her life. Unfortunately for her, though, her mind—and, evidently, several other parts of her body—simply refused to give him up. Probably because the thought of living her life didn't seem like much fun without Rory in it.

"Um, at the risk of pestering you, Miriam..." Rory began, his voice sounding soft in spite of the fact that he had raised it to compensate for the blaring music.

"Oh, by all means, feel free to pester me," she told him. "In fact, pester away. Please."

Good heavens, Miriam, she told herself, *don't beg.*

She took a moment to berate herself for her weakness

where Rory Monahan was concerned. Honestly, she thought. Had she no pride left at all?

Well, actually, Miriam, if you must know…

Then again, it did feel so good to be back in his arms, even if only temporarily. There was nothing wrong with enjoying this momentary reunion, was there? She wouldn't let things go too far. Certainly not as far as they had gone the other night. No matter how badly she might want them to.

When she realized he still hadn't pestered her, she said, "If there's something you want to know, Rory, do please ask. At the risk of pestering me…?" she echoed, encouraging him to finish.

He hesitated a moment, gazing at her face as if he might gauge the answer to his question there, without having to ask it aloud. Finally, though, "If you don't want to dance with me," he told her, "then…why are you dancing with me?"

"Oh, that," she said.

"Yes, that," he concurred.

"That's not pestering," she told him, hedging.

"No?"

"Of course not. It's a perfectly good question."

He waited for her to respond to it, and when she only remained silent—mainly because she couldn't come up with a perfectly good answer to go along with his perfectly good question—he said, "Then why don't you answer it?"

"Answer what?" she asked, still stalling. Stalling lamely, too, she couldn't help thinking.

He inhaled a deep breath and released it slowly, his eyes never leaving hers. "Why are we dancing?" he asked succinctly.

"Um, because the music is so nice?" she replied.

He nodded, but she didn't think he bought her phony sincerity.

"Yes, well, just so you know," he continued, "I can't dance to save my life. You're risking very serious injury to your feet if you continue."

"I think you're doing very well," she told him. With real sincerity this time, too.

"Yes, well," he said again, "when the people are packed together like sardines, it isn't hard to keep time with the music. It's when the music ends and the people begin to separate that things will become a bit troublesome."

Oh, truer words were never spoken, Miriam thought.

But instead of ending, the music grew more raucous, even as Rory spoke his observation aloud. And when it did this time, someone bumped into him from behind, launching his body forward into Miriam's with enough force to make her stumble backward. Where before Rory had settled his hands loosely on her hips, now he circled an arm around her waist and placed a hand at the small of her back to steady her. Normally this would have been a perfectly legitimate reaction, a perfectly innocent touch.

But Miriam wasn't dressed normally, was she? No, she was wearing a Lola Chacha original, which meant that her gown—in addition to boasting sequins and marabou and a side slit that could potentially be considered criminal—dipped as low, both in front and in back, as it possibly could without risk of having the wearer arrested. As long as the lights were low enough that the police couldn't see her, anyway.

Which meant that Rory's hand, when it landed on the small of her back, landed not on her gown, but on *the small of her back*. The *naked* small of her back. And having even that slight skin-to-skin contact with him sent Miriam's temperature skyrocketing.

Automatically her own hold on him—she had settled her hands innocently on his chest—contracted, something that caused her fingers to curve intimately, even possessively, into his firm flesh. Before she could right herself or him—not that she necessarily *wanted* to right herself or him, really, not with his hand on her naked back that way—the person who had jostled Rory from behind jostled him again. This time, when his body was shoved forward, Miriam pushed her hands higher, to his shoulders, which she then found herself gripping for dear life.

She told herself her reaction was simply a result of having responded instinctively, unmindful of the fact that there was little chance she would fall, thanks to the density of the crowd surrounding them. It *hadn't* been because she just wanted to get a better hold of Rory. It *hadn't* been because she wanted to take advantage of even this small moment to touch him one last time.

Really. That hadn't been the reason. She'd just overreacted a bit, that was all.

Rory's reaction, though, seemed to come from something other than a simple instinctive response. Because there was something very deliberate, not to mention very arousing, about the way he had placed one hand on the— quite naked—small of her back and had cupped the other hand over her—equally naked—shoulder blade.

Oh, yes, his movements were very deliberate, Miriam thought as both of those hands on her back then began to dip lower—considerably lower than was actually necessary for keeping her righted. And she knew that those hands *were* dipping lower, not just because she felt the soft glide of his fingertips along the heated, sensitized flesh of her back, but also because she felt his fingertips come to a halt curving over the upper swells of her derriere.

"I'm okay, Rory," she told him a little breathlessly. "You don't have to...to...to..."

"To what?" he asked. And although his voice was all innocence and curiosity, the expression on his face was anything but.

Miriam told herself his cheeks were only flushed because he was embarrassed to have been discovered touching her the way he was touching her—even though he did nothing to remove his hands. And she told herself his lips were only parted that way because the air was close, and it was hard to breathe—even though he didn't seem to be lacking for breath. And she told herself his eyes were only darkening and fairly glazing over because the throng of people surrounding them created a heat that was nearly overwhelming—even though the heat enveloping them didn't seem to be generated by a throng of people at all.

And she told herself that her own response to him— the flush she felt warming her own cheeks, the shallowness of her own breathing, the heat coursing through her own body—was simply a result of the crowd, too.

Unfortunately she didn't come close to believing any of the things she told herself.

The music slowed then, and segued into something by Gershwin, though Miriam was too befuddled at the moment to identify just what the song was. Surprisingly, a number of people left the dance floor then, presumably because they needed more of a rest than a simple slow tune. She waited for Rory to release her and lead her off the floor, as well, but he did neither. Instead he pulled her closer—something she would have sworn was impossible to do—and tucked her head beneath his chin and circled her waist loosely with both arms.

Immediately she was surrounded by the scent of him, a mixture of Old Spice, damp cotton and hot man. The combination was intoxicating, narcotic. And all Miriam could do was relax against him, feeling as if it were the most natural place on the earth for her to be. Their torsos bumped together, their legs brushed against each other, and she didn't think she'd ever experienced a more exquisite sensation than feeling as if she were tangled up with Rory Monahan.

Unable to help herself, but calling herself a fool just the same, she looped one arm around his neck, wove the fingers of the other through his hair and let him guide her body back and forth, back and forth, back…and…forth…

And then she heard him say, very softly, "We need to talk, you and I."

The lights had gone low by now, canopying the entire room with darkness, and something about that must have emboldened Rory. Because the hands that he had linked around her waist suddenly began to wander, skimming lightly over her bare flesh again. His fingers drifted up her spine, then back down. Then they ventured up again, over her rib cage this time, and down the other side once more. And with every soft skim of his fingertips over her back, Miriam's heart rate quickened, her uncertainties multiplied and her confusion compounded.

"Talk?" she echoed. "A-a-about what?"

He hesitated only a moment before saying, "Us."

"Oh."

But instead of launching into whatever he wanted to say about *us,* Rory told her, "This is a, um, a, uh…a rather amazing gown." His voice was a mere murmur near her ear. "What little there is of it, I mean."

"Ah. Yes. Well. It isn't mine," Miriam told him, a delicious shiver of excitement spiraling through her at the way he voiced the comment, and the way his fingers began to make slow spirals over her sensitive skin. "Normally I never... I mean, I'm not usually so... This isn't the sort of thing I customarily..." But she gave up trying to explain, when she was unable to finish any of the anxious thoughts crowding into her brain.

"No, neither do I," Rory told her, agreeing with her all the same.

Somehow he had made sense of her mental meanderings, Miriam realized. And for some reason that didn't surprise her at all.

"I just, um..." she began again. "I mean, I was trying to... It was all because of..."

"Yes, I understand completely," he told her.

And again somehow she knew that he did.

"But you wear it well, Miriam," he said, his voice a velvet caress against her ear, her neck, her throat. "Because you look..." He inhaled deeply, then released the breath slowly, as if he wanted to illustrate the rest of his statement, which happened to be, "You look...breathtaking. In fact," he added further, his voice still sounding a little uneven, "you smell breathtaking. And you *feel* breathtaking." Once again, he sighed deeply. "You *are* breathtaking," he told her. "I don't know why I didn't realize that a long time ago."

Well, obviously, Miriam thought morosely, it was because she hadn't, until recently, been a devil with a blue dress on. An Outer Temptress, so to speak. That was why Rory was responding to her now when he hadn't noticed her before. Not for any other reason than that.

She realized then the folly of her situation—Rory would never want her for who she *really* was—and tried to pull away. But the hand that had returned to the small of her back dipped lower again, to the upper swell of her bottom, pulling her into the cradle of his pelvis. She bit back a groan when she felt how hard and ready he was for her. Or, at least how hard and ready he was for her Inner Temptress.

"We need to talk," he said again. "About us."

She shook her head. "There is no us."

She couldn't be sure in the darkness, but she thought his expression changed then, from one of hopefulness to one of discouragement. "What do you mean?" he asked. "Of course there's an us. There's been an us ever since we…"

She shook her head again, more vehemently this time. "No, there's no us," she insisted. "There's Rory Monahan, and there's my Inner Temptress. Miriam Thornbury doesn't fit into the picture at all."

Now his expression changed again, to one of total confusion. "Inner Temptress?" he echoed. "What are you talking about? Not that I don't find you tempting," he quickly assured her, sweeping his hands slowly over her bare back again.

And all she could think was, *Oh, Rory.*

"It isn't *me* you find tempting," she told him. "It's my Inner Temptress."

He smiled, albeit in a puzzled way. "I still don't understand. If there's someone inside of you who's tempting me, Miriam, then it's *you* tempting me."

As much as she wished she could believe that, Miriam shook her head. "No," she told him. "It isn't me tempting you. It's a fictional creation of *Metropolitan* magazine."

"Now I'm hopelessly confused," he said. "What would a magazine have to do with my feelings for you?"

"It's a long story." She sighed heavily and avoided his gaze. "But when I removed all those issues of *Metropol-*

itan magazine from the library that Mayor Trent wanted removed, I took them home and I started reading them, and there were a few articles that—'' And then the gist of his question struck her, and Miriam narrowed her eyes at him. ''You have feelings for me?'' she asked.

He chuckled. ''Well, of course I have feelings for you, Miriam,'' he said, ''I love you.''

She gaped at him for a moment, feeling, for one scant second, like the happiest woman on the face of the Earth. Then suddenly she sobered. Because she realized what Rory said didn't apply to her. ''No, you don't love me,'' she told him softly. ''You love my Inner Temptress.''

He uttered a sound that very much resembled a growl of frustration. ''Miriam,'' he said. ''What. Are. You. Talking. About.''

As quickly as she could, she tried to explain. She revealed to Rory the crush she had had on him for six months, then described how the magazine articles led her to create what she'd thought was a foolproof plan to lure him and tempt him and make him her own. She told him of her delight that the venture had been such a success, until she realized that he had fallen, not for the person she really was, but for the fictional temptress she had fashioned from a series of magazine articles. She reiterated that he couldn't possibly be in love with Miriam Thornbury the librarian. Because he had fallen in love with Miriam Thornbury the temptress instead.

''So you see,'' she said, ''if you're in love, it's not with me. It's with a…with a…a…'' She, too, uttered a dissatisfied snarl. ''A devil with a blue dress on,'' she fairly spat. ''It isn't with the woman who's fallen in love with you.''

For one long moment Rory only gazed at her in silence, his expression now offering her not a clue as to what he might be feeling or thinking. Then, very softly, he began to laugh. A laugh of utter delight, of total freedom, of uninhibited joy. And when he did, Miriam thought he looked…he looked…

Well. He looked breathtaking. She couldn't help but sigh as she watched him.

And she also couldn't help asking, "What's so funny?"

"You," he said as he pulled her closer. "My sweet Miriam. My erudite librarian. My keen student. My ardent paramour. My bewitching temptress. For you are all of those things, my darling. And then some."

At his softly uttered words, Miriam began to feel a bit breathless again. And a bit dizzy. And a bit contemplative. And then she began to feel very, *very* happy. Because suddenly she began to see that Rory was right. She didn't have to be just one thing. She wasn't just Miriam the librarian. And she wasn't just Miriam the temptress, either. She was many things to many people. Many things to Rory. Just as he was many things to her. And always would be.

All along Miriam had told herself she had to take responsibility for her Inner Temptress's behavior, because her Inner Temptress, for all her alien qualities, was a product of Miriam herself. So if she was so insistent she be responsible for the little vixen's behavior, then why couldn't she reap the little minx's rewards, too?

Rory *must* love all of her, Miriam told herself. No matter who or what she was, because that was the nature of love. Just as she loved all of him, no matter who or what *he* was.

Oh, my, she thought. It was all so clear to her now. Honestly. For an educated woman—not to mention a successful temptress—Miriam truly did have a lot to learn.

And she couldn't wait to have Rory teach her. Mostly because she had one or two lessons for him, as well.

Rory must have sensed her train of thoughts, because he lowered his head to hers, pressing his forehead gently against her own. "So you can see that you are many things to me, Miriam," he said, reiterating his earlier statement. "And I can only hope that there's one more thing you'll become."

"What's that?" she asked, still feeling breathless and dizzy and contemplative and happy.

"My loving wife," he told her. "Will you be that, too?"

"Oh, *Rory*…"

Instead of finishing her answer verbally, Miriam thrust herself up on tiptoe and pressed her mouth to his. Again and again she kissed him, more deeply and possessively with every passing second. Rory responded with much enthusiasm, roping his arms around her waist now and slanting his head to the side to facilitate their embrace.

Vaguely Miriam heard the sound of music and of laughter and of applause. And when she pulled away, she found that the entire population of the Stardust Ballroom—nay, the entire population of Marigold, Indiana—were witness to what was, quite possibly, the most shameless public display of affection ever perpetrated in town. Even Mayor Trent, Miriam couldn't help but notice, was smiling and clapping. Miriam smiled, too. Because right behind the mayor was Cullen Monahan, looking quite flummoxed.

Maybe there was hope for the Monahan clan yet, Miriam thought with a grin.

Then, after bestowing another quick kiss on Rory's lips, she moved her mouth to his ear and whispered, "Let's get out of here."

He nodded eagerly. "I have my car."

She smiled. "Oh, good. I hope you parked it in a secluded area."

Amazingly, not only did Miriam and Rory make it to his car without succumbing to their passion—well, without succumbing *too* much to their passion—but they also made it back to Rory's apartment before succumbing to their passion. Well, no more than some soul-deep kissing at a stoplight. And copping a few feels at a stop sign. And then, once, pulling over to the side of the road in a delirious effort to remove Miriam's panties, only to reconsider and finally—*finally*—make their way to Rory's place.

But once they were at Rory's place all bets were off. And all clothes were off, too, in no time flat. Before Miriam realized what was happening, the two of them were standing completely naked in Rory's bedroom, and he freed her hair and filled his hands with it. Not that it had taken any more than a couple of quick tugs on the chopsticks in her hair—or on the gown she was almost wearing—for Miriam to find herself in that state, though Rory's clothing had presented a bit of a challenge because he'd had on considerably more than she. Not to mention he wouldn't quit kissing her and tasting her the whole time she was trying to undress him.

And even when she'd finished undressing him, he still kept on kissing her and tasting her—not that she minded at all, because she was doing some kissing and tasting of her own by then and remembering all over again just how delicious Rory Monahan was.

And then she stopped remembering anything, because he slowly began to walk her toward his bed, his hands skimming lightly over every exposed inch of her. And of course it went without saying that every inch of her was indeed exposed. Little by little he urged her backward, onto the mattress, then followed her down and covered her body with his.

Oh, this was *so* much better than a car, Miriam thought as he stretched out alongside and atop her. Because now Rory's naked skin was pressed against her own naked skin, from shoulder to toe, and there was nothing—absolutely *nothing*—to inhibit them. Not that either of them seemed to feel particularly inhibited at the moment. On the contrary...

Miriam wound her fingers in Rory's hair as he dragged a line of openmouthed kisses along her neck, her throat, her shoulder, her collarbone. And as she tightened those fingers, gasping, he ducked his head lower, drawing her erect nipple into his mouth to suck hard on her tender flesh. But even that didn't seem to be his final destination, because he moved his kisses lower again, to the underside of her breast, along her rib cage, over her flat belly, into her navel. And then lower still, to her hips, her pelvis, the sensitive insides of her thighs.

So senseless was she with wanting him by the time he began to move his head upward again that Miriam didn't realize his final destination until she felt his mouth upon that most sensitive part of herself. She gasped again at the initial contact, then expelled her breath in a rush of exhilaration and sucked it in again, harder this time. Oh, no one had ever— Oh, she'd never felt anything like— Oh, it was simply too— Oh—

Oh!

Again and again Rory tasted her, teased her, taunted her, until it seemed as if he would never satisfy his hunger for her. Finally, he gripped her hips hard in each hand and lifted her to his mouth, for one final, furious onslaught that very nearly shattered her. Then, as if he couldn't tolerate their separation any longer than she, he climbed back up onto the mattress beside her.

Without a further word he propped his upper body on his elbows, folding one on each side of her head. Then he settled himself between her legs and pushed himself toward her, his hard shaft coming to rest between the damp folds of her flesh without penetrating her. Miriam, barely coherent now, looped her arms around his neck, and met his gaze intently.

"Now," she told him. "Make love to me now."

His breathing was ragged, and his eyes were dark with wanting. But he told her, "I don't have anything. Any protection, I mean. In spite of wanting to talk to you and tell you how I felt tonight, I honestly hadn't anticipated this happening again yet."

"And I'm not a *Metro* Girl anymore," Miriam told him. "Not primarily. So I don't have a condom in my purse this time. Not that I had any more, anyway. Just the one."

In spite of his overwrought state, he chuckled. "Someone sold you one condom?" he asked.

She shook her head. "It was a party favor."

He arched his eyebrows in surprise. "You went to a party where they passed out condoms?" He twisted a stray lock of her hair around his finger. "My, but you are a temptress, aren't you?"

"Actually, it was a bridal shower," she told him.

This time he gaped at her. "Promise me, Miriam, that at your bridal shower, you'll only pass out petit fours or some such thing."

She smiled. "I'm not sure what we'll be passing out at my bridal shower. Depends on who's in charge that day. Whether it's Miriam Librarian or Miriam Temptress or Miriam Hostess, for that matter."

"Right now, at this moment," he said, "I'm hoping you're Miriam Overcome-with-Desire."

"Oh, yes," she assured him, cupping his warm jaw in her hand. "I am that."

"But without a condom..."

"I might become Miriam Mommy," she finished for him.

"Yes," he told her, resigned.

"And you might become Rory Daddy," she added.

"Yes."

"And would that be so terrible?" she asked him.

He shook his head. "No. Not at all."

"Then maybe we should just hope for the best," she suggested.

He grinned. "Maybe we should."

And as Rory entered her, slowly, deeply, thoroughly, Miriam thought that hoping for the best certainly brought the best. Because there was no other word to describe what Rory was.

She closed her eyes as he penetrated her more deeply now, burying himself inside her as far as he would go. For a moment they only lay there, motionless, allowing their bodies to become reacquainted. Then Rory withdrew some, with an exquisite slowness and carefulness that made Miriam writhe with wanting him. Instinctively she shot her hips upward, to reclaim him, and he responded by thrusting himself down toward her again.

This time, there was no retreating, no withdrawing, only a steady plundering of her body with his. She wrapped her legs snugly around his waist, her arms around his shoulders, claiming him more completely, until the rhythm of their coupling generated an incandescent reaction. And somewhere amid the conflagration, Miriam and Rory melted into each other, physically, emotionally, intellectually, spiritually. And as, little by little, they quieted and calmed, she knew they would never, ever part.

For long moments they only lay entwined, their bodies and hearts and souls and minds still joined. Then, very softly Rory said, "As much as I look forward to making love to you in the proper surroundings for all time to come, I think I'll always look back on that first time in my car with very fond memories."

Miriam pushed her hair back from her forehead and gazed intently into Rory's eyes. Then she smiled. "Me, too. As awkward as it was at the time, it was also…unforgettable."

He nodded. "One of these days we'll have to do it again, just for old-time's sake. But we'll use the back seat instead, for logistical reasons."

"And one of these days," she added, "we'll have to make love on one of the tables in the reference section at the library, too." She laughed at his scandalized expression, then added, "And I know just which table to use, too, *Stegman's* or no."

"Why, Miriam," Rory said mischievously. "You've been holding out on me."

"Never again," she assured him. "From now on, no matter what's on my mind—and no matter which one of me is thinking it—you'll be the first to know. And guess what I'm thinking about right now."

He smiled wickedly. "I'm not sure exactly what—yet—you're thinking about, but I'll wager good money I know which one of you is thinking it." He maneuvered their bodies so that they had switched positions, with Miriam lying atop him now. Then he looped an arm around her neck and pulled her down to him for another kiss. "Come here, you little temptress you…."

Epilogue

There was no better time for a wedding, Rory thought, than springtime. Not that he and Miriam intended to wait that long to get married—heavens, no. But having watched his brother Connor plan his springtime nuptials for the last several weeks, Rory was more certain than ever that he and his wife-to-be had made the right decision to marry *now*. Before there was time to argue over whether the bridesmaids would wear pink or peach, before there was time to worry about whether to serve chicken or beef at the reception, before there was time to be concerned if the ushers should wear black or charcoal-gray.

Before Miriam Thornbury got away.

Not that Rory feared she would leave him, but he was an intelligent man, after all, and he knew better than to leave anything to chance. Besides, he was so preoccupied by thoughts of marrying Miriam these days that he scarcely ever got any work done. Not that he minded.

Oddly enough, having his head filled with thoughts of her was infinitely more satisfying than thoughts of…

Oh, whatever those things were that his head used to be filled with. He could barely remember now.

In spite of November's arrival, the weather was surprisingly mild, one of those gifts of a day that the Midwest sometimes received from the weather gods before winter moved in for the duration. Therefore, the garden behind the Marigold Free Public Library was the perfect place to be wed. He and Miriam had planned to hold the ceremony indoors, amid the books and authors they both loved so well, but being outside now, surrounded by the *people* they loved instead, made the ceremony all the more wonderful.

And so many people had come: His sister, Tess, rosy and round with child, along with her husband, Will. His brother Sean and Sean's fiancée, Autumn. Connor and his intended. And of course Cullen was there, too, staying very close to the mayor, who, Rory and Miriam both had been surprised to find, had RSVPed in the affirmative after the wedding invitations went out.

Everyone seemed to be coupling up, Rory thought. His sister, Tess, had started a summer-long tradition for the Monahans when she and Will had become an item last June. Because Sean and Autumn had begun dating shortly after that. Then Rory and Miriam had hooked up. Connor hadn't been long after them, and if Cullen's reaction to the mayor was any indication, then, by Christmas, he, too, would be among the recently engaged or married.

It was just too bad that Rory's oldest brother, Finn, showed no sign of ever joining himself to a woman. Not that Rory was surprised, mind you. Finn, he was certain, would never give up the torch he carried for Violet Demarest, even if Violet would, if she was smart, never show her face in Marigold again. Poor woman.

"That's our cue."

The words pulled Rory from his reverie, and he turned his attention very willingly to Miriam.

"All set?" he asked her, already knowing the answer.

And, just as he had known she would, she smiled and nodded quite enthusiastically. "Oh, yes," she told him. "I've been waiting for this for a long time. Longer even than you."

He narrowed his eyes at her playfully. "I'm not so sure about that," he said. Because he had realized some time ago that, deep down, he had wanted Miriam from the first day he had lain eyes on her. It had just taken him a while to realize that. His brain, after all, had been so cluttered with nonessential information, and he'd had to make room by storing up thoughts and images and memories of her.

He bent his arm at the elbow in a silent bid that she should take it, and Miriam did so eagerly. Her dress was a flowing, snowy gown with a full skirt and long train. It scooped low over her breasts, and in spite of its lack of a side slit, Rory thought she looked very goddess-like in it. Especially with the wreath of tiny pearls that circled her head, and the length of translucent veil that cascaded down to the edge of her gown's train.

"You look beautiful," he told her. He smiled as he added, "Very tempting."

She smiled back. "And you," she replied, "must have been doing some reading behind my back. Because you look like the very devil with a black tuxedo on."

He grinned. "Yes, well, I do confess that I have picked up an issue of *Metropolitan* or two. It's amazing what a man can learn about a woman reading that publication."

"Oh?" Miriam said with interest. "Like what?"

"Well, there was that one headline that said Help Him Find Your G-Spot—Then Go After His! that I found very intriguing. Not to mention educational."

"Mmm," she said. "I must have missed that article."

"That's all right," he told her. "I took notes."

"I can't wait for you to teach me what you learned."

"Oh, Miss Thornbury," Rory said with a wicked smile. "The things we'll learn together."

"Oh, my," she responded with an equally wicked smile. "You are a devil, aren't you?"

"And you, my dear, are such a temptress."

"Then I think we shall both be very happy together."

Rory smiled again as he led her toward the garden. Oh, yes. He was more than certain of that.

*   *   *   *   *

SILHOUETTE® DESIRE™

AVAILABLE FROM 18TH JANUARY 2002

CHILD OF MINE

COWBOY'S SECRET CHILD Sara Orwig

The only way Jeb Stuart would gain custody of his son was by proposing a marriage of convenience to the boy's adoptive mother. One huge side benefit was teaching his new wife to enjoy her own sensuality, but could *she* teach *him* to love again?

THE RANCHER AND THE NANNY Caroline Cross

Rugged John MacLaren didn't know the first thing about making a home for his motherless daughter. He needed help in the unforgettable form of Eve Chandler. She was making his daughter blossom and melting John's icy reserve…

MILLIONAIRE MEN

LONE STAR KNIGHT Cindy Gerard

Billionaire Matt Walker was not a man who walked away from what he wanted—and he wanted Lady Helena Reichard. But Helena was vulnerable, so Matt needed to protect her while he made her *his* forever!

HER ARDENT SHEIKH Kristi Gold

Sheikh Ben Rassad promised innocent Jamie Morris protection. But their passion soon ignited and when he discovered she carried his child, he was determined to convince her to be his bride! Only she could see the man beneath the prince.

ROYALLY WED

THE EXPECTANT PRINCESS Stella Bagwell

When Princess Dominique's father went missing she turned to loyal Marcus Kent. And when Dominique revealed she was pregnant, the ever-honourable Marcus proposed marriage. But was his proposal made out of love for her or duty to the king?

THE BLACKSHEEP PRINCE'S BRIDE Martha Shields

Once she was sure of his innocence regarding the king's disappearance, lady-in-waiting Rowena Wilde agreed to marry Jake Stanbury to help him retain custody of his son. But could she accept only a temporary union, when she wanted forever?

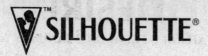
Sensation™

Passionate, dramatic, thrilling romances

AN UNEXPECTED ADDITION Terese Ramin
MY SECRET VALENTINE Marilyn Pappano
SOMEONE TO WATCH OVER HER Margaret Watson
TWICE IN A LIFETIME Merline Lovelace
HART'S LAST STAND Cheryl Biggs
WHICH TWIN? Elane Osborn

Special Edition™

Vivid, satisfying romances full of family, life and love

BACHELOR'S BABY PROMISE Barbara McMahon
SEVEN MONTHS AND COUNTING... Myrna Temte
THE TIES THAT BIND Ginna Gray
UNEXPECTEDLY EXPECTING! Susan Mallery
LOST-AND-FOUND GROOM Patricia McLinn
MONTANA MAIL-ORDER WIFE Charlotte Douglas

Superromance™

Enjoy the drama, explore the emotions,
experience the relationship

THE PULL OF THE MOON Darlene Graham
DR DAD Judith Arnold
THE BABY BET: HIS SECRET SON Joan Elliott Pickart
THE REAL FATHER Kathleen O'Brien

Intrigue™

Danger, deception and suspense

PROTECTIVE CUSTODY Debra Webb
SAVING HIS SON Rita Herron
ECHOES IN THE DARK Gayle Wilson
THE LAWMAN WHO LOVED HER Mallory Kane

SILHOUETTE® SUPERROMANCE™

is proud to present

nine months later

Friends... Lovers... Strangers...
These couples' lives are about to change
radically as they become parents-to-be

HER BEST FRIEND'S BABY
CJ Carmichael
January

THE PULL OF THE MOON
Darlene Graham
February

EXPECTATIONS
Brenda Novak
March

THE FOURTH CHILD
CJ Carmichael
April

Join us every month throughout the
whole of 2002 for one of these dramatic,
involving, emotional books.

SILHOUETTE®

DESIRE™

is proud to present

Millionaires Galore!

Rich, renowned, ruthless and sexy as sin

Millionaire's Club - January

MILLIONAIRE MD *by Jennifer Greene*

WORLD'S MOST ELIGIBLE TEXAN *by Sara Orwig*

Millionaire Men - February

LONE STAR KNIGHT *by Cindy Gerard*

HER ARDENT SHEIKH *by Kristi Gold*

Millionaire Bachelors - March

TYCOON WARRIOR *by Sheri WhiteFeather*

MILLIONAIRE HUSBAND *by Leanne Banks*

Millionaire Marriages - April

MILLIONAIRE BOSS *by Peggy Moreland*

THE MILLIONAIRE'S SECRET WISH
by Leanne Banks

1201/SH/LC26

SILHOUETTE® ™

SENSATION™

proudly presents

36 Hours

*Five books where thirty-six hours
changes everything...*

Come to Grand Springs, Colorado for the holidays

0901/SH/LC23

▼ SILHOUETTE
SENSATION

presents a new heart-pounding
twelve-book series:

A Year of Loving Dangerously

When a top secret agency is threatened, twelve of the best
agents in the world put their lives—and their hearts—on
the line. But will justice...and true love...prevail?

0601/SH/LC18

SILHOUETTE® SPECIAL EDITION™

is proud to present

The Stockwells

*Where family secrets, scandalous pasts and
unexpected love wreak havoc on the lives
of the rich and infamous Stockwells!*

THE TYCOON'S INSTANT DAUGHTER
Christine Rimmer
January

SEVEN MONTHS AND COUNTING...
Myrna Temte
February

HER UNFORGETTABLE FIANCÉ
Allison Leigh
March

THE MILLIONAIRE AND THE MUM
Patricia Kay
April

THE CATTLEMAN AND THE
VIRGIN HEIRESS
Jackie Merritt
May

1201/SH/LC24

SILHOUETTE®

INTRIGUE™

is proud to present

TOP SECRET BABIES

These babies need a protector!

THE BODYGUARD'S BABY
Debra Webb - January

SAVING HIS SON
Rita Herron - February

THE HUNT FOR HAWKE'S DAUGHTER
Jean Barrett - March

UNDERCOVER BABY
Adrianne Lee - April

CONCEPTION COVER-UP
Karen Lawton Barrett - May

HIS CHILD
Delores Fossen - June

Unwrap the mystery

MONTANA BRIDES

Where passions run deep and love lasts forever.

A sizzling twelve book continuity series set against the majestic backdrop of the Montana mountains.

The stories from Whitehorn, Montana capture the excitement of living, with a mixture of romance and wedding fever.

Available from 17th August

Available at most branches of WH Smith, Tesco, Martins, Borders, Eason, Sainsbury's, Woolworths and most good paperback bookshops.

0901/MB/RTL

1 FREE

book and a surprise gift!

We would like to take this opportunity to thank you for reading th
Silhouette® book by offering you the chance to take ANOTHE
specially selected title from the Desire™ series absolutely FRE
We're also making this offer to introduce you to the benefits of th
Reader Service™—

- ★ FREE home delivery
- ★ FREE gifts and competitions
- ★ FREE monthly Newsletter
- ★ Exclusive Reader Service discount
- ★ Books available before they're in the shops

Accepting this FREE book and gift places you under no obligatio
to buy, you may cancel at any time, even after receiving your fre
shipment. Simply complete your details below and return the entir
page to the address below. *You don't even need a stamp!*

YES! Please send me 1 free Desire book and a surprise gif
I understand that unless you hear from me, I will receive
superb new titles every month for just £4.99 each, postage an
packing free. I am under no obligation to purchase any books ar
may cancel my subscription at any time. The free book and gift w
be mine to keep in any case.

D2ZE

Ms/Mrs/Miss/Mr ....Initials.................................
                                                        BLOCK CAPITALS PLEAS

Surname ....

Address ....

....

....Postcode..................................

Send this whole page to:
UK: FREEPOST CN81, Croydon, CR9 3WZ
EIRE: PO Box 4546, Kilcock, County Kildare (stamp required)

Offer valid in UK and Eire only and not available to current Reader Service subscribers to this seri
We reserve the right to refuse an application and applicants must be aged 18 years or over. Only o
application per household. Terms and prices subject to change without notice. Offer expir
30th April 2002. As a result of this application, you may receive offers from other carefully select
companies. If you would prefer not to share in this opportunity please write to The Data Manager
the address above.

Silhouette® is a registered trademark used under licence.
Desire™ is being used as a trademark.